WARNING CALL

THE BLACK PAGES BOOK TWO

BY AUTHOR

DANNY BELL

Publisher's Note: This is a work of fiction. Names, characters, places, and incidents are a product of the author's imagination. Locales and public names are sometimes used for atmospheric purposes. Any resemblance to actual people, living or dead, or to businesses, companies, events, institutions, or locales is completely coincidental.

Ordering Information:
Quantity sales. Special discounts are available on quantity purchases by corporations, associations, and others. For details, contact the "Special Sales Department" at the email address above.

Warning Call (The Black Pages Book Two) / Danny Bell – 1st ed.
ISBN-13: 978-1979994927 | ISBN-10: 1979994927

For Whitton, my hero.

For Amanda, my unwitting mentor.

And for everyone who couldn't see a way out and kept going anyway. I'm glad you're here.

ACKNOWLEDGMENTS

Hello there, book readers. This is me, Danny, the book writer. I'm acknowledging you! Mostly because you have me outnumbered. And then also thanking you! Mostly for reading this book. If you're here, I hope it means you enjoyed the first book, Empty Threat. It is such a surreal moment for me to give everyone a second book in a series. I'm beyond thrilled to be able to do so, and I have a lot more planned, so I hope you're all here for all of it.

One of the hardest things about writing this book was coming up with who to dedicate this book to and what to say. A lot of dedications tend to be only a few words and all kinds of vague. Something like, *"For Jack, the moon"*. And yeah, that's only going to mean something to Jack, but we're all okay with it. Who is Jack and why was he mistaken for the moon? We're probably not supposed to know, and we can still enjoy the story without solving that particular riddle.

But not me! My book, my rules! The best and worst thing about writing is that you can use whatever words you want and in any order. And if I decide to thank a whole lot of people up front, well, who's going to stop me? You? Not likely, you're already reading this, you're too late.

So that's what I'm going to do. I'm going to start thanking people, or at least acknowledging them, even though I know that with the limited space I have here as well as the limited time I have to finish that I am going to forget some people, and I hope they're all cool with that. There are the obvious people, like Whitton and Sloan who have always believed in me from the day that we met, even when I had nothing more than a weird idea and the promise that I would actually finish something someday. Or Amanda, who was kind enough to be brutally honest with me about all of the things I was doing wrong and then generous enough to give me the benefit of learning from their experience. There's Roma who edited the book with care, or Julie who lovingly tries to format the book so it looks perfect, or Kat who beta read the book and gave me honest feedback. People, like Anthony, who gave me tremendous amounts of their time or people, like Misti and Jordan and Claire and Morgan and Matt and Sonni and Osei and Crystal and Shannon and Mor, who just gave me support and love and wanted to see me live my dreams. Then people, like Lauren and Kate and Kim and Courtney, who just inspired me by having the awareness to know they have something to share with the world and then having the courage to do so, even when it wasn't going to be easy. Especially when they knew it wasn't going to be easy.

And then I start to realize that there are so many other people who I haven't even acknowledged on this page who probably deserve to be here. And then I acknowledge two more things:

I couldn't do this alone and I am fortunate enough to be surrounded by amazing people.

And hopefully, so are you.

WARNING CALL

THE BLACK PAGES BOOK TWO

I carefully made my way across the slippery boulders, careful not to touch the walls, particularly the black patches. I'd learned the hard way that there was no such thing as black moss here, getting too close would mean letting loose a swarm of what was likely a hundred thousand minuscule flies, all waiting for the next animal corpse to make their meal. I'd already passed one putrid body of water, far enough from the waves that it could safely grow stagnant. I glanced upwards, feeling a drop of water hit my head. It would rain soon, which would make the area infinitely more dangerous. This entire place was treacherous, honestly, and I wasn't sure what would make someone come here voluntarily.

So I asked.

"Yo, Dawg, what are we doing out here?" I asked my friend carefully, focusing on keeping my balance.

Logan stopped on a large rock and turned to face me. "Did you just call me 'Dawg'?" he asked with a confused smile.

"Yeah, I thought I'd try something different," I replied, looking up to him. "So, Dawg, do you mind if I call you Dawg?"

"I…guess not." Logan laughed uneasily.

"Mr. Dawg, why on earth are we out here?" I asked, repeating my question.

Logan took our conversation to mean that we should take a break, and he removed his backpack and carefully strapped canvas from his back and sat down. I wasn't going to correct him. "Are you complaining now? You love this hike!"

"Not in December!" I countered. "It's gross."

"Don't you regularly travel through hell-scapes filled with nightmares?" he asked.

"Two things can be gross!" I countered, though he had a point. This was a regular beach, not one in The Knowing that might try killing me for walking on the wrong grain of sand. "Also, now that I've heard it out loud, I've decided I don't like it. I'm never calling anyone Dawg ever again; I understand now why I never said it until today. Okay, three things can be gross."

Logan shrugged. "It's cool," he said, removing his water bottle from his backpack. "But what's your problem with the hike? This is probably the most scenic spot we've ever been."

Ordinarily that might have been correct, in fact, I am pretty sure that I'm the one that introduced Logan to this place. We were on the Shipwreck Trail, a coastal stretch in Palos Verdes that was primarily, well, rocks. That's it, just a ton of rocks. The trail started at Flat Rock Point, a cliff top with the sort of view of the ocean that might involuntarily cause that one part of the Jurassic Park theme music to play in your head every time you saw it. The part with the Brontosaurus. Or you could voluntarily play it in your head every time you saw it, the way I did. A steep trail led down to a very small section of actual beach, the kind with sand, before it became all rocks and boulders for the next several miles, occasionally being broken up by a drainage pipe or something else unnatural to the area. Eventually, you got to see a shipwreck. It was really just several tons of rust that you definitely shouldn't try to walk on, but the name of the trail delivers on its promise. You would wrap up around Bluff Cove with a large collection of impacted slabs that just seemed perfect for sharing a picnic on, complete with a trail up to the street, so you could take a pleasant stroll along the cliff on the way back to your car.

And Logan was right! On most days, everything about this hike is magical. The breeze seems to negate the heat from the sun; the ocean is blue and crisp with waves that make a sound unlike anything I've ever heard anywhere else. You might get to see dolphins and sea lions if you were really lucky. But this was not most days. Not a lot of people ever went on the trail as it was, even in the best of conditions, but during the winter months, it was outright deserted. The tide was higher for one thing, which meant more animal corpses and a significantly narrower path. You had a cliff wall to your left, and the ocean to your right, and whatever slippery rocks the beach felt generous enough to place beneath your feet. It wasn't safe, for one thing, and if you got started at the wrong time of day, you'd have to deal with potentially impassable terrain. Not to mention the seaweed that came with the rising water, and the insects, and just all of it. The place didn't smell right.

I gestured wildly to everything. "Which part is scenic? That bird carcass or the rusted-out shopping cart?"

"You, for example," he responded. "That Mermaid costume is legit!"

"No, it's not." I sighed. "I don't even have a tail, just these shiny green leggings. And besides, I met a mermaid. She had gills. I don't have gills. Did you know they have gills? Everyone seems to leave out that part of the story, but they're definitely there. I'm just wearing costume jewelry and fake seaweed. Thank you, by the way, for not making me wear real seaweed."

"Oh come on, can't you see it?" he replied. "The turbulent waves, the foreboding clouds approaching the shoreline—"

"And the rain they bring?" I interrupted. "How are you going to paint if it rains? How are we going to get back to the car?"

Logan smiled the huge, wonderfully stupid smile of his and spread his arms. "Hey, I'm a gambler!"

It was an infectious smile, and I couldn't help but return it. "You're the worst dark and brooding artist ever."

"Don't tell anyone." He laughed.

"I won't," I agreed. "If you answer my question about why we're out here."

"I promise, it's just the painting," he answered innocently. "I needed a model and—"

"You asked your girlfriend's estranged best friend who has never modeled before because you're definitely not working on trying to repair their relationship single-handedly?"

Logan squirmed a little at that. "Yeah," he said, taking an extra-long sip of water. "That."

"Dude." I sighed. "You and I are friends either way, okay? And I'm never abandoning Olivia, I owe her more than I can ever repay, but you have to give us..."

I trailed off as I felt something change in the air. Logan tried to ask what was wrong, but I held up a finger, motioning him to be quiet. There was thunder out over the ocean, but it was rolling, the clouds seemed to be moving unnaturally closer to the shore. I don't like ominous thunder, and I don't like walking out into secluded areas.

That's when the bad things come out.

There are stories of people seeing the impossible when they go out alone. There are stories of those people never returning. Those stories exist for a reason. Over time, we've tried to force them deeper into the shadows with our cities and our disbelief,

It was a skinless horse, surely, but with the torso of, I wouldn't want to say a human given its proportions; but that was the closest thing I could ascribe to it. It grew out of the back of the horse itself, also skinless, but the arms of the thing were far too long and distended with knuckles first leaving their own little trails in the sand before limply slapping on the rocks on the shore. The head was oversized, and the creature seemed to lack the neck strength to hold it up properly; it was maybe two feet wide and rested lazily on its shoulder. Across its entire body, heavy, blood-soaked muscles heaved as crimson lumps pulsated at every movement, sickly yellow veins pumped black blood through it. And while I stared in disbelief at this monster, I saw the eyes of the humanoid head roll to meet my gaze, and with no flesh to indicate what it had done, only the tightening of facial muscles, it smiled at me as a single, deafening thunderclap dispersed the unnatural clouds and restored the waves to their proper place. The horse head exhaled, and a thick, dark cloud escaped from its mouth and nostrils, rapidly corroding everything in front of it.

Logan finally spoke up, snapping me back to reality. "Have you ever—?"

"Run!" I shouted, shimmying up the rock next to his.

"You just said you don't run!" he protested, still staring at the demon horse.

"Have you seen that thing?" I shouted in disbelief. "I was incredibly wrong, I run! You too, you are also a runner. Get out of here!"

I yanked Logan's arm, nearly taking him down with me as we made our descent to the other side of his rock. Our dash away from the monster was anything but, and we used the cliff wall as much as we could to expedite our escape and not break our necks slipping on the wet rocks. We must have angered a million tiny flies as we did, and feeling their frenzied flight as they tried to move into our nostrils and mouths and down into our clothes was a visibly discomforting experience for us both, but moving forward was our only priority. A roar from behind us stopped us in our tracks, and we turned immediately to see what it was. The beast stood atop the elevated rock we'd come from, and I sent a bolt of fire into its path on instinct, which…did nothing. Barely a singe mark where I struck it near its neck. The horse neck, not the other neck. I really don't like things with multiple necks; I've yet to ever meet one that was up to any good.

"I am never going to get used to seeing that," Logan said flatly.

I was about to respond when the horse monster…thing, tried to descend from its perch, slipping instantly and tumbling down hard into the smaller rocks below. The mass of meat twisted in unnatural ways, making it difficult to look at. Logan hurled his water bottle at it as it tried to get back to its feet. The bottle bounced off of it as harmlessly as my fire.

I gave my friend a dumbfounded look. He looked momentarily ashamed and said, "I'm helping."

I took an extra moment to watch the ugly thing, noticing something. It was having difficulty getting to its feet and, between its original spot and where we were now, we had put a little distance between us.

"Oh, awesome!" I cried out sincerely. "It doesn't do well in this terrain; it's going to have a hard time keeping up with us!"

When it made it to its feet, it shook as if annoyed or agitated. One of the elongated arms, with its long fingers and too many knuckles, gripped a stone half my size and launched it in our direction. The projectile sailed over our heads.

"And it's super strong apparently," I added, shaking a shield out of my wrist. "Crap."

"We can talk about that later, come on!"

Logan was trying to move away from the beast, as it was already moving toward us. Things didn't look good for us. With a couple of short turns here and there as exceptions, there was pretty much nothing but open air between the creature and us, and no way out without scaling about two hundred feet of a solid cliff face. It threw another rock at us, again missing wildly, but it only had to hit us once, and that would be that. I was only guessing that my shield would properly deflect something that heavy being thrown at me, but it could just as easily go straight through and pulverize me, so, yeah. I shouldn't rely on it.

"You're the local, you know this area better than me," Logan called back. "How far until the exit?"

"Two miles, give or take," I replied, watching a look of horror spread across his face at that. "But we're not heading to the exit! I have a plan!"

"I've heard about your plans," he said dryly.

"No, this is a real plan," I reassured him. "At least sixty-five percent of a plan!"

"How could you have possibly planned for that thing?" he shot back.

I wasn't exactly prepared to deal with questions right now; I was busy watching for falling debris and making sure I didn't slip and fall into a pile of potentially jagged rocks while at the same time keeping an eye on the nightmare behind us.

"Just get to the shipwreck and get inside of it, it will make sense when we get there!" I instructed.

"Isn't that thing crazy dangerous?" he asked.

How can he possibly be asking that right now?

"Yeah man, I don't want tetanus either," I said impatiently. "But, you know, monster?"

As if on cue, another boulder bounced off the cliff wall hard enough to ricochet into the ocean, causing a minor rock slide ahead of us. This thing's aim was terrible, but again, it only needed to get lucky once for our day to be ruined.

Logan let out a little yelp of surprise and looked back to see our attacker and renew his terror.

"Why don't you just start throwing rocks back at it?" he shouted back to me, panic creeping in. "With magic or whatever?"

I responded a little more annoyed that I expected. "Who do you think I am? And how would that even work? Do you know the spell for that? Because I don't!"

"Dude, I don't know how magic works," he yelled back to me. "You're the first and only magic person I've ever met!"

The creature howled behind us in frustration, either from our unnecessary conversation or from its inability to catch us quickly on this shore. This thought lead to another thought. If it was this unfamiliar with the local terrain and was unable to walk over slippery, wet stones easily, why did it choose to attack me here? I sincerely doubted we were on its home turf, I've never heard of anything worse than an annoyed sea lion in this area, and homeless people sleep down here at night in the makeshift campfire areas. I've never heard of anything like this, especially not locally, and I'm confident someone would have seen it by now. So then it must have made sense that it was sent after me, specifically. But who knew I would be down here, and who has that kind of juice to send something like this after me?

I snapped out of it maybe half a second later than I would have liked, and Logan, who was looking the wrong way, had no idea that the monster with terrible aim was just about to hit its bullseye..

"**L**ogan!" I shouted, throwing my blister shield toward the falling rock before I realized what I was doing. He turned sharply, just in time to see what was an instant from striking him, the surprise of it causing him to stumble backward. I almost fell over myself; I had thrown the shield hard enough that my arm immediately felt pins and needles, and I could have thrown my shoulder out if I'd been a touch more unlucky.

Luck was on my side for once, as it turned out. My shield spun a brilliant violet and exploded in a bright display of kinetic energy, which sent the rock up and into the cliff face hard enough for it to rebound nearly into the ocean, instead creating an impact crater and significant rock shrapnel. Logan's eyes flittered about in multiple directions, his brain trying to process everything he just saw in the past two seconds. That was close. Way too close, and I didn't want to stick around to see how much closer it could get.

"That!" Logan breathed in disbelief, incapable of forming a complete thought at the moment.

"Yes, that," I confirmed, offering him a hand up. I knew what he meant. "Come on; we can see shelter from here."

Logan scrambled to his feet as we rounded the corner in the trail which revealed the infamous shipwreck. We'd have a few precious moments where our pursuer wouldn't have a line of sight to us, but we, unfortunately, would have to be away from the wall and out in the open.

"Can't you do anything?" Logan pleaded.

"I'm open to suggestions," I replied, carefully moving over the stones. "But I only have so much power, and my first frontal assault did nothing to it, so make sure your idea is a good one."

"Olivia said you summoned lightning one time," he began.

"I'll stop you right there, that was the definition of a unique situation," I said suddenly ashamed that I couldn't just rip a lightning bolt from the sky, only to immediately dismiss that shame as stupid when I considered how unreasonable a request that was. "I really doubt I could do it here, and even if I could, this thing appeared with a bolt of lightning. What if it likes being hit by lightning, and I spend all my power tickling it?"

Logan was panting now as we approached the shipwreck. The creature again shrieked behind us, letting us know it saw us.

"What about just dropping a part of the cliff on it?" he suggested.

"Are you insane?" I replied, frustration seeping through my voice. "There are homes up there! We're not dropping someone's house on this thing!"

Another rock landed nearby, not close enough that we were in obvious danger, but this thing was getting used to taking aim, and the practice was going to pay off sooner than later. Logan ducked underneath the shipwreck first, making room for me, and I quickly joined him. It smelled heavily of rotting fish, and I could taste the metal and rust in my mouth as I breathed heavily, trying to catch my breath. We peered out through our little opening as the demon-horse-looking-thing lumbered in our direction. I sighed as I readied my hands and aimed in its direction.

"A little room, please," I remarked to Logan, who did his best to oblige.

I wasn't certain that magic, as a direct assault, was going to work against it. I've learned to conserve my energy in situations like this, rather than throwing around everyone evocation I could think of. At least what I had planned would make sense on paper, so it made sense to toss out a little bit more magic.

I focused on the cold and sent out a freezing cone of ice, immediately coating a large section of the rocks in something far more treacherous than mere water. I mean, it was still water, just worse. Or better. It feels like a point of view position to take.

A second later, all four of its hooves twisted and buckled on the frictionless surface, and the crack its jaws made as they went down was satisfying.

"That's going to keep it busy for about as long as it takes it to remember that it can just breathe that rock melting smoke," I nodded to Logan.

"Why are you giving it ideas?" he asked incredulously.

"It probably doesn't speak English," I lied. I had no idea if it spoke any language, verbal or nonverbal. I don't even know what it is. Ghost horse? Zombie horse? Demon horse? Presumably a horse of some kind. "Whatever, listen. I have one thing I can try, but—"

"Great, do it," Logan agreed quickly.

"But, I don't know if—"

"I promise you, I don't care," Logan interjected again, watching the beast struggle in the ice. "I'm on board with whatever idea you have. I love the idea. It's my favorite idea."

"Dude, listen!" I snapped. "I'm trying to say I have no clue if it will work, and my suspicion is that it won't, so we need to be prepared to run if it doesn't."

"Sorry, just nervous," he said, not looking at me. "Please, what's the plan?"

"No, it's cool; this is a stressful situation," I said. "So, in the books I've been studying, one of the tricks I've learned is, if you have the patience for it and if you learn the right sigils, you can carve them into an inanimate object or sew them into your clothes, whatever. And if you do, you can store the correct spell into said item and hold it like a battery. It's super delicate, and I'm probably not very good at it. I've only practiced on two things so far."

"That's fascinating, and I'm not even being sarcastic, I mean it. Genuinely fascinating. But umm," Logan said, unsure of what to say. "No offense, how does that help us here?"

I tapped one of the gold-looking bracelets I was wearing as part of my costume. It was copper, but the plating made it look gold. "I have one of them right here."

"Yes!" he exclaimed. "Which spell did you save in it?"

"Uh, fire," I said hesitantly. "Like a fire bolt."

Logan looked deflated at that. "Like the one that didn't work earlier?"

"Yeah, kind of," I replied. "Actually, much smaller than the one I shot earlier. As I said, it requires finesse, so call it baby fire bolts."

Logan slumped back into the interior of the shipwreck and let out of a moan of frustration. "Please tell me this wasn't sixty percent of a plan!"

"Sixty-five percent, actually," I corrected him, almost immediately wishing that I hadn't. "And, yes, it was. But dude! Listen! I've done this nearly every day for the past seven or eight months. One baby fire bolt every day, over a lot of days might add up to one pretty good fire bolt, right?" He started to look hopeful, when I added, "Or it might just be a baby fire bolt. Or hundreds of baby fire bolts. I have never done this before, you know. One way or another here goes. You might want to put your head down, just in case."

I removed the bracelet and heaved it into the air in the beast's direction, and realizing how far off I was, I sent a small gust of wind along with it, sending the bracelet harmlessly into the creature's side. It bounded off and made a clinking noise as it landed on the ice-covered stones. The beast stopped struggling for a moment to examine what had struck it while Logan and I stared, waiting for something to happen.

"Oh right, I need to unlock the spell," I said, feeling stupid that I forgot such an essential element. I extended my will to the bracelet and "Let me just—"

FWOOSH!

In terms of difficulty, it was the magical equivalent of blowing out a birthday candle to unlock the spell in the bracelet, but when I did, I was instantly flung backward, along with Logan, as a bright light and intense wave of heat threatened to suck the oxygen directly from our lungs. A sound, like an incinerator at a crematorium only a hundred times louder filled our ears, intensified by our enclosure inside the shipwreck. Logan was pressing both palms to the side of his head to try and block out the roaring winds and that threatening crackling sound. I had no choice but to do the same as I sat up and looked out to see what was happening.

My mouth hung open in disbelief at what I saw through squinting eyes. In front of me was a tower of flame, maybe ten or twelve feet in diameter and unnaturally dark and thick, swirling rapidly like a tornado and jetting hundreds of feet into the sky, reaching higher than I could see. As overpowering as it was,

I couldn't look away, and maybe fifteen seconds later or so it just vanished.

Logan crawled up and out of our little, rusted refuge as I did the same, and the two of us stared dumbfounded at the devastation. There was a pool of magma that now slowly rolled toward the ocean, and in the center, was the charred, ashen skeleton of the former horse creature that crumbled and broke apart as we watched, leaving no trace that it ever existed. I looked up to see the clouds had parted where the flames had obliterated them. There was a smell in the air, like soot and ozone, and it hurt to breathe, but only a little.

I felt like I just unlocked a new title. Elana Black: Monster Incinerator.

Logan stared at me like he had a million questions, his face full of fear and awe and more feelings and emotions than he could process right away. I could relate. I didn't mean to do this; I didn't even know it was possible! Part of the hill cliff was on fire, but thankfully none of the homes seemed immediately threatened, and when you live in an area this wealthy, you'd better believe they had things like municipal safety services taken care of. The fire department was a mile or two inland at most, and there was no way that every single firefighter in a ten-mile radius wasn't on their way here right now, if not the Coast Guard. There might not be anything now, but a minute-long tower of a sky-splitting fire was going to get a lot of attention.

Which reminded me, we had to leave right away. "Come on, man, we don't want to be here," I said to Logan, trying to thread the delicate line of insistent and gentle. "There's going to be a lot of questions that we're not going to be able to answer."

"You can just do that?" he asked in disbelief.

"To be fair, no," I said. "That thing took me most of the year to make. I'm usually just okay with the shield thing and maybe a 'Whoosh!' or a 'Fsssh!' Or, you know, yeah. Smaller stuff. I get your point though."

"Whoosh is smaller stuff?" Logan asked as he mimicked my poor imitation of wind.

"Seriously man, ask me anything you want later over pancakes or something, we need to—"

"Go. Right," he said, getting a handle on things.

There was a drainage pipe not far from the shipwreck, maybe a five-minute hike away. It wasn't the way I'd usually take out of here, but this wasn't the usual hike, and I was thankful for it for a change. It was an eyesore against the rest of the landscape for sure, but it was also the most popular access point to the shore due to the fact that tons of concrete had been poured into the crevice and smoothed out, roughly, to resemble steps. It made it the safest way in and out; it was just utter hell on your quads. The steps seemed to be made for someone seven feet tall, which meant that every step required a pinch of climbing, and considering the steep incline, it wasn't uncommon for people to stop halfway and pretend to turn around to admire the view and snap a picture on their phone, when what they were really doing was catching their breath. Or at least, that's what I usually did.

Not today though, we had to keep going until we were out. I already heard helicopters approaching. We'd be hidden from their view for the moment as long as they were trying to cover the blast area and the newly formed magma, but it would only take one person deciding to scout around to put our faces on the news, and I was looking to avoid that. So we climbed, as safely and quickly as we could, until we reached the top, nearly collapsing, drenched in sweat. I felt a little better about the fact that Logan was also panting and struggling to catch his breath, at least I wasn't the only one. I then felt bad for feeling good about a friend's discomfort, but I'm working on some things. I'm sure he'd understand what I meant.

For my part, I'd been distracted the entire climb out with thoughts of Logan and what had just happened. Not the safest thing, I know, but I couldn't help it, and I couldn't blame Logan for his reaction. He was a trooper, all things considered, and the fact that he hadn't run away screaming from me was a testament to what kind of person he was. I wasn't even sure how much I should be freaking out at my own power, at the moment. I've heard plenty that wildlings are dangerous, but maybe they had a point if that was the kind of thing I could accidentally do. If I'd used this in a more populated area, or if I activated it while I was wearing it, or any one of a million other careless things I probably would have done given enough time, I could have caused real damage. Of course, they didn't have the right to go around killing whoever they wished, and I'd never forgive…whoever they were for that, but maybe letting everyone run around unsupervised wasn't the best method either. I didn't have the right answer, not yet, and it would take me a lot longer to figure it out.

Logan had heard stories, certainly. Olivia had told him all about our adventure in The Knowing fighting Jason, for example. And he was surprisingly open to the idea of The Knowing, which was a surprise. He didn't freak out too much when he saw some basic magic either. If anything, he thought it was awesome. It was easy, but concerning. It's nice when someone can look at the weirdest parts of your life and simply say, "Okay," and be done with it, but when those same parts are a constant source of anxiety and uncertainty for you, it's unnerving to see it handled so freely by someone else. You can't help but wonder if they're just trying to be nice, if they don't understand, or if you're just the one making too big a deal of it.

But nope. Logan saw me nuke a demon, and the facade cracked a little. I think he meant what he said earlier, he genuinely believed in me to handle whatever was coming, but that nearly got him killed. And when Logan saw the full extent of my power, beyond what even I knew I was capable of, he hesitated for a moment. I saw it in him; he wasn't sure if he recognized me for a second. He was a little afraid of me. Logan is a friend, and I don't want him or anyone to be afraid of me. The world has enough fear; I'm comfortable with never seeing anyone afraid of anything ever again.

"Elana?" Logan wheezed out to me, and I only just realized that I was staring at my feet, clutching my knees.

"'Sup?" I managed through labored breaths, looking up. Parked on the street ahead of us was a dark black limousine, and standing at its rear was a child, who was maybe eight or nine and dressed in a chauffeur's uniform, regarding us with a stern expression. He silently made a motion for us to get in.

"Well played," Logan remarked to me, nervously trying to make a joke of the situation as we walked toward the car. "Our entire childhood was spent being told not to accept rides from strange adults, but no one ever—"

"I really do wish you'd come along," a fatherly voice interrupted from inside the vehicle. "I'm not a man who likes to be kept waiting."

"Oh yeah?" I said, as we approached the car door. I looked in, trying to get a peek at who was inside past the tinted windows which had been rolled down just a crack. "And why would we do that, mysterious guy who rides around in stretch limos and employs children as drivers?"

The window rolled down further to reveal a middle-aged man in a crisp suit with an unnatural tan, who looked in my direction with a kind smile, but impatient, tired eyes.

"I'll save us both a lot of time, Elana, and just give you all the reasons," he began. "Because you don't want to answer a lot of questions about the fire you just started. Because we've both caused each other a lot of trouble and we'd both do well to figure out a way to help each other. And lastly, the one you won't be able to say no to, it's because—well, I knew your mother."

It might have been the exhaustion, or just the unexpected and totally casual way he said that which caught me off guard, or some combination of the two, but I suddenly felt far more vulnerable than any horse demon on a rocky beach could ever make me feel. I tried to reply, sought to say anything, but my voice caught in my throat, and one syllable alone made it shakily past my lips.

"Mom?"

3

If this man had wanted me to move, he chose the wrong words, because I was frozen stiff. He had said so much, and I wasn't able to process it all. The word that broke my heart immediately was "knew". *Knew*, not know, not met, not any other ambiguous euphemism to indicate that I was wrong in what I somehow always suspected to be the case, that my mom wasn't alive. No one had mentioned her in…I couldn't remember anyone mentioning her, actually. I never had anyone to bring her up to me because no one knew her. Since I was old enough to remember, there had always been a feeling that I was missing something, but I had also been content, or at least convinced myself that I was content, in the knowledge that she wasn't coming back. To hear it from this stranger—so very calmly—did something to me. He had no right.

Figuring out who he was also ended up on my mind, involuntarily, because of what else he said. He knew my name, that part couldn't have been a guess given that he was waiting for me in a place that was pretty out of the way. But he accused me of starting the fire. Had that been a guess? How could he have known for certain? No, he probably didn't know, he was just putting the pieces together. He was aware that I was capable of magic, and now I was leaving the scene of what was clearly an unnatural event. Unless he sent that creature after me, in which case, could he have been watching somehow? Would he have expected me to survive the encounter? If he did, he'd been over-estimating my ability already because without the bracelet I don't think we would have. The beast was strong, and that black mist it breathed was able to make stones wither like dying plants almost instantly, and it had been immune to my standard magical arsenal.

The other part though, that left no mistaking it. This man was with the Gardners. Or whoever controlled them. Or at least he was tangentially related to them somehow. It didn't matter, he wasn't to be trusted, and he was affiliated with the people who tried to make my life hell and had been responsible for nearly every bad thing I'd had the misfortune of being a part of lately. In fact, I was certain they had to be responsible for whatever just happened on the beach just now. I wasn't certain how they did it, though the Aos Si implied it was possible previously. I didn't know if they pulled something out of The Knowing, or if it had always been here, but remained unseen, or something else entirely, but the details didn't matter at the moment. It made my blood boil to think that these monsters would know my mom or have the nerve to mention her to me. There was no chance she'd be associated with their sort of business.

I mean, probably. I never knew much of her. I had a birth certificate, and it had my parents' names on it. Rosheen McCarthy for my mother, Frank Black for my father. My dad never signed it, and finding any information on him was impossible. Even the service I used to dig up my family tree came up with nothing, they said they'd never see anything like it before. Maybe the names of the birth certificate had been fraudulent, or the records were all misplaced somewhere. That proved to be false later when I was given a death certificate for her. She was real, and she was gone. All the same, looking into the two of them had been fruitless, so logically I had no idea who my mother would or would not associate with. But I always believed I had to get the good parts of me from somewhere, and it was always comforting to believe that the best parts of my mother survived her and ended up in me. That seemed like a selfish thought, but I never cared, and I still didn't now. Whether or not it was a fiction, it was my thought to hold.

"Hey, are you doing okay?" The voice belonged to Logan, but I only half-heard it. I tried to take in my senses around me. The faint smell of burnt—

You know what? Screw it. I don't need clarity.

I reached down and plucked a fist-sized rock from the earth and threw it with a shout at the limo, causing both the man and Logan to jump, startled as my projectile shattered the window of the door which had been held open for us.

"Whoa! Okay, easy there. It won't do to just try and break all my windows," the man said, surprise in his voice. I noticed the boy hadn't flinched. Shows what he knew. I'd been aiming for the man's face. "You finished?"

In response, I found another rock and the man put up both hands in surrender.

"Okay, that was my fault, dumb question," he remarked. "But what say you throw rocks at me when we're safely away? Unless of course, you don't feel you need to know what I have to say."

He was right, and I hated it. I dropped the rock, knowing full well he knew something that I couldn't find elsewhere, and I had to know what it was. Logan gave me an 'Are you sure?' look, and I nodded to him that it was okay. We stepped toward the car, and the child put up a hand, indicating that we needed to stop. With a wave of the man's hand, the shattered glass rose back up to the window and repaired itself, leaving no trace it had ever been anything but whole.

"Not him," the man said. "Only you."

"Like hell!" I spat. "If you think I'm leaving him alone after all of this, you're out of your mind!"

The man made an exasperated look and sighed, motioning the two of us in. The child gave a nod and moved to allow us inside.

"Not yet," I said, putting a hand in front of Logan to stop him from moving forward. "One more thing. Your word that you're giving us a ride directly back to our car, and that you'll take no action against us on the way there."

"Of course, no harm will come to either of you if you comply," he replied, and we cautiously got into the limo, the child closing the door behind us.

I had a better look at the man now. He had the tanned and weathered look of someone wealthy who frequently took vacations and spent them on boats. He sat across from us, tailored black suit, a spotless white dress shirt, and a crimson red tie. If not for the fact that he had the look of someone who sold real estate to celebrities, I would have guessed he was running for Congress. I knew better of course, and I fixed my eyes on him, paying attention to his every move.

"So, uhh, who's the kid?" Logan asked nervously, trying to break the tension. "Are you sure he should be driving?"

"He's my muscle," the man replied evenly, still locking eyes with me. "And he's more than capable of taking care of himself."

"Does he ever talk?" Logan continued.

"He speaks when it's time, and believe me compadre, you don't want to hear what he has to say," the man said, before addressing me. "Elana, would you remind your friend that he's here as a courtesy to you and our drive is not a long one?"

"What do you know about my Mom?" I asked coldly.

"Plenty, but answers like that are a perk of the job."

I barked a bitter laugh at that. "You think I'd come work for you?"

"Why not?" he asked. "Your life would certainly be improved by gainful employment in an environment which would nurture your natural talents. For one thing, you'd dress better."

In my anger, I'd forgotten I was still in costume. "Not a chance," I said defiantly. "I'm a Mermaid now. Mermaids are cool."

"I'm not an expert on cool," he conceded. "But you know what I've always thought was cool? Surviving. Making a difference and being part of a team. And I'm offering you all of that right here, right now."

"And sending skinless centaur-looking demons out of the ocean after me is what? Part of your screening process?"

His eyes narrowed on me. "What did you say? Describe it to me."

"Don't play dumb; you know exactly what—"

"Pretend I don't," he said urgently, but softly. "Tell me what you saw."

I wasn't sure why I was indulging him, but I was impatient enough to spit out an answer. "Dude, we're playing it like this? Fine. Skinless horse, glowing red eye, breathed something black and putrid. A human torso grew out of its back, but the proportions were all wrong. Would you happen to be missing one?"

He stared at me in awe now, leaning in. "And you killed it, with that tower of flame?" He made a motion with his hands, like an excitable child describing a TV show.

"Yeah, that's right," I answered suspiciously. Was it possible he didn't know? A grin spread across his face, and he clapped his hands together in applause, lounging back into his seat.

"Wow! Just…" His face a mixture of amusement and disbelief. "And with no rod, staff, wand; nothing like that? Do you know what you just fought? Be honest with me now."

I remained silent for a moment, not wanting to give him anything, but I had to admit it finally. "No, I don't."

"Kid, you need to accept this offer more than you realize," he said smugly.

"And why didn't you offer this to me in the first place?" I asked.

"Look, I've made it a long time, and I know better than to pick a fight when I don't need to," he said earnestly. "Cards on the table? You've more than proven yourself. You're resourceful, you've got more grit than most of the people under my command, and you've made some pretty powerful allies. Not all friends, exactly, but allies. You took down Jason, which I will admit to being intrigued by. My money most certainly would not have been on you, but that's my shame to bear. I underestimated you. As did Bres, which again, wow. That stunt you pulled with him indeed bloodied our noses. And the simple fact is that, no, we can't just let you continue the way you've been, it's too dangerous for all of us, but if we can teach you the right way to do it, guide you, we can maybe both get what we want. If not, we'd have to stop you, and that would be a real shame."

"Nothing you can say or do can stop me," I said trying to show him that I wasn't intimidated. "Your entire army couldn't stop me." That might have been too much.

"Do you know why I am not too terribly mad about the deal you bound Bres to?" he asked. "I'll tell you. It's because you've left him with very little to do, and that's not our problem. That's yours. Because for as big and bad as he can be when he's working, I will tell you this, and hey…look at me. Right in the eyes, and you tell me if I'm lying. There is nothing in this great big world of ours or any other that is more dangerous or more frightening than Bres when he gets bored."

I shuddered at that; I couldn't help it. He wasn't lying; I saw it when the deal had been made. I knew then as I am aware now, he's going to do his best to make me pay, and I saw his life. I am more than assured that he won't let this go. I glanced away, for just a moment, and that was his opening.

"I knew it," he said, snapping his fingers. "There it is, I see it on you. You know the storm that's coming. And it's all starting to click in your head what we can do for you. Strength in numbers, am I right? If you can't beat 'em, join 'em! But that's not why I want you to accept this offer. I want you to gracefully, thankfully accept my very generous offer because you know deep down inside of you that what we are doing is not only necessary, but it is right. And because you know that for all your good intentions, you might do more harm than good, and you need the guidance we can offer you."

"You're full of crap," I said harshly.

"Excuse me?" he asked, taken aback.

"Your entire sales pitch, your whole duty spiel, it's crap," I told him. "Oh, you definitely practiced this before you got here, for sure, and it was pretty good, but you're trying to give me just enough to make me think you're telling me everything. Which of my friends are you worried about? You're not sweating the artists, or bookstore owners, or Elves, or even Celtic gods. Okay, maybe you're sweating a little with the Celtic gods, but I know what really scares you," I said proudly. "The Knowing took my side, and it wasn't supposed to do that, was it?"

He shifted uncomfortably in his seat. "You're not wrong, but—"

"And that whole trying-to-scare-me-with-Bres thing?" I said, cutting him off. "Come on dude; you think I've never been negged before? I already beat him, you dope! And if you didn't notice very recently, I'm not the same person I was earlier when I did this! My arson skills have leveled up considerably. But do you want to know the worst of it? The part that really offends me? It's that you sit here and try to appeal to my sense of morality to get me to join a band of murderers! I don't even know how many innocent people your group has killed! How many children? Oh god, please don't tell me you've killed children because I'll put you in the ocean. Jesus, did you offer Lucia a deal like this before you did who knows what with her?"

"Lucia Cruz is a very, very particular situation," he snapped.

"No, Lucia is a person, and she's my friend!" I shouted back at him. "She is not a situation to be dealt with!"

"You don't know what you're talking about," he said, trying to recover.

"Maybe I don't, but I know this," I told him, not letting him look away. "You don't have anything to offer me. My mom wouldn't want me to trade my soul just to know about her life a little better. Whatever else she did, she produced me, and I'm not here by accident. Anything you think you have for me, I will take. I will come for it. I'm coming to save my friend from you. I will beat you into dark, damp earth until you give me your hand and I rip every dark thought from your head and make sure her name stays out of your mouth until the day you die. As long as any little boy or girl out there has a reason to be afraid of you, I'll never stop coming for you."

"Don't be stupid," he said suddenly full of anger, the facade starting to slip. "You don't come for us; you hide from us. You run from us because if you're not with us that's your only chance of seeing another day. You are one person, do you get that? And not even a particularly strong or significant one at that. I am here as an act of charity! You should be thanking me for the rest of your days for what I'm offering you! What you are seeing is me as patient as you will ever see me, and I am not someone you want to push."

"It looks like we're here," I said flatly as the car stopped.

The man composed himself. "I'm going to," he said, pausing to find the right words. "I'm going to give you time to reconsider your answer."

"Probably not going to happen."

"Well, you say that, but I have something for you as a show of good faith," he said producing a small wooden box from a compartment next to him. "This was something your mother held very dear, and I am certain she would have wanted you to have it."

I had reached for the box before I was able to stop myself, taking it from him and looking down at it. It was an oak box, maybe six inches by six inches, with familiar wood carvings etched into it. I opened the box to reveal a silver chain necklace bunched lazily behind a silver Dara knot. This was the first piece of my mother I'd had in my entire life. It took everything in me not to cry.

"If you're lying about this—"

"I'm not," he cooed. "For whatever else you think I am or who and what I represent, I would not lie to you about this. That belonged to her, and now it belongs to you."

I opened the car door and moved to get out as quickly as I could, slamming the box shut. The man grabbed my arm, just enough to stop me.

"Hey! Hey," he said producing a business card from his coat pocket, handing it to me. "My name is Roger. You call me when you know it's time, alright?"

I crumpled the card in my fist as I got out of the car, a single tear managing to escape from my eye.

"Keep away from me," I said yanking my arm away from him.

He didn't say another word as Logan and I stood in front of Big Sister, the limo driving past us, a full-grown man sitting in the driver's seat where we'd previously seen a child. It drove away leaving me alone with a friend, an old car, distant sirens, and a piece of something that I thought I'd never see.

R ain beat down on and around me. Not right away, it took a little bit, but I had been standing there unsure of what to do or where to go for a little bit. The wind had been picking up around me, biting the exposed parts of my flesh. The sirens cut through the air in the distance along with the news copters creating far too much noise for such an otherwise tranquil area. Logan stood nearby, unsure of how to comfort me or if he even should. I barely registered any of it. I just stood there dumbly holding my mother's necklace staring at it inside of the box. I had no reason to believe Roger; he worked for the people who terrorized my friends and me earlier this year, or rather, much more likely, they worked for him. He had that air of authority around him. He also felt like a car salesman, and I didn't trust him on just about anything else he had said, he was definitely hiding things from me. With this though, I knew he was telling the truth or at least the more immediate parts. I felt a connection to this necklace. Not emotional and not magical, something more intimate.

This necklace belonged to my mother.

Eventually, the rain came in the sort of drops that were unreasonable, and Logan gently asked if we should leave. I agreed and opened the driver side door, grateful that Logan had been holding onto my phone and keys during the hike. We sat for a moment, quietly, before I put a key in the ignition without turning it over. Someone suggested food, and someone else agreed with the idea. I was barely there; I wasn't sure who said what. Life doesn't always give you notice for when it wants to hit you for the big moments, and when those moments come, sometimes all you can do is react and adapt and hope that when the moment is in the past that it didn't knock you to the ground and run over you. Right now that reaction looked a lot like going to eat recently promised pancakes.

The traffic trying to get off the hill was a nightmare. Cops, ambulances, and fire crews had all been called to the scene, not the residents who suddenly felt the need to flee their homes. Once we were down the hill and toward PCH, the traffic had completely cleared up, and I was already feeling a bit better, at least well enough to speak like a human again. I promised Logan the best pancakes in the area, and it wasn't long until we reached our destination. Logan seemed surprised as we passed The Original Pancake House and, I mean, I'm not about to knock their pancake game. Pancakes are kind of hard to mess up in the first place, and they had so many different combinations of pancake toppings that they were insulated from critique. One of the options was something like a pancake bowl that they filled with butter, but if you didn't want to try this one, if you didn't like the blueberry pancakes, well, you should have tried the chocolate chip pancakes. And if you didn't like the chocolate chip pancakes, well, you should have tried the bacon pancakes. And if you didn't like the bacon pancakes, well...why wouldn't you? Everyone likes bacon, don't they? You're not weird and different, are you?

Nope, that place was too gimmicky for me. That's why we were going someplace equally gimmicky, but in a different sort of way. Logan and I were headed to the Black Bear Diner. Their only gimmicks were serving more food than any one person should eat in a single sitting and plastering bears on everything. Every inch of every wall was covered in assorted bear art. Surrounding the building, including the parts not visible from the street, were bear totems as large as real bears engaging in activities from playing guitar to scuba diving. If you're trying to make sense of any of it, don't. The answer is bears. And yeah, this place was cheesy, but it was exactly the kind of cheesy I needed at the moment. Not a bad cheesy, but a gouda—no, I'm not making cheese puns now. Besides, I wasn't lying when I said this place had the best pancakes.

"I'm buying that bear hat. I need to buy that bear hat," Logan said approximately two seconds after we had walked in the door, nodding toward the merchandise stand. I didn't feel the need to stop him. Our wait was thankfully short, and perhaps due to the utter mess the two of us currently looked, the hostess politely sat us in the back away from the majority of the patrons, allowing us to talk in private.

"So, the pancakes, huh?" he said, glancing at the menu.

"Yeah, they're pretty good," I replied.

A few uncomfortable moments had passed before Logan tried again. "You, uh, seem to be doing a little better now," he managed. "Is there anything you'd like to talk about?"

I considered that for a moment. "Not particularly," I answered. "But that doesn't mean...It doesn't mean we can't talk, though. I'm just not eager to talk about everything, but that I get that you have questions. I mean, I also have questions, honestly."

A waitress came then and took our order. Logan ordered the pancakes, I asked for a breakfast plate. Our server was polite, but

I could see in her eyes that she thought I looked like a crazy person.

"No pancakes?" Logan asked after she left.

"Pancakes are a happy food," I replied. "I'm not sure how I feel right now, and a lot just happened. I need to eat, sure, but I'm not sure I'm in the mood."

"I understand," he said thoughtfully. I could see him thinking, trying to gather his courage to say what he wanted to say. "This might be personal, but can I tell you something?"

"Always."

"So, my Dad has always been kind of racist, and he hates that I'm a set designer instead of, well, any job that would require a tie and keep me in an office all day, every day. And he really hates that Olivia isn't Japanese," he began. "And my mom isn't much better. Every weekend she takes those charter buses down to the Native American casinos. My dad spends the weekends alone most of the time. She still lies to everyone about me, even when it makes no sense to do so. She tells strangers that I'm single and that I'm going to be a lawyer. Did you know that she tells people that she's my sister?"

I shook my head no, not sure how to react to that bit of news.

"There's plenty of things they've said and done, plenty of things to make me feel like I'm a bad son or that I'm not their son at all," he continued. "But that's not the entirety of who they are. Dad hated that I was in an art college, but he came to my showings, and one of my pieces is in his office. He always wanted to know how I was doing; he tried to learn the same theory I studied, or pretend like he wanted tips on how to sketch. He didn't want to learn how to draw, but he wanted me to think that he did. And my mom! When I was a kid, my mom used to be the queen of gift cards. We always had a ton of them, mainly to local grocery stores and department stores. So, she would lie to our extended family or just anyone she happened to know when they needed money, she said she got them from work, but she didn't. That was just her way of giving people access to the basics, food, clothes for school, whatever, without making them feel guilty for taking money. She still does that sometimes, just not as often."

"That sounds like a complicated childhood," I said awkwardly, not sure what to do with that information.

"It was," he admitted. "But I love my parents, deep flaws and all. I'm telling you this because you don't know your mom, but until now I think you never really knew how much you'd missed her, and that's not to say that you didn't want your parents around, just…I know that I'm not saying this well. Look, you're still holding the box!"

I wasn't sure that I agreed with him on the first half of that statement, but he was right that I hadn't let the box out of my grasp except to drive.

"I'm just trying to say that regardless of how your mother knew that guy, no matter how her necklace got into his hands, even if it was something appalling, there must have been a lot of good in there too. And even if there wasn't, I'm glad for whatever series of events she took in her life, because they created you. And you're a good friend who has done good things."

"You're a good friend, too," I muttered, looking at the box, letting those words sit in the air. I brought the box up to the table and studied it. The carvings on the box were intricate, depicting leaves and tree branches, and I knew that I'd seen them before, but I couldn't tell you from where. I unlatched the box, removing the necklace and letting it dangle in the air, suspended by the silver chain tangled between my fingers. The way I saw it, I could believe in her or believe the worst of her, and until I was proven otherwise, I was going to choose the best. Besides, she wanted me to have this, and she took steps to ensure that I got it. That had to mean something, didn't it?

I put the necklace on without a word, and Logan said nothing either. There was more of an acknowledgment, and we moved on. Our food came, and with another parting look of concern from our waitress, I took a fair-sized bite of hash browns and asked, "So, did you want to talk about what happened? On the beach?"

"I mean, I have questions, but only if you're up for it," he said.

"Sure, let's do it."

"Okay, big one then to start," he said quickly. "What the hell was that thing?"

"No idea. Seriously," I answered.

"Okay, but the guy in the car, he seemed to have an idea."

I finished chewing another bite. "Yeah, it looked that way, sure. But I don't know how much we can trust that guy. I'm pretty sure he sent it after us or one of his people did. It's far too much of a coincidence that he just happened to be there when we left."

"Yeah, that was pretty creepy, so was that kid," Logan agreed.

"Anything else?"

Logan seemed to hesitate before he spoke. "Yeah, and this might sound rude, all things considered, but do you think that guy had a point? Being around people who can do what you do, teaching you and looking out for you? I mean, you didn't think your bracelet was going to do all that, if we'd been anywhere else when you used it, it could have…"

He didn't want to finish the sentence, but I understood what he was asking. "Just because one side is wrong, it doesn't make the other side right," I answered. "I don't know how I feel about it, not fully. But his people have killed innocents, presumably kids. He might have a point in there somewhere, the most convincing evil usually does, but what he's really asking from me is to compromise. And putting aside that, no, I'm not going to ever be cool with hunting people down because they were born different, there's an important question in there. Why is he trying so hard? Even before I did everything he's worried about, Bres was under orders not to kill me. It's pretty obvious that he believes in the prophecy stuff with Lucia and seems to think I'm involved somehow, but why not just say that? What's with the stalking and job offers?"

Logan had a big mouthful of pancake now when he answered. "Hey, seriously? I don't know nothing about no prophecy, and I am for sure not qualified to talk about whatever that whole whatever you just said was. I'm still getting used to the fact that magic is real and today you just added concrete evidence that monsters are also a permanent worry."

I breathed a sigh, half in relief that this conversation was wrapping up and half because I was just reminded that my life was too crazy for most people to entertain, even people who wanted to.

The rest of the conversation after that was lighter and friendlier. Neither of us was in the mood to chat further about the heavy stuff, and both of us were fine with changing the topic. Our topics included the validity of these pancakes receiving my made up award of best pancakes in the world, how Thanksgiving went for us both, and if monsters are real, and sometimes they run around, then who or what else is out there because we just couldn't help ourselves. Okay, maybe Bigfoot is real? How about ghosts? I heard about a giant moth one time, where did that thing come from? Was it real or was it just a regular-sized moth that someone saw way too close to their face? Things had been getting weird over the past few months, and I'd been attacked more than once, sure, but I hadn't actually stopped to think about it mainly because no one else was around to corner me and force me to consider what it meant or what was even real. The bipedal cats were for sure real though. They were adorably bloodthirsty.

On the way out, Logan spotted his hat and upon seeing the price tag decided with a grimace that he did not, in fact, need to buy it which meant that I would purchasing a bear hat in the near future as his Christmas gift. I stopped him at the jukebox near the front door and removed a couple of dollars from my bag. "Hold up; I have a tradition here, a game if you're up for it," I said with a grin.

"And this game involves the jukebox?" he asked, quietly musing to himself as he inspected the machine. "Any good indie stuff in here? Beach House? Angel Olsen? Maybe American Football? Holy hell MGMT has been around for ten years? Okay, I'm old

"It does," I replied, ignoring his muttering. "So you know that game with the demon in Sandman, with the dueling microphones and the one-upping and all that?"

"Of course, I am a wolf, I am some guy on a horse with a spear, yadda yadda."

"Right, yes, perfect. So, we're going to play that, but with music. One of us picks good songs, the other picks awful songs, and we try to counter each other. Of course, we won't be here to hear everything."

"Which kind of makes you the demon, given that you're willing to inflict awful music on a family friendly establishment."

"If I am to be the demon, then allow me to begin by stating the rules," I said letting the machine suck up the dollars. "We are given three songs for a dollar, which we will choose in alternating order. This jukebox has been connected to the internet, so while originally it was designed to play a lot of Woody Guthrie and Frankie Lymon, over time it has stored, like, everything. If anyone ever downloaded a song from the internet, it's still lives on this machine. You can't download anything new though; you need to use what we have. In the end, the light of your three songs has to overpower the darkness of my three obnoxious songs. Are you ready?"

"Yeah, okay, I think I got this." Logan nodded, a smile spreading.

"Good, then the opening move is mine!" I said in an approximation of a demon voice. "I am 'All Star' by Smashmouth, faux inspirational, meme-inducing."

Logan cringed as he saw it added to the playlist, giving me a look of betrayal. I knew he hated that song. He took a second to get used to the scrolling display, before selecting a song. "I am 'Outro' by M83. Creative inducing, meme erasing. Also used in, like, every fan trailer for a reason, but yeah, sorry, your turn."

I already had my next pick. "I am 'Photograph' by Nickelback, rock by committee, devoid of creativity. A song no one wants to hear, yet everyone has heard."

"I am 'Mr. Brightside' by The Killers, carefully crafted and enduring, a song everyone wants to hear," Logan said, scrolling to it without hesitation.

"I am 'Faith' by Limp Bizkit, never needing to have existed, distorting the work of a better man, screaming inappropriately and unnecessarily as I corrupt even the purest of lyrics!" I said triumphantly picking the worst song I could think of, still using my ridiculous demon voice. "And what will you be then, Dreamlord?"

Logan thought a moment and then added his song to the playlist, stepping aside to show me how he rounded it all out.

"'The Sign'?" I asked, now in my regular voice. "I don't get it."

"I just like Ace of Base." He shrugged.

As we jogged to my car in the parking lot, Logan nervously sang to himself something about my being dragged somewhere and that I belonged there. It took me a moment to get what he was on about. We got into the car, and Logan asked, "So, who won?"

"There are no winners when you're minorly annoying," I said, turning the ignition over and backing up. "There will be times in your life, young Logan—"

"I'm older than you," he interrupted.

"—that things will seem impossible to get through, like being attacked on a beach by a D & D monster and fighting for your life with only the husk of an old ship for protection. Then that moment will pass, and you will find yourself eating breakfast in the afternoon at a bear themed diner before retreating to the comfort of your home. And I am just about ready to head home."

"You mean head to work?"

"Smartass," I teased sourly.

5

The Book's End, formerly my home away from home, is now just my home. It is also a constant source of jokes from several of my friends. Though I hid it pretty well at the time, I was hurt when Olivia asked our mutual friend, Teague, to be her new roommate instead of me, particularly with what caused her to be in need of a new roommate in the first place. But, all things considered, it's still worked out. Kind of. To start with the positives, rent is significantly cheaper than living in a proper apartment. Rent prices are out of control everywhere, and it's not like anyone works in a friend's book store for the money. More than that, I'm not really worried about getting to work on time. I wake up, clean up, open up. It's as simple as that. And I'm surrounded by books all day, every day! If I want to read something, I can just order it to the store. There's also the coffee maker, which means that every day when I get up to brew a fresh pot, it counts as work, and there's no such thing as making too much. Stealing a muffin every day is just one of the perks of living where I work. Before moving in here, the majority of my income went to rent and books and snacks, so I found myself with triple digits in my bank account slightly more often than I had in the past.

It isn't all great, though. For one thing, the loft space where I sleep isn't exactly private. No one would know I was up there if I didn't announce it or make a ton of noise, but there's no door during the day either, and you'd be surprised how much you're willing to pay for a door. The shower situation is less than ideal. We have a shower, which is better than you might expect out of a bookstore, but said shower was also built nearly twenty years ago by twenty-year-olds who didn't know how to build a shower. There are better showers outdoors at the beach. The water pressure sucks, and you're lucky to get two minutes of hot water. The loft space also doesn't seem built with a permanent resident in mind, which presented challenges. Sleep is a toss-up most nights, as you'd be surprised how often people knock on the door at the most inappropriate of hours. We also have cats who don't understand the concept of two in the morning, and attempting to forbid them from any area would only ensure that they would stop at nothing to occupy that space. Then there were the times you'd just like to go home and relax, and that meant walking in on your boss while she was working.

Times like right now.

Logan and I entered the shop to see Claire hard at work, revamping the snacks portion of her business. She had recently managed to buy an open-air refrigeration display from a storage auction for a couple of hundred bucks, and I can't remember the last time I'd seen her that excited. I didn't understand, she told me. These things typically cost in the thousands, and all the big chains have them, and this fits the counter area perfectly! We're going to be able to keep milk and juice and sandwiches and everything down there! And it was a turbo something or other which is pretty much the best brand you could buy. It was practically brand new; she couldn't believe no one else tried to outbid her. I know my limitations, and my knowledge of esoteric refrigeration is an area that I am most certainly limited in, but the important part to me is that she knew it was good for business and, if it had her this giddy, it mattered to me.

"Hey, we're back," I said simultaneously announcing my arrival with the door chime. "How's the new display coming?"

Claire turned to look at us, adjusting to the sight of me as she did. "Put a pin in that; I think we need to have a conversation about this."

"Oh, this?" I asked, glancing at my costume. "I'm a mermaid now. Mermaids are—"

"Elana was modeling for my painting," Logan interrupted.

"Ah. Okay, I wasn't sure if this was going to be your new everyday look or something," Claire replied, relief evident in her voice.

I gave Logan a look to show my annoyance at being cut off, which he didn't see because he had already turned away from me to pick up a comic book.

"Nope, only on Mermaid Tuesdays," I replied. "So, whatcha doing?"

Claire's eyes lit up, remembering the display. "Yes! Check it out; we're stocking the healthy stuff now!"

I spotted a favorite of mine, though calling them healthy was a stretch. "Oh rad, we have chocolate covered acai berries," I exclaimed. "And you're planning on leaving me alone with them every night, because I am totally trustworthy and wouldn't dare steal from the store no matter how much I craved sustenance."

"Wait, did you just pronounce them 'Ah-Kai' berries?" Logan asked.

"Yeah, why?"

"They're pronounced 'Ah Sai Eee."

I thought for a second and responded, "Ah. I see," I waited for a second, proud of my joke and waiting for a reaction. One never came. "One day I will understand what these Hu-Mans call humor."

"Right," Claire said, changing the subject. "We have Green tea, ionized water, Kombucha—"

"Gross," I said out loud without meaning to.

"It's not gross! It's one the healthiest things you can drink!" Claire protested.

"Believe it or not, healthy things can taste gross," I argued. I guess this was the fight I was willing to pick today.

"It's a traditional drink in Japan—" Claire began.

"Nope, that's Kombu," Logan said, taking a side in our great debate. "You're thinking of kelp tea, my grandma used to make it, and it was also gross. What you're selling is disgusting snot water and your customers are fools for drinking it."

"See?" I exclaimed, giving Logan a tiny high five.

"Do you have any idea how many Dan Brown novels I sell every month here?" Claire asked Logan. "Dan Brown alone plays my utilities. I sell what the people want, no judgment. All hail Dan Brown."

"Claire has a point, without Dan Brown I'd be in an office somewhere," I conceded. "All hail."

"Glad that's settled, you want to get cleaned up?" Claire asked moving back to her display. "I need to get out of here in, like, fifteen."

Heck! I absolutely forgot that I had promised to close tonight. I wanted nothing more than to shower and pass out for twelve hours, but that wasn't happening now. "Yeah, sure, let me just walk Logan out," I said, hoping that I hadn't given anything away. When we were out of earshot and into the parking lot, Logan eyed me suspiciously.

"You're not going to tell Claire what happened today?" he asked.

"Later, probably," I replied. "She's about to head out, and I don't want her to spend the whole night worrying. She's getting out more now that I live here, but still not as often as she should. I'll tell her tomorrow."

"All right, you got this. I'll tell Olivia you said hi," he said offering me a goodbye hug.

"Thanks, please do," I said returning it, before exchanging our final goodbyes as he ordered a ride home. Once back inside, I offered hurried apologies to Claire as I ran to the back to get as presentable as possible in the short amount of time I had, which amounted to throwing on a hoodie and keeping the shiny green leggings. By the time I wiped off the last remains of patchy, sweat-ruined mermaid makeup I had come back out to the shop front to see that Claire was already packed up and ready to leave. Whatever her plans, she was in a rush and took off in a hurry.

The rest of the afternoon until closing time was, thankfully, relatively slow. A couple of Santa Monica City College kids had accidentally wandered too far inland and studied in peace and quiet at one of the tables for several hours. I sold a board game to some guy in his forties who told me far too much about his inability to find a decent brick and mortar store in the area that carried anything worth buying. A couple of neighborhood regulars bought cocoa and cookies and wandered around the store for the better part of an hour without purchasing anything else. So mainly I felt like I was on babysitting duty more than customer service. The Christmas rush would start soon, but not quite yet.

The time came to close up, and I drew the curtains and locked the doors, prepared to ignore everyone else for the rest of the night. I had a couple of text messages. Logan was letting me know that Olivia said hello, which I didn't entirely believe even though it felt good to hear. Ann was asking me if I wanted to see the Eternity Pilgrim Christmas special in the theaters at some one-night-only special event thing. I said yes, hoping that I didn't forget between now and then. And with nothing else on my phone immediately urgent, I set the ringer and alerts to silent and prepared to get to work.

I still wanted to catch up on that sleep, no question, but all of my free time as of late had to be devoted to getting caught up on not only the books I had, um…let's say, "inherited from Jason", but also the stack of study materials I was given by Chalsarda and the Aos Si. I still didn't know his name, which irked me every time I thought about it, but ultimately it didn't matter. At least not for the moment. They had both been tremendously helpful over the past few months, and I'd especially became fond of Chalsarda. Beyond the fact that I'd somehow become friends with a badass warrior Elf who was trying to teach me archery and occasionally went to the movies with me, she was also just a genuinely cool person. Eight-year-old Elana would have freaked out if she had known what she was in for as an adult.

There was a lot about these books and, well, everything else that I had to learn. For one thing, you shouldn't just pick up one of these books and start reading them for hours at a time. You totally can, but you'll also probably go mad in the process. There was a circle of serenity I learned how to create and sit inside of, which offered a measure of protection. The voices that I heard while I was reading before, they're echoes of the history of the tomes. As it turns out, the older a thing is, the more powerful it is. But the knowledge, not the pages, are the important things, and throughout history, knowledge is transplanted from one dying book into another as a means of preserving that which had been discovered and known. So what might appear on the outside as a guide to finding old bottles in mineshafts might actually be a step by step guide to creating wards to hold off all manner of super-spooky baddies.

And the weird thing was, not everyone could read them; there was no rhyme or reason to it that I could see. Of the friends who saw what I saw in the books, and not the original printed text, Olivia was about to read it as clearly as I did, not that she could understand much of any of it. Logan would see bits and pieces every so often, but for the most part, he couldn't. It came and went with him. Claire, Teague, and Jason—not evil Jason; my friend, Jason, who will definitely change his name to something else because I asked nicely—couldn't see anything. Ann hasn't ever tried, so who knows? But there was no real common denominator between them which explained why some people could and some people could not. It was frustrating, to say the least.

Oh, and speaking of frustrating, there was the matter of the aforementioned wards! I could understand the concepts beyond why a ward worked, what it was meant to do, and nearly every mechanic behind it. It was like the "Them Bones" song, but with magic. The problem wasn't in anchoring the spell, or weaving the lines, or anything like that. It was simply a matter of power, and I simply didn't have enough of it. I was trying to gift wrap a car with a sheet of newspaper. And my lessons were going all right, my magical well was getting deeper all the time the more I practiced, just at an excruciatingly slow place. I've heard countless stories, both in fiction and now second hand, of Wizards and Witches and Sorcerers and Magicians all turning bad or suffering a heavy consequence because of their rush to gain power. In the past, it never made sense to me, you already have magic, so why burn yourself out trying to get more through a shortcut? But now that I have the knowledge of how to offer even the most basic protection to the people I love, and I am unable because I'm not strong enough, I get it.

Not that I'm ever going to make any deals for power. I've seen how that works out, I mean, come on. I'm just saying that I understand.

So I decided to spend the evening trying to work on what I knew I could. My bracelet was gone, so I decided to make a new one. Maybe not fire this time, but I'd learned a new spell recently and given the less destructive potential it seemed like as good an idea as any. I looked through my little costume jewelry box, thinking I might try something different this time, but rings were too small, and the only possible earrings that I could have etched the proper symbols into would have been absurdly big. It also occurred to me that I might not want to rip a hoop earring out of my head in the heat of battle. I had a necklace, but it was pretty special to me, and I didn't feel right about the idea of scratching it up. So unless I wanted to go with an anklet, and I did not, another bracelet seemed like the best idea. I had also been working on my jacket, but as I learned the hard way the first time, sewing sigils into a garment was way more work than just chipping away at cheap metal.

The spell that I had in mind was unexpectedly complex. It turns out that fire, earth, water, ice, wind; these are all grade school level spells. Evocations are what they're called. Anything that created a quick something from nothing. Easy to conjure, very temporary, and wild by nature. It was super cool that I could just set things on fire and then also put out that fire with a stream of water because I am so sorry that I set that thing on fire I swear it was a total accident; but it turns out I was overconfident in my abilities by a generous amount. If magic were cooking, throwing around evocation magic was like scrambling eggs, serving it with toast and bacon, and then calling yourself a chef. Yeah, you made food, but it was sloppy and quick and required the barest mastery of cooking. For my part, I managed to turn the stove on without burning myself most days, both literally and metaphorically.

What I was considering storing in this bracelet was...sap. Yup, tree sap! It's not an elemental force, not primal and basic, so somehow it took way effort to produce. It was an earthy spell and definitely felt more druidic than anything else I have tried casting yet, but apparently, it is possible to cast bees. That would be way more druidy. As fascinating as that was, I was not prepared for the fallout of what would happen if I cast bees incorrectly, and sap seemed to have a lot less potential for unintended destruction. Probably more like a ruined carpet or something. Both came from life, and anything involving something living or life giving was significantly more difficult. Not impossible, you just had to be careful and understand there was a lot more to it. I'd also have to be careful not to overload it the way I did with the fire spell, lest I encase myself in amber by mistake or something. I figured that I might as well go through the motions of getting started on my arts and crafts projects before settling in for a night of study. I instinctively went for my jacket as I had nearly every day for the past half a year, and stopped after a second remembering the flame tower.

I considered for a moment that the jacket was potentially also packing far more of the spell inside of it than I'd ever anticipated. That said, what I'd been storing in the jacket hadn't been really anything dangerous like it had with the bracelet. And if it had gotten to that point, well, it was already there now. Eh, why not? I carefully felt for the spell woven into the jacket, trying my best to understand every inch and nuance of it, asking it for permission. It felt like reading a book by spelling out every word in your head. When I was done I released the small amount of energy as I painstakingly cast a now very familiar spell, and the jacket seemed warm to the touch, letting me know I wouldn't be able to store anything else into it for the night safely. Next up was the hard part: Creating a bracelet from scratch. It was a headache. The first time I tried, I went through maybe eight or nine bracelets trying to get it right. I had bought a stack of them from the flea market at Alpine Village. They weren't very expensive, and at the time I thought I was just going to create an arsenal of magical jewelry. It turned out that I had grossly underestimated the difficulty of engraving magical sigils into low quality metal.

I set up shop, first opening up an encyclopedia about infectious diseases which turned out to instead be an encyclopedia of various sigils. I was certain this would prove to be one of my most useful books over time. I used a fine point marker to draw the little symbols first, carefully. Confident that I had them just so, I used my hand vice to attach the bracelet to my desk, turned the crank just enough so that it wouldn't move, but so I wouldn't ruin the bracelet either. From there I went to work with my little hammer and chisel. Tiny little dings into the metal, slow and deliberate. It was the better part of three hours to finish, but I hadn't made the mistake of trying to rush through it as I had before and, by taking my time, I finished it in one shot this time. I took my prize to the sink in the back, carefully cleaning it in solution and examined it. Yup, it was good, or at least as good as I was going to manage. My shoulders ached, and I was mentally exhausted, but there was still one last task I had to accomplish. I almost considered letting it go until the next day, but decided that would just be a waste of an evening. I concentrated the same way I had with the jacket, only with the degree of difficulty turned up a notch or two, and released the tree sap spell into the bracelet. It glowed for a moment, turning warm, indicating I was done.

I trudged back upstairs and looked at my chosen studies for the night. *Spagyrics: The Alchemical Preparation of Medicinal Essences, Tinctures, and Elixirs*. When I couldn't immediately decide if that was the normal title of a magical book or not, I decided I'd done enough for one evening. "Book learnin' is for nerds," I said with an enervated sigh, collapsing into my bed. "All the cool kids are—"

I yawned slowly, closing my eyes, not bothering to finish that thought. It's not like there was anyone around to hear me make an attempt at humor anyway.

J ust because I wasn't forcefully dragged into The Knowing while I slept as often these days didn't mean that I was sleeping well, exactly. I woke up groggy in my bed, still clothed from the night before. An optimistic thought ran through my head almost as soon as I opened my eyes. At least I didn't have to open the store today. My immediate thought after that was crap; I totally forgot that I promised to open the store today. Okay, so maybe it wasn't so bad. I might have enough time to go back to sleep for a little bit. I checked my phone and…ugh. We open in an hour and twenty, give or take. I let out a shout of frustration, which felt like the best way to start my day. Or scare the cats. One of the two.

With my morning protest out of the way, I forced myself out of bed and put myself on autopilot, getting everything ready for the day. I fed the cats out in the back, brushed my teeth, put fresh coffee on—all the mundane things someone who lives in a bookstore does to wake up. I love working here, and for as much as I was in a morning mood, I clearly understood the benefits of being able to wake up at my job. I was certain by the time I managed to have breakfast, caffeinate myself, and allow fresh air and hopefully sunlight inside, that I'd be in much better spirits. One would assume that to be the case anyway. How often do you see someone with fresh coffee in one hand, a muffin in the other, bathed in pleasant weather and they're still in a bad mood? Okay, maybe it happens, but they probably have other things going on, and it's not fair to put that kind of pressure on muffins.

I glanced at my phone and I had two minutes to spare. I decided that I didn't want to miss the uncommon opportunity to get the store open on time for a change. I unbolted the door and swung it open, nearly falling back at the sight of a woman towering over me. Someone had been waiting at the door, but not outside at a reasonable distance, checking their phone or anything like that. A woman, who was easily a foot taller than me, was standing at the door so closely that her nose might have been touching the door.

"Jeez!" I exclaimed, stepping back startled.

The woman looked down to regard me. "May I come in?"

"What?" I asked, still off guard. "Yes, of course, we're open now. Welcome to The Book's End, how many I help you today?"

"I understand that this is a business," she remarked, still studying me. "But it is also your home, is it not?"

"Yeah, how do you know that? Do you know Claire or something?"

"So, then it is only polite that I request your permission before entering," she continued. *Where was that accent from?*

"Either way, door is open and I'm on the clock, so you're welcome to join me," I said, walking behind the counter.

The woman entered and cast her eyes to every corner of the place as Jameson and Koala dashed past me from the back of the store and began to furiously rub on her legs and purr with deep contentment.

"Oh, hello little ones!" she cooed as her face turned up in joy.

"Wow, they, uh…" I began, taken off guard. "They really like you."

"Jameson. Koala. You will be blessed with long, happy lives. Now run along and play now, children," she cooed to the cats who immediately turned and trotted happily toward the back door.

Okay, so cats like her and obey her commands. Oh god, please tell me more weirdness didn't just walk into my life. "So, how do you know Claire?" I asked hopefully, silently praying for a mundane answer like high school, the gym, or prison.

"I don't," she said confidently.

It was only just now that I got a good look at her and a wave of panic swept through me. She was tall, nearly a foot taller than me. I'd picked up on that when she was at the door, but maybe it was the sun in my eyes or the fact that I wasn't fully awake yet, but I hadn't pieced together the rest of it. I would have placed her in her early forties, a couple of years older than Claire maybe, but she looked as if she had been assembled in a factory. Something was decidedly not human about her, and it was unsettling that I couldn't pinpoint what it was. She had thick, straight hair that was the kind of blonde you only seemed to see in eighties movies. Her eyes were a deep sapphire, and aside from an amount of gold that would have bordered on excess on anyone else, I noticed something else. White shoes, a white pleated linen skirt, a white blouse.

Oh…no. "Did Roger send you because I wouldn't accept his offer?" I asked, not breaking eye contact.

She raised an eyebrow at that, as the beginnings of a grin touched the edge of her lips. "No one ever sends me anywhere," she said bemusedly.

I wasn't ready for a fight, especially not when some hapless customer could wander in any second now. And something about her felt decidedly not human, what if she was Fae like Bres? A fight with one of the Fae could get ugly in a hurry for everyone around. Mostly for myself.

"Kind of stupid for one Gardener to come alone," I said shaking the blister shield out of my wrist. I was trying to sound confident, but I was terror-stricken by the unknown elements here, and it was all I could do to bluff. "It didn't go so well for the last one who came at me alone."

The woman couldn't help herself as she let out a small laugh. "You fashion yourself a sorcerer?" she asked, and with a dismissive wave of her hand, my shield was gone. Just gone! "Child, sorcery is but one of my domains, and you are no more a sorcerer than any of those pretenders you are so quick to associate me with. The people of this realm wield magic that is not their own."

I stiffened as she spoke. "Okay then," I said slowly. "If you're not a Gardener, then what are you."

"Goddess."

Of course you are.

"Well, December is free coffee for deities month, so lucky you," I said, trying to force a laugh.

"Is it really?" she asked. "Because I would love to try the house blend."

"It is now," I said, moving to make her a cup. Whoever she was, goddess or no, she was severely out of my league, and the best thing I could do was to keep her talking.

"Please make yourself a cup as well and join me, we have business to discuss."

"Cream or sugar?" I asked pouring the cups. She indicated a quick no as I brought them over. "So, shouldn't I know who I'm doing business with?"

"Indeed. I am Freyja," she replied, sipping her coffee. "And this is quite the beverage you've made."

"Thanks, I've been practicing," I said taking a sip of my own.

"You don't believe me, do you?" Freyja asked, warmly somehow. Not disappointed, or angry, or defensive. "Even with everything you've seen and done?"

"No offense, but I've met a lot of magic users lately, and it's not like someone wouldn't just claim to be a god if they wanted to look bigger than they are. You're definitely stronger than me, but that doesn't mean I have to believe whatever you say at face value. I met a guy named Bres earlier this year, and I'm pretty sure he wasn't the Demon King."

Freyja chuckled at that. "Oh, the things I could tell you about Bres," she said taking a sip. "Did you know that historians mistranslated, and he's actually the Lemon King?"

"That doesn't make any sense," I snapped back. "Citrus trees aren't native to—Oh damn it."

"Maybe one day we'll both understand what these Hu-Mans call humor," she replied with a smirk. Wait, I just made that joke yesterday. Was she spying on me?

I shook my head, trying to understand what was happening. "Okay, so let's say I believe you, and you're telling the truth about being Freyja, Norse goddess of love," I began.

"Among many other things," she responded.

"Well, then what you could you possibly want with me?" I asked.

"To kill my brother."

I didn't know how to respond to that. It was said so casually, and the people who are generally casual about fratricide aren't what I would call good people. I very much went out of my way to prevent death, not act as its agent.

"At the risk of pissing off a goddess," I said, practically shaking. "No. You'll need to find someone else."

Freyja looked as if she expected that response and lolled back in her chair. "I am sure you are hesitant to take a life, as much as I am loathed to ask this of you."

"Well, yeah, obviously. I don't want to kill anyone," I said, trying to articulate my thoughts. "But, like, I'm not just unwilling, I'm unable. Your brother is Freyr, correct?"

"He is," she confirmed.

I sighed. "And how would you even expect me to kill a god? And why?"

My head perked up as I heard the door chime, announcing a visitor. I saw one of the better parts of the past year walk through the door, my new friend Chalsarda. She looked significantly different than the first time I saw her at that party. Well, we both were, honestly. Both of our dresses were fancy enough that I'd call them costumes. At the moment, she had traded the evening gown for skinny jeans with a leather hip satchel firmly attached to her thigh, and a baggy, vintage t-shirt for the band The Pixies, which made me laugh a little inside at a joke that I didn't quite understand immediately. Her blonde-brown hair hung freely, and she was currently making absolutely no attempt to conceal her elven ears. I had asked her once about why she didn't conceal her ears most of the time she was here, and her answer made a surprising amount of sense. She asked me how many everyday people I thought saw her and their immediate thought was that elves were real and they should freak out? The answer was of course, none. This city was weird enough as it was; at worst she got disapproving looks, and at best she had people asking where she bought them. Anything that did know she was Fae was something she could probably handle and, if it wasn't, trying to hide the ears wasn't going to matter anyway.

Chalsarda looked ready to offer me a greeting when Freyja turned around as well. In the second that their eyes met, a flash of surprise washed over my friend's face and, in an instant, she was on one knee, offering a deep bow.

"Goddess! Forgive my intrusion; I meant no offense!" she exclaimed.

I began to say something, but Freyja held up a hand and stood gracefully. "The offense is forgiven," she said to Chalsarda. "Now rise and wait outside until my business with Elana is concluded, is that understood?"

Chalsarda rose to her feet just as quickly, eyes still facing toward the floor, nodded her head and turned to leave.

"Hold on, no way," I said, and the tension was suddenly palpable between them.

Freyja turned back to face me and, as she did, a wide-eyed Chalsarda pursed her lips and quickly shook her head no. "Chalsarda is my friend and she was invited, so you don't get to just order her outside like a pet."

"Oh?" Freyja said, regarding me.

"Okay, let me put it another way," I said, trying to diffuse the tension. "I see three seats at this table, and she was to be my guest. Now we can have three people sitting here, enjoying a drink, or just two of us, but it won't just be you and me all by ourselves. I trust her counsel, and to that, you're asking something that I am adamantly averse to even considering. So if you want that conversation to continue, you'll let me decide who is welcome in my home or not. Deal?"

Freyja offered a quick glance back at my friend before turning back toward me. "I apologize, you have shown me hospitality in your home. I was wrong to disrespect your friend in that manner. Please, won't you join us?"

Chalsarda offered a nod, with her hands crossed in front of her at the waist, and joined us at the table, looking more uncomfortable and unsure of herself than I thought was possible.

"Chai tea?" I asked, and she responded with a nod. I returned with her beverage and sat down at the table with the two of them. "So Chalsarda, Freyja was just telling that she wants me to kill her brother."

Freyja looked visibly perturbed at that, and Chalsarda immediately choked. She looked mortified by her reaction and did her best to recover her composure.

"To answer your earlier question, the how is less important than the why. Are you familiar with Ragnarök?"

I nodded. "The Norse myth about the end of the world, right?"

"I am not mythology, I am history," she said tightly. "I am the past, present, and future. The gods are forever, but we cannot last. Ragnarök refers not to the end of the world, but the end of the gods. Nevertheless, it is the story of something that hasn't happened yet, but is destined to come to pass. All of us will die, save me. I am to be the witness, the last of us."

"I am truly sorry," I said. "I'm still getting used to the idea of fiction not being fiction; I didn't mean to imply that your story meant any less to you than anyone else. I have questions, though. For starters, how are you here?"

"It is all right, most have forgotten us, all of the gods, really," she started. "You have been to The Knowing, as you call it. The land before creation, some call it creation itself. We know of it as Ginnungagap, and yet others call it something else. The simple answer, as far as I can tell, is that we were here first. You say mythology, a better way of saying that might just be the first stories. We are all so very ancient, and we span across many worlds. Walking between them is second nature to us. But in the end, like everything, we are stories. And though we are all aware of our roles, we are biding our time until the end. We cannot change the outcome. But, you…" Freyja let that hang in the air.

"You want me to prevent Ragnarök? By killing your brother?" I asked incredulously.

"Precisely."

I rubbed my temples. "That makes no sense," I said considering everything. "And even if it did, which again it does not, wouldn't the job of god killer be better suited to, I don't know, a goddess?"

"There are certain parts of us which are inescapable," Freyja said sadly. "The gods can't escape their fates, at least not directly. We all have a role to play. I am forbidden by something beyond myself, beyond even the All-Father, that prevents me from doing this by my own hand. But if you were to do it, the rules will change."

"And why me?" I asked. "Why at all? With your brother specifically, I mean."

"How many stories have you already changed? What is one more?"

"Okay, I almost feel like you're being intentionally evasive at this point, but why your brother?"

"Do you think I want Freyr to die?" she snapped. "This is simply the best chance for everyone. I have spent years trying to find another way, and this is it! Freyr is the first of us to fall to Surtur, after that all is lost. They all know this, know they cannot win, but will fight anyway. If Freyr is killed before Baldur's dream, the end will never be signaled. We will all be given our own path, and I will be free to kill Surtur myself."

I was wondering at the moment if it were possible for the gods to go crazy. Why not just kill Loki, who kills Baldur? Why not have Frigg ask mistletoe to protect her son? Why doesn't Frigg just ask it already, if she knows that's how her son dies? I was missing something. "I want to help you, I really do," I said finally. "But killing is wrong. I'm not a murderer. There has to be another way."

"You keep interesting counsel," Freyja responded, fixing her gaze on Chalsarda. "Perhaps she can convince you of the unfortunate necessity of sacrificing the few for the many."

Freyja looked back to me and placed the backs of her hands on the table. "I would appreciate it if you thought on this before you gave me an answer. I have a token I would like to give you, as a tribute for my slight earlier." As she spoke, a soft golden glow formed in her palms and, from nothing, golden strands formed and wove into each other, creating a solid gold brooch that resembled an acorn. "My gift to you. You have but to whisper my name to it, and I will come to you. I expect that if you use this, you will have good news for me."

When she finished her weaving, the golden object hit the table with a thud that implied more weight than you would expect from an object the size of my fist.

"Thank you," I said, trying to be polite. What else do you say when someone gives you a chunk of solid gold?

"You are very welcome." Freyja nodded, standing up to leave. "And before I go, I have one more piece of information that might help you come to a decision. It is possible that my brother has heard of my intentions to choose you as a champion. He likely knows because I told him as much. And to that end, he has already chosen a champion of his own to stop you. That champion would be Kodran Osvifsson, and I believe he may have already begun his campaign of permanently stopping you. Tell me, Elana, have you seen anything strange lately?"

7

"What were you thinking?" Chalsarda let an arrow loose, pulling the string just a bit too tightly. Her whole body was tense, not that it seemed to be affecting her aim at all. "Did you have any idea who she was?"

I shrugged, hoping to appear aloof in an attempt to hide my embarrassment. "She might have mentioned it," I replied as Chalsarda quickly nocked an arrow and released it at her target dummy. With everything else that had been happening in my life, I got my schedules confused and forgot I was supposed to train today. I could try to blame the fact that hardly anyone else has worked retail while also training in archaic forms of combat, knowledge of magic, and enough studying that even I started to resent reading; but I had done this to myself. It was my decision, was still my decision, to do whatever I could to be ready for whatever was waiting out there for me, and I thankfully managed to get a pretty good head start with better assistance than I could have hoped for.

"That was one of the single stupidest, most foolish acts I've not only ever seen from a mortal, but could ever have hoped to see from one," she chided, before softening her tone. "Thank you. It's not everyone who will stand up to a goddess for you. You are a true friend, but you did not have to do that."

"I was happy to do it."

Chalsarda shook her head. "You're not understanding. You really didn't have to do that. My people have a connection to her and several of the other gods, but my kind is, well, less important than other elves. I doubt she'd ever have known my name had you not mentioned it to her. She'd have forgotten my face the second she turned away from it, if you hadn't interfered."

"It didn't matter who she was," I said plainly. "You can judge a person's character by how they treat people who can do nothing for them. I believe that. She was willing to compliment my coffee and give me gifts and crack jokes because she needs something from me. She treated you as less than a person because she didn't need anything from you. In my book, that's a strike against her. I can't stand people who take advantage."

"That is noble of you; it is a quality I admire in you. But it is shortsighted," Chalsarda said, taking a much more controlled shot with her bow. "She is not people. She is something greater. Many of the elves see her as their creator, those that have chosen that pantheon anyway. My behavior was a sign of reverence and respect to those who believe in her; at that moment, I was a representative of all of my people. It was also a matter of safety, in case you forgot who she was and what she could do to us."

"So that was *really* Freyja?" I asked, trying to question her without being disrespectful. "As in, the Norse god? Like a god... a, for real, god?"

"Indeed, that was The Fair One," Chalsadra replied with a nod, hanging up her bow and removing her quiver. "To her people, she is the goddess of war and sorcery, beauty and love; even gold and crops. And for some reason, it seems as though every-

one who follows that pantheon worships Thor. I don't understand it myself."

"Love and war?" I asked. "Those things seem to be at
odds."

"Well, it just means that she's a lover, not a fighter," Chalsadra remarked thoughtfully. "But she's also a fighter, so you
might want to take her seriously."

I stood a moment trying to take in the idea that I might have
just pissed off someone I'd read about in mythology as a kid. I
might have just been looking at it through the lens of a child, but
Freyja never seemed like the type to ask someone to commit
murder. She'd been quite different than what I would have expected entirely, the more that I thought about it.

"Quit stalling," Chalsarda said, instructing me. "I've set
your targets, now hit them."

"You know if I ever split an arrow it's going to be on accident, don't you?" I asked, slipping on my quiver and picking up
my bow. "You're an elf; I'm a human."

"My being an elf only means I have the vision to see an arrow being split a mile away and in the dark. You have a list of
reasons why you can't split the arrows yet, and your eyes have
nothing to do with it. To start, you don't follow instruction and
wear your quiver on your hip, not your back."

"Come on, that's just your preference, admit it!" I teased.
"Every archery-based hero I've ever seen wears it on their back.
Hawkeye, Legolas, even Robin Hood all wore the quiver on their
back."

"We've talked about this," Chalsarda said impatiently, adjusting my quiver to my hip the way a mother might need to help
a child get dressed. "Different worlds have different rules. Sometimes the rules are big, like the ones that have access to magic or
super science, and sometimes the rules are small, like when it's
not completely stupid to have a quiver on your back. The people

of those worlds have different rules, and on their worlds, an arrow is drawn faster from the back than the side. But your world does not care for the fanciful whims of legendary archers, and so you must be taught the proper way. Draw from your hip, nock, and shoot."

"Fine." I pouted. "But you have to admit it looks cooler on my back."

"It does," she conceded. "But I'm not teaching you to look cool; I'm teaching you to survive. Now aim and shoot."

I stepped up and did my best to remember all the safety tips I'd been shown. Chalsarda was right about different worlds having different rules. I never saw Robin Hood use a wrist guard and, if he'd been shooting in my world, his arm would have been shredded to the bone in a matter of weeks. There were so many steps to shooting. Where to rest the arrow, how to stand, how to release, when to move your head. I followed all of these steps admirably and, as expected, I missed the target completely.

"Breathe in as you pull, out as you release. Go again," Chalsarda commanded. I repeated the steps, focusing on the breathing, releasing another arrow and at least this time I made my way to the neighborhood of the target, but nowhere close to splitting an arrow. "Better. Go again."

I had an idea and I've done something similar before, so I decided to go for it. After nocking my arrow, I reached out with my senses for the arrow Chalsarda marked as my target; the arrow that I was meant to split. I focused on it, and with the smallest bit of power, I traced an invisible line back to it in my mind, releasing the arrow in concert with a fraction of my normal wind spell. The arrow darted along the path, hitting the target with a considerable thump and splitting the arrow Chalsarda set for me.

"Ha! Yes!" I whooped in triumph, turning to celebrate only to have my box snatched angrily from my hands.

Chalsarda stared hard at me, her posture tense and coiled. "Have I taught you nothing or did you think I was just dumb and blind and wouldn't see you cheat?"

I hadn't expected this reaction from her and it startled me, even scared me a bit. "Calm down; there's no harm done, I thought that was pretty neat. I split the arrow, didn't I?"

"Magic is not a shortcut; it is a single tool of many!" she shouted at me. "The point was not to split the arrow."

"Then what *was* the point?" I retorted.

"Come with me."

She marched away from me in a huff to the middle of a clearing on the expansive grounds. I followed, and she instructed me to sit on the ground across from her. I did, and she produced a key from her pouch and handed it to me.

"You've been keeping up with your magical studies at least?" she asked in a harsh tone.

"Of course," I said, meekly taking the key.

"Then, you know what to do," she replied, sitting across from me.

This was a training practice, an augury. It's maybe one of the things I'm the worst at, and this exercise was a two-part practice. I was to divine the where in the house this key fit, and when I did, I was to determine if using this key would be harmful or beneficial to me. I wasn't able to tell specifically what would be there, but if it were, say, a pack of rabid dogs, it would be a bad feeling. Birthday cake and balloons, it would be a good feeling. It was about feeling and sensing more than anything else, but it required intense concentration.

I held the key in my hand, shutting my eyes and preparing the mental gymnastics needed to find what door or chest or box the key fit. My own method, calming my senses, was an advantage here normally. I saw the yellow and red patches through my eyelids as the sun shone on them. I felt the cold of the steel key in my palm. I smelled the floral scent of—

Suddenly my cheek burned and my eyes shot open as Chalsarda slapped me hard across the face. My eyes went wide, and I reactively grabbed at the offending area.

"Why are you stopping?" she asked me plainly. "Continue."

The look she gave me said this wasn't open to debate, so I closed my eyes to concentrate again, trying to ignore the stinging sensation. Another slap, almost immediately and in the same spot. A tear came out of my eye involuntarily.

"Why are you stopping?" Chalsarda repeated.

"You slapped me!" I shouted incredulously.

"And what will your enemies do?" she asked.

"Friends don't slap each other!" I retorted.

"I am your friend, but while I train you, I am responsible for more than your feelings. I am responsible for your survival. If you can't handle a slap, you won't survive. If I am to accept that burden, I am your teacher first and your friend second. I would gladly slap you a thousand times if it meant preventing your death. You only get to do that once."

"This is different!" I shouted back. Something flipped in me, and I didn't know how to back down. "It is just…different when you're fighting!"

"Very well," she said standing. "Then we'll fight."

"What? No!"

"Are you my student or not?" she asked harshly.

"I am, but—"

"Then you will do as I say, and you will fight me. Come," she said walking toward the front of the home, the place we first met. We marched up to the front door, stopping just below it at the foot of the steps, and Chalsarda handed me a dagger.

"I don't want to stab you," I said, feeling uneasy about the weapon.

"Don't worry, you won't," she said confidently. "Magic is what you prefer, then use that. Use anything you have. Get ready."

Chalsarda walked the length of the walkway away from the door, far enough away that she had to shout for me to hear her. "Today you are the defender of this house. Your only goal is to put me on my back," she shouted as she began to strip. Soon she was wearing only bandages wrapped tightly around her chest, wrists, and feet like an incomplete mummy. "My goal is to put you down and get inside. I am one unarmed elf, running straight at you. If you can't stop me with magic and weapons, then you're not ready for a real fight. In ten seconds we will start, and I will not stop until one of us succeeds."

I didn't realize it before, but I was shaking. I really didn't want this, no matter which way it went, I wasn't going to like it. I wasn't completely in control of my powers all of the time, and evocations are dangerous. I might accidentally really hurt her. Or she makes it to me, and if what I suspect is true, she hurts me to make a point. I tried to steady my breathing, tried to focus, but it was too late. Without a word or a warning, Chalsarda was off in a dash. I sometimes forgot how blindingly quick she was, but she still needed her footing. I sprayed the ground with a thin film of slick ice directly in her path, but she was in the air as I did this, almost as if she expected it. It was sudden, and I wasn't used to changing gears so fast, but I tried to switch to a gust of wind, hoping to knock her out of the air. No good. In mid-leap, she twisted her body and seemed to flow through and around the wind. Damn it! Just like that, she was upon me, inhumanly fast, but then again, she's not human.

I tried to shake out a shield, but she chopped a forearm down onto my wrist, fizzling it out before it could materialize. I barely had time to yelp in pain before her body twisted and she kicked me in the stomach hard, sending me tumbling back until I slammed into a support pillar. She was really trying to hurt me! She was moving up, and this time I did get my shield out, maybe a half second before a flurry of blows came in my direction. Most were hitting the blister shield, until she kicked at one of my legs, sending me to one knee with a white-hot pain in my calf. I kept the shield raised, feeling helpless. The door was right there, why wasn't she going inside? Why couldn't I do anything here? Why did I ever think I'd be enough to save people? Why won't she just—

"Stop!" I screamed, a torrent of power surging out of me, leaving me empty. Even my shield evaporated. I opened my eyes, and oh no. Oh god, what have I done? In front of me, by inches, was a cloud—No! Not a cloud!—a solid, white wall of permafrost maybe eight feet high and double that across. I had no idea how far it went. My friend was in there! I raised a hand to bang on the ice, to do anything, when I felt the cold steel press against my neck. I stopped, afraid of what any movement would do to me.

Labored breaths heaved from behind me, and through them, I heard a voice. "It is not that you are incapable, it is that you are unwilling," Chalsarda panted. "You lack focus, patience, and control. And if you can't or won't change, it is only a matter of time before you hurt someone, or they hurt you."

"I believe you've made your point, Chalsarda. Wouldn't you agree, Elana?" The voice was unmistakably that of the Aos Si.

The knife left my throat, and I turned to face them both, hearing the dagger fall from exhausted hands. Chalsarda looked pale; she was sweating profusely and looked like she might fall over any second.

I glanced back to the ice and then to her. "How did you—"

"Not now," she interrupted quietly. "Don't ask."

"Are you alright?" I asked her.

Chalsarda smirked at that. "Are you?"

Despite the throbbing pains in my forearm, calf, and stomach, I was positive that she had taken it easy on me. Nothing was broken, for starters, and there was no question that she could have broken my arm right away if she had wanted to. I'm pretty sure that the continued use of all my limbs meant that we're still friends. I decided to just give her a nod and try to tough it out.

"That will be all for the day, Chalsarda, I will have someone attend to the mess," the Aos Si said, dismissing her. I was never clear on the nature of their relationship, but the way he was with her was almost like she was an assistant who was only around to earn college credits, and he knew she couldn't leave. I'd never seen him ask for anything unreasonable or degrading, but I've always had the sense she was with him begrudgingly. Like a job that she couldn't quit. I could relate. Of course, neither of them would talk about it, so, for now, it was just a gut feeling.

"Elana, would you come with me?" the Aos Si said to me, seemingly ignoring the ice. "I believe we have much to discuss."

I gave him a look of acknowledgment, and we moved inside where I was able to collect my belongings. I followed him upstairs and into his study, and once the door closed, he sat, ready to talk.

"I understand that you had quite the interesting visitor," he said, more statement than a question.

"Freyja," I agreed, taking a seat, exhausted.

"I've never been fond of the Norse gods. It's all violence with them, all the time."

I wanted to debate that, but one of the nicer members of their ranks just asked me to kill her brother, so I wasn't sure I could make a case at the moment.

"You've been getting stronger, this is good," he continued. "You're going to need that strength."

"For anything specific?" I asked. "Or for just the unending wave of nightmares that seems to follow me?"

"Elana, you will need your strength for so many things. For the enemies you managed to make at your own party. You'll need your strength to protect everyone you've placed under your protection because when someone or something decides they really want to hurt you, they won't come for you, they'll come for them. You will, of course, need your strength for the end. But I suppose you'd really like to know about the more immediate threat you're facing."

I wasn't sure what he meant by that, and I let him know as much. "Are you talking about Freyr? The Gardners?"

"I am often amazed at how quickly you make enemies," he said with a chuckle. "No, I'm talking about something much worse. I am referring to that which returned from the abyss for you. I am talking about the Nuckalavee."

The Aos Si waved a hand toward his mirror, and as I watched, the mirror became hazy and muddled, and when it became clear again, I saw it. The image of a city, apparently ravaged by war, but something unnatural was happening. That was a thick, black cloud covering everything, and soldiers wearing a uniform I did not recognize, falling, one after another in horrific ways. The smoke seemed to fill their bodies, causing them to seize and disintegrate. Others were torn asunder, and as they fell, the smoke rose to meet them, claiming their bodies. It was awful.

"The last time it attacked, more than a hundred years ago now, it came for a young man named Thomas Haring. He'd made a deal with, well, let's just say the wrong sort, and knowing what he was to face, he thought he'd be rid of it in the middle of battle. He'd made it all the way to Sulva Bay in fact. But there is no escaping the Nuckalavee, it will find you. And young Mr. Haring managed to get his brothers in arms killed for his greed."

The focus shifted in the mirror, and that abomination I'd faced on the beach was visible now, dragging a screaming man with him into the water. "And now Elana, the Nuckalavee is coming for you."

8

When the Nuckalavee had finished dragging the sol-
dier into the water, the image faded in the mirror,
and I merely saw our reflections again. The Aos Si
had the look of a man who wasn't sure how he was going to pay
his dinner bill.

"So, that was terrifying, but you, uh, didn't need to show
me that," I said. "Unless the intent was to show me the bullet
that I dodged. I already killed that thing."

"No, you didn't," he said softly.

"Yeah, I totally did. By accident, I think, there was a lot of
fire involved, and I may have permanently scarred a piece of the
great Southern California landscape, but it was pretty dead."

That got a small chuckle out of him. "Oh, to be young again
and be blissfully unaware of that particularly painful lesson," he
mused to himself.

"What lesson would that be?" I asked.

He looked at me, and for just a moment there was sadness
in those ethereal blue eyes of his as he gave me his answer. "Bad
things never die. The worse it is, the harder it sticks around. I've

always heard this in reference to memories and stains, but I suppose in your case it applies to monsters."

"So, okay, I'm confused. I watched it disintegrate," I said, feeling the worry that comes with a sixth sense of knowing the bad news before it's delivered.

"Well, let's walk through it, see if we can't answer some of the questions that you'd like answered, and maybe answer some of the questions you didn't know you needed to ask," he said, motioning to the chair near his. "And please, sit already. You must be exhausted."

He wasn't wrong, Chalsarda had beat the hell out of me, and I'd dramatically drained my reserves with a showing of ice. My fear was sitting down and being too tired to get back up, but maybe I should risk it. I sat down and, yup, that was it. Oh god, I knew I was sore, but there it was. "I have no idea what's going on with any of this, so I'm game."

"Very good. Now, to begin why don't you tell me why you think the Nuckelavee was defeated?"

"Well, umm," I replied, looking for the proper words. "Flame tower."

"An eloquent answer to be sure," the Aos Si replied sarcastically. "But start from the beginning. How did you come to cast this, as you say, flame tower and why did you cast it?"

"Okay, so, in my studies I figured out how to create items with spells in them. Not exactly magic items or anything, I haven't figured out how to create boots that let me fly or anything like that, I just figured out how to store a spell for later use. Since fire was the easiest for me, I began with that. I made a bracelet to practice on and saved fire in it."

"And how often did you do this?"

"I don't know, exactly," I answered, trying to think about it. "It usually takes about a day or so before I can safely try again, and I made it a habit so…two hundred times, give or take."

The Aos Si blinked hard in disbelief at that.

"Two hundred?" he asked. It wasn't often that I elicited surprise from him, and it was oddly satisfying. "That was not the answer that I was expecting. That must have been spectacular, no wonder you thought you'd killed it. Describe the spell, if you would."

"It was intense. Frightening. I didn't know anyone could do that, let alone me," I said truthfully. "It was like a tornado; centered and unmoving, but swirling unbelievably fast. It split the clouds in the sky and turned the rocks where the flame was centered into magma. It lasted maybe fifteen to twenty seconds, but it felt like forever."

"And now you've learned what magic upon magic is. All magic is three dimensional and amorphous, all at once. It is not flat; it is not binary. It is a swirling mass, it is perfect, and it is chaos. When you store a spell within a spell, it grows exponentially. So, what have you learned?"

"Smokey the Bear hates and fears me?" I asked sarcastically.

I don't think the Aos Si got that reference. "I see. And the Nuckalavee?"

I shook my head. "Reduced to ash. Even that blew away. Nothing left."

"What happened next?"

"I managed to climb my way off the shoreline," I said. "I had a friend with me. When we made it out, a man was waiting for us, said his name was Roger. I think he was supposed to be the big, bad end-boss of Gardeners or something. He made me a job offer, gave me this necklace and said it was from my mother."

"Oh? And what did you tell him?" the Aos Si asked, perking up in his seat.

"I told him to suck eggs," I replied sourly. "For as much as he tried to make himself out to be the good guy, he's still responsible for leading a pack of murderers. It wasn't a hard choice to make."

"No, I imagine it wouldn't be with you," he mused. "So, tell me about your visitor."

"Oh my god!" I exclaimed, before correcting myself. "I mean, not literally. I really have to stop saying that, I think. Jesus! Wait. Ah, never mind. Freyja! Yeah, I got a visit from the Norse goddess of everything, and you know how they say you should never meet your heroes? She was way different than what I remember reading as a kid."

"Well, this should be interesting," the Aos Si said with a grin. "How so?"

"Well, I didn't remember Freyja being a jerk, for one thing. She was not particularly cool to Chalsarda," I began.

"Do you know the history of the Elves and Freyja?" he asked.

"Chalsarda told me that some of her people believe that she created them," I replied.

"In a sense, yes. There are many origins for the Elves, and everything else for that matter; and all of them are correct. Freyja created some of them."

"Hold on; I remember this. The Elves live in Alfheim, right? I thought that belonged to Freyr," I said, wishing suddenly I'd read any Norse myth past middle school. "Or does he just live there?"

"I thought you would understand by now," the Aos Si lectured. "In some of the stories, it was Ull who created Alfheim. In some, it is Freyr. In others, Freyja. But they're all so old that they're all correct. But even then, we're talking about one type of Elf. Do you know how many there are?" I shook my head no.

The Aos Si stared through me as if to make a point and only said, "A lot."

"Yeah? Well, do any of the old stories talk about how Freyja wants me to kill her brother?"

"They most definitely do not," the Aos Si replied. "That is certainly interesting, but not surprising. The gods are almost always equal parts mad and capricious."

"Aren't you an Aos Si?" I asked suspiciously.

"Some are more capricious than others." He shrugged. "Did Freyja mention why she wants you to do this?"

"To prevent Ragnarök."

The Aos Si leaned in toward me, his fingers creating a steeple. "More interesting still! And how do you feel about doing this?"

"I'm not going to, so I feel nothing about it," I replied. "I'm nobody's assassin."

"Though it's troubling to know that you may have made enemies with a goddess," the Aos Si said patiently. "What I meant to ask was, how you felt about preventing Ragnarök?"

I knew the answer right away, but I still hesitated in answering. "Yeah, of course. Right? It's the end of the world, death of the gods, why wouldn't I want to stop that?"

"And are those gods worth saving? They're not exactly known for having the best interests of anyone in mind except themselves."

"Well, even if they're not, what about all the people?" I asked. "Ragnarök claims a lot of innocent bystanders."

"Would it make a difference if I told you that Ragnarök would not claim your world? That not a single person you grew up with would ever even know, that not one place you've ever called home would be touched?"

"Of course not," I snapped.

"No, I didn't think it would," he said. "Still, it's a moot point. You're no match for a god. Freyja was sending you on a suicide mission. Still, I think it's time I give you something, follow me."

I followed him out of the room and into the basement, through a wine cellar, through a false wall, and then down into a sub-basement before arriving in what I could only describe as a magical armory. The room was sprawling, long and twisted, and filled with ancient tomes, crystal balls, staves, and more. "Chalsarda does not believe you are ready for combat, and I agree. But I think trouble will continue to find you one way or the other, so you might as well defend yourself. Elana, I have a confession to make," the Aos Si said, strolling through the room. "I have withheld much from you, to see the limits of your natural ability. I feel it is important to take your time with magic, rushing toward strength will only lead to ruin. But you have reached a limit much faster than I would have expected, a limit which tells me to continue your training at this pace would produce only diminishing returns. So today we choose an implement for you."

"I'm going to get a staff?" I nearly shouted, suddenly excited. "Facing down a Balrog all Gandalf-style like 'You shall not pass' and holding it over my head?"

"Of course not, that's absurd!" the Aos Si responded in shock and disgust. "A staff is far more power than you're capable of handling. Maybe you're not ready after all."

"I am, I promise," I responded quickly, suddenly feeling like a kid at Christmas. "Please, what were you thinking?"

He regarded me for a moment before continuing. "Very well, as I was saying, you are in need of an implement. You should never be in battle without one. And a staff is off limits to you at this point. You're still on training wheels, and your first staff is one you create. To just give you a staff would be to rob you of a precious experience. There are many reasons why you should not have one yet, and that you are not capable of wielding one is not the least of those reasons. Spellbooks are an option, certainly. For those with sharper minds who cannot hold the power they want, pulling the spells straight from the pages is an excellent choice when conservation is critical. And while I do not doubt dedication to research, you lack the capacity to learn more esoteric languages. Perhaps in a couple of hundred years or so. No, a spellbook is wrong for you. Orbs, a reliable choice for pulling in energy and expelling it quickly, but no, that's a bad idea. Orbs are far too fragile and unstable, and you do not tend to stay put in a fight. I can't afford to give you a new orb every time something tries to eat you. There are wands, of course, but you lack the attention to fine detail required to make use of one. I'd sooner expect a dog to learn calligraphy!"

I looked around at the room full of objects and tried to see what was left. "So if staves, books, orbs, and wands are off the table, where does that leave me? What can I have?"

The Aos Si walked over to a cabinet and opened its door to reveal the treasure inside. "You can have a rod," he said with a smile. Several rods about the length and thickness of my forearm hung inside, made of different materials, bone, steel, ivory, bamboo, stone; some had a glass at the end, some had gemstones embedded in the base. They were all similar and yet wildly different at the same time, and I couldn't decide which one to stare at.

"These are so cool!" I shouted. "Do I get to pick which one is right for me? Is this one of those holy grail style tests? Do I have to figure out which one speaks to me?"

"Nothing so complicated as that," he said opening a drawer beneath the cabinet and removing a rod I hadn't seen prior. "You get this rod."

I took it from him and examined it. Roughly the same size as the others, it had a bit of weight behind it. The rod was made of some heavy wood I wasn't familiar with. No gemstones or glass. At the end of the rod was a rounded sphere of wood, carved and smoothed out, enough to be slick to the touch. It looked like a coffee table leg.

"Thank you," I said graciously. Protector or not, showing ingratitude to the Fae was a bad idea.

"Do not think you have been cheated," the Aos Si replied. "Each rod has a use and a function; it is a tool. This is the tool you need right now. Do not be distracted by baubles."

"Of course, I'm sorry if I gave the impression that I was not excited, I just don't understand," I said as diplomatically as I could. "What is this rods function?"

He smiled at that, excited to explain even if he didn't want to show it. "This rod acts as something of a limiter. When you cast, you expend more energy than you actually use. Stray strands of magic fly out in every direction and dissipate into nothing. It's wasteful. This rod will train you to focus. It's not that you need more power, it's that you need to use the reserves that you already have properly. Additionally, this rod will naturally attract those stray bits that do fall through the cracks. When you are attuned with the rod, that magic will flow back into you as well."

Wow. "That is, uh, wow," I said, studying my coffee table leg shaped rod. "That is really, really cool! Does everyone have one of these?"

"No, even the most simple implement takes mastery level craftsmanship to produce. Many magic users have to go their whole lives learning without an implement."

My mind began racing with the possibilities of what I could do with this, and that conflicted with the staggering implication that, for as useful as this was, it was still in the bottom tier of what an implement could be. So now I know two things for certain: I have a long way to go magically, and if I ever see anyone with a staff I am going to run like hell. "There is something else I need to show you. If you'll come with me back to the study," the Aos Si said, closing the cabinet.

By the time we arrived, I was still considering my rod, examining it, getting used to it the way someone might get used to a new cell phone. It didn't exactly come with instructions, but I could almost harmonize with it. That was the best way I had to describe the feeling, anyway. I could see tiny bits of magic, like dust in a sunbeam all around me, and the rod seemed to absorb them at a glacial pace. It was fascinating, and I felt like there was so much more to learn about this mysterious hunk of wood.

"So back to your more immediate concerns, the matter of the Nuckalavee," he said, looking through his shelves for a particular book. Opening it to a section in the middle, he handed it to me as he asked, "Would you read this, please?"

It was a poem that read:

From the briny depths, on fetid knees,
Destroying crops and withering trees,
I'll tell you the tale of the Nuckalavee

No man survives its warning call,
No weapon forged can slow its crawl,
No blade, nor axe, nor cannonball

It only sees flame; it only breathes death,
It steals lives, and souls, and babies' breath

It will not rest until you are under the sea,
The Nuckalavee, he comes in threes

"I only saw one of those things," I said, handing him back the book.

"Well, no one said all three come at once," the Aos Si replied. "Throughout history, it has been said that no one has defeated it, but it has appeared in what you would know today as Ireland, Scotland, and Norway, though it will chase you anywhere as you've seen. The reason, however, is not that it wanders, it is that it is three beings living as one. If you do not strike down all three, it will eventually be whole again. It is unrelenting, perhaps one of the most unrelenting things in existence. Running from it will only make things worse for you and everyone. It will raze cities to get to you if you are its prey."

All of sudden my new rod wasn't making me so confident. "I don't know if I can defeat it," I said soberly.

"Neither do I," the Aos Si agreed.

"Is this part of what you're supposed to do for me? Can you defeat it for me?"

The Aos Si looked me directly in the eyes and spoke slowly. "You know that because of my nature I am unable to lie. I can play with words; I can allow you to take the meaning from them that you want to hear and be under no obligation to correct you. So know this, and know I am sincere when I say it: I cannot kill the Nuckalavee for you. I did not say that I won't, or that I can be persuaded. I cannot. But that does not mean that I cannot help you, that I cannot share what knowledge I have of the creature. But when you return, you will be without my help. With what I know, you might even win. You'd be the first person ever to do it, but someone always has to be the first, right?"

Okay, this sucks. I have to fight an unbeatable horror not once, but three times; the one lucky, sucker punch shot I had at beating it is now gone, and my only backup is a wooden club.

"Let's take this seriously," I said, sitting down and trying not to panic. "What can you tell me?"

"Well, to start, it has weaknesses. It will only chase you if it's seen you, but once it does, it won't stop. Fresh running water will slow him down, which is good," the Aos Si said thoughtfully. "Of course, running water also shorts out your magic too, so that might not be great. It can't cross running fresh water though, so you'd get away from it for a little bit."

"Wait, seriously?" I asked. "I have access to magic, and I can be defeated with a garden hose?"

"Have you ever tried to cast in the shower? I wouldn't, if I were you. Oh, you could always just contact the Mither O' the Sea. Part of her job is specifically to hold the Nuckalavee under water. Of course, she is only available during the summer. Think you can make it six months?"

I sighed audibly. "Anything else?"

"It hates gold. It's terrified of it. But it would take a significant quantity of gold, actually, to harm it. You can also burn seaweed to make kelp."

"What does that do? Does it ward it off or something?" I asked.

"Well, if you make kelp from seaweed, it will immediately stop chasing you—"

I breathed a heavy sigh of relief. "Oh awesome, that's easy enough, you should have led with that."

The Aos Si pursed his lips and continued, "It will immediately stop chasing you and go on a rampage, mindlessly trying to eradicate everything around it."

I let out a curse in frustration, feeling helpless. He continued, "And not that I enjoy piling on the bad news, but while it wouldn't be unreasonable to assume that the Nuckalavee was sent after you and no one else, it also wouldn't be unreasonable to suppose that it is coming for both you and your loved ones. After all, you made quite the show about protecting your friends and the innocent, something that I am still dealing with, by the way; so what better way of getting to you than by getting to them?"

"I have to get back and warn them," I said standing up. "I'm sorry, I don't know when it will return and—"

"A week," he said. "Well, it can appear once every seven days. So you have another five days, give or take."

"Okay," I said to myself, thinking out loud. "Okay, that's not immediate, but it's still not a lot of time to think of something."

"But I'm sure you will," he said with a nod. "Take Chalsarda if you require her aid."

"She would be a big help, I'm sure, thank you," I said sheepishly. "For everything. I may not have entirely trusted you when we met, but you've gone above and beyond for me, so maybe I was wrong. Thanks. I need to go."

"You're quite welcome, but I believe there is one last piece of business to attend to." He was eyeing my bag expectedly, and I suddenly remembered.

"Oh! Right, sorry, here," I said, removing a large, thick mason jar full of milk from my sack and handing it to him. "This has been out of the fridge for a while though, and it's pretty warm, so I'd...okay, yeah, that's happening."

The Aos Si, typically so elegant and dignified, had popped the top off of the mason jar and began to chug it messily, gripping the half-gallon jar with both hands as he did, milk sloshing across his cheeks and down onto his clothes. Without another word, I began to back out of the room and leave him to his drink. I wasn't quite sure what I'd just seen, but I knew it was time for me to leave.

9

Parking was difficult here, which was not unusual, and it was in part my fault. After what had happened with Jason (the bad Jason, once again, not my friend Jason), I set up a code word with my friends, and everyone knew that if I were to ever text, or say, or in any way use the word obstrigillate, they were to drop everything and head to Olivia's home. No questions asked. After a few harrowing tales from Claire, Olivia, and myself, well, they still didn't quite buy into it. So I lit the fire pit in Olivia's backyard up with magic, and that did it. Seeing is believing, I guess. Everyone agreed to be sworn to secrecy and agreed to my new code word rule. This was the first time I had to use it.

I probably should have used it when I was a little closer and not the second I got back with Chalsarda. The narrow driveway to the house could fit two cars naturally, and a third behind them that would block the sidewalk. Up here no one was going to complain a whole heck of a lot. Unfortunately, Claire's delivery van was blocking almost the entire driveway, which meant finding somewhere else to park. Chalsarda could have probably scaled the side of a mountain with ease right now, but I was still pretty tired, even if my wounds had been healed on the way back through The Knowing. At least that place still liked me, even if I wasn't sure about Olivia. She's been cold and distant ever since the incident with evil, jerkface, bad guy Jason, but she's at least been semi-cooperative and cordial. I think that while she has an issue with me, she acknowledges now that there are other things to worry about that aren't going away.

"It will be nice to meet your friends finally," Chalsarda said as we parked.

It just occurred to me that she hadn't met them yet, though that wasn't exactly her fault. Her time here with me was limited to whenever the Aos Si allowed it or when she had free time, which wasn't often. It wasn't like there hadn't been opportunities for her to meet everyone, we'd just never gotten around to it. Not even Claire, despite her visits to the store. Just unfortunate timing, I guess.

"Yeah, that's going to be the one good part of this," I agreed. "I just wish that introduction wasn't going to be immediately followed by the phrase, 'Run for your lives!'"

The front door was open, so we let ourselves in to find Ann in a valiant, but futile effort, to educate Teague and Claire about nerd lore. The three of them didn't seem to notice us right away as they sat on the couch, watching an episode of Eternity Pilgrim. I felt a twinge of sadness mixed with excitement as I realized that this was a rerun from the most current season and I hadn't seen it yet. I hated spoilers, but I couldn't help but watch for a moment. The Pilgrim was in some sort of lab, probably in the late eighties. He was studying a big series of equations scribbled hastily in various colors. A middle-aged man in a lab coat with a bushy mustache was hurriedly talking to him.

"So you see, Pilgrim! If I'm right, there are multiple timelines! What we are experiencing should not be!" His voice was frantic and cracking.

"This is remarkable," the Pilgrim said, nodding his head. "Truly remarkable."

"So you agree with my findings?" the man asked.

"What?" the Pilgrim asked as if distracted. "Oh, no, I meant this dry erase board. It's remarkable."

"But in the last episode he was in the present, so if this happened thirty years ago, wouldn't he already know what happened?" Teague asked, clearly exasperated.

Ann leaned in, visibly excited to talk about her favorite show. "Because that's not how it works! So you're viewing this show from an A-to-Z perspective, with the rest of the alphabet showing up in the right order. But really on this show, time is this mutable thing—"

"Did you say mutable?" Claire asked with a small laugh.

"It's a word!" Ann protested.

Ann and Teague could not have been any more different. Ann Bancroft was the only person I knew who was smaller than me, and she also happened to be a bigger fan of Eternity Pilgrim. Given how much I liked that show, that was hard to admit, but it was true. Once in high school, we all got name tags printed for a school-wide testing event. The printer cut off everyone's last name after three letters and went last name, first name. So I was Bla, Elana. Olivia was Moo, Olivia. And Ann was, unfortunately, Ban, Ann. For the remainder of the year, she was the butt of banana related jokes, but her reaction was to get in anyone and everyone's face who dared. A lot of people dared. High school is like that. Now she's a comedian, and you make fun of her at your own peril.

Teague Chetty was the person in this little group I'd known for the shortest amount of time, Chalsarda excepted. She was a makeup artist who met Olivia on the set of a student film they both worked on a couple of years back. She quickly got along with everyone in our little group and beyond, but Ann especially somehow. If Ann were one extreme of the nerd spectrum, Teague would be the complete opposite. She was still artistic in her own way, however. Despite being friendly and kind, she didn't deal with conflict well, which is probably how she got stuck watching a show that involved neither cooking challenges or home renovations.

"Oh god!" Claire exclaimed, startled, putting a hand on your chest. "How long have you two been standing there?"

I was embarrassed and wanted to laugh all at once. I was lost in my own head for a moment and didn't realize that we were right behind everyone in silence. Chalsarda had followed my lead and didn't say anything, so it looked like two people crept up behind the couch and everyone. I wasn't sure how to transition away from that.

"Hey," I said, offering a small wave. That was probably good enough.

"Cool ears!" Ann said, standing up.

"Thank you." Chalsarda smiled, nodding her head.

"Chalsarda, these are my friends Ann, Teague, and Claire," I said, making introductions. "Claire owns the bookstore that I kind of work at, slash live in right now."

"It is lovely to meet you all." She seemed to be in etiquette mode. "I am terribly sorry this is our first chance to meet, Claire. You have a lovely store."

Claire seemed to appreciate that. "You too. Elana has told me a lot about you."

"I'm sorry, how do you two know each other?" Teague asked.

I'd never introduced a mythical being to my friends before, and even though I'd prepared for this, it still took me off guard. "Chalsarda is a new friend who is…teaching me archery, and—"

"I'm an elf from the land of faeries who is in service to a Celtic deity, and he has assigned me the task of preparing Elana to defend herself against the forces, people, and things that are less than people who would see her come to harm," Chalsarda finished for me, giving me a small grin at the end. "And yes, we're also friends."

Everyone except Claire seemed in shock at this, myself included. Claire's tolerance for the weird was pretty high these days.

"I was going to ease them into that," I muttered.

"No, you're not. An elf, that is. Can I touch your ears?" Teague asked, visibly annoying Chalsarda.

"I always thought elves were short," Ann mused.

"Why would you think that?" Chalsarda asked.

I heard the door open behind us as Jason (aka good and not-likely-to-murder-us-all Jason) walked in, followed by Olivia and Logan. "Hey, sorry we're late," Jason said, squeezing past us with two bags of groceries. "I had to grab these two, and I didn't know how long this was going to be, and I didn't want to get into a situation where, you know, we'd all get hungry and couldn't pay attention or, like, we'd be in lockdown mode, and there wouldn't be enough to eat. Who's your friend?"

"Her name is Chalsarda, and she's an elf!" Ann beamed.

This wasn't how I pictured introductions going, and I was becoming more embarrassed by the second.

"Hey, that's great. My name is Jason Kelly, a human. A pleasure to meet you." He extended a hand to her, which Chalsarda briefly shook.

"Wait, why aren't more of you freaking out about the fact that an actual elf is standing here with us?" I asked.

"Well, you know, we've seen you do magic a whole bunch of times, so our world view was already shattered months ago," Jason casually explained as he adjusted his glasses. "And then all the stuff you've seen with Olivia and Claire, I just kind of figured you'd show up with someone like this eventually. I was thinking it would be, like, a sexy vampire or something, but an elf makes sense too."

"A vampire?" I asked incredulously at the sound of the dumbest possible answer.

"Can I ask you elf questions?" Ann practically begged.

"Of course." Chalsarda smiled.

"Okay, so if you're an elf, are you super old and live forever?"

"I'm two hundred and seven, which is still young among my people, and nothing lives forever."

"Do you live in a forest, and why don't you ever see houses in the woods where the elves live?"

"No, I live in a house that is not in a forest, and there are many types of elves who live all over. And for why you don't see elf houses in movies, maybe small production budgets?"

"So you have the same travel powers as Elana?"

"I am able to travel, but I do not have what Elana has. I travel with the help of an item."

"Are you a vegetarian?"

"No, but I don't see why that is an elf specific question."

Olivia sighed and interrupted and stepped between the two of them. "Hi, it's nice to meet you finally. And this is very interesting, but Elana just gave us all the code for the world coming to an end, so would it be alright if we got to that?"

"Yeah, right, sorry. It's great to see you," I said, offering Olivia a hug and getting one from her in return that felt awkward.

Everyone grabbed a seat in the living room, and Ann turned off the television so I could address the room. Even though it was an audience of the people closest to me, I didn't feel comfortable having the spotlight like this.

"Thank you all for making it here, I'm glad you're all safe," I began. "Not that you would have been in danger immediately, but I'm still happy that you're safe, because..." This wasn't going well, so I took a deep breath and tried to center myself. I needed my senses now before things got any worse, so I turned my focus on other, more normal, things. The remnants of spearmint gum in my mouth from earlier...the familiar stain on the carpet as I looked down...the cold sweat forming on my palms as I opened and shut my hands...the smell of leather and musk from the protective layering under Chalsarda's t-shirt...the sound of an impatient leg that was not my own, bouncing up and down. It took a moment, but I found my calm.

"I'm sorry this is what it took for us all to come together," I said now more calm, my voice steady. "Logan and I were attacked on the beach recently by a monster I now know is called the Nuckalavee."

Olivia looked at Logan in disbelief. "You were what? When did this happen? Why didn't you tell me?"

"It just happened yesterday," Logan said defensively. "And Elana killed it, so I thought it wasn't a big deal and that she could tell you about it."

"That's not how...you don't just get to..." Olivia was flustered. I hadn't realized she didn't know. "We're going to talk about this later." Her voice was firm and upset.

"It turns out it's not dead," I continued. "It appears three times; it's never been killed before, and, this is the worst part, it might come after all of you to get to me."

"Why would it do that?" Teague asked. "We don't even know what it is, why is it even after you?"

Chalsarda spoke up to answer that question. "The Nucka-lavee is one of the worst demons in existence; no one knows exactly where it came from or why. It emerges from the sea, but beyond that its origins are a secret. It chooses a victim and relentlessly hunts them down, destroying all in its path until it has found them, then it drags them into the water, never to be seen or heard from again. It is infernal and inhumanly strong, heavily resistant to magic. It hasn't been seen for over a hundred years, but now it seems to be controlled by a sorcerer named Kodran Osvifsson who has been tasked with killing Elana. Anyone who would summon the Nuckalavee to kill a single person genuinely does not care about the collateral damage they would cause in the process."

"Wait, did you say Kodran Osvifsson?" Ann asked quizzically. "As in The Stone Sorcerer?"

I knew that I'd heard that name before! The Stone Sorcerer was the worst! It's rare for me not to make it through a book, but I got halfway into book one of that series and had to put it down. There was no way that I was reading nine books of that garbage. Kodran was supposed to be this sorcerer who existed in the age of the Norse gods. Because of his wild magic, he was fated to die an early death. So he made a deal with Freyr for immortality, and in the process made an eternal enemy of Hel, but there was a catch. The further he strays from the mountains, the weaker he becomes. And that's about all I know because I gave up on the series when I found out how much of a casual jerk he was. He was completely indifferent to civilian deaths, he was utterly self-absorbed, and honestly, it felt like the author was trying to be an edgelord with how aloof the character was. It must have worked because there were nine of those books, but it wasn't for me.

"You know who is doing this?" Chalsarda nearly popped out of her seat.

"Just…just the character," Ann replied, her eyes unusually wide behind her glasses. Chalsarda looked ready to pounce, which took more than a couple of people by surprise.

"So, to be clear, a fictional character is trying to kill you in the real world with a demon that may or may not be real?" Jason asked.

"Well, yes. But also, no," I answered, trying to get everything straight in my head. "But also, yes. The Stone Sorcerer is fictional, but then again nothing is, but it is except we're looking at fiction wrong, but you know what? Let's keep this easy. A character in a book series is trying to kill me. And maybe all of you. Sorry."

"And you just found this out?" Olivia asked.

"Of course, the minute I knew, we came back and called this meeting," I rebutted.

"And what's your excuse for not telling us about the first time you fought it?" Olivia's voice was cold and accusatory.

I didn't have the chance to reply, though I wasn't immediately sure how I could. Claire jumped to my defense nearly as soon as she finished asking her question. "Hey, that's not fair. I know you're upset, and I am too, but it's understandable at least. This just happened yesterday. She thought it was dead; maybe she wasn't ready to talk about it."

Claire gave me a side glance that said I wasn't completely off the hook for later. I'd looked Claire in the eyes after it happened and hadn't told her, and she had pieced that together.

Olivia looked ready to fight the entire room. "And what if she was wrong? What if it hadn't been dead? Or worse, what if it hadn't come alone? We're all worried that it could come after any one of us, what if this Conrad guy or whatever had just sent half a dozen things after us instead of one?"

No one said a thing, not even Chalsarda, who looked to be carefully weighing her words.

Olivia continued, "That's my point though, we could have all been killed this weekend, and we didn't get a warning." Olivia turned to look at me. "I don't have a problem with the insane crap that happens to you, but I have a problem with you thinking you can make choices that can affect our lives without being bothered to consult us first, just because you have access to magic or whatever and we don't. Like we're all your sidekicks to be protected, and we can't be trusted with the big decisions."

"That's not...I mean...I don't." I could feel my face immediately heat up at that, any calm I had was shattered. "I don't think I'm any better than any of you!"

"I don't think that you do, but I do believe that you have a problem with trusting us, and I believe that it's going to get one of us hurt," Olivia said evenly. "I think you feel like you have superpowers now and subconsciously that makes you feel like you have to do everything, and whatever decision you make is going to be the right one. You can't keep hiding things from us."

I wanted so badly to be furious. Olivia had no right to think this about me after everything, let alone call me out in front of everyone. Everyone! Especially knowing what she does about my social anxiety, not to mention the fact that I've literally saved her life, and I'm in the middle of trying to do it again! I wanted so badly to be righteous and tell her how much it's hurt that she's been so distant toward me all these months, that she was utterly wrong in how she was straining our friendship when I'd been thrust into a new and impossible life. I wanted to do all of those things, but I could not. Because she was right. For everything else, for all of my good intentions, I was hiding something from her, the knowledge that she is to die, and I wanted to save her on my terms without having to burden her with the knowledge I'd been given.

I put my head down and took a couple of deep, silent breaths before looking up to meet her gaze, and I choked, "Olivia, I love you, and I hear you, and that is why you and I need to speak in private. Now."

There was a silence in the room. With a handful of sincere words, I'd made everyone feel as uncomfortable as I'd felt. Olivia's face was unreadable. I want her to, no, I needed her to say something.

"You have got to be kidding me," she said in disbelief. Okay, I didn't need her to say that. "Are you completely missing the point intentionally?"

I felt guilty. "You're right, okay? I have been keeping things from you, and I know that's not my choice to make, but what I have to say isn't for everyone to hear. You have to trust me. Just listen to what I have to say, and if you feel you need to tell the world, I won't stop you, but I just—"

I couldn't finish. It wasn't just that what I had to say was something I was uncomfortable telling Olivia, and it was that, I'd been trying to pretend that it wasn't real. Or at least not immediate. The truth was, I didn't know. It could happen five minutes from now or never, but if I were to vocalize it, it would become real.

"Hey," Olivia said, her voice softening. "Hey, it's okay. Fine, we can talk in my room. But Logan is coming with."

"Are you sure?"

"I am. For one thing, he's my partner, and I don't want to hide anything from him. And for another," Olivia looked directly at Logan as she finished, "I feel the need to prove a point."

Logan and I both accepted that as we left the room. I made quick apologies to the others as I followed the couple.

I always liked what Olivia did with her room. She had a way of making even the biggest mess feel intentional, whether it was or not. She wasn't dirty in the same way her previous roommate had been. No dirty clothes or old food containers were left on the floor, nothing that would make the room smell or anything that would get you sick. But her style in her personal space was differed from the rest of the house. Where the common areas were always very tidy, the bedroom was controlled chaos. It was fun and kinetic; welcoming.

But not today. Today it scared me. It felt inescapable and claustrophobic. There are worse things than having to come clean to someone you love in a safe space, but I didn't have a clue what they could have been at that moment.

Olivia wasn't waiting for me to speak, she got right to it. "So what do need to say?"

"So much," I breathed. My heart was racing at the thought of this. Logan, to his credit, was doing his best to be invisible in a cramped space. "How do I...how am I supposed to tell you that you're supposed to die?"

The color rushed out of Olivia's face at that; she looked ten pounds lighter suddenly. Brittle enough to crumble.

"What did you just say?" Logan snapped, his voice laced with the sort of anger that one had when they hoped they could scare their fears away.

"I figured it out during everything before, the Aos Si confirmed it after. He warned me. He did it in riddles, and when I understood, he just..." I choked a little. "He's warning me of something inevitable! At least, he thinks so."

"Start over, why me? Why would he care about me enough to tell you I'm going to die? And how? How could he know? How does he think it's supposed to happen?"

"It's tied into Lucia," I said, sitting on her bed. "A whole lot of people think she's supposed to be some kind of savior. I don't even know what she's meant to save us all from. It's why she was taken. It's why she's still alive. As for how he knows, I don't know, but he can't lie. I watched a vision of you reaching out for Lucia, and when you reached her, you—" I stopped mid-sentence. I don't care; she doesn't need to know the details. "You reached up into a light, and that's when it happened. You die so Lucia can live."

"You've known this whole time?" It came out as a pale imitation of her voice. I'd never heard her like this before. "Why wouldn't you tell me?"

"Because no one should have to feel like this!" I sneered, pounding a fist into the bed. Anger that I'd been holding back, anger the unfair nature of life was now at the surface. "No one should have to feel this pain and uncertainty! So, I kept it from you, I kept it from myself! And do you know what else I did? Maybe the worst thing of all, I stopped looking for Lucia! Because what if he's right, and you're going to die? And what if I'm wrong, and I can't stop it? What if I can't fight fate? Huh? What then?"

Olivia wanted to give me an answer, her mouth moved, and she struggled, wanting to say something, but settled on, "I don't know."

My words were coming through gritted teeth. "The day I came for you, I made a choice. I could save Lucia, or I could save you and Claire. It was one or the other, and it was an easy choice. You were going to die, but Lucia was being held prisoner, but at least she would be alive. I told myself that every day afterwards, that decision was on me. I had the chance to finish it, to end her suffering, and I didn't. But I knew what she was going through, and I knew that she needed saving. And then, when I thought the dust had settled and we were safe, I learned what saving her meant, and I swore to myself and without hesitation that I would save you. Not Lucia. You. It was all I could think about."

"It's been nine months," Olivia said in realization. "It's been more than that. It's been most of her life!"

"I know that! But what was I supposed to do? I'm not proud of it, but there's been a lot to focus on. Getting stronger, looking for the kids, or just trying to live a normal life. If I keep busy, if I'm doing something, then at least I'm not turning my back on my friend for nothing."

"I had no idea," Olivia said, sitting next to me. I put my head on her shoulder, and she didn't push me away.

"There's something else," I said after a moment, sitting up. "Logan and I met someone at the beach. He's, I don't know, the Head Gardener or something. He tried to offer me a job, he seemed weirdly desperate in a way, I couldn't tell you exactly how. I turned him down, but he gave me this."

I sat cross-legged on the bed, facing Olivia and she did the same, facing me. I removed the necklace and handed it to her. "It belonged to my mother."

"Oh my god," she said, turning over the necklace in her hands. "How?"

"I don't know, but it's real."

"You were there for this?" Olivia asked Logan.

"I was, but this definitely wasn't my story to share," he said.

She nodded at that. "Would you mind going into the living room and checking on everyone? I need to speak with Elana alone."

"Of course, Olly," Logan said, kissing her forehead before walking out.

Olivia sniffed back a tear as the bedroom door closed. "I hate that name," she said.

"I know," I replied. "Logan knows too."

"I had no idea about any of this," Olivia said softly. "You could have talked to me."

"I probably should have, I miss you," I replied. "But I don't regret holding it in, either."

"I'm not mad at you, I don't think I ever have been, but I've been disappointed. Frustrated. You walked out on me and left me in danger when I asked you not to. I have always been there for you, and when I was really afraid, you bailed on me because you knew better. Do you remember what happened that night?"

"I'll never forget," I said sadly. Olivia and I had only barely rescued Claire from Bres. If I hadn't spoken up when I did, I'm certain that Bres would have slit Olivia's throat. I still had the occasional nightmare about it.

"Neither will I. I was nearly knocked unconscious, and by the time I realized what was happening, I had my hair in the hands of a maniac and a blade to my throat. And you left me defenseless. And when Jason came for us, all I could think was that if you were still there, you might have been able to do something."

I didn't have words for her. I knew she felt hurt, but I never considered all of that from her perspective. As long as I've known Olivia, I've never seen a person who could be frightened. I saw a hero. Someone invincible. Lionhearted. Everything I always wanted to be and never felt I would be. Or could be. It never occurred to me that she saw me that way now.

"I cannot imagine how hard all of this is for you right now," she continued. "And I know you're trying to do the right thing. You always have, and I'll bet you always will. I want my friend back; I want the biggest worry of your life to be what show to watch next. I want to trust you. I don't know how quickly all of these things will happen or if they ever will. But if I'm going to forgive you and move forward, you have to promise me that you will see things differently. See things from your perspective, but then step back and see them from ours too. Because right now you have a room full of people who believe that you're going to keep them alive, and they need you. Promise me you'll consider them."

I let the words sink in. I wanted to fix what was broken. I wanted it so badly that I didn't consider what the price might be. "I promise," I said. I hoped I wasn't lying.

"Are you sure about this?" Claire was pensive, and rightly so.

"Of course not, but it's really our best option," I replied heavily. "Hiding isn't an option unless we're okay with countless people getting killed until the Army drops a nuke on the Nucka-lavee."

"I don't think the Army drops nukes, that's more of the President's deal," Ann mused as I gave her a look. "Not the point, got it."

Collectively we came up with a plan, and it wasn't the smartest plan, but it was what we had. Kodran was clearly an a-hole, but by all rights, he shouldn't have the power to summon something like the Nuckalavee and send it across worlds until way later in the series, even if he had help from Freyr. Which meant if I could get to him and appeal to his good nature earlier in the series, maybe he wouldn't summon a horror machine later on. Of course, he already summoned it here, and we weren't sure how that would work, but I know that I'm capable of changing stories, so we'd just have to find out.

My attempt to send everyone to safety was a resounding failure. Most of my friends had found a reason to stick around. Ann was our lore expert, and without her, we wouldn't have known, well, anything about what we were walking into. Chalsarda understood far more about the limitations of what was possible with magic than I, which came from hundreds of years of exposure to that world. She didn't understand the feeling of magic flowing through, of creating something from nothing. That wasn't something she'd ever be familiar with, but from an academic perspective, it would be decades before I'd be at her level. Claire owned the bookstore I happened to live in, which was the best place to stage our trip. And Olivia, well, she just insisted. I wasn't really able to say no to her at this point.

That put five of us sitting in a circle in the back of The Book's End with a used copy of Rocky Road, book one of The Stone Sorcerer. Opening ways into books and TV shows without just falling into them required a bit more patience, but it was just as easy as the way I'd always done it in the past. Getting things into those worlds and The Knowing was more natural, in fact, though bringing things back remained just as unlikely an occurrence as ever. That said, I wasn't thrilled about the idea of opening a portal in front of everyone, it gave me anxiety. I wasn't sure why. Chalsarda was able to travel on her own just fine, Olivia and Claire had already been in The Knowing, and Ann would probably just think it was cool. Still, I wasn't sure I'd do great with an audience.

I skipped ahead to the last chapter. Kodran had already thwarted the rogue Valkyries plan to claim the four Dwarves holding up the sky. Just hearing that was the plot from Ann made me glad I never finished the first book. The last chapter didn't do it any favors either. If anything, his victory made him more insufferable. Blah blah blah, derogatory comments about a woman he slept with, blah blah blah, something about not crossing him because he's an immortal, blah blah blah, humanity is stupid and doesn't know how great it is that he—oh finally, the opening! That was getting painful.

"Everyone take a step back," I said carefully standing up, holding the paperback in one hand, not taking my eyes off of the portal. When they had all given me ample room, I cupped a hand under the gooey black beginnings of an idea made whole and placed it on the ground, imagining it as a stairwell, smoothing out the edges, allowing it to become semi-solid. I could make doors, stairs, whatever, but having a look at a staging area seemed safer in this situation.

"Well done," Chalsarda nodded in approval.

"Thanks," I said, gently setting the book down at the foot of the stairs. "Okay, so this should hold until we get back, as long as no one takes the book out of the room. I'll mask the way back from the other side, so nothing wanders into the shop. Chalsarda and I will be back in—"

"And Olivia," Olivia interrupted.

"No," I said.

"Yes," she countered. This was debating at its finest. "You agreed to let me come with you. And here we are!"

"I meant, like, to the store!" I protested. "You'd be defenseless in there, not to mention we're on our way to see a guy who is trying to kill us. No part of this is safe."

"I think we both know why I'm not afraid to go in with you," Olivia replied sternly.

She meant the prophecy. Her logic was probably that if she were supposed to die somewhere else, she would be safe until then. That's not at all how any of this works, but I didn't have a chance to argue before she continued. "So I guess if you're still worried, you two will just have to do a really good job of protecting me."

"It's her choice," Chalsarda offered. "Even if we survive this, it's not going to be the last time your friends will be in danger. Why not let her come? Could be good practice."

"Me too! And you actually need me! Not that you're not needed," she apologized to Olivia. "Not what I meant, just, I have a reason to come with."

"You're not coming!" I nearly shouted, fed up. "Dangerous! Monsters! Death!"

"No, listen!" Ann insisted. "I read the books, so I might recognize things that you don't! And if Olivia is safe, why wouldn't I be? Come on! I want to see what it's like! I could be your Comrade!"

I wanted to tell her that this wasn't a TV show, I wasn't the Pilgrim, and she could really get hurt, but I didn't have the chance. "Of course you can come," Chalsarda said.

At first, I was angry, but I think I needed that to happen. I wasn't anyone's boss, and I especially didn't have the right to tell Chalsarda what to do. "She's right," I said, taking a breath. "None of you have to ask me permission for anything. This is your life. You can come along if you like, but I can't promise that you're going to want to do it a second time. Claire, does that mean you're coming too?"

"Nope, someone has to keep the store open. Good luck," she answered.

Olivia and Ann peered down into the impossible hole in the back of the store; I was unsure of what they were trying to see. "So we can just walk down? Is it safe?" Ann asked.

"Not at all, but yes, that's how we get in. Just like any other set of imaginary stairs. Okay, so listen up, this part is important.

If we get separated for any reason, stay close to Chalsarda, and she'll get you home. I have a problem in there. It's difficult to explain, but it's like I'm trying to walk with seventy-foot legs. If I don't concentrate while I'm in The Knowing, I can just be somewhere else entirely. For you three, it will be less, well, fluid. So if I'm just gone all of a sudden, I didn't mean it, but I don't know how quickly I'll be able to find you again either. Any questions?"

Ann raised her hand. "Should we bring weapons?"

"Not unless you want something to think you're worth challenging," I replied, leading our descent into an impossible place. "And here we go, our tour of the void begins. If you look down, you'll notice an unending sense of dread."

It was unnaturally humid in The Knowing, which made me regret my jacket and book bag. It felt like everything I was wearing was clinging to my skin, afraid that I might leave it behind. We weren't blessed with much visibility or a bright sun to balance out the weather either; we had an overcast and blood orange sky to enjoy. When I traveled this way, there wasn't a blinking arrow hovering in the sky illuminating my destination or a yellow brick road leading me on a predetermined path. There were just feelings, a sense of the wrong way and the less wrong way. I was never quite sure which was worse, the feeling that there were many paths to take but having no idea about the danger level of each or the feeling like I had right now, that there was only one way in, and to deviate from the path would mean being forever lost in uncharted territory.

I've strayed from the path in the past, and it's always been instant regret. For as strange and beautiful and terrifying a place as The Knowing could be when you were intentionally there, it was still infinite. Parts of it welcomed me and guided me, but those parts couldn't be everywhere and everything all at once, and my working theory is that they guided me not toward the safest paths, but the ones my mind could accept and handle. This place contained everything that had ever been imagined, but there were some pretty messed up imaginations out there.

I shuddered and was grateful for the humidity. It was uncomfortable, but I understood it. And besides, it was made aware to me that I didn't have a choice in walking this path, and I didn't want to think about what was invisible to us, surrounding us if we strayed.

"So, what else can you tell us about the books?" I asked Ann, trying to get the unknown out of my head.

"Who cares about that?" she practically shouted. "There's a whole world under the bookstore!"

She had a point, and it took her response to make me realize that with my focus being on the path, I hadn't been really paying attention to her since we entered. This had to be overwhelming; I didn't blame her for not wanting to talk about a book series that she already wasn't a fan of.

"Well, yes, it is, but no, it isn't, but yes, it kind of is," I answered.

"It is a world between worlds. Its location is more of an idea than anything else," Chalsarda explained. "The world we are currently between is the one you have knowledge of, and anything you could tell us may prove useful later."

"Yeah, that makes sense, this place is just, you know." Ann looked around at everything, and did a little spin on her heels to take in a three-sixty view of it all as we walked. "No, you're right, so just anything I can think of? Okay, no one calls him Kodran except the gods or any of the supernatural things, he presents to the rest of the world as Kenny something or other. I forget his last name. He passes for a forest ranger up in the Shasta Cascade, and the idea behind that is that it allows him to remain near the mountains so he can operate in secret. His home is in

Dunsmuir, which is this small town at the foot of the mountains, but his real home is in a cave behind a waterfall that he manages to keep hidden from the rest of the world. And sometimes he takes meetings at a place called the Stone Lagoon out near the ocean. Seems a bit on the nose, but I'm not a novelist, so what do I know?"

"I told you people hid in the mountains." Olivia smirked at me, and for a moment I saw a bit of my friend again.

"Oh! Yeah, I should have said this one before we left," Ann said in sudden realization. "I mean, we're not there yet, so technically I didn't forget. Just so you know. It's fair to say that I thought of this in time, I think. And, yeah. You should know this."

"What is it?" Chalsarda asked warily.

"He hates elves. It's a very specific hatred, too."

Chalsarda sighed heavily as if she expected this. "Let me guess: because of Freyr?"

"How did you know?" Ann asked.

"You mentioned in the shop earlier that he made a deal with Freyr for immortality, correct? To some elves, and I suppose in this world that may very well mean all elves, Freyr is king. Granting a human a lifespan longer than the one possessed by the elves who support him would be seen as an insult. I'd wager that he's made lifelong enemies of the elves, and if he's been around long enough, I can only imagine that rivalry is sufficiently bitter."

"Wow, that was it." Ann was surprised by the answer. "Yup, exactly right. Are you sure you've never read the books before?"

Chalsarda grinned at Ann and pointed wordlessly to one of her ears.

The path soon gave way into what seemed to be a town made entirely of stone, as far as I could tell. The structures and roads were carved or constructed from the same gray rock, with no wood or glass to be seen anywhere. Even the doors, when a building had one, were stone. It was a ghost town, spectrally quiet in a way that made me uncomfortable. Even ghost towns had the ambient noise of insects or the chill of a breeze. This place felt hushed.

Our way through began to narrow and the margin for safety forced us over a short, arching bridge that overlooked a dry river bed maybe twenty or thirty feet down. The way through didn't feel right, beyond the unease I was feeling from this place, something else was present. Chalsarda seemed to tense up as well and notched an arrow, so at least it wasn't just me. Olivia and Ann got the impression something was wrong as well, and they both hurried up toward me, while Chalsarda brought up the rear. With no choice, we continued across the bridge and just as we passed the halfway point we heard it. The sound of something heavy and clumsy, scaling the rocks and bringing with it a smell like a forgotten, still lake.

Two hideous, hulking creatures the same color and texture of the stone, almost imperceptible for a moment, climbed out of the ditch and stood at the base of the bridge, blocking our path. Olivia let out of a little shriek of surprise as we got a better look at them. Each of them stood maybe six-and-a-half feet tall, with exposed, distended bellies betraying slabs of inhuman muscles. Thick, dirty claws, like rusted spikes, replaced fingernails. One of them smiled and revealed rows of jagged teeth resembling the clash of swords in some medieval battle. It said in a voice like a bulldozer, "What 'ave we 'ear, brother?"

"Silly 'umans what didn't pay the toll, brother," the other said in an equally gravelly voice.

"And don't forget the elf, brother!"

"Of course, brother! Wondering, 'ow long 'as it been since we had 'uman?"

"Several moons, brother! Several moons! And we've never 'ad elf!"

Chalsarda already had an arrow drawn and pointed before they could finish laughing among themselves. "Stand aside," she commanded.

The laughter turned sour as they looked down to scowl at us. "Or what? You know the rules! It's our bridge, you 'ave to pay our toll!"

"I do know the rules," Chalsarda agreed. "As do you. Trolls must ask for their toll before we begin to cross, not after. You are owed nothing."

"You'll give us our toll, or you'll be sorry!"

"I see two children trying to extort a hunter and a powerful wizard," she began.

"Extort?" one of them questioned.

"Rob. Steal from," she continued. "In any event, I think it is you two who will be sorry."

"Maybe we'll just 'ave our meal of you all right now!" one of them threatened.

"Tell me, you regenerate, correct?" Chalsarda asked.

"What's that?"

She audibly sighed in frustration. "Grow body parts back. Heal good," she explained.

"Yeah, that's righ—" A howl of pain echoed all around us as an arrow buried itself messily into the eye of the one on the left, and in the blink of an eye Chalsarda already had another arrow drawn. The troll went down to its knees, clutching at its face as the other stared in shock.

"How long does it take to regenerate an eye?" she asked coldly.

The other troll looked back and forth between its brother and us, sneering and growling. "We 'ave many brothers, and you'll 'ave to pass through here, we knows it! You'll pay us in triple next time or we'll 'ave your bones!"

"That sounds a lot like you're doing the reasonable thing and standing aside," Chalsarda remarked, training the arrow on the troll. "We'll be on our way then if you'd be so kind."

The troll reluctantly stood aside, and we hurried across the bridge as Chalsarda kept her bow in her hands, arrow trained until we were well past.

"Keep moving; someone surely heard that," she instructed.

We bunched up, hurrying out of the city as quickly as we could without running, until we made it a safe enough distance away that Chalsarda allowed us to rest.

"Did I hear you right?" I asked, panting slightly. "Did you just refer to them as children?"

"Indeed, full-grown trolls are much larger and don't need to rely on intimidation. They stand at their bridge, and most people are too terrified to refuse to pay the toll."

"That was nuts!" Ann exclaimed. "You straight up shot him in the eye!"

"Yeah, that seemed a bit much," Olivia agreed shakily. "They were horrible, but did it have to be his eye?"

"It will grow back, and I had to make a point," Chalsarda claimed, strapping her bow to her back. "Wounding them and hurting their pride is the far better alternative to killing their young. The Knowing may be infinite, but you never know when you'll run into them again, and the trolls are not likely to forget. Meanwhile, we still need to come up with a plan for our return."

"Possible dumb question here," Olivia asked. "Why didn't we just pay their toll?"

"How would you have paid them?" No one answered, and Chalsarda spoke as if she'd made her point. "And that's why."

We made the rest of the trip in relative silence. I didn't think there was anything else to worry about immediately, but that couldn't have been an easy thing for Ann to experience. First time in The Knowing and she watches a troll take an arrow to the face. Perfect. I'm sure that will never come up again. It's precisely why I didn't want her to go with us. Something happening to one of my friends would be bad enough, but I didn't want her traumatized after this. Olivia has at least been through the thick of it with me before, I was less concerned about her. I guess it's not like she handled everything she saw particularly well, but she was still here, which was nice, probably.

"Can you teach me to do that?" Ann asked expectantly.

Chalsarda grinned at that. "If it were up to me, I would love to. I am tasked with training just Elana for the moment, unfortunately. But perhaps one day."

Okay, so not traumatized. I guess I don't know anyone after all.

"This is it," I announced, stopping in front of a stone pillar clouded by shadow and surrounded by nothing, all covered in etchings that had long ago eroded to the point where it was unreadable.

"Is there a hidden door here or something?" Olivia asked, scanning the obelisk.

"Something." I grinned, excited to show off, like the reveal of a magic trick.

What we were going to see was potentially dangerous, and we weren't here on vacation, but I decided to have fun when I could. I could see the seam in the film of what passed for reality here, and I raised my hands above my head to get the edge of it, gently and almost surgically slicing a line in the air and through the rocks as if they weren't there; parting the veil from this world to the next. When my hands were spread apart as far as they could be, I lowered my palms to the ground and, as I made contact, a hole was made, giving a view of a lush mountain tree and a waterfall in the middle distance. The crisp air immediately hit me like an air conditioner turned on full blast.

I turned back to the group smiling, anticipating the lit-up faces of my friends who were in awe of my ability to tear the fabric of space and time with my bare hands. Instead, I got a nod of acknowledgment from Chalsarda who thanked me briefly and instructed my friends to let her go first, just to be safe. Seriously, nothing from these two? Archery gets a reaction, but interdimensional travel gets squat. I felt oddly ripped off by that. Well, I thought it was cool at least.

When we were all through the portal, I got a better look around. Well, a look and feel, for that matter. The world itself felt wounded somehow. The air around me felt like touching pain that was not my own, though I felt like I was likely the only one who sensed this. Aside from that, the scenery was breathtaking, though if I had seen this area under any other circumstance, I'd be wondering if rescue crews were on their way. There was no trail or path anywhere that I could see, no sign of wildlife either. There was a lake in front of us—ice cold, I imagined—though in no danger of freezing. I was suddenly grateful for my coat. The high cliff face walls nearly blocked out the gray, overcast clouds, and gave the illusion that the waterfall was pouring from a bleeding sky. The trees in the area were bare and leafless, though the area was not without its fair share of green by way of moss covered logs, which were themselves covered in a thin layer of ice. A cold snap likely had hit the area, and it looked like no one had been around to see it.

"Be on guard, someone has moved through this area recently," Chalsarda casually remarked.

Man, I am just super perceptive lately!

"That looks just like…!" Ann breathed out in an excited, harsh voice. "Are we really in the book? This is almost exactly as I pictured it! So does this mean we can go anywhere? I want to see space! Or meet the Pilgrim! Not dinosaurs, that would be stupid. Unless they were the talking, smart dinosaurs. Wait! Why haven't we gone into a comic book specifically to get super powers?"

I laughed at Ann in spite of myself. I didn't mean to, but how could I not? This was the exact same reaction that I'd had, only now I had the benefit of being on the other side of excitable for a change.

"Yeah, if that's how it was described, that's probably it," I told her, grinning as I did.

"Sorry." Ann blushed. "This is just the most unreal thing I've ever seen."

"You're standing next to an elf, you've seen me cast magic, and I just took you on a stroll beyond the veil separating your world and everything else; a waterfall is the most unreal thing you've ever seen? Even by definition, I just showed you what was actually unreal."

"To be fair, this is my first time in a fictional world as well." Olivia was poking at a tree absently as she said this. "I never read the books, but still this is somehow, I don't know, tangible. It feels wrong though, doesn't it?"

"What do you mean?" The concern in Chalsarda's voice was genuine.

Olivia looked pensive and didn't answer for a moment as she tried to find the words. "Have you ever watched a medical video? Dental surgery, huge zit popping, guy breaks his leg falling off a bike...anything like that? It doesn't hurt you, not in the same way the person you're watching is hurt, but your empathy for that person causes a sort of phantom pain. Your teeth hurt just watching someone get a root canal, you know?"

"Yeah, I feel it too," Ann agreed. "Like a miasma radiating from the sky."

"Good word." I offered Ann a small, quick high-five. "But yeah, I'm glad it's not just me. I mean, I'm not glad that the world feels like it's in pain, but I'm glad I'm not the only one picking up on it."

Chalsarda seemed to consider this. "Just me then," she observed. "Odd. Something to keep in mind, certainly."

We followed Chalsarda, carefully, around the lake and up a series of increasingly elevated rocks that were smooth and flat at their base. My guess was that this was the work of Kodran, and he had made himself a nice little stairway up to his lakeside view apartment. That was also a cave, apparently. When we reached the ledge, it was probably a hundred feet or so above the water, with maybe another twenty or thirty feet of sheer rock face above us. There was a break in the rock wall above us, and from that break came the torrent of water that utterly blocked the mouth of the cave into his home.

"Riddle me this," I asked sarcastically. "When is a door just a surefire way to get hypothermia?"

"It's actually supposed to be pretty warm in his cave, part of his magic, but yeah, not the point," Ann conceded. "This is intentional. The running water is supposed to act as a brief short circuit to any casters who might enter or to serve as a cleanse for stray pieces of wild magic. The books spend an uncomfortable amount of time describing him standing shirtless under the water for that purpose."

That was genuinely concerning. The magic trap part, not the shirtless guy part. I'd heard something similar with the Aos Si, which meant that my rules for magic shared at least one aspect with the rules from this world. More to the point, if my magic were shorted out, even a moment and he caught me off guard, I'd be completely defenseless.

"Is there another way in?" Olivia asked.

"There is," Ann answered slowly, looking up and around as if she were looking for something. "But I might have completely forgotten what it was."

"No need," I said shaking a blister shield out of my wrist. "Huddle up if you want to stay dry."

I held the shield up with both hands over my head like an umbrella as Ann crowded in next to me, then Olivia, and we walked through. Chalsarda opted to simply jump through the falling water. My blister umbrella didn't do as good a job of protecting them from the water as it had me, but good enough. The cave was, as Ann had mentioned, unusually warm, with the feeling of being a comfortable distance from a fireplace anywhere you moved inside of it. Minus any electronics, the first room of the cave felt like a studio apartment. An apartment with stone walls and braziers hanging from ceilings too high for anywhere in LA, but still an apartment.

"How did he get a couch up here?" Olivia asked of the fluffy sectional sofa. Among other things you wouldn't expect to find in a mountain cave were bookshelves, a coffee table, a bed, an ice chest (the old wooden kind that you had to dump ice into), and just about everything else you'd expect to find in a bachelor's home, including laundry that somehow missed the wicker bin.

"Uh, Elana?" Ann's voice was on the precipice of panic. "I need you over here, now, please. Now. Like, right now! Oh my god, why aren't you here? Seriously, now!"

I was running toward her voice immediately, as were the others, but that didn't stop her from rambling. She was around a twisting pathway that opened up into another room, lit by more hanging braziers, and all at once I saw what had her so spooked.

"I just had to see it for myself," she began, eyes fixed on the room. "I wasn't sure it was real, like really real, but now I...I..."

In the room were maybe twenty or so statues of people, but something was off about them. Some of the statues looked to have been bound with rope and lay on the ground, the faces pained. Others stood shackled, looking defiant. A couple of them appeared to be elves. Some were dressed in armor, others in street clothes, and everything in between.

"Later in the books, i-it talks about this," Ann stammered. "He did this to them."

I was struck by how familiar the magic from them felt. It's hard to explain, but I could feel the spell-work heavy in the air. Not that I would even know, or want to know, where to begin on how to do this, but the framework of it, it had the same flavor as magic I had performed.

"Are they dead?" I asked, my stomach dropping as I did.

"No," Chalsarda answered thoughtfully. "But they aren't alive either. No one touches them or goes inside, just to be on the safe side."

I considered that. They weren't dead at least, that was good. Or if not good, it was something. This would be a horrible way to die. To no one in particular, I asked, "Is it reversible?"

"Reversible, yes, but not by you. Not by a long shot. This is a combination of Thanatology, Animacy, and mastery level Earth command," Chalsarda began to explain. I had taken a Thanatology course in high school, but I had the feeling she meant something else. "This is vile; I don't like it. We need to leave, immediately."

A man's voice interrupted her then, the sound of it echoing across the cave walls. "Of course it would make sense that *you* don't like it," he said, emphasizing the word so that there was no doubt about who he was addressing. "And yeah, after the day I've had, I'm just going to go ahead and say you all made a big mistake coming here."

12

There was something dark and invisible rising within him as he said that, and it was growing.

"Kodran! Wait!" I shouted, anticipating how quickly things could get out of control. "I'm just here to talk, I swear!"

Kodran was a slight man, but even through his loose clothing, I could tell he was physically imposing despite his lack of height. His forearms and biceps were packed with the sort of muscle that you only ever saw on people who worked with their hands for a living. His youthful appearance was a lie. Golden blonde, messy hair and the sort of yellowish, wispy beard that would not look out of place on the kind of guy who would enthusiastically corner me at a party to explain my craft beer to me. He was an immortal though, so maybe once upon a time, he was mansplaining mead to shield maidens.

"One of Freyr's goons and three wizards break into my home to talk?" he sneered, and I heard Olivia yelp, which distracted me long enough to get caught off guard by the rocks which seemed to form around my feet, immobilizing me. I looked back to see that Olivia, who had been closest to a cave wall, was now shackled to the wall at her wrists by rocks which looked as if they'd always been there that way. Chalsarda managed a little hop to her left, smoothly pulling an arrow into her bowstring as she did, and Ann had somehow succeeded in possibly just falling out of the way of the trap.

"I am not of Freyr and hold no allegiance to him!" Chalsarda shouted.

Olivia's voice was a mixture of annoyance and disgust. "And we're not wizards, you jerk!"

Kodran had a look a parent might when they knew a child was caught red-handed. "I will not tolerate lies in my home! You're an elf with an arrow pointed at my head, of course you're with Freyr. And you three, you reek of wild magic, especially this one," His eyes fell on Olivia, before moving back toward me. "And you're carrying a shield formed entirely out of pure magical energy. And you're not wizards?"

He kind of had a point. "Okay, so maybe I'm a wizard, I'm still not sure how I'm supposed to identify to be perfectly honest," I admitted, stammering through my words. "But I'm the only one, and I, dang my feet are really stuck. Oh! Good job with the Valkyries and the Dwarves and stuff!"

He looked struck for a moment at that. "How could you possibly have known what I just went through?"

I sighed, knowing this would come up eventually. "We're not from here, but I promise we're not here to hurt you, only to talk. Now can you release us?"

"That doesn't answer my question, and I definitely do not trust that one. So let's do this," he said, arrogantly walking straight up to Chalsarda as if an arrow wasn't a moment away from being released into his face. "You are Fae, and you're unable to lie. You're clever with your words, but if you want me to listen to what your friends have to say, you will answer me this: Who do you serve?"

Chalsarda grimaced at that and her grip on the bow wavered for a moment. "I cannot say."

"Sure you can," Kodran coaxed. "Just give me a name."

"I told you, I cannot."

"Without a name, you could be working for anyone, and who knows what kind of danger I'd be in? So I'll ask once more, and then I'm done with all of you. Who is your master?"

Chalsarda began to sweat and looked visibly pained. "And I will tell you once more, I cannot say! I did not say that I don't want to say, that I do not know, or that I refuse to answer. I am bound against saying his name. I can only tell you that I do not serve Freyr and I did not come here with the intention of harming you."

Kodran chewed that over for a moment. "There's definitely a story there, and you might be the only elf in the world who doesn't serve Freyr, but I suppose that will have to do for now."

The bonds underneath my feet and those pinning Olivia to the wall crumbled, and the dark energy coming off Kodran dissipated. "Just as well, I've had enough fighting for one day. Come on, let's have our chat somewhere more hospitable."

Kodran beckoned us to come with him, and asked, "Since you know my name, maybe introductions are in order?"

Chalsarda answered before anyone could say anything. "We're not giving our names to a sorcerer."

"Figures."

The four of us cautiously followed him out of the statue filled room and back through his bedroom, living room, and kitchen. It just then occurred to me that I hadn't seen a bathroom, and thoroughly grossed out decided never to never think about that ever again. "Coffee? Tea? Sit anywhere you'd like," Kodran offered as he moved toward his ice chest.

"We'll pass on the drinks, if it's all the same to you," I replied, and then noticing that Ann was about to plop down on his couch, I added, "And after what just happened I think we'll all stand. This shouldn't take long."

Ann caught herself and bounced back to her feet, trying to play off the motion.

"More's the pity," he said, returning with beer. "I was hoping this one might be willing to lie down later."

Kodran winked at Ann as he said it, and her face instantly reacted with a twist of disgust so apparent that her glasses slid down her nose. "Ew."

He shrugged at that, and sat down in an exhausted heap, taking a sip of his beer. "Well, you wanted to talk, so talk."

"Full disclosure, I'm not going to be able to disclose everything fully," I began. "For reasons. That said, I'll get right to the point. In about twelve years or so, is that right?" I asked Ann, turning toward her. She gave a noncommittal shrug that told me I was more or less correct. "In twelve years or so you're going to summon the Nuckelavee, and we're here to ask you very nicely not to do that."

There was a pained sound of beer being choked on, going down the wrong pipes, and coming up through the nostrils.

"I'm going to what?" Kodran finally choked out. "How could I even...what am I doing? I have a living, breathing lie detector right here. You there, long ears, yes or no. Is this true?"

"Yes," Chalsarda answered impatiently.

Kodran let out a whistle at that and laughed. "Why the hell would I do that? I mean, I'm a bastard, sure, but I'm not a murderous bastard."

I thought back to the room full of people trapped in a prison of stone and considered his statement debatable.

"Not yet," I said, hoping I found the halfway point between honest and confrontational.

"Okay, let's say I summon the Nuckelavee, which nitely wouldn't do, but let's say I do." He sat up at this so big and bad that I need to summon one of the most unholy things in creation?"

"Me."

He barked a laugh that seemed forced and asked, "You and what army?"

I cringed at the joke and trying to stay on track I answered, "No, just me. You know what? It was kind of a dirtbag move."

"Sounds like it," he agreed. "And what could possibly make me do this? It doesn't add up. I could just kill you right now; I think I'd even have a shot of taking all of you in one fell swoop. Summoning the Nuckelavee is something I'd do if I wanted to raze a city. Hell, maybe a state. So what makes me swat a fly with an A-bomb?"

Magically I wasn't punching at his weight, that I was sure of, but I didn't like the implication all the same. I focused a little bit more on my shield as I answered him. "I really don't know exactly when you make the turn to full blown evil, only that Freyr asks you to do it, and—"

His eyes narrowed at that, and I realized what an incredibly stupid thing I'd said almost as soon as I said it. "Did he now?" Kodran asked me, locking eyes. His words came out more deliberate, immediately changing the tone of the conversation. "Well, let's just review then, yeah? In the next dozen years or so, I summon a beast which will kill anything in its way to get to you. I don't want to kill anyone, but the fact that you're sitting here means you've survived at least the first incarnation; so I might have underestimated you. And if Freyr gives me a direct request, I will be unable to deny him, the same way your bodyguard here can't name her master. But I think I see a way out for both of us."

"What's that?" I asked cautiously.

"I turn you to stone," he said nonchalantly. Then, sensing the hostility of the room continued. "Hear me out! Twelve years will feel like twelve seconds to you, if that. And if you're already trapped, there's no need to send the Nuckelavee after you, so random strangers won't die in the process. Your friends even get to go home. When Freyr asks for you, you're already here. Easy, right?"

"Except you're still handing her over to a Norse god for execution!" Olivia shouted. "You could just not do the murder summoning thing!"

Kodran shrugged at that. "My way seems easier."

With that, he sprang to his feet and extended a palm toward me, and what looked like slow-moving dust appeared out of the air and flew in my direction. I lifted my shield on instinct, and to my horror, the purple sheen was replaced with opaque stone. I dropped it in surprise, and it crashed to the floor with a thud, the transformation completing entirely by the time it reached the ground. Everything next happened in a blur. An arrow struck Kodran in the shoulder, staggering him, but it shattered on impact. I hit him with a gust of wind, sending him toppling over the couch, and he stood up quicker than I would have thought possible holding what looked like a machete carved from stone.

"I can tell you where to find the Anvil of Broker!" Ann shouted at the top of her lungs, and as quickly as it began everyone stopped moving. "Brockor? I don't know how to pronounce it."

Thick, adrenaline-fueled breaths left Kodran as his brows furrowed and he stared at Ann. "The Anvil of Brokkr? What do you know of it?"

I could see now that under his shirt where the arrow struck his shoulder was as pale as the cave walls around us.

"I know you're looking for it," Ann said, trying to project confidence. "And I know where it is. Give us your word we can leave safely, and I'll tell you."

"It was destroyed years ago; you have nothing!" he seethed.

"Yeah, I thought you might say that," Ann replied. "But I didn't just make it up, so obviously I must know something. If you want to know what that is, make me a deal."

"No, you couldn't have," Kodran answered uneasily. "Do you know what you're offering me? If I have the Anvil, at best you're trading a little bit of time for your friend in exchange for the certainty that I'll be able to wipe you all off the map no matter where you go. I'd probably be able to give Freyr himself a bloody nose with what I could do with that."

Ann shook her head. "Not by itself, it's just one part of the puzzle, and you know that."

Kodran nodded in agreement. "That was a test, you're right. The Anvil is nothing on its own. Fine, you have a deal."

He stepped forward to shake hands with Ann, and before I could react, she stepped toward him as well and clasped hands. She looked pained for a second like maybe he gripped her hand too hard. They released, and Ann turned her gaze to me, looking a little sick in the process.

"Get out of here, and I'll meet you in a moment."

My hand was inching its way toward the rod in my book bag as I answered her, "No way, you'd be defenseless, I'm not doing that to you."

"I'm not asking you to go far, just outside of the room. This is a place of power for him; he's not so tough outside of this room. No offense."

"I'm still standing here," Kodran said annoyed.

"Leave Ch—" She stopped herself. "Leave our archer behind with me, and you two just get on the other side of the waterfall. When I give the answer, we'll meet you. If he goes back on his word, you have a better chance of saving me out there than in here, even if it means coming back for me."

"I'm not a villain, I did just kind of save the world." Kodran sighed. "I'm not going back on my word."

I hated it, but her logic was sound. I was the one he wanted, and if nothing else he was a protagonist in a book series, so there was at least a little bit of nobility in him. Not much, but if he were going to go back on his word, it would be a lot more tempting with me in the room. Chalsarda gave me a glance of approval and kept her arrow trained on Kodran, decidedly pointing the arrow at his head this time.

"Come on," I said to Olivia, moving her before she had the chance to protest. We walked straight through the waterfall this time, no time for cover. Soaked and cold, we waited anxiously for what felt like minutes, before Ann emerged, followed by Chalsarda.

"Ohmygod! Ohmygod!" Ann was hyperventilating now; hair pressed to her face from the waterfall, the veneer of cool completely gone now that she was out of the cave.

I gripped her in a wet hug as tight as I could, utterly relieved to get her out. "Don't do that!" I nearly shouted at her. "You idiot, I'm supposed to get you back safe!"

"Let's move before he changes his mind," Chalsarda said grimly.

The way back down the stones was especially treacherous given how wet we were from the waterfall, the stone steps made slippery under our feet, and the shivering made us unstable. Chalsarda did her best to get us down, and we made it back to the tear without incident. He'd kept his word, or maybe he just didn't want to risk a fight with another prize in sight. Either way, we were safely back in The Knowing, which was something I somehow didn't expect I would say today.

We rested in the relative safety and warmth of our spot just inside The Knowing, drying off clothes and wringing socks of water. "So, what was up with that Anvil thing?" I asked Ann, once we'd all settled down.

Ann shrugged. "He was going to find it in book three, either way; I just told him what he was going to find out anyway. But you know, it's a shame that no one told him that Hel is already there and has plans for the Anvil. That's probably going to suck for him."

"You just probably altered the entire series!" I laughed in disbelief. Laughter that I hoped wouldn't turn into panic. "Oh my god, that's...I don't even want to think about how big that ripple is going to be!"

"It's true," Olivia confirmed, smacking her socks on a boulder. "When I found out about Elana's travel thing, she saved a clerk in an Eternity Pilgrim episode, and when she got back, that woman was the new Comrade. And you wouldn't have thought that would have made a significant impact, but then, hey. New character!"

Ann jumped to her feet, her face in utter shock. "You went into Eternity Pilgrim! No wait, you met Charlie? No! Wait! Shut up! Charlie was dead?"

"Yup," I admitted sheepishly.

"I knew I wasn't crazy!" she shouted. "I remember there being two episodes! One where she died, one where she was alive! No one believed me! Oh, hold on. She was dead!"

"Yeah, totally dead," I agreed.

"Now she's not dead!" Ann sat back down, reeling.

Chalsarda came over to us, looking a bit more relaxed, but her expression was still less than enthused. "We all need to be a bit more careful." She was somber in her tone. "We've all been reckless today, and while I'm glad we're all still alive, it could have gone much worse for all of us. Ann, you especially. No more putting yourself in danger like that. I'm not going to bother training someone just to see them die. It would be a waste of time for us both."

"So you're going to teach me?" Ann asked.

Chalsarda smiled slightly. "Like I said, perhaps one day, if I'm ever relieved of my duty. You have the heart for it, after all."

Ann beamed with pride at that, and that seemed as good a time as any for us to go. We had to head home, and unfortunately, that meant crossing through troll town. It felt like it would be best to do it while we were all feeling pretty good about surviving. Good vibes and all that. The city was, however, surprisingly quiet as we made our way through it. It wasn't until we were nearly to the other side of the town that we saw it. Dozens of troll corpses of various sizes, some as small as the ones we'd faced earlier, some seemed like they could have been nine or ten feet tall if they'd been standing. Many were dismembered. None of them had a head attached to their body. And standing in the middle, slouched down was a man in a black suit with a scythe in one hand who was crying. No, not crying. Laughing. And the laughter grew, genuine laughter filled with amusement. The man stood up straight and turned to face us, a mad smile on his lips and his suit covered in blood.

"Can you believe it, Elana?" Bres asked, looking me dead in the eye. "The poor bastards had me surrounded! They never stood a chance!"

His laughter echoed across everything as he laughed at his own joke. It sounded like it may never stop.

13

Terror seized me, and I instantly reached out into The Knowing, looking for any help, any advantage. Nothing came. That's the problem with infinity, I suppose. You can't be everywhere at once. And whatever forces or parts of this place had helped me in the past weren't here at the moment.

"Well, I'm waiting," Bres said impatiently, spreading his hands. "Is there anything you'd like to say back to me? Any clever retorts or, oh, I know! How about a speech? You're pretty good at those, you know!"

I spun on my heel and locked eyes with Chalsarda. "Get them back, now! Don't try to fight him, don't wait for me, just go!"

"Oh come now, don't be stupid." Bres sounded genuinely annoyed at that. "I'm willing to put up with a lot of annoyances from you, but stupidity isn't one of them. I won't go down in history as the man outsmarted by an idiot."

I turned again and yelled at him, despite myself. "From what I can tell, you're not going to go down in history at all!"

His nostrils flared at that, and a deep breath later he chuckled and wagged a finger at me. "That's how you got me last time, running your trap, getting under my skin. Not this time. You learned quite a bit about me, didn't you? Kicked about upstairs for a bit, eh? But you didn't get everything."

I pulled my rod out of my bag and held it outstretched in his direction with a trembling hand, using my other hand to shoo everyone behind him. I wasn't happy that they were still here, but if they weren't going to run, I needed to get between them. "What are you talking about?"

Bres looked at the rod and nodded in approval. "Not bad, and this makes much more sense than the damned Vorpal sword. I'll bet you didn't even have to steal this one!" He stared at me for a long second, and then continued, "Fine, you remember our deal? You're using the ways, and that's good! What's even better is that I know the ways better than you, so there is literally no place that you can hide from me. And your friends, sure, I can't kill them. You're friends with Elana, I presume? Right, you're off limits. But you, Elana, I can slit your pretty little neck any time I like."

A thought occurred to me, and if Bres had a tell, I was starting to think I figured out what it was. "Then why haven't you?" I asked, lowering my rod. "I mean, look around us! If ever there was the time, this is it. I'm helpless, and I know it! Do you just like sounding scary? I'm starting to think you like the idea of sounding intimidating more than actually, you know, doing the violence. Oh man, seriously, when I first saw you here I was ready to crap myself, and I mean that. But you're not doing anything! Which means you probably can't, right? Did you honestly just slaughter a bunch of trolls to scare me? That's messed up, man; you should feel ashamed of yourself."

Bres chewed his bottom lip, a hand resting on his waist. "Oh, clever as always, right?" he asked with a smile. "I know about your meeting with Roger Nill, and it is true that he told me to not to put a hand on you. But you're wrong about the whole 'why' portion of why I haven't taken your head, because hey, when have I liked being told what to do? No, you've got it all wrong. All wrong."

I studied him for a moment. He was acting like he knew something that I didn't, and that was more frightening to me than anything else at this point. The last advantage I'd want him to have is a plan. A tiger doesn't need to lay traps to be a fearsome hunter. "Then what is it?"

"Oh it's a few things, to be sure," he continued. "It could just be that I want to toy with you. Make you suffer for what you did to me. And that is part of it, definitely. The real answer, though, is that the worst I can do is kill you, and in the ever-increasing list of things that I know, I know that something is coming for you that can do much worse than that."

"The Nuckelavee," I whispered.

"Well, I think you can just say Nuckelavee. You don't call me The Bres, do you?"

"You don't want to know what I call you," I said half-heartedly.

"I'm sure I could guess. Along those lines, can you guess why I made a pile of troll corpses for you?" he asked, and then without waiting for more than half a second added, "Oh, it's too good, no guesses! So I killed all the trolls! All except one, who in exchange for his life, went home to get help from the grown-ups. And of course, to finger you as the big scary meanie who killed all of his brothers."

I was so angry that I almost couldn't get the words out. Bres made a mocking gesture at how flustered I was until I finally managed to ask, "So you just killed them for no reason? Why? Why would you do that?"

"I didn't say there was no reason; there was a perfectly good reason! To make the trolls in this area your new mortal enemy!" he proclaimed. "And because it was funny. And I might have just taken all this time speaking with you to give them time to get back here because, yes, yes, that looks like them now. Now who's the clever one? Luck be with you, Elana! You're pretty strong, right? You can handle a few trolls, I'm sure. Actually, make that all of the trolls. Ta!"

Bres then casually walked away.

Well off the path, I could see home, just as the ground began to rumble with the imposing sound of an army of trolls stampeding toward us from the town, and even now, we could see buildings quake and foundations shudder.

"I hate that guy!" Olivia seethed.

With each second the rumbling grew louder, and the ground began to quake.

"Run!" shouted Chalsarda. "I'll slow a couple down, but you mark the path! Go!"

The severity of the situation gripped everyone suddenly, and I took off in a dead sprint, Ann and Olivia keeping pace easily with me. I heard the distant squeal of trolls doubling over in pain, but I didn't dare look back to see what was happening. The pounding of the mass on ethereal dry earth told me all I needed to about not stopping. Before I could worry about whether or not Chalsarda would catch up with us or not, she appeared beside us, running as effortlessly as I would have walked.

"We're not going to make it," she said grimly.

I wanted to say something in response, but I was a little too busy wondering whether or not I had asthma to say anything. Our entrance was nowhere nearby, but ahead of us stood a frosted glass door, attached to nothing with no visible hinges.

"That looks like our only chance out of here," Chalsarda remarked.

"Wasn't...there...before...!" I wheezed as we approached it.

It felt like a trap. Like Bres had herded us toward it. I stopped in front of the door as Olivia gripped the handle.

"Wait," I managed.

Chalsarda directed my attention toward the area we had just fled, and what I saw could only be described as a tsunami of mutant elephants. More trolls than I could count, some of them ten feet tall easily. All of them bearing down on us and bloodthirsty. "No time," she said, and before I could react, I felt strong hands grip me by the jacket as I was tossed through the door.

There was a feeling like stepping off a curb that you expected to be a few inches from the street but was, in fact, a few feet, and instead of the street it was the deep end of a swimming pool. I fell for only an instant like that before being dumped onto my friends Olivia and Ann, who were themselves on a hardwood floor. I heard a sound like a sandwich baggie being zipped up, and I turned to see Chalsarda hop through a tiny rip in reality that burst into nothing like a popped soap bubble after she landed in the room with a little hop.

I followed her gaze to see Roger; I guess his last name was Nill (if Bres was to be believed), staring at us in mild shock from across a large desk that seemed to be carved out of some ancient, petrified wood. Seated across from him was an older gentleman with a thin pencil mustache who was wearing a tuxedo of all things. It took me a second, but I realized he reminded me of a middle-aged Vincent Price. In that second, however, an enormous woman with sharp features and chopped silver hair, inexplicably in full-plate armor shouted a wordless challenge and unsheathed a sword that looked like it weighed as much as I did and leveled it at Chalsarda. With her free, gauntleted hand, she backhanded a chair in a show of power, obliterating it. Chalsarda simply nocked an arrow.

Roger tried to break the tension by standing with a chuckle, saying, "Well now, look at that! I completely forgot about my... uh, 7:43 appointment!"

The man in the tuxedo motioned a hand in a downwards pat motion, and the armored woman cautiously sheathed her sword, but did not break eye contact with Chalsarda. Roger walked the Vincent Price look-alike and the warrior princess out of the room with apologetic promises about rescheduling, while Chalsarda helped the rest of us to our feet. I noticed on their way out that Roger was playing the pronoun game with his guests, careful not to say their name or any identifying information at all. It wasn't terribly difficult; he was speaking the way an NPC would speak to a character in a role-playing game. Very generalized.

I took the time to look out of the wall-sized windows in his office as well, and I noticed the wide, disbelieving faces on Olivia and Ann as they did the same. I didn't know if we were in The Knowing, but it certainly didn't feel like Earth. There was a city out there, though none of the buildings came close to being as tall as the one we were in. It was dark outside, but in the distance, past the buildings, were luminescent, violet rolling hills, which threatened to intrude upon the deep spinach-green of the night sky. And there were stars! So many I could never count them all, and it all just seemed to go forever.

"What is this place?" Olivia asked breathlessly.

Roger power walked back across the length of the long office toward his desk. "I assume," Roger said, allowing heavy emphasis on the word. "That you all did not inter-dimensionally travel into my office and interrupt a meeting to discuss the view."

"Who were those people?" I asked, turning to face him. "And did that woman seriously have plate armor?"

Roger looked mildly frustrated at that and stacked a few papers to put into a drawer; he continued, "And furthermore, I will go ahead and assume you also didn't just pop into my office to discuss the attire of my guests, as that would be quite rude. And unless someone would like to try a third time." He paused at that and looked into each of our faces. "I'm going to go ahead and assume that you all came here without an agenda, and now that my schedule has been cleared, I don't have one either. Hi, I'm Roger."

He walked over while he spoke and extended a hand to Ann, which she nearly accepted until both Olivia and me smacked it down simultaneously. A look of shock crossed her face, but not Roger.

"No handshakes," I said sternly.

"Very well then, introductions at least. Elana Black, Olivia Moore, and Ann Bancroft I know, but you," he said turning around to face Chalsarda who hadn't moved from the spot she landed on. "You, I do not know. I'm Roger Nill, what can I call you?"

"You may call me a friend to them, and that is all," she said flatly.

"I'm really getting a sense in here like you all don't trust me, which is funny considering you broke into my office," he said with a small, frustrated laugh that lacked any joy. "But I am always willing to be the bigger man, so if you'd indulge me for a moment, I'd like to take this unexpected visit and turn it into a tour of sorts."

I looked into the faces of my friends, unsure of what to say to that. It was just starting to occur to me that Roger's willingness to work with me might be the only thing that got us all out of here in one piece. No one else knew where we were, and come to think of it, we didn't even have any idea where we were either; and if this went wrong, there wouldn't be a cavalry to come to our rescue

"Come on now, what's that look?" Roger asked. "Yeah, you, the elf especially. What? Are you actually planning on trying to fight your way out of here? You'd never make it, believe me, not that you'd need to. If I wanted you dead, any of you, I could have done it long ago; I'm trying to play nice."

"Yeah, you, the human with the hair dye," Chalsarda mocked. "Do you know who I serve?"

"I do indeed," Roger agreed. "And killing you would make things mildly complicated, very temporarily. Do you think we have time to worry about every god and would-be god here? They all want something different, each one of them hates another one. For as pissed as your master would be, I'm sure at least a couple of others would be happy to see him annoyed."

Chalsarda showed nothing at that, and either she was unafraid to die, or she was just focused on getting everyone out of here alive. Or she was terrified and just really good at hiding it.

"I want to see," Olivia spoke up in a voice that commanded the room. Then, a little quieter, but sharper she continued. "I want to see what possible excuse you could have for everything your people have done to my friends, to me, and everyone else. I don't want to believe that anyone out there could be that awful for its own sake. I want to see you justify yourself."

Roger pursed his lips and snapped his fingers, pointing at Olivia. "Now that is great news," he said and looked around. "Who else?"

Chalsarda looked ready to protest, but I stopped her. "She's right. We're here; we might as well. Olivia deserves to see if she wants."

I gave a look to Olivia, who smiled slightly in appreciation at that.

"All right, open minds, that's what I'm talking about." Roger smiled. "Okay then, follow me, we'll get started. Can I get anyone anything before we get started? Diet Coke, coffee, arrows?"

"Just get on with it, and know that I'll have my eye on you," Chalsarda nearly spat.

Roger moved to the back corner of the room and pulled what I had not previously recognized as a door away from the wall, and at that moment I had to stop myself from jumping out of my own skin when I realized that I hadn't noticed that creepy kid from the beach earlier was standing silently in the corner, wearing his little suit. His face was emotionless, but his eyes followed me, and there was a danger in them when he saw that I'd noticed him.

We followed Roger into a vast, brightly lit hall, with windowless doors lining either side. "So that door into my office, let me guess," Roger remarked as we walked. "Bres?"

"Something like that," I replied uneasily.

"He's a child, I swear. A real S.O.B. if you'll pardon the language. I didn't even notice it, if you can believe it." There was a small laugh filled with frustration at that. "He's loyal, to an extent. He fights for the cause, he does what he's told, but Bres'll always push back where he can. The Fae are tricky like that, aren't they?"

The question was directed at Chalsarda who didn't respond. We stopped in front of a door that I could not have differentiated from the others for the life of me. None of the doors were marked in any way; nothing was numbered. The doors were all the same size even. Roger opened the door to reveal a windowless room with a conference table and several chairs. He flipped off the light switch, and despite the light source from the hall, the world inside vanished, only to be replaced with void and a glowing orange spire about three feet in height, suspended in nothing.

"Everything is done for a purpose. Everything," Roger said, stepping into the void. "Stories are told, revered, forgotten, revisited, or not; not that it matters. Once a thing is made, it has been made. Even if something is undone, it was still done. We have been set upon a path, and for quite some time that path has grown dark. But there is a light at the end if only we do not waver, there is one who will save us. 'Show me a hero, and I'll write you a tragedy', am I right? Well, would it surprise you to know that we've been staring in the face of our protagonist all along? Because we will surely need a hero very soon, and we know where she is."

Roger looked me in the eyes with hope and weariness, and for just a moment he didn't seem like the salesman. Sincerity touched his words. "Elana, I think it's about time you learned what it means to be the chosen one."

I couldn't help myself. In spite of everything, the danger we were in, the current company, and the severity of Roger's words, even the creepy void room; I barked out a laugh at that.

"You idiot!" I practically shouted incredulously. "I'm no chosen one. I can barely feed myself actual meals on most days, let alone be responsible for the weight of the world on my shoulders. Besides, this isn't a story, and I'm not your protagonist. My story is my own, same with my choices."

"Well, that's not what I said." Roger sounded perturbed at that. "But agreed, at least in part. You'd make a terrible protagonist, and thankfully you are not the chosen one. But you're wrong about this not being a story; everything is a story. Once upon a time, they lived happily ever after, ad infinitum. Wherever a hero or savior is needed, there's a story behind it. You and I, and everyone here, are merely players playing our part."

"I think I speak for everyone here when I say we have no idea what you're talking about, and speeches are boring," I replied.

"And that brings me to why we are here in this room," he continued. "I could tell you, but you and I both know that you'd never believe me anyway. Sometimes show is better than tell. So please, you three, approach, but do not touch until I say so."

"Why not all four of us?" I asked suspiciously.

"This works out best for all of us," he answered patiently. "For one thing, this is not for her. But at the same time, due to your inability to trust me fully, I imagine you'll want someone you trust watching your back while you're away."

I was skeptical, but Chalsarda gave me a reassuring nod that told me that she wouldn't let anything happen to us as long as she was around, and with looks of my own to Olivia and Ann, we cautiously stepped into the room to find ourselves walking on nothing that was visible. It was disorienting, but I adjusted quickly.

"Now, all together, I want you three to place your palms on the top in unison; that part is important." Roger spoke in a voice that sounded more like a yogi than a car salesman now. "And you will be shown another perspective."

The three of us exchanged one more nervous glance, and in motions that mirrored each other we placed our palms on the—

I see myself! I am much younger, but that's me! And I'm laughing! And I smell awful. I'm nine? Maybe? I need to brush my teeth; they're caked in plaque. I forgot how bad I used to be about that. I am in a bedroom, one I recognize. A musty old unicorn blanket, boxy CRT Sony television on top of the dresser, and is that an order form for the Scholastic Book Fair? I haven't seen one of these in...This bedroom belongs to Lucia! No, it doesn't. That doesn't ring true in my head. I look at the black, curved mirror of the television, and I understand. I am Lucia. I remember, and I forget. And I—

I was just in Elana's head! But she was so much older. That's new! Maybe that's the new thing I can do! I've told her so much about where I've been and about all of my new friends. I want her to come with me one day, or I want my friends to come here. I haven't liked keeping secrets from mom and dad, but they don't believe me. Elana believes me. She wants to hear another, and I start to tell her about the time I met a kid who was trapped in Santa's body.

I am thirteen. Middle school is out; I'll be in high school after the summer. I'm not ready for it. I'm ready for dragons and robots and mad scientists, but I'm not ready for high school. I know what most of the kids say about me. They're wrong, but that doesn't matter. It still hurts. Elana hasn't changed at all. She gets picked on for being my friend, and I hate it. If I were stronger I would stop letting her hang out with me, but I need her or else I'm alone. Olivia isn't mean, but she is embarrassed to be seen with me. When she invites Elana to do things, she does it away from me, and I make her uneasy. I can tell. She doesn't believe me, and she wishes that I wouldn't talk about things that she can't do. Like right now.

"So then what happened?" Elana asks, and I can't stop the story now, not when she's this excited.

So I tell her. I tell her about how the kids in the treehouse built a plane out of playground equipment, and how we dropped water balloons filled with anti-zombie juice made out of chemicals and candy onto the big kids and teachers, and they went back to normal. I tell her about the woman in the white suit who was always watching me, even though no one else saw her.

"That doesn't make sense," Olivia said. "You can't make a plane out of playground stuff, and there's no such thing as chemicals in real life! Those are only in cartoons."

"Well, maybe not our playground stuff, but theirs can!" I counter.

"Whatever. Elana, are you still going to play carroms with me at the park?" she asks our friend. Olivia loves it when the rec center puts out the carrom boards during the summer. I already know I'm not invited.

Elana looks nervous at that, and she doesn't know how to answer. "I've got to go home; mom is taking me with her to Costco. Have fun!"

Her expression softens at that, and her eyes light up. "Don't forget BookIt tomorrow!" Elana says with a grin, referring to our summer reading program. Every time we do a book report for summer school, we get a free personal pizza coupon. I feel myself smile in return and, in that moment, I wish she could do what I do, and I feel lighter, like taking off a heavy backpack.

I am in high school now. Nothing is cute anymore. The pressure to lie is more intense now than ever. I don't. Most kids don't care. Some zero in on me. Like the one who just threw a runny shake in a Styrofoam cup at me. I remember being excited for a whole day that our cafeteria sold milkshakes at lunch. An older boy says something about my body, and what he wants to do to it. His friends laugh, my face grows hot. I immediately try to forget it and walk away. A tiny voice cracks as it shouts out a challenge. I turn to see a student who I would swear was ten-years-old if not for her clothes and that she's on the quad at lunch. She

cranes her neck up to yell at the boy. He mashes a tater tot into her hair. She sharply lifts a steel toed boot up between his legs. The boy howled, his face crimson. His legs shudder, and he falls to a knee, breathing hard as a crowd of kids whoops and shouts.

The small kid looks at me with frightened eyes and starts to run, smacking me on the arm to join her. Soon we're behind the music room, out of breath and filled with adrenaline.

"I don't like bullies," she tells me.

It's the first thing I hear from her to me, and I look at her like some kind of minuscule superhero, and once again I have that familiar feeling of a weight being lifted from my shoulders. I thank her, and she looks at me in shock. She can't believe she just did that! She didn't know that would actually worked, and she never wants to do it again. Her giant glasses, half the size of her face and perpetually falling off her nose, clash with her black lipstick and goth style. Her name is Ann, and she asks if I'm the weird one everyone talks about. We both laugh at that statement, and we find one of the lesser used bathrooms to clean the milkshake out of my clothes and hair. She asks if I'm friends with Elana. I tell her that I am, and she confirms that she shares an English class with her. She tells me about the Sci-Fi/Fantasy club that meets in the K wing on Thursdays at lunch, and that they have a strict no shake throwing policy. I promise to join her sometime.

A year later or so. The parking lot of a mini golf course. Olivia is on the verge of yelling at me. She's been so patient with me for so long, she claims. She's my friend, she claims. But I'm acting crazy, and she doesn't know if I'm doing it for attention or to try *and be cool or if I'm actually crazy. She doesn't like the way I influence Elana. It's fine if I want to be a freak, but she already has enough problems around people, and I'm making it worse for her. She tells me I'm selfish. I tell her I'm not lying; she's just mad because she can't do it too. Now she's really yelling at me. She shoves me and tells me to grow up. I want to prove it to her. I want her to see how stupid she is for doubting me. I am more angry with her in that moment than she'll ever know. I want her to know what I can do so she'll shut her stupid mouth and never come between my friend and me ever again. I feel light again. A little too light, and I collapse. Olivia is concerned, apologetic, scared. She tries to help me. I don't want her help. She helps me up anyway.*

Now it is night. Another day, not far from the last one. I had a bad day at school. None of my friends were around. Kids kept asking me about what I did. I told them. They were mocking me. I knew it, but I became insistent. That only made it worse. Soon I was screaming at them. Some kids knew it went too far. Some took it further. I just didn't want to be different. Or I wanted everyone to be different. I was afraid and lonely and unable to process how to make it from minute to minute. I felt lighter than I'd ever felt before. I woke up in an ambulance. Then I woke up in a hospital. I woke up a third time just now. There is a woman in a white suit speaking with my parents outside of the room. They look concerned, but more than concerned they look tired. I know by the looks on their faces that I'm not going back to school. I am now thinking that Olivia might have been right, I should have kept to myself, and now I'm in trouble. The television is broken,

and if it weren't, I would escape right now. But there's nothing to escape to. I close my eyes, and I hear them clearly. They don't know that I can hear them.

The woman is assuring my parents that they have a special place for people like me, that they can give me the help I need, but that they will continue my education and foster my creative energies. It's in Oxnard, not far from here. I'm now thinking about the X-Men. My parents are hardly listening. I want to yell at the woman to stop drilling. She's already hit oil. I don't because I'm still weak, but that's the only reason.

My parents tiredly nod in agreement and, in that moment, I cease to have parents. Their choice, not mine. They gave up on me.

The woman comes to my bed. She has warm, dark skin that reminds me of umber colored wicker, and it stands in stark contrast to the brightness of her clothing. I have seen her before. She is unmistakable in that ridiculous all white three-piece suit.

She kneels down at the side of my bed and, when she speaks, there is warmth in her voice. "Lucia Cruz, you are very special, do you know that?" She is middle-aged and, now I realize, motherly in a way that I'd almost forgotten exists.

"I have seen you. Many times," I tell her.

"So then, we understand each other. I know you are telling the truth," she tells me.

"Who are you?" I ask her.

"My name is less important than my function, and in time you will not remember it, nor will it be important to you, but I will tell you both if that is your wish." She strokes my hand as she says this, and I let her.

"Please, tell me," I respond. It brings a smile to her face that touches her eyes.

"My name is Folayan Harris, and I am here to tell you that of all the stories you've seen, of all the heroes you've met, that

yours is the most important story of them all. You are going to be the greatest hero of them all. You, Lucia Cruz, are going to save everyone."

I consider this in my bed. I'm not ready for this news, but I'm not ready for my parents to give me away either. I'm not ready to go back to a school where everyone thinks I'm crazy. I'm not ready for anything. I'm numb.

"What do you need from me?"

"I need you to tell me that you're ready for what is coming, that you will help in the way that only you can," Folayan says.

"I'm an orphan," I tell her grimly. "I'm ready when you are."

That pains her, and she strokes my head and says, "You will not be alone where we are going. Come on up now. I will take you away from this place. You are not sick, and you do not belong here."

"Thank you," I say, and I mean it. Hearing those words heals me in a way that I didn't realize that I needed.

"I have a son, not much older than you. I think you will get along," she tells me.

"What's his name?" I ask, holding her hand as we walk hand-in-hand out of the room.

"Jason."

Now I am eighteen. I did not get to have a prom. I would have liked a prom, but I can't have everything I would like. I would like not to go back to the hospital, but I have to. Elana is coming to visit me again. They give me drugs when I'm at the hospital, for my own good. I need to keep up the disguise. No one can

know that I'm okay, it's my secret identity. I appreciate that she comes. I do not appreciate what it does to me. I do not appreciate the trips. Even through the haze, I can tell that she's going to be like me soon. She always was, though, just like I was always going to be me.

Everything was always going to be what it is, and I find comfort in that knowledge. Everything will be what it is supposed to be. I was never supposed to have a prom. That is okay.

I've lost track of time. It doesn't matter anymore. No one comes to visit anymore, which I never thought I'd miss. I never thought I'd miss the drugs or that horrific trip, but I miss what they symbolized. That I was remembered and loved. I am feared, and hated, and flattered in this place, but not loved. I am needed. I am necessary. Not everyone believes that. I found that out the hard way. But the right people believe that, and we will proceed.

I know a Bres, who is not Bres, but he is. That's not surprising, not even that interesting. I've also met an Ares, who is not Ares, but he is. A Balor, who is not Balor, but he is. A Ceto, who is not Ceto, but she is. There's probably one here for every letter of the alphabet. Whatever, Bres doesn't like me. He wants to kill me. He might be able to. We won't ever know for sure because he won't try. He's been asked not to. He doesn't believe the ancient texts and scrolls. There are some who do and don't want to. Those ones are easy to spot now, Bres is not one of them. Bres only believes in the job.

He has killed before. No one would ever need to tell me that for me to know, it's all over him. He is a monster. He is hell. He protects me. Protects me until the last day, that is. When I ask him if that's my last day or everyone's, he laughs. It is some-one's last day, he says, and he laughs harder when I ask him who. Right now he is taking me to my lesson. It's the same lesson I've been studying every day for...I don't know. For a long time. I am reading about some stone bending sorcerer, but I am not to focus on going there or bringing anything here, I am to focus solely on the magic in that story, hold it in my mind, and not let go no matter what else I read. It's a concentration exercise or something.

They have magic now. So I do. Magic suspended at five points around our world, anchored by five lamps. The magic is now shared between worlds, attuned to everyone who can do what I do. I've been thanked. I've been told how many lives this will save, how all of my friends will be able to fight back a little easi-er now. I don't have friends here, and I don't care what they do. I'm tired, and I'm glad never to have to read that book again.

Time doesn't work here. Or it works too well. I learned that to-day. It feels like I've been eighteen for years, and I have. I've been eighteen as long as I needed to be. Today I am nineteen. I've grown up, but with bittersweet news. I am dying. I am the chosen one, though not sure who chose me, but I am also dying. I spread my light far and wide before they found me. I put the light into people who needed it, and people didn't want it, and people

who may never know they have it. I spread it around the world. I spread it far into the past and so far into the future that my name will be forgotten by the time many people discover it. But I spread too much. Before my metamorphosis, I will need some of it back, and it will need to be given freely and with love. If not, I will die, and I will never fulfill my destiny.

There is one who is viable. And the texts and scrolls and prophecies that have brought me so much comfort in my life now bring me heartache. Everything was always going to be what it is. Everything will be what it was supposed to be. Elana Black will be dead. She will save me, she will give me back her light, she will give me her life, and she will save everyone. I will miss her, but she's been gone a long time, and this was always going to happen. It is no one's fault.

She's so close! She's right there! I don't know that I want to do this anymore, there are some who believe there's another way, or that they can prolong it, or something! Elana is going to come for me! She's going to...

No. No, she left me. They practically put out a welcome mat for her to me and she left! Why? I've given her a piece of myself! I gave her friendship! I...no. No, she doesn't owe me anything. Our friendship has been dead for years now. I was friends with a child. We are not children anymore. Besides, everything will be what it is supposed to be. Elana will be dead, and I will be a hero. I don't want to be a hero, but I will be one.

I'm on my way now. Soon we will be in...

"Careful now, you don't want to be in there too long, do you?" Roger asked as the lights in the conference room went on. There was no void, just a conference table and chairs. Ann was doubled over, dry heaving. Olivia was weeping openly; thick tears spread across her face. I felt a sense of vertigo.

"My name is Elana Black. My name is Elana Black," I could hear myself repeating reassuringly, convincing myself eventually.

"They're fine, I assure you," Roger said to Chalsarda. "The experience does a number on you, but it's perfectly safe. Hits everyone a bit differently, though. Think of it like the saddest movie you've ever seen. They just need a moment."

The world stopped spinning so much, and I was able to ask Chalsarda, "How long were we away?"

"Less than twenty seconds? I wasn't counting, I'm sorry. What did you see? Do you need help?" she asked.

"Perhaps we'd better have this conversation in my office and away from this room," Roger suggested.

Slowly, and with some help, we did as he asked, though Olivia never stopped crying the whole time. Ann merely looked sick. For my part, I felt shame, and dread, and more regret than I thought possible.

"So, now you know," Roger sounded resigned as he said it. "If we're going to save the day, we need you."

"She's here!" I shouted at him, losing my temper. "She's here right now!"

"Yes, she is, and she is going to die without you," Roger explained.

"No, that's not the only way," Olivia weakly tried to explain.

149

Before I knew what I was doing, I shook out a blister shield from my wrist. "She's right. You think it's the best way, but there are a hell of a lot of people who disagree with you. Now bring her out here, and give us a chance to find another way!"

The child walked out of the corner and slowly stepped toward me, eyes unblinking. His lips began to curl up in a snarl like a protective dog.

"Elana, put that away," Roger cautioned me, his tone suddenly very nervous. "Setanta, stand down."

A hungry aura began to emanate from the child, and his walk became a sprint.

"Setanta, no!" Roger shouted.

The child swung a haymaker at me, which would have been adorable if not for the presence of foreboding waves of dread coming off of him. I put my shield up at the last second, and it was like being struck by a train. My shield evaporated on contact, and before I could register what had fully happened, I was off my feet, through the plate glass window, and falling down, down, down.

I saw stars in front of my eyes before I realized half a second later that I was looking at actual stars. There was a whooshing sound through my ears, and my hair whipped wildly in front of my eyes.

Where am I? I'm falling!

I'd never been afraid of heights, but I was immediately paralyzed with the feeling that I was going to die horribly in a matter of seconds and there was nothing that I could...

My jacket! My mind was racing desperately in my final moments for any sliver of hope no matter how slim. My jacket was all I had left, and I'd never tested it, and this was one hell of a way to find out what would happen when I did. I narrowed every inch of my mind into activating the spell I'd sewn into its lining, and it was like blowing out a birthday candle with a leaf blower. The entire jacket seemed to come to life, enveloping me, and then...

The world was massive swirls of violet dancing across my eyes. The shockwave deafened me. I tried to sit up; my first go was unsuccessful. I struggled to breathe for a second, and I was reminded of a Vonnegut quote: 'Everything was terrible and nothing wasn't pure hurty pain.' At least that's how I think it went. There might have been a double negative in there. I might have been in far too much pain to care.

The pain was good though. Dead people don't get to be in pain, at least as far as I know. As if the universe was punishing me for trying to find the silver lining, a length of rope tied to a small weight landed on my stomach, further knocking the wind out of me. That was enough to jolt me upright and see the devastation. Beneath me was a car whose make and model would now and forever never be recognized, it looked like a wrecking ball had been dropped straight into it. Between me and the flattened vehicle was an Elana shaped pillow with all the swirling violet energy of my Blister shield. And this wasn't The Knowing; this was Van Nuys! Not even the good part, this was the butt end of Van Nuys! As far as I could see down the block in either direction, every window on every car and building had been blown in, or in some cases out. Mostly in. All except the tiny building I was in front of, it was dirty and looked abandoned, and at any other time, I would have ignored it entirely. I craned my neck to look up from where I fell. Okay, the word "fell" might have been a bit generous. Either way, I spotted it, what seemed like a hole in the sky, the broken, jagged glass window high in the air. Wow. Yeah, okay, that was pretty high up there. Yup.

The blister popped underneath me, and I rolled without dignity from the top of the ruined car to the asphalt. What time was it? People would probably be here soon. My ears began to ring, at least that might have meant my hearing was coming back. I convulsed and shook, bracing myself against the car to prop myself up, my legs were unsteady, and the left one, in particular, kept trying to bounce uncontrollably. Something similar happened to me in middle school once, and I was suddenly reminded of it. Back in the sixth grade, I used to race Olivia to school on bikes. I had no family and a very loose definition of guardianship, so things like a bicycle weren't exactly going to be under the Christmas tree. My bike sucked. It was heavy, and sort of dangerous, and covered in stickers. Olivia was taller, and her bike wasn't found in a bin behind a discount carpet center, so she always had the edge and won every single time. Not by much though, she was always willing to let me keep up, but she was faster. One morning I'd had it, and I cheated, and I stuck a long, many branched dead stick between her spokes before we could start, and I took off. I still expected her to catch me once she got the branches loose, but I was going to enjoy the head start while I could.

I rounded the corner and flew down the hill on the sidewalk, racing on Yukon Avenue, past the nursery, and toward school, standing up on the pedals and pumping into them for everything I was worth. An older woman, a school teacher if you can believe it, backed out of her drive too quickly for someone with the blind spot her fence had created for her, and with no time to brake, I slammed into her car and flipped head over heels clear onto the other side of her car! And just because life is funny like that, it happened in front of a cop who just happened to be driving past. When his lights came on, I actually thought that I was the one in trouble. The teacher couldn't stop apologizing, I couldn't stop insisting that I was fine, and because eleven-year-olds are invincible, I actually was; and throughout it all, my leg would not stop shaking. It felt like everyone except Olivia had wanted to forget that whole incident happened, and everyone just sort of went on their own way. I eventually managed to ride the bike to school at a wobbly, glacial pace. I was nervous about riding bikes for a week.

I thought remembering the story would distract me long enough to try and walk into the building, to come up with a plan to reach Olivia and the others. It worked for a whole three feet or so. My leg stopped shaking, but so did the rest of me. I collapsed in the middle of the street, unable to move. I wasn't even sure if I were injured or not, but either way, my body refused to keep walking. Given recent events, half of my brain decided this was reasonable. The other half of my brain shouted about the danger everyone was in, but even that was drowned out by the voice that told me I'd just used up all my usefulness walking away, albeit not very far, from an impossible fall.

I thought the adrenaline might keep me up, but when it crashed so did I. I realized that I was on my back, and the street was uncomfortably close. The hole in the office window looked out of place in the night sky, and it made my view of the universe itself feel like something manufactured. The ground was hard and uncomfortable on the back of my head, but my situation didn't change. I worried about cutting myself on broken glass, but I suddenly had the very pragmatic thought that if the worst that happened to me after that fall was a few glass scrapes, I'd still be way ahead. I wanted to get up, to fight back and run in and save the day against all odds, and that was a pretty good last thought to have before I shut my eyes.

"Well, we haven't met like this in a little while." The voice belonged to the Aos Si. I nearly fell over from being startled. "It's nice, isn't it? You, doing something foolhardy, and me, keeping you company while you're unconscious."

I turned to glare at him. "God damn it, dude! Do you always need to make such an entrance?" I asked with the sort of fleeting anger that one only has when they've been surprised.

"Of course not, it's just more fun that way."

I got my first look around now, and towering over me in a way that gave me vertigo just to look at it, was a building, shimmering and brilliant. The crown jewel of the skyline I'd seen the first time I'd met the Aos Si. "This is…"

"Yes, now you're getting it," he said with a knowing grin. "But that's not what I want to show you. Look there."

I followed his gaze to a ball of light on the ground in front of the building. "I don't get…"

"No questions yet, focus and understand." His voice was firm, but not angry. I did as he asked, and an outline appeared around the brilliant light.

"Me?" I was astonished. I was shocked I even managed the question.

"Indeed." The Aos Si nodded his head.

"They showed me something, something that contradicted you," I began, trying to form the question.

"Keep watching," the Aos Si said patiently. From the front doors of the building I saw a light, similar in size and scope as my own, exit the front doors, and a moment later something brilliant which dwarfed those two followed behind it.

This was misdirection.

"Why are you here?" I asked suspiciously. "Why now? You haven't had to meet me like this in a while, I've just come to you."

"Well, it would be within my right to check in on you after you've borrowed my elf for so long,"

I didn't care for the way he referred to my friend, but there was another question there.

"How long?"

"By your standards?" he asked. "Four days."

"Four days?" I shouted.

"Oh, good news, they're waking you up! A pleasure chatting with you, Elana," he replied, fading from view.

The Aos Si was gone, replaced by a throbbing pain in the base of my skull. I tried to open my eyes and closed them again almost instantly. The darkness was better for the moment. I could hear Ann attempt to use every expletive she could after the word holy.

She was up to eight now; it was impressive.

Olivia was frantically questioning if I was dead, and if not, how did I live through that? That seemed like a good question; I was looking forward to telling her when the world wasn't pain. Chalsarda assumed I likely had an enchantment of some kind, though she wasn't sure what I could have possibly had that did this. Way to ruin the surprise. Well, not completely. Chalsarda added that she was certain I wasn't dead because, if I had been, they would have known it. That was weird. It was weirder that they seemed to understand what she meant.

"Shut," I muttered weakly.

"She's waking up!" Olivia shouted about six inches from my ear, kneeling at my side. "What are you trying to say?"

"Shut up," I said quietly, eyes still closed. "Everyone just shut up your faces area."

Olivia practically yanked me out of my skin to an upright position and gripped me tightly in a hug. "How are you not dead?"

"Magic," I replied weakly, hoping I didn't have a neck injury for her to aggravate.

Everyone gave me a hand to my feet, and I took stock of my aches and pains, which was shockingly not many. My left knee felt like it might have been tweaked a little, and my back was stiff as hell, and I needed to pop it, but that was it. Oh, and an errant sneeze could have immediately knocked me down. I had absolutely nothing in me at the moment.

I tried to block out the flurry of questions from everyone and instead forced out a question of my own. "What day is it?" It was weak, but they paid attention.

"Is that a head injury question or a real question?" Ann asked.

"It's Thursday!" Olivia shouted at her phone. "We were gone for a few hours! How is it Thursday?"

I sighed, and somehow that morphed into cathartic, long, sustained yelling. "Why did he have to be right?"

"Who?" Chalsarda asked.

"You know who," I replied a little more annoyed than I would have liked.

"Dumb question, probably," Ann asked. "It looks like a literal bomb went off here. Where are all the upset car owners? The cops? Anything?"

"This area belongs to some powerful people," Chalsarda replied. "My assumption is that no one is going to hear about anything that happens here if they don't want it to be heard about. Still, it might be wise to leave."

After a long walk away from the wreckage and an even longer Lyft ride with a completely unfazed Lyft driver, we found ourselves at Fred 62 in Los Feliz, because apparently, it was 3:30 in the morning and we all needed to eat, and there weren't a lot of great options that time of the morning. For all the weirdness, I was confident they wouldn't be pleased with Chalsarda's archery gear in the middle of the diner, a problem she solved by walking around the back and leaping to the roof to stash her bow and arrows. I was going to suggest the trash cans. Her solution made more sense. The only person who was going to steal her gear from the roof while we ate would be a brooding, street level superhero. And though our universe apparently had eldritch horrors, magic wielding book nerds, and probably Norse gods, I was still pretty sure we didn't have superheroes. Also, this is Los Feliz; it would be a terrible place for superheroes.

The weird little quasi-retro diner was empty of customers at the moment, which was ideal. We got our choice of table and took something in the corner, just to be on the safe side, though no one seemed up for talking until we ordered. As we sat, I glanced at a wall filled with portraits of Hollywood legends past, and I had the overconfident thought that I could meet any of them if I wanted to, and then without intending to, I ended that thought with the harrowing realization that I might not live that long.

I didn't give my order a second thought, I abandoned all grace and went straight for the breakfast burrito. With everything. I needed food, and no part of that thing was about to survive its encounter with me. Chalsarda ordered an Ahi tuna Freshwich, which seemed to be all of the healthiest items in the building wrapped in a spring roll, which made me question my greasy food option for a unit of time so insignificant that scientists don't know how to measure it. Ann and Olivia however, looked hungrier than I'd ever seen them. Ann ordered a Bossa Nova waffle and a chocolate peanut butter malt. The moment her food came, it made more sense to me that magic existed than that she could finish all of that. She called it a celebration of survival for her first mission. Olivia ordered a Juicy Lucy, which was already a monstrous burger, and added a side of mac and cheese. When the waiter foolishly asked if she meant like a little side instead of fries or something, Olivia firmly, but politely, made her order clear.

She wanted everything as she had ordered it; no skimping, no "little" anything. Good day.

"Okay, so." My words hung sloppily. "I, uh, don't even know where to begin. I mean, do we have to?"

"Yeah, kinda," Olivia responded, sympathetic to my frustration.

I knew I was being a little immature and tried to soften up. "Okay, yeah, we do, I guess, but Jesus! What a mess. I'll answer, but I don't want to go first. Anyone have any ideas?"

"You fell out of a window, and you're not staining the sidewalk," Ann offered, shoveling in a bite of waffle. "Did you catch the rope or something?"

"No, but thanks for trying." I gingerly offered a tiny fist bump to my elven friend, a gesture that seemed to confuse her for a moment. "Actually, it was the coat. I've been storing my shield in it every day for a while now. Never expected it would be used like that!"

"Could you do it again?" she asked.

I shrugged. "Probably not, but it's not like I have any way of knowing without trying. When I store a spell in something, there isn't a meter to read; I can just tell if it has magic left in it or not. I can still tell there's some juice left in the jacket, but I have no idea if that means I used one percent or ninety-nine percent of what it had."

Ann's eyes lit up in realization. "Ooh! Can I try it on? You can throw baseballs at me!"

"If it means I don't need to have baseballs thrown at me first, sure," I replied. "Okay, so yeah, I actually do have a pretty big question."

"Shoot," Olivia mumbled through a mouth full of burger.

"I know how I got out of there," I said, holding a single serving of coffee creamer high over my head and dropping it onto my plate. "But how did you three get out of there?"

"Right, sorry to let you down, there's no cool story behind it or anything. He just let us go," Olivia remarked.

"Just like that?" I asked.

"Just like that," she confirmed.

"Well, not exactly just like that," Ann waffled.

I eyed Olivia, trying to read her. "What do you mean?"

"Tell her," Chalsarda said plainly.

"Yeah!" Ann said excitedly. "So Roger was actually pretty freaked out that you got punched out the window, and that weird ass Solomon Grundy kid ended up backing down, but not before Chalsarda tried to catch you with a trick arrow thingy and Olivia —"

"I think she wanted me to answer," Olivia interjected. "And I think what they mean is that I promised I'd talk to you about the whole Lucia thing."

"You didn't make any deals, did you?" I asked nervously.

"No, just talk. About, you know, my thing," she answered to my relief.

"Yeah, well, not now." I shifted uncomfortably in my seat. I was starting to stiffen up, which couldn't be good. I needed a hot bath, and I wasn't going to get that at the Book's End. Maybe I could swing by Olivia's place after this and...oh damn it, I totally forgot. "Has anyone reached out to Claire?" I asked.

"Oh dang! Four days!" Ann said in realization. "I'm probably fired!"

"I need to call Logan, he probably thinks we're dead." Olivia was already pulling out her phone.

"I'll text her, but I think we have a bigger problem than that," I said gravely.

Chalsarda nodded. "The Nuckelavee is coming for you in just a couple of days."

Ann invented another expletive.

16

After our meal, and at an hour that made absolutely no sense to any of us, Chalsarda excused herself to return to the Aos Si with the promise to see us again before the Nuckelavee arrived. Ann made her own way home, having had more than enough adventure for one day. Or week. Or whatever. It was unclear. Claire didn't return my text, but that wasn't unreasonable given the hour. After suggesting we continue our conversation at her place, Olivia helpfully reminded me that I had left a portal to somewhere beyond the veil open in the back room of our bookstore and, after four days or so, it was entirely possible that we could return to a building full of hyper intelligent octopi or something, and that was more than enough reason to change my mind about heading home.

The Book's End was lit only by the recent memory of moonlight. We were still a good hour or so away from sunrise, and the streetlights in the area were on a permanent summer schedule, so right about now they thought the sun was out, and their job wasn't needed. Olivia and I entered the shop quietly, just in case Claire was asleep, having kept vigil for our eventual return or something...but no such luck. She must have gone home, and good for her. A bookcase was, however, moved in front of the door to the room with my still open portal, so that was thoughtful at least. Satisfied that at least for the moment there wasn't a horde of trolls on the other side of the door, mostly on faith and a general lack of interest in finding out, I set about to flipping light switches and making the place generally a little more hospitable for a conversation.

"Do you want anything?" I asked, making my way around the shop as Olivia collapsed into one of our more comfortable reading chairs.

"Can I steal one of those Kombuchas?" she asked.

I cringed internally, considering for a moment which side the rest of our friends would land in that low stakes civil war. Team Sluice Juice would have probably been Claire and Olivia for sure, and likely Teague, since she was all about juicing and farmers markets and all of that. Chalsarda too, I could see her being into it. The Not Gross Team would have been Logan and me for sure, Jason maybe. Likely, actually. I think that man lived at Arby's; he didn't strike me as the type to ferment mushrooms. Ann, if I'm being generous to myself? She was probably okay with it, but I'd like to pretend at least to give my side a...

"Did you fall asleep standing up?" Olivia's question snapped me back to reality.

I yawned hard. "Almost, but yeah, help yourself," I said absently.

I noticed the twinge of annoyance from Olivia that told me she wasn't interested in getting back up, so I made sure to grab her a beverage while I grabbed a bottle of water.

"Danke," she offered, tipping her glass in my direction, tapping the edge of my water bottle as I sat down as well.

"So, ready to talk about the stuff and things?" I asked, hoping secretly that the answer was no.

Olivia extended her sip of her drink. "Yeah, I guess we're getting right into it then, huh?"

I shrugged.

"Things and stuff it is—" Olivia was cut off at the sound of a scream coming from the back side of the shop, followed by the sound of something slamming into the back door. My friend's eyes shot open wide, and I was on my feet in a second.

"Stay here!" It came out in a forceful whisper.

I reached into my bag and grabbed my rod, comforted by the weight of it in my hands. I didn't know what was happening outside, but if it wasn't supernatural, I was probably okay to just bludgeon it.

I flung open the back door to the shop, and without the light it was difficult to tell exactly what I was seeing, but one thing that was absolutely clear was that of the two people in front of me, one of them was a man wearing a stark white suit, white t-shirt under a white blazer tucked into white slacks. He was gripping the wrist of a woman, though I couldn't immediately see her face. It didn't matter; his eyes lit up when I came through the door.

"Elana Bla—" he began.

I didn't stop moving.

There was a yelp of pain as I smashed the rod into his forearm. I was aiming for his head, but he dropped the woman's wrist and raised his arm defensively at the last moment. He stumbled back, trying to put distance between us, genuine shock on his face. I pushed past the woman and swung a second time, this time catching him in the shoulder and sending him to a knee with another grunt. You can call it aggressive, but monochromatic-besuited, magic murder men who know my name are on my 'Beat up first, maybe also beat up later' list.

I went to swing a third time before stars exploded in front of my eyes and a smell like burning hair filled my nostrils as my body seized and I went down.

"Ah, Christ!" the man moaned, getting to his feet. "Took you long enough!"

"Not my fault, I was expecting magic, not a smiting!" she replied. "And since when can you not handle one little—"

"One move and you're dead." I heard Olivia's voice and looked up, struggling to stand.

The woman's eyes showed pure shock. It's possible they expected me to be alone.

"It's okay, we're not here to hurt anyone," the woman said slowly.

I managed to get to my feet and recover my rod, making my way behind the woman where I noticed that Olivia was holding our brownie scooping spatula to her back. I suppose anything is potentially deadly, especially if you can't see it.

"She's telling the truth," the man said shakily. "We're here to take you to safety."

"Okay, so two giant problems with that," I said as I began to draw in as much residual power into my rod as I could. "The first being the obvious, that there is approximately a zero percent chance of me trusting anyone in that suit, and the second thing, and this one is really important, so please pay attention here," I let the words trail off as I contained my annoyance.

An uncomfortable moment later, the man tried to ask, "What is the secon—"

"What the hell is with you people and not just talking to me?" I yelled louder than I should have this early in the morning.

"If we had just asked you, especially dressed like this, would you have believed us?" the woman carefully asked, keenly aware that something metal was poking into her back.

"Fair point," I conceded. "Now piss off. I literally do not have time for this. If you come back, I'll make sure you're eaten by a Bugbear. Like, a really big one."

I could see the man mouth the question, 'Can she do that?' at the woman.

I don't *think* I can, but who knows?

"Please, just hear us out," the woman pleaded. "You see his uniform? We're actually still authorized to hurt you and your friends, and we haven't. I mean, after you tricked Bres into making that deal, pretty much everyone in this world is off limits from the red and the black suits. We didn't bring a team, we haven't kidnapped your friends, and even now I just hit you with a few volts to stun you. We really do have good intentions here, I promise."

I considered for a moment that people with good intentions don't typically stage attacks in order to blindside you, but I also wasn't ready to fight two Gardeners with Olivia nearby.

"Fine, we can talk inside," I said, giving Olivia a nod. "Besides, I think they know better than to try anything past these doors, it's why they called me outside. They're not willing to risk summoning and fighting a god."

That got the two of them to exchange looks of concern and confusion. The inside of the shop was no safer than the outside, but I might as well plant that seed of doubt now in case they might have been thinking about pulling some crap later on. If I treat them like they know they should be afraid of, they might act accordingly. Or they'll turn on us and set the store on fire anyway.

Olivia lowered the spatula, and when the woman turned around to see the offending weapon she had a sour look on her face that said she knew she'd been had. Olivia in response menaced her with the spatula, waving it over her head and approximating what she likely thought was a scary face. I shook my head in bemusement and beckoned everyone inside.

"The mastery on these wards are unlike anything I've ever seen," the woman breathed out in disbelief. "I can't even detect them!"

I decided against telling them I still hadn't gotten around to creating wards for my home since getting my rod. I nodded to the reading area and announced, "Have a seat, but don't get too comfortable, I kind of hope you leave soon and are hit by several buses shortly after. Coffee?"

"Do you really have this place under a god's protection?" the man asked uneasily.

"What do you think?" I asked, not lying.

"I'm legitimately not sure," he mumbled.

"Let's keep it that way. So, who are you?" I asked as everyone sat down.

"We are Gardeners," the woman began.

I sighed impatiently, interrupting her. "I kind of got that part already; I meant who are you two specifically and why are you here? And why aren't you in a suit?"

"It's just a uniform; I can take it off. We thought if it looked like only one of us was, sorry, not important. My name is Yviene, and this is Florian. We came to get you to safety."

I had the chance to look at them now, and I doubted either of them was older than twenty. Maybe younger. Florian wasn't a large man; he was maybe an inch taller than I was. He had short blonde hair in a Caesar cut; his hair was nearly white, in fact, and a rounded baby face that practically screamed, 'I am *too* a grown up!' Yviene was the opposite. She had a long face and angular features that were framed with straight jet-black hair. A beanpole might have been the best way to describe her. If I'd met these two under any other circumstances, I wouldn't have thought they would be a threat to a puppy, let alone to me. That uniform, though, gave me an instant disdain for them, and I wanted them gone the moment I learned what they were up to.

A thought suddenly occurred to me, and I let it fall out of my head as I remarked, "No one knows you're here, do they?"

"I wouldn't say no one," Florian replied defensively. "But yeah, this isn't exactly official or anything."

"And what exactly is this?" Olivia asked.

"We told you, a rescue mission," Florian said. "Besides, there aren't a whole lot of people left who are really allowed to act."

"That's the second time you two have mentioned that," I remarked with suspicion. "Explain."

"Do you really need me to say it? I know what you did," Florain said with an uneasy chuckle. "The deal you bound Bres to. Everyone knows."

I narrowed my eyes on him. "And what do you know about it?"

"Everyone and anyone you care about, Bres and those who answer to him are to bring no harm to," Florian answered. "But he didn't count on you caring about just, you know, people as a whole. And it turns out, a whole lot of reds and most of the blacks answer to Bres by way of chain of command. God, at least that was limited to just this world and not, like, every world! Can you imagine?"

"Yeah," I said flatly. "I can."

"So anyway, Bres is magically prevented from hurting the majority of people directly, but those under him aren't. But if they do, they'll be breaking a deal on behalf of Bres, and no one is stupid enough to do that. So, turns out you kind of neutered them as far as this world is concerned."

Whoa.

"But that's not why you came, is it?" Olivia asked.

"Okay, so you know how everything wants to kill you lately?" Yviene asked. "That's not good for anyone, especially not you, and definitely not Roger Nill, and everyone else who believes that the Lucia girl is going to save everyone. They want to keep you alive long enough to sacrifice you to her. You're a kid in the woods being fattened up on gingerbread for the witch to bake later. That's it."

"And why do they want to do that?" I asked. "I know why they want that, but why do you think they want that?"

"They told you she's some chosen one or something, right?" Florian asked. "She's not. She's maybe one of the chosen ones, but no one bothers to ask who did the choosing or why. Really, she's just someone who is just stronger than the rest of us, that's all. And they used her to open up a hole into a world with magic so we could have it too. And that's not even unique, people with enough power have been pulling stuff from other worlds into this one for as long as anyone can remember. It gives us an edge. Our job is dangerous enough as it is, having magic, ray guns, super powers or whatever is sometimes the only thing keeping us alive! Except, this time." His voice trailed off.

"Except this time what?" I pressed.

"So, you're a wildling, and I don't know how much you've learned on your own, what you know, and what you don't, so I'm going to give you the CliffsNotes on this." Florian was unsure of his words, or at least he seemed unsure of how to communicate what he wanted to say. "Alright, so yeah, there's this sort of spark inside everyone with the ability to travel, this light that never goes out. And on very, very rare occasions you can give some of it to someone new, create a wildling. But it takes a whole lot of skill and power to do that, and then if you could, why would you want to? But for the most part, you're either born with power, or you're not. No rhyme or reason as far as anyone knows, you just can or can't. Until Lucia, there was actually a tale of a man who gave his light to twelve special people in his village who went on to be great defenders of the land."

"And after Lucia?" Olivia asked.

"Um, well," Florian mumbled.

Yviene wet her lips and answered for him, "We don't actually have the number. It's impossible to tell. She made wildlings not just all over the world, but all throughout history. We only know this because most of what we record is outside of this reality, but we don't even know how we've been personally affected! You're all like an infestation at this point!"

"That's perhaps the wrong word to use," Florian interjected. "I don't think Yviene means any offense by that, it's just that wildlings are given power without responsibility and, left unchecked, they can do a lot of harm, and it's sort of our job to make sure they don't, and when there are more of you than there are of us...our jobs can get a bit hectic."

"As one cockroach to another, do you mind getting to the point and telling us what this has to do with anything?" I asked.

"Fine, I mean I was getting to that, it's just that you need to understand how powerful Lucia Cruz is," Florian continued. "She did all that and still opened a portal into another world to borrow their magic, and on top of that, she did it too well. Imagine that what typically separates one world from another is something like the door to a bank vault. Right now, what separates this world and the one supplying our magic is little more than gossamer."

"The Stone Sorcerer world?" I asked, and Yviene nodded in agreement. "And why is that bad?"

"It's a world filled with monsters, and beasts, and vampires, and werewolves, and all sorts of crazy junk! And your world had none of that, but it sure does now." Yviene was on the point of exasperation. "And I mean, sure, things from other worlds have always managed to slip through here and there. It happens, and we deal with it, that's just part of the job. An angry ghost, a dretch, a Wendigo; those things make their way here and it's just a bad day for us. But now you're on the verge of just opening the door entirely, maybe even merging that world with this one!"

"Okay, definitely sounds bad," I agreed. "And you want me to do what? Close the door?"

"Are you out of your mind?" Florian shot the question at me like an accusation. "Have you been paying attention, of course not! If you shut the door, we all lose our magic. No, Roger and the people who actually believe in this chosen one trash need to give her a jumpstart. That's why you're alive. She's a dead battery; she just needs a tiny bit of light to get back up to full, and then she's practically unstoppable. Unfortunately for you, that kills you."

"And aside from my love of the arts, why do you care what happens to me?" I asked. "If I'm off the board, I can't give my light back to Lucia."

"Yeah, killing you would just solve the problem, sure, but we're not murderers. Think about it: If Lucia can do that to one world with a fraction of her power, imagine what she can do to every world at full power," Yviene said gravely. "And you're one of the only people with that kind of connection to her, so it has to be you. Our plan is to keep you locked away until her time is past. If she doesn't get that extra juice at just the right time, in just the right conditions, her window will close, and she won't be able to ever again. We need to run out the clock. Infinite worlds aren't in danger; you get to keep living, everyone wins."

I chewed on their words a moment. "And Lucia dies, right?"

"Honestly?" Florian said sadly. "Probably, but we don't know for sure."

"You're leaving something out," Olivia interrupted. "Intentionally."

Everyone in the room faced her quizzically at that. "You've talked a lot about our world and what kind of danger we're in, but what happens to these other worlds when people start to drain them? You let it slip earlier, this isn't the first time. If you already had magic in the past, why did you need to do it again?"

"Yeah, I'd like to know that as well." My words came out hostile, but I was proud of Olivia for catching that.

Florian's cheeks grew red at that, and he looked at his feet. "That's not...that's not the important part right now!"

"I really think it is," I pressed. "What happens?"

Yviene's words came out hurried. "What you have to understand is that we protect countless worlds and—"

"What happens?" I asked again, my voice now a command.

"They're eventually drained," Florian admitted, now resigned. "Sometimes it takes hundreds of years, sometimes only a couple of decades, but those worlds aren't meant to have enough resources for two universes. Eventually, they just run out. We try to make it a point to borrow from a world no one is going to notice, but they screwed up this time and picked a book that ended up being a runaway success. And before you ask, we measure that time in their world, not yours. A thousand years can be five minutes in your world, depending on how the story goes."

I needed a second to take that in. "You're...you're killing an entire world so you can throw around fireballs? That can't be right; please tell me that's not right."

"It isn't power for its own sake!" Yviene protested. "Think about how many lives you've saved with magic or even just your own! We use this to protect many worlds and, yes, one dies a little quicker than it should, but think about—"

"No," I said flatly, standing up. My hands gripped the rod tightly enough that I was afraid it might splinter. "I'm done. I'm not going to pretend to know what the right answer is, at least not right now, but whatever you're planning isn't something I'd be okay with. I'm offended that you thought I would be. There's a part of me that really wants to believe that you're both too young and stupid to understand how craven and heartless you're being, and despite knowing that you have more than enough experience on me, I need to pretend you still have even a shred of humanity in you, so I don't just send you both through the walls by force. Get out."

They both stood in protest, and Yviene tried to make her case, saying, "You don't understand! No one is going to just let you walk up there! It's not just Gardeners either; it will be Pacifiers, Librarians—"

"Fine, you give them all a warning from me," I said through clenched teeth. "They have my friend, and I'm coming to save her. And I'm ready and willing to fight whoever I have to in order to make that happen. And if you think I can't, you remember the name Jason Harris and then tell me what you think I'm capable of. Now get out before something bad happens to you."

The pair looked at each other and at me in disbelief, then without a word made their way out the back door. I slumped down into my seat.

"That got a little dark, didn't it?" Olivia asked carefully. "You know, bringing up their dead co-worker as a threat and all?"

I shrugged. "Yeah. Maybe. I don't care. I am just so sick of all of them. Besides, we have what? Two or three days until I'm probably dead anyway? I just need sleep at this point."

Olivia adjusted herself in her chair. "You know, we never did find out who sent them."

"Doesn't matter, don't care. Good night. Morning. Something."

The weekend came much sooner than I would have liked, and I found myself dreading it more with each day. I've become surprisingly comfortable with the idea of being attacked by things that common sense says shouldn't exist, but there was something particularly unsettling about knowing in advance the day you might die. I hated having to deal with this on someone else's schedule, knowing that I had no other option. If I ran, people would die. I couldn't come after it; I had to wait for it to come to me. It was the worst. The majority of my time was spent resting, studying, and planning. We sent Teague, Ann, Jason, and Logan on a road trip to Lake Havasu for the day, with the feeling that three hundred miles inland or so was probably far enough. Teague and Jason were a no brainer. There was absolutely nothing they could really do to help at the moment, and they would just be in danger if they stuck around. Logan was the difficult one. He wanted to stay with Olivia, but she convinced him to go away for her sake. He wasn't happy with it, but ultimately relented. Ann, however, was more pragmatic. She wanted to help and understood that one day that might be possible, but for now she'd just be a liability. With Kodran, it made sense for her to come with, she was the subject matter expert. But this was just going to be a straight up fight, and she wasn't equipped for that at all.

Chalsarda came back to help, and I never doubted that she would. She was open with me that she felt powerless against this sort of thing, but she would help however she could. Claire was the one who helped come up with a battle plan. We'd be driving north of LA about five hundred miles to a remote cove in Albion. The town of Albion itself was less than two hundred people, and there were miles and miles of secluded beach where you could be completely alone. The whole idea was to get innocents out of the way, and this was as good a spot as any. Away from the highway and people was the only option. Claire also insisted on taking us in the work van, that she made as cozy as possible with pillow toppers and blankets. She refused to let me drive on the grounds that I needed to conserve my strength and that Big Sister probably wouldn't make it anyway. Olivia also insisted on coming with, not only to keep an eye on me, but to help Claire with driving duties. It would be an eight-hour drive in the best of conditions, and they were taking a van that was not built for speed.

I wasn't entirely comfortable with being waited on, and that's exactly what this felt like. It felt like the closer we got to leaving, the more everyone wanted me to conserve my strength and focus on getting ready, but it also felt like no one expected me to make it through. That could have just as easily been all in my head as it could have been true, but that didn't change how I felt about everything. I didn't know how I was going to beat this thing, but I didn't plan on dying either. I had too many people counting on me, and getting killed now would affect more than myself. The door would probably be wide open on hurting my friends, for one thing. Lucia would be killed, if the Gardeners could be believed. I'd never have the chance to find Lainey and Jaden, not that I really knew what to do with them when I found them. Then there was just the general work I did, helping where I could, trying to save who I could. It's not like there were a lot of people stepping up to give me a break and take over. A year ago, my biggest responsibility was keeping two cats fed, and even that was only occasionally. Responsibility sucks.

It was around three in the morning on the day we headed out. There was a lot of uncertainty about when and how the Nuckelavee would come for me. If it was anchored to the same spot, and we were five hundred miles away, that could be disastrous, but what I'd see from the Aos Si made me think that wasn't likely. It was probably going to show up wherever I was. Then there was the matter of it coming back after seven days. If it came back at the same time, exactly seven days later, we should probably leave pretty early in the morning to get up north to time it out right. Then again, it could have just shown up at any time, so who knows? There's not a rulebook that comes with this thing. I know, because I looked. Just a handful of tales and sightings. None of it was comforting.

When I woke up, it was sunny out, at least that I could see. The van had no windows in the back, but I could see clouds patching blue skies as I opened my eyes and looked up into the cab. The gentle hum of tires on paved asphalt as the van seemed to make its way down the uncontested was almost enough to make me want to go back to sleep, especially with an abundance of padding surrounding me. It was too late for me though; I was awake now, and I knew it. Claire was driving silently with Olivia in the passenger seat, Chalsarda seemed to be quietly fiddling about with her bow.

"You're up," Chalsarda observed.

"I am?" I asked sarcastically, trying to smooth over hair that was now pointing in every direction.

"Looks like it," she replied. "How are you feeling?"

I stretched and sat up as I answered, "Physically? Pretty good, I guess. Better definitely. I think the jacket took most of the hit."

"And not physically?" Chalsarda asked.

"I mean, fine? I think? I don't know; it really feels like you're all way more freaked out about this than I am," I answered.

"Of course we're freaked out!" Claire practically shouted from the front. "I'm driving you five hundred miles up the coast to fight a demon! It's a little weird that you're not more worried."

"That's not fair at all; I never said I wasn't worried," I protested. "I'm just trying not to lose my head over it. And it's not the first time something weird has wanted me dead."

"Have you at least come up with a plan?" Olivia asked.

I realized that for all my reading, I really hadn't. "There are things that can hurt this monster or slow it down," I began. "The problem is they're all impractical or could just get other people hurt."

"Such as?" Claire asked.

"We can burn seaweed, but then it will just attack everything and not just me. It can't cross fresh running water, but if we go inland far enough to find a stream, then it's going to probably kill anyone it finds along the way. Kodran could also just die, it would give up if we did that, but I'm not really the murdering type, and time hasn't done the job for me. Also, I don't think I could kill him. Dude is, like, way stronger than me."

Everyone rode wordlessly for a moment. Olivia broke the silence first, saying, "Yeah, that definitely sounds like you don't have a plan."

"But we'll figure it out, I'm sure," Claire added, trying to be optimistic.

"Thanks," I said, not sure what else to say to that. I looked at Chalsarda who looked like she was trying to keep her hands busy, and I asked, "What about you? What do you think?"

She put her bow down, and looked back at me and said, "The honest answer is that I don't know if this creature can be defeated by us, and I don't know what we're going to do once we find it. However, I am not allowing myself to think that way. I'm not ready to die, so I won't. And I'm not ready for you to die either, so I won't let that happen either."

"I have to ask," I said, still bothered by something. "Why isn't the Aos Si here? He's supposed to be my guardian or whatever, right? Is his version of protecting me really just giving me a stick and wishing me good luck?"

"I'm here on his behalf; I'm your protection."

"But you just said that you don't know how—"

"I know what I said," Chalsarda interrupted sharply. She relaxed a little and continued, "He can't be here, and I can't tell you why. I would like to, but I cannot. He also would prefer it if you don't die today, for what that's worth."

"And how would he feel about you dying today?" I asked.

Chalsarda blinked at that, not expecting the question. "It is …different," she began. "I am more of a tool, where you are an —" She winced hard in pain, waving me off when I tried to ask if she was alright. "I apologize, that was my fault. Sometimes I try to push the boundaries of what I am allowed to say, and I just learned a new limit."

"Everything okay back there?" Claire asked.

"We're fine," Chalsarda answered curtly.

"Hey, you don't have to say anything more, I'm sorry," I said, rubbing a hand on her shoulder. "I trust you. You're a friend, one of the crew, right? You're risking your life for me; you don't owe me anything else."

She smiled at that, but there didn't seem to any joy in it. She raised a hand to my shoulder and pulled me into a hug. It felt like the kind you get from someone who is saying goodbye.

A couple of hours later, we parked at a scenic ridge with a walking trail down to a cove. The high ground seemed like as good an advantage as any we might get in this fight, and I didn't imagine we'd get more than that. We crossed a river on the way here, which was surprising and potentially helpful, but it also seemed like the only populated tourist attraction in the area, and the whole idea was to get as secluded as possible. We ruled out any advantage that might have given us in favor of not subjecting campers to the horrors of an ocean-dwelling demon horse.

After we had parked, it seemed like everyone needed to stretch and take a breath. Chalsarda walked to the edge of the cliff, and closing her eyes, took in a deep breath and smiled. The smile didn't reach her eyes. I thought about saying something to her for a moment, but I thought better of it. The sight of the ocean got her attention in a way that made me feel, for just a moment, that none of us were here in her eyes. Instead, I got my jacket and bag out of the back of the truck, throwing them both on. I would have expected the weather up north to be more like my last beach excursion, but the skies were blue, not gray. There were no clouds of note, just the sparse patchy white spots dotting the horizon. If not for the impending doom, this is exactly the kind of place I would have enjoyed a hike, mermaid costume and all.

It was at that moment that I seized up. The gravity of all of this was suddenly weighing down on me, I understood that this was insane! I shouldn't be here; I don't even know how I got here to begin with! I've been pretending for so long, and now I was going to die. I didn't beat it the first time, not really. I sucker punched a baby. Now I have gods and sorcerers and trolls and an army of suit wearing jerks who all want me dead, and they're going to hurt my friends, and I got a couple of children so lost that not even a Celtic deity knows where they are, and I...and I ...know that I'm not a hero! I'm not! I work in a bookstore! I shouldn't be looking for—

"Hey! Hey, it's okay." The sound of Olivia's voice comforting me snapped me back to reality. We were behind the van, and she was rubbing my arm. "Talk to me; it's fine."

I saw her now; she looked concerned, if not outright worried.

"It's not fine!" I choked out quietly. "I can't do this. I've been acting brave, but I'm starting to see, this isn't something we can win! You, and Claire, and Chalsarda need to get in that van and just drive away, okay? It doesn't care about you, but if you're still here, it might."

Claire came around to the back then, and asked, "What's happening back here?"

Without removing her hand from my arm, she turned toward Claire and said, "Elana just needs a moment."

I snapped away from them both at that, and started to yell, "No! That's not it at all; you don't...you haven't seen what I have, this is serious! We can't beat—"

Two hands came to rest on my shoulders, firmly, but comfortably. "Stop," Chalsarda told me softly.

I did.

"Come with me," she said softly, and we walked close to the edge of the cliff, out in front of the van. She sat cross legged in the dirt, maybe a couple of feet from the edge, and I did the same. I realized now that I'd started crying and did my best to wipe my suddenly puffy eyes. Chalsarda looked out over the ocean and said, "The ocean always has a special place with me. Any ocean actually, it doesn't matter."

"I didn't know that about you," I replied.

"There's a lot that you don't know about me."

"Well, you've been around almost two hundred years longer than I have, that might have something to do with it." I tried to make a joke, but the words cracked in my throat a little.

Chalsarda chuckled anyway. "It just might," she said. "But you trust me anyway. You stood up to a goddess for me, you've invited me into your home, treated me like family. Yet, I work for someone whose name you don't know; I keep secrets from you; so why do you trust me?"

"You're my friend," I said quietly.

"And you are mine," she replied, smiling at that. "But exactly why are you my friend?"

I had to pause at that. Not because I didn't know the answer, but because I wasn't expecting the question. "Does it matter?" I asked sincerely.

"In the end, no, I suppose not," she mused. "That is not to say that I wouldn't like an answer anyway."

"You got it backward," I began. "I know you've been given a job, and I'm it. So how you treat me isn't what I look at. No, from the very first time you were ever here with me, in my world, I've seen how you've treated others. Do you remember the first time you came to see me?"

"I do, I was trying to test your endurance. We went to Columbia Park; you wanted to show me the fire truck. You failed every test remarkably; I thought I didn't have enough years left in my lifespan to train you properly." She laughed.

"Yeah, I remember too, I thought you might need to take me to a hospital. But that wasn't the part that I was talking about.

There was a little boy, remember? He walked up to us and asked if you were an elf."

"His name was Ali. And yes, that does happen, sometimes," she agreed.

I nodded. "But it was how you treated him. You let him touch your ears to see they were real. You tried to show him how to throw rocks. You jumped into a tree, but I think you might have just been showing off at that point or you were just trying to let me catch my breath or something. But I mean, you made him smile. You were nice to him. And when he asked how he could be an elf, do you remember what you said?"

"I told him that I'd been born an elf, and he had been born a human, and that one was not better than the other," she said thoughtfully. "That he was Ali and I was Chalsarda, and the world needed us both the way we were."

"But that wasn't all," I continued. "You said that if he lived a life that was brave, and kind, and good, then one day he might join other elves as one of them."

"I shouldn't have told him that," she said under her breath.

It was a true statement, though. She was incapable of lying.

"I'm glad you did, though. It was the first of many examples of why I wanted to be your friend. Not for how you treat me, but for how you treat everyone, even little kids in the park that you'll probably never see again. I don't know everything about you, but I know you're a good person."

Chalsarda looked now as if she might cry herself. After a moment, she said, "Thank you. I'm not always sure if...I don't always know if I...thank you."

We sat for a minute or so, and she said, "My master doesn't go out of his way to help many people, but he helps you. And not just because it is his duty, he's fae, and he's a god. If he wanted to give you the bare minimum, you'd know it." I didn't say anything at that, and she continued, "Life is short. For you, for me, even for him. Everyone always wishes there was more time in the end. He wouldn't allow you here if he didn't believe in you. I wouldn't be out here if he didn't believe in you, come to think of it. He sees a lot of heart in you, as do I. If he didn't, we might just both be locked in a dungeon until it was time."

I craned my neck at that. "Time for what?"

Chalsarda blinked at that, but before she could answer, I saw familiar clouds gathering in the distance, dark and ominous things, bringing thunder and lightning rapidly toward the shore. It was time, but something was off. Something was very wrong, and I felt sick as I realized my mistake.

"What's that?" Olivia asked as she and Claire walked over to us.

I stood up with Chalsarda and looked off into the distance. "That's the Nuckelavee. But I screwed up. Really, really badly," I said, my words coming out a little harsher by the second. "The first time it found me, it must have locked onto where I was and, even then, it took it a little while to climb out of the ocean, and when it did, it was still a ways behind me. But now, it figured out where I was, but we went zipping past it at seventy miles per hour, and now, well, now it thinks I'm way back there. Back by the river. Back where all the people are."

18

We were all back in the van, frantically racing back the way we came, but I was almost certain that we were too late. What's worse, I couldn't accurately predict any kind of pattern from the Nuckelavee. I knew that it needed to see its target, but it worked both ways in that once it saw what it was after, it would never give up. I had no idea how intelligent it was or where it would go when it didn't see me. Would it stay put? Would it venture up and down the coast or maybe travel inland? It was a remorseless killer, I'd seen that much with my own eyes, and that was the one that I actually defeated. The version I took down had killed a platoon, or a legion, or whatever you called that amount of soldiers. This incarnation was supposed to be bigger, more horrible. I couldn't imagine what campers would do if they came across it.

"Hold onto something!" Claire shouted, possibly unaware that there was nothing to hold onto in the back of her cargo van.

"Why?" I asked, half a second before I was jostled over as the van began to rock up, down, and side to side.

Claire's knuckles gripped the steering wheel hard; her biceps bulged as her arms struggled to keep control of the van.

"When someone dramatically yells at you to hold on," Claire shouted unsteadily, focused more on the road than my plight. "Don't ask why!"

Chalsarda was crouched now, trying to avoid hitting her head on the roof of the vehicle, but even she was struggling to keep her balance now. If not for the immense padding in the back I was certain I'd earn a concussion before the fight could begin. I stopped fighting it after a moment and opted to stay as flat as possible on the mattress. It helped some, but I was sure to have a few bruises later on. This continued for a several, agonizing minutes until the van lurched forward sending everyone, including Chalsarda, into a whiplash. I rolled into the back of the passenger seat, bouncing off it.

Claire gave the van gas, then tried to put it in reverse, and neither action was doing any good. The van was stuck.

"What the actual, literal, physical hell, Claire?" I demanded, trying to gather my bearings.

Chalsarda opened the back of the van, and I nearly rolled out of it and managed a look at Claire's handiwork. We were, in the loosest possible terms, driving along the coast, but on extremely uneven ground that wasn't meant to be walked on, let alone driven over at high speeds in a too heavy van. Parallel to us were train tracks, though they looked as if they hadn't been in use for years. Maybe a couple of hundred yards away was the river that led into the ocean, and the tracks that created a bridge over it.

"Highway wraps inland a couple of miles," Claire mumbled, trying to clear her head. "We had to get to the beach, right?"

"Jesus," I breathed. "I mean, yeah, that was the right move, but...dude."

Chalsarda slung her bow over her shoulder and addressed us, saying, "Unless anyone is injured we need to move. Every moment the beast is out there, lives are in danger. Olivia, Claire, this will be dangerous, you don't have to follow us."

"Yeah, screw that," Olivia said flatly. "We're already here, aren't we?"

No one seemed to be a hundred percent after that, but everyone was on their way, and no one had time to argue. We made it about halfway before we heard the screams and the unsettling crunch of metal. My stomach sank at that. "Hurry!" I shouted to everyone, and in remarkably unhelpful fashion, I added, "Try not to roll an ankle or anything!"

Chalsarda gave me a look that unquestionably said, 'No, you especially, Elana Black, who is not good at hiking or running, should try not to roll an ankle.'

I shook out a blister shield and gripped my rod as we rushed toward danger, running across the uneven hillside. Between my weapons, my friends, and the setting, I probably would have felt like a proper hero if not for the authentic sense of dread that a bunch of good people were about to die because of me. Fighting monsters would be a lot more fun without all of the lousy dread.

Below us was the result of a monster throwing a tantrum. Camper RVs were overturned, rocks and trees had been moved with incredible force. More to the point, the culprit, the Nuckelavee, was right in the middle of it all, apparently looking for something, and was more than frustrated at not being able to find it.

"You fought that thing?" Claire asked incredulously.

"Last time it was a bit smaller, and it wasn't holding a spear, but yeah, that was it, sure." This one looked so much worse somehow. For one thing, it was angry and definitely more agile. Oh, and the six-foot long rusty spear wasn't making it look any more approachable either. This instance of the Nuckelavee was enormous, maybe fifteen feet high and twice as long. And we still had the high ground on it like I had wanted, but it was too much of a good thing. There was no safe way to get down in any reasonable amount of time, at least not from this side of the bridge. I began to wonder if I could just cross the bridge and win when I realized what the beast was doing. It was stabbing the side of an RV to the horrified screams of children inside.

I took a deep breath and turned to Olivia, asking, "So you know how I said that once the Nuckelavee sees me, it won't stop until it has me?"

"Please tell me you're not going to do something utterly stupid," she replied.

"Hold this," I said, handing her my rod and flinging my shield at the monster. It bounced off its hide with a disappointing, almost inaudible thud. I willed it back immediately as both the horse and human heads turned to look at me, the glowing crimson eye on the horse was bright, even from up here.

I took a hard swallow, realizing now what I'd done. "Okay, so, it's real now," I choked out, filled with instant regret. "This is really about to happen."

As if in response, it yanked its spear out of the side of the RV with a terrible screech of metal on metal, and hurled it up the hill at us. I raised my shield on instinct, but Chalsarda grabbed me by the hood of my coat and pulled me toward her roughly, a split second before the spear tore the air where I'd been standing before planting itself in the earth a hundred yards behind us or so.

"I thought it was supposed to drag you into the ocean, not slice you in two!" Claire exclaimed.

I did too.

Any relief that I might have felt from not being impaled was gone the moment the RV suddenly caught on fire where the spear had been removed, and the screams of children were very much audible again. The Nuckelavee was trying its best to climb the side of the hill as well, making its way steadily toward us. My head began to feel tight; I knew this was getting out of hand, though I don't know what I was expecting.

"You two, get back to the van. I don't know what I was thinking, there's nothing you can do here, and it's not safe. Chalsarda, we have to get down there," I said in a huff.

She offered a wordless, determined nod and scooped me up, sprinting headlong down the rough hill straight at the Nuckelavee. It happened so fast that I had no time to do anything but scream and grip her with panic-fueled strength as she kicked off the ground at the last moment in the face of the ravenous monster, before planting a boot on top of its horse head and launching us both skyward, tripping up the surprised beast in the process. I instinctively shut my eyes tightly, and when we'd stopped moving my heart threatened to break a rib or two if it didn't calm down.

"The hell's the matter with you?" I managed through shallow breaths. Looking back up the hill at the dizzying height we'd just dropped, a few hundred feet at least, and in the middle of it was the twisted mass of skinless flesh and bone of the Nuckelavee trying to right itself and get back down the hill.

Chalsarda furrowed her brow at me. "How did you think I could get us down the hill?"

"I don't know! I thought like, maybe you'd tie a rope to an arrow and we'd maybe swing down or something!" I gasped.

"Do you see any rope on me?" she snapped. "Now focus! We have maybe a moment before it's here. What's your command?"

The word command struck me a bit weird, but I didn't have time to dwell on it. "Get whoever is in that camper to safety, I'll stay here and, I guess just try really hard not to die."

"I'm on it. By the way, are you missing something?" she asked as she began to sprint toward the flaming camper.

My rod! Of all of the stupid, easily avoidable mistakes I could have possibly made today, I just made the one that crippled me. Okay, so if it wasn't bad enough that I am about to fight for my life against an unstoppable demon horse that is actively pissed off at me, I have to limit my magical output severely. And despite my best efforts to keep innocent people out of this, I once again didn't think my situation through, and someone else is cleaning up my mess. God, I want a do-over so badly with all of this that I could just scream!

Alright, I need to stop beating myself up, something else is already trying to do that for me. I either need to think this through or wait to get dragged into the ocean, but I have to decide now. So, okay, surroundings. Lots of driftwood around, the beach itself is somewhat dirty, a few large stones in the water. The hills are lined with patchy, thick brush and loose dirt, but not much in the way of rocks or anything. None of this is helping me, what else? That RV was likely to keep burning for a little bit, but that feels more like an obstacle for me than a danger for this creature. The bridge, which separated the river from the ocean's beach, was supported by dozens of support beams made of a mix of sturdy wood and rotting steel that likely hadn't taken the salty breeze into account when the structure was built.

And there goes the Nuckelavee. I watched as it lost its footing and tumbled hard down the hillside, obliterating any flora in its path. Its hooves were unable to negotiate the terrain, its elongated arms flailing wildly as it reached out for anything to grip, the twin howls of surprise that escaped both of its throats; it would have been comical if it wasn't so unsettling. It came to rest with a heavy, sickening thump and the sounds of hundreds of bones all cracking at once.

Then, suddenly, that was it. Was that it? It couldn't possibly be it, could it? We'd traveled all this way, gotten all worked up over an unstoppable demon, and it just fell down and died? I stared at it, unmoving for a couple of minutes at least, but it didn't move either. Chalsarda was nowhere to be seen, the fire on the RV had been put out as well. Everything else aside, for all of the chaos just moments before, I suddenly felt very alone. There were no screams, no howls, just smoke and gentle waves lapping at the base of the bridge. Unconsciously, I began to walk toward it, barely aware of the blister shield I still had on my wrist.

It was hideous up close. Like a ton of spoiled meat left to bake in the sun, like the exposed refuse of an industrial hot dog factory. Worse than that was the smell. It had exactly the smell you would imagine it to have, nauseating and vomit inducing all at once; the sort of smell I was afraid would stick to my clothes forever just by being around it.

"I hate you so much right now, Kodran, you giant turd," I muttered to myself. "I'm super glad this thing is dealt with, but it feels just more than a little…"

A crimson eye, blazing with the very fires of Hell, hot enough for me to feel its heat through my clothing, shot open in concert with the disturbing sound of bones and sinew reconnecting, reforming at an alarming rate before my very eyes. It was nearly impossible to tell without skin, but I swear I saw the human head smile with sick glee. The thing's arms moved like injured snakes and grasped at my legs with sudden bursts of speed.

"No!" A scream escaped my lips involuntarily as I closed my eyes and reacted, my palms extending toward the earth and casting a wind spell before I could think twice. There was a sound, something like a muffled explosion, and I opened my eyes to a cloud of dirt and sand obscuring my vision, but I could still the Nuckelavee tumbling head over heels through the air before it arched in the air and slammed into the hillside with an earthshaking thud. I shouldn't have been capable of that! I looked at the ground where I could see a fresh hole, one that had gone deep enough to double as a grave.

I thought I heard a sound like a distant choir, but the sound was replaced by Chalsarda shouting my name as she sprinted toward me. I stood there, dumbfounded, trying to understand what had just happened. I didn't feel drained. If anything, I felt like I cast a minor amount of wind.

"What happened, how did you do that?" Chalsarda asked, wide-eyed.

"I...I don't know," I mumbled, searching my hands for clues.

"Your bag!" she exclaimed, I could hear it again, muffled under the books and canvas. I reached into my bookbag, and removed fist sized golden brooch that Freyja had given me last week. It seemed like a soft, melodic song, like a hopeful choir was coming from it for a moment, and the sound faded.

"I forgot I had this," I said, bewildered by everything.

"Elana, not now," Chalsarda said nocking an arrow, and I looked up to see what she saw; the Nuckelavee charging at us from down the river, its broken body healing as it ran.

"I've got a plan," I said, suddenly confident. "But I'm gambling hard on my power boost not being a one-time thing. Are you ready to do something really dumb?"

"Just give the word," Chalsarda said, firing an arrow into one its legs. The arrow merely stuck and didn't seem to otherwise faze it.

"We're going to drop a bridge on it," I said. "I'm mostly sure it was going to come down one way or the other anyway."

"Sounds like a plan," she agreed, without stating an opinion on exactly how good of a plan it was or not. She was already sprinting away from the beast and toward the bridge before I could say the word.

I took off after her, but her speed was blinding compared to mine, and even though much of the sand here was compacted, it was still slowing me down enough to worry about my balance. I pumped my legs hard, sensing the creature gaining on me, though I didn't dare turn around. Just as I began to worry that I legitimately might not make it in time, my foot caught a soft patch of sand, and I slammed into the river's shore face first. I scrambled instantly, trying to get to my feet almost the second that I went down, but something wet and hot gripped my ankle with incredible strength. Before I could react, I was being pulled roughly across the sand toward the ocean, and I screamed at the realization.

The Nuckelavee ignored my cries, and I struggled to free myself from its grip in any way I could. I threw my shield at it, but it missed wildly. I began to kick at its fingers with my free foot, but it ignored it. I was hesitant to hit it with a spell, at least at this distance. If I cast at regular strength, I could be potentially hurt if I missed, and if I did something like I had with the wind gust, I might just kill us both. I could hear arrows plunging into its hide, but if it was affected at all, it wasn't showing it. It wasn't until I listened to the sloshing of water that I realized where we were.

"Chalsarda! Get clear!" I shouted, and looking up just long enough I prepared to cast a bolt of fire, but not into the beast. I was looking past it. I began to silently pray for a miracle as I let loose with the burst of flame. It struck the wood, instantly igniting it, but not as I had hoped. It wasn't charged or anything, and the Nuckelavee ignored it.

Oh, no!

This wasn't good. This was my whole plan. Lure it under the bridge, drop everything on it, hope it dies. But at this rate, I

simply couldn't do it. I was about to drown in a matter of moments if I didn't come up with something and quick. I began to
hyperventilate. I couldn't stop, I couldn't get my breathing right.
I began to claw at the west sand, and in a moment of pure des-
peration, I felt into the earth with my senses, searching for anything that could help, and the ground began to quake. Slightly at
first, but then the sound of a choir began to emanate from my
bag, and I understood.

With a shout, and the knowledge that if this didn't work it
was over, I released every last drop of energy from my well, extending my consciousness into the ground, and I felt it move
through the earth and toward the support beam like the pain of a
pinched nerve traveling from your back to your hands. The
bridge groaned and swayed, and the Nuckelavee stopped just
long enough to recognize what was happening. There was a
sound like an inhuman roar as the now flaming bridge creaked
and imploded, large sections falling in every direction. The
Nuckelavee let out a screech of its own, but did not let go. I desperately pulled my hood down over my face and contorted my
body to lie face down in the sand.

This was going to hurt.

The jacket did its job admirably, in that I wasn't impaled or
squished, but with every unseen bit of falling debris it felt as if I
were being struck by a car, or being pummeled by a heavy
weight. I cried out, I was in agony, but I didn't dare move. It was
over almost as soon as it began, though maybe not exactly as I
had planned it. The hits just stopped coming. The was just one
issue. Throughout all of this, the Nuckelavee hadn't loosened its
grip.

19

I couldn't breathe through all the dust and smoke, but I still didn't dare to move. I had absolutely nothing left in my well, and my body quivered at the exertion, panic, and adrenaline, but the fact that my leg was still caught in the inescapable grip of the creature had me rigid with fear. The fear that this devastation somehow wasn't enough, that I was truly out of options. So I stayed still, kept quiet, and waited, hoping that maybe it would forget me, or just get it over with, or just anything. Anything but making me wait. The waves were lapping at my face now, and with my options being that I drown or try to stand, I pulled back my hood and turned my body to look at what I'd done.

I had trouble processing the results of my actions. Tons, literally tons, of wood and twisted metal piled sloppily, providing a new and fresh, but obscene, view of the ocean that had been obscured by the structure. Either the water or the fall itself must have extinguished the flames, but all of the wood had fallen, every last plank, but the steel support beams, rust and all, all remained standing, save for one. I knew it instinctively; it was the one I had touched. One particular beam, one with a spot that had been weakened just a bit more than the others by the decades of rust that the ocean breeze brought it, had cracked and toppled over, had impaled the Nuckelavee with a metal spike that jutted thirty or forty feet into the air. Impaled might not even be the right word, the beam was nearly as wide as the monster, and had nearly cleaved it in two.

"Dam," I said, unable to stop myself from making the joke in spite of the situation, and I was embarrassed instantly despite the fact no one had heard me. The majority of the debris had stopped maybe a couple of feet from where I lay, but even the stray bits would have been enough to kill me if not for the protection of my jacket.

The horse head wheezed heavily, and I snapped back to attention. It wasn't dead. I sat up and saw the arm of the Nuckelavee, pinned at the elbow by the metal railing of train tracks. Leaning in, I tugged at one of the fingers, trying to pry my leg free. I almost didn't register what happened next.

I was in the air; then I was slammed into the earth with a force that almost took the wind out of me, coat protection and all. Then it happened again, and I realized that the Nuckelavee was trying to knock me unconscious by smashing me into the ground until I stopped moving. It had little more than a forearm to work with, and most of the fight had gone out of it, but it was determined to take me down with it. It may have been losing strength, but it was still hurting me. A lot. When that didn't work, it passed me from one hand to the other, a terrible screech of pain filling the canyon as it did. Thick, viscous blood seeped and pooled from its wound into the ground underneath the wreckage, steam rising from the rubble as it did.

With a new hand gripping my torso, the Nuckelavee brought me up to its hideous, skinless human face and hissed at me; its labored breaths hot in a way that reminded me of looking into a pot of boiling pasta.

That's when the Kombucha got into my mouth.

More accurately, that's when a bottle of Kombucha exploded on the back of its head, and a fair amount of it splashed onto my face and got into my mouth. We both looked up in time to see a second bottle strike it, this time in the back. I fumbled in my bookbag, still hanging off my shoulders, trying to take advantage of the distraction. The Nuckelavee shouted a bestial challenge at my barely visible friends, Claire and Olivia, moments before their entire cooler struck it near its wound, causing its disposition to change from rage to agony.

I found what I was looking for. I pulled out the gold brooch and held it above my head for just a moment. The Nuckelavee saw the gold and understood, I could see it in its eyes, but before it could react, I shoved my entire arm into its gaping maw. It clamped down on my forearm, but with the protection of my coat it couldn't bite through, only hold my arm in place. Good. I released the gold down its throat, figuring it had to be afraid of gold for a reason. It was. It apparently had an excellent reason.

I saw the terror in its eyes as it released me, choking in panic as I rolled painfully and awkwardly away from it through the debris. Large chunks of putrid fat began to bubble and slough off its body as its skin steamed and boiled before darkening and finally catching fire. It screamed, briefly, worse than anything I'd ever heard before going silent and falling still. Even then I stared at it, waiting for its next move, waiting for anything. Nothing came.

It was probably dead. For real this time. Better to get back from it, just to be safe.

I became aware that Olivia and Claire were shouting at me from the hilltop. I couldn't manage much more than a thumbs-up in their general direction, but that seemed to calm them down some. Claire shouted something that I couldn't entirely hear, but understood as they would make their way to me. I felt like that was reasonable, but I didn't have the energy to get excited about it at the moment. I stumbled a few yards away from the growing fire, the carnage, all of it before stopping to catch my breath, my hands on my knees. I was acutely aware of the pain in my leg where I'd been gripped by the Nuckelavee. I didn't have anything protecting my shins, and now I found it difficult to walk. Assuming I didn't have massive internal injuries, and I wasn't ready to assume that just yet, I was going to be sore and bruised for a very long time.

I heard coughing and turned my neck to see Chalsarda climbing over the wreckage. "That was some plan," she said, making her way toward me. "Dropping a bridge on me. I'll bet it never saw it coming."

"Oh god, I didn't mean to." I only just now realized how far ahead of me Chalsarda had gotten, and I was immediately grateful that she seemed to be fine. "That wasn't the plan, not exactly. I'm really sorry; I'm just glad you're not hurt."

"And you as well," she replied. "How did you do that though? Was it the jewelry?"

"Probably," I replied, not sure if I was ready to sit down or not. "I kind of felt into the ground for the stuff, and felt the thing, and then did the other thing, and…yeah. Don't ask me to articulate right now. Words are hard. You got the kids to safety?"

Chalsarda looked as if she had swallowed a lime whole, and it was slowly making its way down her throat. "I got the children to safety, yes, but you should know that—"

"This was quite rude," a powerful voice interrupted. "What exactly do you think you were doing here? Is this how you treat all your gifts?"

"Oh hey, it's Freyja, the Norse goddess of most things," I said, mixing up internal and external dialogue for a moment. "Hold on, how are you even here?"

"I can be where I please," she replied. "But to answer your question, I am here because you abused your *Singasteinn*."

"The what?"

Freyja motioned toward the corpse of the Nuckelavee, and my gold brooch sort of popped through its neck and flew straight into her hand. "Your Singing Stone. Do you know how rare these are? Loki and Heimdall would kill you if they just saw what you did. Well, come to think of it, Heimdall could have seen this, it's entirely possible. Good luck. Now, let's see," she continued, studying the trinket. "You've been using it sparingly, which is good, for your sake, but it seems you are only able to tap into its power when you're afraid. That's interesting and not in a good way. It says something about you. You've used her, three times? Yes, I can see ice, wind, and earth, all evocations. She likes that much at least, though you have not given her the chance to sing, not really. Interesting that the elf frightened you more than the Nuckelavee. Perhaps you've not taken this threat seriously. Hmm? She doesn't believe you have the talent to sing with her. Well, now that's hardly fair of you, is it? You've yet to hear her sing! And besides, do you not trust me? I know! I made you a very pretty pin and everything, she should be proud to wear you. Maybe she just doesn't understand fashion. No, don't say that. You are very pretty. Yes, you are!"

She was talking to a rock. She told it that it was pretty. And she insulted my fashion sense. That shouldn't have been too confusing to me given everything else, but I felt I was missing something here.

"Chalsarda, do you know what's happening?" I turned to look at my friend, but saw that she was kneeling, her head deeply bowed.

"Elana, pay attention when I am speaking," Freyja said sharply. "Now, I'll ask you this: Why are you here?"

I turned my attention back to Freyja, who was now cradling the brooch like a beloved pet. "What do you mean? I'm here because of you!" I didn't expect to shout the answer, but I was under a lot of stress. "You let your brother think I was going to murder him, and his idiot friend summoned an unbeatable sea demon to mess me up! I'm out in the middle of nowhere trying to make sure no one else gets hurt!"

Freyja raised an eyebrow at that. "Why are you fighting it at all? Kill his champion and be done with it. Then you can focus on my brother and Ragnarök."

I flared up at that. "Are you out of your mind? Are you crazy because you're an immortal or because you just never learned how to hear the word no since time immemorial? I'm not a killer! I'm not killing Kodran or Freyr, and even if I wanted to, which again, let me reiterate that I absolutely do not want to do that that thing, I am not capable of doing that thing!"

"You should consider your tone," Freyja said tightly. "And what do you think the Singing Stone was for? It is not enough to kill a god on its own, but it would certainly give you a fighting chance."

"You lied," I countered. "You said it was a gift. You said I could contact you by speaking your name into it."

"Neither of those statements were lies; I fail to see your issue."

"You handed me a weapon! I could have hurt someone!"

Freyja seemed offended at that. "I offered you so much more than that, but it is becoming increasingly evident that you are either too dense or too childish to understand the responsibility being offered to you!"

"Responsibility?" I spat, having completely lost my cool by now.

"Elana! Please," Chalsarda pleaded in a harsh whisper without raising her head.

"I'm sorry, but no. This is crap," I exclaimed. "You thought this would motivate me? Because of you, I've had to uproot my life and put my friends in harm's way. Your entire plan is stupid! And it makes sense, and I'll tell you why. Because you, Freyja, are the goddess of war, and if there is one thing that the world has never, ever needed, if there is one utterly stupid concept in all of history, it's war. So, however this makes sense to you, it doesn't make sense to anyone else. I'm out here trying to survive, trying to help where I can, and as long as I live, I will never understand things the way you do, because I am not like you. You don't give a damn about anyone or anything besides your pantheon's continued existence!"

Freyja was still at that, unreadable. "So that's it, is it? We can't see eye to eye because we're not the same?"

"Pretty much."

Freyja inhaled deeply through her nostrils somehow standing up taller than she already was, something I hadn't thought possible. "Then, child, allow me to help you understand my point of view. I'll offer you another gift. I shall allow you to feel the smallest fraction of the love I feel."

In an instant, I felt submerged. I felt like my body was cooking from the inside out, like my body was an eggshell incapable of holding in pure emotion. It was ecstasy and agony, but it was far too much. Tears involuntarily flowed down my cheeks, my chest heaved, and I would have sobbed if I were able to breathe. "I don't care, do I? I care more than you will ever know, Elana Black." Freyja's voice was hard and pained. "I am eternal, and cursed, and eternally cursed. I was not there at the beginning, and you understand now why that is so much worse. Without me, there was no one who held dominion over love, no one to accept that responsibility. I am the mother of humanity! And when they love, I am pleased, and when they fall, I feel it every single time."

"It hurts!" I cried out. I was on my knees now, unable to move. Every part of me saw what she saw, felt what she felt. I wasn't meant to experience this, and I knew how wrong it was intrinsically.

"Goddess, please stop," Chalsarda said meekly behind me.

"That's good!" Freyja shouted in approval. "It hurts because you care! The more you care about the wellbeing of others, the more you care about their lives and hopes and fears and births and deaths, the deeper it will hurt. And Elana, you are about to feel a deeper hurt than you've ever known. Do you feel that? That is the pain I felt when thousands were burned alive at Pompeii. And that? That is the pain I felt when Bill Greenwood died here, moments ago, protecting his children from the Nuckelavee. Know that they feel the same. Know that I have felt this pain countless times, and will feel it countless more!"

I screamed now, aware that the scream itself should have hurt, but that pain was lost to everything else. This was infinite and circular. It never ended, but it was always beginning.

"Enough, Goddess," Chalsarda stood as she said it, her voice louder, but trembling.

Freyja's voice deepened, booming across the canyon. It knocked me over, not that I otherwise moved much. I was in the fetal position now, unable to form words.

"Now feel the pride I feel for humanity as they move ever forward, indomitable as a species, always striving to advance! Feel the disappointment I feel as they continually break each other down, destroying themselves, stunting their own advancement, shunning and killing the best amongst them! And tell me how anyone carries all of this inside forever because I—"

Chalsarda drew an arrow and pointed it at Freyja, her eyes wide with fear for a moment before narrowing, and shouted, "Freyja, you will stop this now!"

Freyja's eyes flashed with anger as she turned her gaze from me, abating the pain for a moment. "Elf! You would dare command me by name? You threaten me with violence?" Her voice was accusatory, yet as afraid as Chalsarda must have been, she refused to show it.

"For her sake, I would," she replied.

"This is madness! Know your place, elf, and bow down," Freyja demanded. "Yield your weapon."

"I will not."

Freyja released her hold on me entirely, and turned her full attention to Chalsarda. "You will, elf."

"I tell you again. I will not. And I have a name, and you will respect it and use it. My name is—"

"I know your name," Freyja sharply interjected. "I know everything about you, Chalsarda of Verisia, daughter of Aeleth. I know your tribe, I know of your heartbreak, and I know of your deal. I know of your mistakes. Do not presume there is anything about you that I do not know. Now, answer me truthfully, child. Do you threaten me as a duty of your master?"

Chalsarda's eyes widened at that, but she answered immediately. "No."

"And do you think you have any chance of harming me?"

"Truly, I do not."

Freyja seemed to be staring through her now. "Then I would ask, are you aware of what I could do to you, without fear of repercussion or reprisal?"

Chalsarda swallowed hard, but her bow did not waver, and she did not look away. "I am."

"My final question then, what I wish to hear from your own lips," Freyja said firmly, almost invasively. "Why? Why would you insult a goddess and invite your own destruction?"

"Because she is worth it," Chalsarda replied without hesitation. "Because she would do the same for me or anyone else in pain. Because I am her friend and she is mine, and I have so few of those left. But mostly, because you are wrong, and I would rather be destroyed doing the right thing than to bend knee to a tyrant."

If there was anger to be found in her face, Freyja was hiding it well. "You are every bit the stupid, impetuous, stubborn child that she is," Freyja said after a long moment. "Fine, you may share her suffering if you care so much."

Chalsarda dropped the bow and collapsed with a shriek, and I knew in an instant what she was feeling. "Stop!" I managed, unable to look at Chalsarda.

"I will not," Freyja said directly.

I tried to move, to get to my feet, but when that failed I just said, "Please, I'll help you! I'll work with you! I'll do whatever you want, just don't hurt my friend!"

Freyja seemed to consider this and stopped. "Rise," she said to us both, and I somehow found the energy to stand, albeit on wobbly legs. "You say you will help me?"

"That's what I said," I agreed.

"No, this will not do," she said sadly. "You agree to help me under duress. That is not the help that I wish. I want you to understand the situation for what it is, and I want you to want to help me. I hope that I have taught you a lesson here, today, and I will await your answer. Now open your hand."

I did, and she placed the singing stone in my hands. "She is still yours until she decides not to be. Take care of her, whisper nice things to her, and do not rely too much on her, for your sake and hers. I can be patient, to an extent, but you have less time than I. Now say thank you."

The words barely came out of me. "Thank you."

Freyja turned to leave before stopping and turned to face me one more time, tears in her eyes. "Elana, there is just one more thing. Do not ever presume to tell me how I feel ever again. To-

day I have excused you for your youth and passion. I will not be
so generous again."

20

It was an uncomfortable ride home, in more than one way. Chalsarda wasn't ready to talk about what happened, and neither was I. I offered her my thanks, which she briefly accepted, and after that we were silent. What Freyja did was inhuman and unnatural. It was an assault. I was attacked in a way that I wasn't prepared for, and I wasn't sure how I would recover. It made me sick knowing that Chalsarda experienced that for even a moment on my behalf. She didn't deserve that. No one does. There was a part of me that wanted to have sympathy for Freyja for having to carry that around, and that part of me was quickly beaten back when I was reminded that she forced that pain onto the two of us.

I would have tried to sleep on the way back if not for the fact the van had been a near casualty of our adventure. I'm still not sure how Claire managed to get it back off the hillside, but the shocks were toast. The area was remote enough that by the time emergency crews were on the scene, we had cleared out, but the main road was still blocked off, which meant we got to find out what every single bump and crack in the road felt like.

Coupled with my laundry list of injuries, they didn't feel great and they made sleep impossible. Which meant I had to be awake and painfully aware of everything I'd just experienced. Claire and Olivia weren't entirely sure what had happened, but they respected our need for silence. Still, it wasn't an easy drive for any of us.

We arrived home at a frustratingly late hour, and I was the first to be dropped off. Chalsarda took the opportunity to get out as well. I reiterated my thanks, though at this point what I really wanted to say was sorry. That I regretted that she was hurt, and that while I appreciated her immensely for what she did, I truly wished she hadn't. I wanted to tell her that I knew how brave she was, how afraid she must have been, how difficult the choice must have been given what her family would have thought. I wanted to say a lot of things. I said thanks. She acknowledged the thanks, and she left.

I walked into the shop, and by all rights I should have wanted nothing more than sleep, but I knew as soon as the lights were on and the door shut behind me that there was no chance of that happening. I had too much on my mind, too much anger at those kids being orphaned because petty small-minded idiots thought violence was a solution to a problem that didn't exist. I was furious at the games everyone seemed to love to play. I was terrified that I couldn't do anything to stop it. So I did the only thing I could think to do, I put my hands to work.

My first task was getting around to something I'd meant to do forever: Actually protecting this place. I gathered the books I needed and followed them to the letter. If I was going to ward this place, I was going to do it right. The rod was incredibly useful for this task because, as it turned out, the Aos Si was right. I was spilling excess energy all over the place. I must have been in a mood since I managed to weave not one, but two wards over the shop. I didn't have the finely tuned skills to ward against specific people, at least not yet, but anyone not a human or an elf was going to be hit with a pair of evocations in the form of water and electricity. I'd do better later, but for now, I very pleased with myself given this was my first successful attempt. Not the kind of thing you can Instagram, but I didn't need anyone else to know about my achievements to feel good about them.

I still had plenty of juice left over, from the residual energy I'd wasted in the shop and not from my own well, that had been long spent; so I got down to the daily task of charging my bracelet and coat. I had never expected that I'd rely on the coat as much as I had, but it has saved my life twice now in the past week (two weeks? I can't even keep track of weeks anymore) and I was smart enough to realize I'd been lucky. It wasn't like I had a plan for being punched out of a building, I don't know anyone who has a plan for that. But it worked out for me all the same. Still, I could only get lucky so much before I would really need to start trying to plan for the unplannable.

After that, I began doing anything and everything to keep my brain distracted. I tried to scry for Lainey and Jaden, knowing full well nothing would come of it and they weren't anywhere that I could see them. I've also never successfully managed to scry for anything, but I knew it was possible. I tried to read, for fun and not study, but my heart wasn't in it. I even organized the shop and played with the cats, but eventually, I knew I'd need to really face myself and think about what had happened.

I climbed into bed, trying not to cry. Maybe tomorrow.

I woke up the next morning, not to the sound of an alarm that I definitely didn't set, and not to the sounds of Claire opening the shop, but the sound of my phone ringing. I almost forgot that people still called other people. I definitely forgot that I set my ringtone as the Adventure Time theme song. My phone beckoned me to grab my friends, and then there was a line about distant lands or something. It was six AM on the dot. The caller was unknown because, of course, they would be. I declined the call, certain that no one was evil enough to call me at six in the morning on a Sunday. My faith in humanity was misguided, as they immediately called back. Two more declined calls later, and I got a text message from the same number that lets me know that Domino's has received my pizza order and they're on their way. The text read:

Pick up the phone, Elana.

"You don't tell me what to do, Domino's," I mumbled, silencing the next call the second it came in. After another I shouted incoherently, scaring away Jameson, who I hadn't realized was there. Another rejection, another text. This one read:

This is Roger Nill. Answer the phone so I don't have to go over there.

I tried to reply with just about eighteen letter Fs when the phone rang again, and I accidentally picked up the call. "Rise and shine, kid!" The enthusiasm he offered was far too intense for this hour. I shouted wordlessly for a full ten seconds in response. "I'm sorry, did I wake you?"

"Is Domino's pizza a front for the Gardeners? You have to tell me if it is," I demanded.

"Always with the jokes. You need coffee, so I'll make this quick," he said not answering my very real question. "We have a date and a location. If you're looking for your friend, and you're looking to do the right thing, we'll be in the square. It is my understanding you've been there a few times now."

I had been there, once when the Aos Si showed me what was to come, and another time when The Knowing practically forced me into the middle of the city. "I'd ask how you know that, but you're not going to tell me, are you?"

"I surely will not," he agreed. "Next Sunday night, incidentally. I assume you can clear your calendar for this."

"For ritual sacrifice, you mean," I added. "You know, you have unrest in your own house. Two baby Gardeners came by asking me to stay out of sight until the whole thing was done."

He chuckled on the other end of the phone. "I'm aware. So, I can take your sharing of that information to mean that you're on my side rather than theirs?"

I rubbed at my eyes. "I'm still looking for the side that wants to beat you up and save Lucia with me, but I'm happy to go it alone if I have to. It just means Lucia and I won't have to share our victory snacks with anyone after we win."

"You cannot possibly be this dumb." He sighed. "How many times do I have to tell you? It's you or her! Now, if you show up, my people will clear a way for you, but it's going to be a fight. You were frighteningly accurate when you said there was unrest in my house. Everyone has an opinion on this, and plenty of people feel strongly enough to go to war."

"Don't call me dumb, you dumb, uh, gibbon," I said sleepily. "You gibbon-faced dummy."

"Pay attention, this is serious, and I have a lot to prepare for," Roger snapped. "It is my understanding that you have a friend who can, let's say, give you a ride here?"

"I hate you. But like, actually hate you. Like I want bad things to happen to you, and pretty much just you," I complained.

"The elf. She has her own unique way into The Knowing, make sure she can bring you along."

"I hope you poop yourself, and then you slip on the poop, and then some of the poop goes into your mouth, and you get poop sick."

There was a long silence at that, until he finally said, "That's disgusting."

"Next Sunday is Christmas Eve, a-hole!" I shouted at him.

"And on Saturday you're fighting your last round with the Nuckelavee, but I don't set the schedule," he replied. "If you still need help with that, by the way, you know my terms. And hey, congratulations for—"

"Hanging up now. Help me by throwing yourself into the ocean."

I absolutely hated that I was awake at this point, but I was even more upset that I knew I wasn't going to fall asleep. I stretched hard and looked at Koala who curiously stared back, and I said to him, "Okay, good deed time. Come on, let's eat."

I honestly thought I might sleep in until noon, but if I was up, I was going to do something good for a good person. I knew it wouldn't really make up for the damage to her van, but I knew Claire probably didn't want to get up and do any of the busy work either, so I got to work. I knew her schedule. The store opens at ten on Sunday, which means Claire is up by eight, leaves by eight-thirty, and gets to the shop at nine. I'd give her the fun news in a bit, but for now, I'd take care of everything I could.

After feeding the cats and putting on some music, I got going. Over the next two hours, I managed to turn off my brain and organized the place in a way that I could be proud of. I thought

I'd done a decent job last night, but now it was like, wow. Around eight I sent the good news to Claire and went back to work. By nine-thirty I had all of the online orders packed and ready to ship, and I couldn't think of a single thing I could have done more to help out for the day. At least Claire would be able to relax during her shift, something I intended to spend my time doing as well.

I threw on a change of clothes without showering, and headed out before Claire could arrive. I wasn't trying to run away from her or anything; I just needed a day free of anyone who'd been with me during the past couple of days. I gave her a wave as she pulled her motorcycle into the parking lot. I didn't have anywhere specific to be; I just wanted to leave.

I stopped at a coffee house and had a cup of oatmeal while I figured out what to do next. I was in that uneasy mood where I didn't want to be around anyone and craved company, and I was trying to come to terms with what I actually wanted. Instead, I decided that what I needed was to be normal for one day. No magic, or battle preparations, or fantastical worlds. I wanted to catch up with my friends who I sent away and just talk about eighties hairstyles or bears or what flowers are safe to eat or anything except what's been going on lately.

Which is why I shouldn't have been surprised when I got a text at that exact moment from Ann asking me if I was still alive. I confirmed that I was, and she informed me that I needed to come over to her place immediately. I asked if it could wait until tomorrow and was met with the word 'NO' in all caps, followed by a generous amount of exclamation points. I looked at my half-eaten cup of oatmeal with despair and threw it in the trash, realizing with a degree of frustration that I probably wasn't going to get what I wanted today. I sent her a text letting her know that I was on my way.

I wasn't upset with Ann, not even annoyed. She's my friend, and she's asking for my help, so I'm going to help. Obviously. It's who I am. But there are times I just need to recharge and take care of myself, and this is one of them. To anyone on the outside, I'd probably look massively irresponsible. A mythological goddess is trying to recruit me as an assassin, a shadowy organization is seeking to convince me to kill myself, and in about a week or so an unbeaten, undefeatable demon will rise out of the sea to try to kill me...again. For the third time...damn. If I'm being reasonable, I should be doing everything in my power to prepare for the utterly unfair amount of challenges that are about to crash into me. But like I keep telling everyone, I am not reasonable.

The way I figure it, I am very likely about to die. I don't really have much in the way of affairs to settle, everyone I'm really close with already understands the situation, even if they haven't accepted the reality or they just don't comprehend the fact that I'm not invincible and I've been scraping by with impossible amounts of luck. I can't keep this up, and I'm going to need to start getting smarter about how I approach the unknown or it's going to destroy me. And no part of this means that I'm giving up by any means. If anything, I'm dead set on taking down as many bad things with me as I can. But I just know myself, and I know that at some point I need to clear my head or I'm going to burn out or make a mistake.

I pulled up to Ann's place, and she was already outside waiting for me. Before I could park, Ann was waving at me from the sidewalk, looking somehow less rested than I was. I parked and got out, studying her carefully.

"Hey friendo," I said cautiously. "You doing okay?"

Ann blinked heavily at that and yawned, before replying, "Yeah, totally. I think so. We got back at three, I think, we saw a lake. It was fine. We weren't attacked by demons or anything. I think I'm okay, haven't slept in a couple of days though. Got some laundry done. I'm probably not fine. But I mean, maybe."

"And would you like to talk about it?" I asked.

"Yes!" she shouted, then quieter, she added, "Yes, I need to talk about it. For sure. With you. Please."

"Sure, of course," I replied. "Inside, or in my car, or...?"

"Inside would be great!" It was clear that she had to stop herself from shouting again and added in a near whisper, "I'm so tired."

It was a feeling that I could intimately relate to, and with a reassuring rub on her shoulder I walked her into her apartment, stuffy and poorly lit as it was. There was a stale odor that seemed to come from everything, but with the piles of clothes, and boxes, and sewing equipment everywhere, it felt like it would be impossible to pinpoint the exact origin of it. Dust danced in a sunbeam, which made it through an exposed, pulled curtain, and if not for how exhausted Ann looked, I would have opened a window and let some light in. Almost immediately after walking through the door, she collapsed in a heap onto her overstuffed sectional sofa. I moved a pile of folded laundry and joined her, and waited for her to speak. Of course, if she just fell asleep right then and there, I would have also considered that a positive outcome to the trip.

Ann sat up and rubbed her eyes with her fingers under her glasses and said, "I'm sorry, this is just stupid and strange, and I think you kind of told me this happened to you too." She sighed. "So, you remember telling me how you can Know someone?"

Ah, crap. "What did you see?" I asked.

"Kodran something-something Osvifsson," she said slowly. "I can pronounce his last name correctly now, that's something, I guess. I'll get back to you with a funny middle name for him when I'm able to think of a good one."

"Oh no, in the cave with the deal and the—"

"The handshake and the thing, yeah," Ann finished for me. "I wasn't sure what happened at the time, but then I saw that Lucia could do it in that weird vision thing, and then just the entire past day I haven't been able to get his crap life out of my head. I Knew him, didn't I?"

"Yeah, you kind of did, homie," I said sympathetically. "You know, the first time I did it, I was freaked out for weeks. You seem to be handling it better than I did at least. The good news is that you'll get the hang of it really quick, and you'll only share when you want to. Although, I don't remember Lucia Knowing anyone, did we get different visions?"

"We were looking at the whole of her life, so yeah, probably. Is this what it feels like to do drugs?"

"Kind of a broad question, and I'm not really a big drug person, so, maybe?" I answered, then trying to be helpful, I continued, "I once had a hundred-and-two-degree fever, and drank a bottle of Robitussin, and passed out with my face in a couch cushion, and I thought I was talking to Falkor. Turns out it was this dude I was seeing, and we never saw each other again after that."

"Oh right, Dexter, freshman year of college, right? Did either of you ever apologize or anything?"

"Nope, he blocked me on Facebook, I instantly deleted his number out of embarrassment," I replied. "This was like six years ago, and I legitimately forgot his name until just now, and I think it's kind of weird that you remembered it, to be honest."

Ann chuckled at that. "Shut up; it's not weird to remember things. Dude was super creepy anyway. He was just a little too into Sonic the Hedgehog."

"I also forgot that detail, so thanks for that reminder as well." I laughed.

"Hey, for real though," Ann said after a moment. "You need to be careful with this guy. I saw too much, and he's not a good person. He's done good things, but he's let some terrible things happen as well. Deep down, he's a coward, and I didn't expect that. He's lived a very long life, and part of that is because he's immortal, but only part of it. He lets people suffer and die if it seems like he might have to put himself in harm's way. I've seen him run from danger at the expense of innocent people; I've watched as he's kept his mouth shut and let other people pay the price for his mistakes. But he's strong. Stronger than I really think any of us know. He's had lifetimes to gather strength, but between the books and what I saw in his head, he's trying to ramp up his power levels in a big hurry because he's afraid of something. I couldn't see what it was, but it has him freaked out."

I was silent a moment, and I didn't want to say it out loud, but I felt that if I didn't then, it would just burn a hole in me. "A man died yesterday. His name was Bill Greenwood, he had kids. The Nuckelavee killed him because it was looking for me, but I place the blame on Kodran. He knew what he was doing when he sent it after me, and he did it anyway."

"I'm so sorry," Ann said nervously, unsure of herself, and tried her best to stifle a yawn. "Are you okay?"

"No, not now, but I'll get there. I'm not beating myself up over this one, but there is plenty of anger there to be sure," I replied quietly. "I wanted to turn my brain off for the day, try to be normal for five minutes, but I can't do that. Not until this whole thing is done."

"That's good, it's not your fault." Ann suddenly closed her eyes at that, falling asleep in the middle of the conversation, her head tilting lazily into her shoulder as her brain quit for the day.

I took off her glasses so she didn't roll over and break them in her sleep, and I found an Eternity Pilgrim themed fleece blanket in her laundry pile, and threw it over her before tucking a pillow between her chin and her shoulder. I'm glad she passed out, she needed it.

I walked outside knowing full well that I was going to have some uncomfortable conversations before this week was done, and I knew where I needed to start.

21

"**Y**ou're wrong. Right now, in this moment, you are wrong, and you need to be told that you're wrong."

I wish I could say that I wasn't half expecting Logan to say that, but I mean, I was at least sixty percent expecting that from him. Maybe sixty-five percent. It was Monday night, and I had less than six days until I'd faced the Nuckelavee, mostly likely for the final time. One way or another. There was a lot I needed to take care of before the week was done, and this was pretty high on the list. So I wasn't about to leave without challenging him on it.

"Dude, in what way am I wrong?"

"This is exactly what Olivia was upset with you about in the first place," Logan explained, leaning across the island in his kitchen. "So let me see if I have this right. My girlfriend also has magic or something inside of her, not to mention Ann and you know, me. Your Celtic god mentor says that Olivia has to die in order to save your grade school friend, who is also magic, but the bad guys who are also magic, say it can be you or it has to be you, that part I'm not super clear on. And if one of you doesn't save her, then I guess she dies or something, but I don't know what happens past that, I'm also not clear on that part. Right! Yes, and this happens on Christmas. Can't forget that part. Am I good so far?"

"That was a healthy amount of exposition, but yes," I agreed.

"If you could not be sarcastic for a whole ten seconds, I'll get to the part where you're wrong," Logan continued. "I don't want Olivia to be hurt, and neither do you, and we have that in common, and I love you for that. But you don't get to make her decisions for her, and neither do I. And asking me to keep this from her, asking me to keep her away from whatever you're doing, is wrong. You need to trust her."

"Should I go?" Jason asked from the couch in the living room. "I mean, if you two need to talk, that's totally fine, I promise."

"Nah, you're cool," I remarked, before adding. "Just don't repeat any of this to anyone."

Jason looked unsteady as he answered, "Mum's the word, but that kind of proves my point. It just feels like none of this is my business and, like, maybe you two have a lot to unpack here. And I promise you, I will really not be hurt if you ask me to leave, and our pizza is getting cold, I've had this episode of Collapsing Stars paused for a pretty long time, and I just know that I can't go on Facebook now, or Twitter, or whatever because yeah, it's the season finale, and there are definitely going to be spoilers, and yes, okay, I could just not look at my phone, but what else am I going to do?"

"If you're uncomfortable, we could just catch up later," Logan offered.

"I'm not that uncomfortable, but I do have questions." Jason stood up and walked over to us at that. "So, and this is an important one, are we going to be attacked by a demon on Christmas Eve? Because I am genuinely concerned for your safety, but I was planning to be in town for Christmas, and my parents are in France, but I have a brother who is visiting, and he's not the nicest guy, but I also don't want to see him or me dead, so it's really important to me that I know we're not going to be attacked by a demon."

"You're not getting attacked by a demon. At least not this demon, I can't speak for all demons," I poorly reassured him.

"Okay, that's good. And am I magic? Because I'm feeling a little left out of the whole magic thing?"

Oh, I had something for this!

"First, you're already magic, so shut up. But there's a way to check!" I reached into my book bag and pulled out a worn, old book and handed it to him. "So, I know that we tried something similar to this a while ago, but some things have possibly changed, so yeah, open this and tell me what you read."

Jason's eyes widened looking at the title, and he said, "Oh, now this is going to be problematic." The book he was holding was titled *Life with Women and How to Survive It* by Joseph Peck M.D. He immediately looked flustered at it. "Okay, so first off, this looks like it was written in the fifties, and we've come a long way since then, and I don't think this book is something that we can really learn from, and yup, that is offensive. You definitely cannot say that to another human being and, and there are pictures! This man is supposed to be a doctor! And another person was paid to draw that out, and—"

"It's a manual for all the different types of vampires that exist," I said cutting him off. "All of the very real, different types of vampires."

Jason suddenly looked very afraid at that. "No way."

Logan took the book and read it for a few seconds. "She's right, all vampires. Just a whole bunch of 'em."

"So magic, elves, gods, and demons all exist, and now you're telling me that there are also vampires?" he asked.

"Afraid so, buddy," I replied. "And pretty much everything else."

"If you two are lying to me that would be...well...mean," he mumbled sadly.

"Wouldn't do that to you, promise. And yeah, the books are charmed or something to prevent people who don't have whatever it is that I have from finding out all this stuff by accident," I explained as understanding as possible. "That's why we see vampire stuff, and you see the ramblings of a sexist senior citizen from sixty years ago or so."

Jason put the book on the counter and said, "Okay, look, I'm not magic, I probably shouldn't be hearing most of what you two have been talking about for the last half hour, and I'm pretty hungry. So really, I should go, it's okay. I'm taking the pizza, too."

I felt a little bad for him at that moment, like I'd intruded on his evening and made him feel excluded, and I said, "Just don't get bit by a vampire on the way to your car."

Why am I like this?

Both Jason and Logan looked at me in stunned disbelief, and Jason asked, "Why would you say that? Why am I only just now getting warned about being bit by a vampire?"

"No, it's fine, I was only kidding, there aren't any vampires in this world," I tried to reassure him. I didn't know if that was true or not.

"Are you sure?" he asked, more than just a little upset at this point. "Because I'm probably going to have a weird dream now because of you!"

"I'm certain," I said. I was not certain.

"I'm going to go now," he said, his eyes showing a mixture of disappointment and looking for approval.

"Would you like a hug?" I asked.

"Yeah, okay, that would be good," Jason replied, accepting goodbye hugs from both Logan and me. Then, on an uncomfortable note, added, "Bye."

By the time he left, I was kind of hoping that Logan would have been through with telling me about how I was betraying my best friend.

"So, vampires. That's creepy, right?" I asked.

"Dude, don't run away from this." Logan sounded tired as he said that. "This is the mistake that you made last time and I forgave it, but I know how impossible your situation must have felt. And Olivia forgave you because she loves you like family, and the last thing she ever wants is to be upset with you. But you have to know by now that you're not alone, and you won't have an excuse this time if you shut everyone out. This isn't your decision to make. And it's not mine either."

I stared at him and asked, "And how would you feel if Olivia chose to let herself die?"

Logan took a deep, pensive breath through his nostrils and said, "I'd feel terrible, but—"

"No! You'd stop her! You'd sacrifice yourself if you could, wouldn't you?" I suddenly shouted, losing control for a moment.

He flinched at that; I don't think he was expecting that kind of reaction from me.

"Yeah, I would," he answered after a moment. "But let's start over. Walk me through it, help me understand. Start from the beginning."

I took a breath of my own. "I'm sorry for shouting," I told him. "Can we sit down, so we don't debate over your kitchen sink?"

Logan agreed, and we walked over to the couch, where he shut off the TV.

"Okay, we're cozy now, no distractions, and Jason took all of the pizza and I let him," Logan said eyeing the coffee table. "Damn it. Okay, still a little hungry, but whatever. Talk to me."

"From the beginning? All right, well, the first time I was ever in The Knowing was shortly after Olivia and I beat up Jason. Not our Jason, you remember the other one. I went there in a dream, it was a frightening place, but I wasn't frightened, you know what I mean? So that was also the first time I met the Aos Si. It was bizarre, he was bizarre for sure; but I guess that makes sense, right?"

"If I met a Celtic god I might use other words, but sure, bizarre is acceptable."

"Fair," I agreed. "So he showed all of this symbolic imagery, not that I understood what I was looking at, at least not for a while. He offered to help me understand, but the whole thing felt off, and I left without realizing what I was looking at."

"What were the images?" he asked.

"Well, they weren't just images, they felt like they were actually there," I corrected. "A tree, red and burnt. It had one rapidly growing branch with an olive at the end of it, extending toward two crossing beams of light."

"I can see how that might be confusing. So did he tell you when you went back?"

"He actually wasn't there when I went back," I replied.

"Oh?"

"Yeah, the best I can tell, The Knowing pulled me in directly, something I've since been informed just simply doesn't happen."

Logan looked as if a word had caught in his throat before he replied, "I was about to say that sounded weird, but the whole thing is weird, so please, continue."

"The Knowing just sort of herded me to a city, I thought it was decaying, but that wasn't it. I was lead to the tree, the olive, and the light again. It wasn't empty either; I found that out the hard way. I saw something…disturbing."

Logan looked troubled by that. "What did you see?" he asked.

"I'd prefer not to talk about it, I'm not proud of how I handled that, and I don't think it's relevant anyway. I saw the Aos Si again in The Knowing, but I wasn't near the city or anything. He didn't show me any of the imagery from before either, but he was busy trying to teach me not to get killed by Bres, and we were on kind of a time crunch. In fact, I figured out that Olivia was supposed to represent the olive, kind of out of nowhere, after I had defeated Bres. I felt simultaneously like a genius and an idiot all at the same time. You know, the way I feel most days."

"Wait, you figured it out, but when did you know for sure?" Logan asked.

"At that party where I met Chalsarda," I said. "The Aos Si took me aside, answered some of my questions. I told him that I understand my name meant tree, Lucia was the light, Olivia was the olive. I figured out the metaphor. He confirmed it was all correct, and then he showed me something. It was a mirror, but instead of seeing myself, the Aos Si, or the rest of the room, I saw the imagery as I saw it before, only now, instead, it was all moving so fast. The branch grew faster than it should have been able to in a year, the tree was in pain and possibly dying, and when the olive touched the light, it was no longer a metaphor. Not imagery, not an idea. It was Lucia. It was really her! Older than I remember, but radiant and, sorry I don't know how to explain this, but she just seemed whole. She was overflowing with energy, and she was flying! And with a wave of her hands, the city itself was healed, and it too was whole. But the olive was gone, it was destroyed. I'm sorry, I need a second."

Logan remained quiet while I took a moment to breathe and to focus. "I wasn't in a good place when I saw that. My first thoughts weren't about Lucia or all the people she would save, they were about Olivia, and I swore to myself that I was going to save her. I didn't know how, I didn't know when, but I had a purpose. You said Olivia sees me as a part of her family. Olivia is my sister. She has always been there for me more than anyone I've ever known. She's more important to me than myself, and there are times when I'm afraid of what that means, what I'll do for her. A year ago, that meant just going to her parties when I'd rather stay home and watch a movie. Now it means I'll fight things that I should run from. Do you know what happened after that?"

"No," he said softly.

"I'd just learned that my friend was fated to die, and a Celtic god asked me to address a room full of beings that were beyond my ability, at the time, to comprehend. Imagine a masquerade ball full of sprites, and immortals, and elves, and impossibly beautiful people that may or may not have been people; just every crazy thing you can imagine, all in one room, all dressed to the nines, and every single one of them is staring at you as you stand on a balcony, waiting for you to address them, to offer a toast, or maybe just go insane. They're waiting for something. That's what happened to me. And right then and there, I didn't care about any of them. I was mad about every innocent person who had ever been terrorized, lived their lives in fear because of the Gardeners, or myths, or monsters, or whatever, but mostly I was mad that Olivia, my best friend, was fated to die because of something that neither of us had ever asked to be a part of. So, I threatened them."

Logan blinked at that. "You threatened them?"

"Yup. Every single last one of them. I got overconfident, or arrogant, or self-righteous, or something, but whatever it was, I lead with my chin. I let them all know that if they ever even thought about harming the innocent, I'd be the greatest enemy they'd ever know. Which, you know, no. I'm not even close to their power level; I don't pose a threat to any of them, and yet, ta-da!"

"That's astounding, sure," Logan said thoughtfully. "But hold on, back up. You said that Olivia was fated to die?"

"That's what the Aos Si said, yeah."

"When?" Logan asked.

"What do you mean, when?" I asked. "Weren't you paying attention?"

"I mean, I've heard that he confirmed what everything meant, and he showed you a magic movie mirror, but did he actually say that she was fated to die? Who told you that?"

I didn't have an immediate answer, and I had to think about it. He had to have said that, right? "I don't...I'm not sure, exactly," I stammered, wracking my brain for the answer.

"Well, okay, let's come back to that. Do you have any other evidence that any of this is real and not just some insane ruse?"

"We've gone over this, man. It's why we're fighting."

"We're not fighting, we had a disagreement, so just tell me again."

I rubbed my temples and took a deep breath. "Yeah, as I said, the Gardeners showed me the same thing, but more than that. I saw it through Lucia's eyes. I was, and yeah, this is not going to make any sense at all, but I was Lucia. So were Olivia and Ann, we all experienced it. We were Lucia. I don't have a way of proving that it wasn't all just one big lie somehow, but I know deep down it was real. And Roger, the head Gardener guy, he was talking about fate and prophecy or whatever. It's all over the place there, but not all of them believe it."

"And what were Roger's words exactly, why did he say it had to be you?"

I shook my head at that, and said, "Not him, Lucia. The reason I have this power, the reason Olivia and Ann have this power, comes directly from her. She was a child with far too much power that she didn't even know that she had. She spread it not just to her friends and the people around her, but throughout time! I was in her head when it happened, and I still can't fathom how she did it. My own personal theory is that she's the Queen of the Wildlings. A lot of people just have that power who aren't supposed to have it; I think she's the reason for the aberrations. And even with as much as she gave away, she's still immensely powerful, but she's like a dead battery. She needs some of it back to give her a jumpstart, get her back to full power. We get her back to full power; she saves the day. If we don't, she effectively bleeds out and dies. She knew intimately what she did, and she knows that it's not just the power, but how and why it's transferred. It has to be done with love as the reason, but she didn't have anyone growing up. I was her best friend, and when she was gone, there was no more love in her life. I'm the only one it can be."

"Or Olivia," Logan added. "Or even Ann for that matter."

I remembered what I saw in Lucia's memory. "I don't know, man. Ann was cool with her, but they didn't meet until way after she and I did, and she was gone like a year later or something. And her and Olivia were technically friends, but I saw their time together, it was strenuous at best."

"But this isn't about Lucia, it's about Olivia, right? You know what Lucia's perspective is, but is Olivia willing to give up her power with love in her heart, it would work, right?"

Damn. He was right.

"Here's the way I see it." Logan pressed his fingers together and looked at me seriously. "A being who can't lie hasn't actually told you anything, he's let you come to your own conclusions, and a person who can lie has told you that it has to be you. Either of them can have their own agenda, and now you have to decide who you trust, if either. There's something we're missing, but you don't have a lot of time to find out what it is."

I really didn't, but I knew who to ask.

22

When I got up around three-thirty or so, I knew right away that my sleep pattern was going to be decidedly screwed up for the remainder of the week, but this was something that I had to take care of on my own, as soon as possible, and at full strength. That meant charging my coat and my bracelet early, and getting as much prep work done before turning in just long enough to recharge my well. I let Claire know that we'd have to switch shifts for the day, and while I felt bad about making her close on a Monday and open alone on a Tuesday, especially the week of Christmas with the extra rush and all, it couldn't be helped. I gave her a vague answer about needing to prepare for the Nuckelavee, which wasn't a lie, but it did hide some of the dumber elements I had planned.

I had put aside a set of books as soon as this whole mess started because the worst possible thing would be to need to travel into that dumb world and realize that some fifteen-year-old was enjoying that book somewhere and I couldn't find a Barnes and Noble that had a copy anywhere. I popped open my trunk at the foot of my bed, and I found the second book in the

Stone Sorcerer series, "Blacksmith of the Night," and started to read the first chapter. I genuinely didn't care about the rest of the book, I just wanted to find a spot early enough in the story that I didn't disturb things too much, and since I wasn't taking anyone with me this time, I could just gently enter through the book without going through the effort of a portal this time. That would, of course, break my deal with Bres, and I wasn't quite ready to do that just yet.

The first chapter seemed pretty straightforward. Kodran is waiting in a diner in Dunsmuir for someone who's going to ask for his help with whatever I presume the call to action is in the story. It's a woman, because of course it is, and he makes an unhealthy amount of observations in his mind about what he thinks she's like in bed, because of course he does. I almost wanted to shout out loud that he needed to get it together and pay attention, but I stopped and reminded myself that wasn't why I was going in. I didn't have to read any further, I had my plan, and thankfully I found a way in near the beginning, so if my timing was right, none of this would really be an issue.

Before I prepared my way in, I grabbed a blank sheet of paper, and a marker, and made a sign.

DON'T OPEN! DEAD INSIDE!
Also, I made another portal,
back soon.
—Elana

(Seriously, I'm not actually dead inside, it was a Walking Dead joke. I'm fine. But also for real, stay out. Just in case. You never know. Love you, Claire!)

I realize I could have grabbed another sheet of paper and just started over without the joke, and potentially worrying my boss and friend about the state of my mental health, but whatever. Stream of consciousness is my jam and, also, I have somewhere to be. I made a door this time, one made of oak and reinforced with steel. When it was good and ready, I did one last check of everything I had in my bookbag, let it slump across my chest as I threw it on, and headed in before I could talk myself out of it.

Bres would be a concern, obviously. Some guys you wouldn't want to run into in a dark alley. The Knowing was like ninety-nine percent dark alley. If he wanted to hurt me in there, I don't really know what I would be able to do about it. The last time around I had back up, and it didn't matter. I only survived because he wanted to toy with me. At this point, none of that mattered, and I had to just assume that he would enjoy my suffering more than just outright killing me. That was a chilling thought, and one I didn't want to dwell on, given everything else ahead of me. And that was an even more chilling thought. Of all the things wanting to see me hurt or dead, somehow the half-Fae, filled with equal parts magic juice and hate, wasn't scary enough for me to worry about at the moment. I'm sure he'd hate that.

I made it as far as my first stop without incident. Perhaps Bres thought I'd just get killed right here and now, and he'd get to sit back and watch, and maybe eat whatever the Fae equivalent of popcorn is. Elderberries? I actually don't see why it couldn't just be popcorn, now that I think about it. Magic popcorn?

Stop it, Elana. Focus.

I stopped at the stone city, making sure not to disturb even a speck of dust inside its borders, and I shouted, "I would like to talk!"

Dread filled me the instant I did, knowing full well there was no turning back at this point. There was nothing for what felt like an eternity, but when the ground rumbled, my stomach sank. Okay then, here we go.

A lone troll, well over double my height, stepped from around the corner and, though reading the facial expressions on a troll was likely a skill that I was unqualified for, this one felt decidedly like angered bewilderment. It kneeled down to try and meet my eye, and in a thunderous voice that triggered every instinct to turn and run, asked, "Are you out of yer bleedin' mind? Are you tryin' ta get eaten?"

I stood my ground, trying my best not to show fear and said, "I am here to make things right."

The troll furrowed its brow at me and said, "You killed many of our young, you can make it right by sittin' in a stew!"

"I didn't kill any of your people, I promise," I said. "Look at me, closely. Do I look like I could kill a troll?"

The troll studied me carefully, for a moment, and finally said, "Look, no, but you smells of magic. Magic can hurt real bad."

"I agree, magic can hurt, but I did not use magic to hurt your people."

"Melkree said he saw you. Are you callin' Melkree a liar?" he asked.

"Perhaps Melkree is mistaken," I replied. "Maybe if you invite me into your city and take me to him, he could see me up close and tell you for certain? And if after we meet he still insists that I am the culprit, I will agree to be in your stew. Do we have a deal?"

The troll considered that thoughtfully, and said finally, "Well, I would like stew. Right then, come wit' me."

I crossed the threshold into their city and panic spread through me, but I refused to show my fear, even now. To them, fear would look like guilt. I had a plan, one based largely on their fear of magic, but if it didn't work out, I didn't have an exit strategy. But if it worked, the gains would be enormous, and I had nothing to lose by gambling right now given my almost certain death was just days away anyway.

I had to practically run to keep up with the troll's steps. As we moved through the city, I began to see more of them popping up from around corners and in shadows, their faces a variety of expressions, but definitely not joy. Nope, not that one! By the time we reached what I could only guess was a city square, the number of trolls that had joined us began to block out the sunlight from overhead. They were massive already, and now many of them were perched on top of buildings to get a look at me. There wasn't enough room for all of them.

We stopped, and the trolls had formed a circle, a heaving mass anxious and excited to see what was going to happen to me. The troll instructed another to find Melkree and bring him to us. The sheer amount of trolls here was staggering; I didn't know if I could count them all, even their muttering was louder than most concerts I've attended.

"I don't think I'll make enough stew for everyone," I joked. I don't believe that the troll took it as a joke.

"Many of us are angry, others sad," the troll replied. "Today will be good."

The noise died down as a smaller troll, no more than six feet tall, was brought to the center of the circle, his eyes went wide as he saw me.

"Hello, you must be Melkree," I said pleasantly.

"That's 'er!" Melkree shrieked. "She's the one what killed the others!"

The murmuring took on an ugly tone, one of anger.

I found my nerve and said, "I'm sorry, Melkree, could you repeat that for everyone?"

"You killed my friends! Lopped off they heads, you did!" he yelled.

I looked at the troll who brought me in and asked, "I believe I can prove my innocence, will you allow it?"

"You will be stew if you don't." His grim expression told me how much time I had.

"Because I'm a wizard, correct?" I asked Melkree.

"Yeah! That's right! You killed 'em with magic!"

I puffed up my chest and walked into the middle of the circle, proclaiming, "Everyone! My name is Elana and, as your Melkree has identified me as, a wizard! In my bag, I have a magical item which will prove my innocence." I reached into my bookbag and produced my rod, lifting it high over my head. "Does anyone know what this is?"

"A rod!" a voice boomed from the crowd.

I kept the rod over my head and shouted back, "Correct! But not just any rod, this is the Rod of Truth, and it glows when one holds it and tells the truth!"

As I said that, I tried to concentrate on the rod and willed a minuscule amount of power into it. The rod began to glow and, either my announcement or the shine, caused a gasp to fall over the crowd. "But if one holds the Rod of Truth and they lie, they will be consumed with an eternal fire that will burn them forever and not extinguish, even past death."

Again I made the rod glow, and Melkree looked terrified. I looked back to the troll who walked me into the city and extended the rod to him. "Do you smell the magic from this rod?" I asked. He nodded, and I offered it to him, saying, "To hurt you here would mean my death. I invite you to test the rod for yourself. Hold it and tell the crowd something they all know to be true."

The troll grinned at that, and with a hand far too large for the rod, held it delicately and proclaimed, "My name is Zangu!" I caused the rod to glow, and he dropped it in amazement. "The rod works!" Zangu shouted to the crowd.

The mob was conflicted and stirring now.

I picked up the rod and, riding that wave, I held it over my head and, in a voice as loud as I could muster, I screamed, "I have never harmed a troll!"

I put a little bit of extra glow into that one for effect, and then, sensing I had them, I walked toward Melkree and extended the rod to him. "If not me, then perhaps you will tell everyone, Melkree."

The terrified troll's eyes darted around, knowing he was trapped. "I-it was her! She's lying! It's a trick!" Melkree was backing away from me now, but when his back bumped into the crowd, they shoved him back into the circle hard enough for him to fall on his face. They were chanting and agitated now, calling for him to take the rod.

Zangu brushed past me, even the innocent gesture nearly knocking me down, and he lifted Melkree into the air and demanded, "Who killed them, Melkree? Tell me!"

The smaller troll squirmed and stammered in Zangu's grip, looking for an exit. Zangu slammed him into the ground a couple of times as he repeated his question. Finally, sniveling and petrified, he screamed, "It wasn't her! It was a man!"

Zangu put him down and Melkree continued in a softer voice, "It was a man who smelled like a demon. He promised to let me live if I promised to say it was a lady with red hair."

"Coward," Zangu snarled at Melkree. Melkree began to beg as he was dragged away.

The crowd was stunned and began to disperse at the news. Some were furious with Melkree, but many weren't sure what had just happened. Zangu kneeled down again to look me in the eyes, and said, "Never believed Melkree, bad liar. But 'ad to prove it."

"Not his fault, at least not entirely," I said, putting away my rod.

"He lied to us. He must pay," he replied, and I suddenly realized that I didn't want to know how. "You have to pay, too. You have to pay the toll."

I nodded, and reached back into my book bag, pulling out a smaller bag. "And along those lines, I would like to bargain."

I had his interest.

"When I was here last, my friends and I were surprised halfway across a bridge. We didn't know that a toll would be required or even that anyone lived here. We meant no offense; we just didn't know that it was expected."

Zangu barked a laugh at that. "The 'umans never do! Sometimes we chase them, sometimes we eat them."

I was disturbed by that, wondering how many accidental travelers didn't pay the toll, but I pressed on. "I will provide you a bounty of tolls, enough for every human to safely pass through your city for a year. In exchange, I will tell you how and when to find those responsible for the attack on your people, and more than that, I will return once a year to pay the tolls again."

I then dropped the bag, which held roughly fifty dollars' worth of pennies, nickels, dimes, and quarters, at my feet and let it hit the ground with a thump for effect. "Where I am from, this is the most valued currency in all the land." It wasn't technically a lie, American currency is one of the strongest. "I assume you care more about collecting your tolls than you do fighting with people who don't mean you any harm. This will help to bridge relationships with the humans. Do we have a deal?"

Zangu licked his lips, and said, "And you promise to tell us who attacked the little ones?"

I smiled at that. We had a deal.

Dunsmuir was a small relic of a town, and the moment I stepped into it, I was grateful for my coat. There was a stone's stillness to the air and to the town, as if nothing was supposed to happen here, and so it all just stopped moving. There were Christmas lights up in the town, it was also December in this book at this time I supposed; but they were infuriatingly sparse. As if the whole quaint little hamlet would have been better off if they just hadn't bothered with lights at all. I wasn't far from my destination, in fact, I could see the brick built corner building that was the Cornerstone Cafe just a block away or so, along with a whole street full of other antiquities. Like the old train clock in the middle of the sidewalk and a marquee for the California Theater, a building that I suspected was as old as the town itself. Even the hotel looked like it had been built during World War II and everyone just decided that, yeah, that was good enough. No need to ever maintain it ever again.

I was standing in the middle of the street, but I doubted that I had to worry about being struck by a car or even seen, not because of the low layer of fog that reached my ankles; I just found it hard to believe that more than a few-hundred people lived here, which is why it was probably perfect for Kodran. Off in the near distance, the Shasta mountains loomed over the town menacingly, and I was glad that I wasn't facing Kodran where he was strongest. Not that I thought this would turn into a fight, but that was kind of the point. I wasn't meeting The Stone Sorcerer; I was meeting Kenny. And Kenny didn't want to out himself in town as anything other than a douchey park ranger with a crappy beard.

The bare minimum of what could possibly pass for snow crunched under my feet as I approached the building. I saw him inside, sitting at a booth in the back, drinking coffee and writing in a notebook. He was one of three customers, so maybe it was just too cold to go out to eat. I pulled my rod out of my bag and tried to gather as much residual magical energy as I could from the air around me. The air was practically drenched with it, and though most of it felt stale and fading, there was more than enough for what I wanted to do. I tried not to think about how many times someone had to cast around here, or what kind of magic had been used, considering who I was dealing with. Kodran was the kind of guy who turned people into statues, and that was on the low-end of his potential for atrocity.

Enough magical energy had gathered in my rod in about a second, but I gathered just a little bit more anyway, just because. He must have sensed it, because he looked up just in time to see me standing in the doorway, looking right back at him, as I unleashed a huge gust of wind directly into the restaurant.

23

The destruction was immediate and obnoxious, but more than that, it was satisfying. Utensils and napkin holders were the hardest hit, but the plates and cups weren't spared either. Even the tables and chairs had been pushed askew. If it wasn't nailed down, I caught it. The waitress and customers were startled and confused by the surprise gust of wind, but not Kodran. We locked eyes for a moment, before I cheerfully, and with my best impression of embarrassment, apologized profusely and made sure to shut the front door and inspect it to make sure that it would stay closed.

Kodran stared at me incredulously as I confidently strode to his booth and took a seat opposite him, seeing up close now the mess I had made of his coffee and how some of it had landed on his pages, but mostly it was on his shirt and lap.

"Hey there, Kenny! Thanks for meeting with me today, it's been too long!" I announced, just loud enough to be overheard by anyone who cared to hear.

"What the hell are you doing here? What do you think you're doing, throwing around magic like that in public?" he asked in a hiss. "Did you really just pretend to be a damsel in distress to get me out here like this? Do you have any idea how badly cocoa stains?"

"Okay, that's a lot of question, so in reverse order," I began, whispering back to him. "Not as bad as coffee, which I was pretty sure you had. No, she's still coming, but who the hell still says damsel in distress? Making an entrance and getting your attention, and finally, I'm here to give you a warning."

Kodran found a few napkins and was busy dabbing at the brown liquid that was seeping into his clothing and the notes, the ones that remained on the table at least; and with an annoyed smirk, he began to ask, "Oh? What warning would that be, E—"

"Don't," I said flatly cutting him off. "I'm not even going to bother threatening to out your identity to the town and telling the world where your dumb little cave is hiding. I seriously do not care about any of that; I'm telling you that saying my name would put all of these people in danger, and for the sake of everyone here, do not say my name."

He stopped playing with his shirt for a moment and really paid attention to me for a moment, and in a quieter voice asked, "You're serious, aren't you?"

"Deadly."

"Okay then, She-Who-Must-Not-Be-Named, what do you want?" he asked.

I had to pause at his joke. "Wait, do they have Harry Potter books here?" I asked, then with a second revelation I asked, "And you've read them?"

"The kid's books?" he responded. "Yeah, you can get those books anywhere in the world, and I've got a lot of time on my hands. Immortal, can't die, and my day job is a park ranger? Seriously, I'm not kidding about the free time, but you've managed to find the one time I don't have any, so what do you need?"

"Kenny, here, you'll want a little ice water for that," a waitress said, putting a glass down next to him. Her name tag read Nancy.

Kodran's face instantly lit up with a smile that wasn't fake, not exactly, but it was practiced. "Thanks, Nance. Maybe a refill?"

"You got it. Would you like a menu?" she asked, turning toward me.

I put on a practiced smile of my own, and replied, "I'm okay, thanks. I'm not able to stay. But I wanted to apologize for the wind! It really made a mess in here!"

"Oh, not your fault!" she said almost apologetically. "Wind is wind, we don't always get it here, but I've seen it bad. Ha! Seen the wind! You know what I mean."

I gestured to everything in the restaurant and agreed with my eyes, and we shared a brief laugh. "The wind's a force of nature, and it's not obligated to give us a warning, you know?"

I returned the reassuring sentiment, mirroring her expression, and offered, "Thanks, Nancy."

Nancy appeared to appreciate the banter genuinely and wandered off to take care of the other patrons, but when I looked back to Kodran, his expression had become grim, almost menacing.

"Don't even think about it," he growled in a low, barely audible tone.

I almost choked at that and had a hard time keeping my voice low as I replied, "Oh, are you kidding me? You think I'd ever harm an innocent person? And really, now is when you're going to get all protective of your city? Fine, let's get into it then. You really want to know why I'm here? You killed an innocent man."

239

He made what I assumed would be the same face if I tazed him, and he sputtered out, "No I didn't! You can't just say things like that!"

"You did," I reiterated, my tone harsh. "His name was Bill Greenwood. He was a father of two, and he died protecting his children."

His face softened, realization dawning on him. "The Nuckelavee?" he guessed.

"Yeah, round two," I confirmed.

He nodded somberly. "I see you got away alright," he observed.

"Wrong, I didn't get away; I triumphed. But it doesn't feel like much of a win considering I didn't get to Bill in time."

Kodran looked away from me and swore under his breath. "There's still my plan," he began, but his words lacked conviction.

"People still die that way, myself included. I'm trading Bill's life for the lives of others, and we both know that doesn't work for me."

"Just go back and get to Bill in time," he said soberly.

"What?" I asked.

"Yeah, go back. Do it, just this once," he repeated. "I know you're probably not supposed to mess with your own timeline or whatever, but—"

I laughed in spite of myself. "Do you think I'm a time traveler?" I asked.

"Yeah, something like that." His voice was meek, like he didn't have the answers, but was trying to push through the conversation anyway.

"You're a jerk," I said incredulously. "Is this just how you always are? This is why I hated you from the first time I even heard of you. You are far too comfortable with civilian death. You always justify it. Freyr or whoever was too strong to stand

up to, best not get in their way, right? The building was already
on fire, they were already as good as dead, no need to risk getting burned. The Valkyries have them marked; it's their fate to
die, there's nothing you can do. You know what you can do?
You can try! It might hurt, it might really hurt! It might even do
worse, but you can goddamn try to stick up for the little guy just
once when it's inconvenient. Jesus! Even now, you're willing to
fire a gun, unconcerned with who it might hit because someone
bigger than you ordered it, and because you can't see that far
ahead. But guess what? I'm telling you right now, I've seen who
it hits! And if innocent lives matter that much to you, or even at
all, you'll find another way. Or you'll tell Freyr to eat bugs the
next time he gives you an order. Or you'll just take responsibility
for your own crap for once, because you have to know deep
down that every bad thing that has happened to you since you
made your deal for immortality has been your fault. Stop letting
other people pay for your mistakes." I was infuriated at this
point, rambling without an end in sight, unable to stop. "I'm just
…I'm giving you a gift, do you see that? I'm telling you who
your stray bullet hits, just this once. I'm telling you what happens, so if you still go down this path, I'm not going to regret
what comes next."

There was a heavy silence in the air between us for a moment. I didn't think I'd spoken loud enough for anyone to hear,
but you never know.

Kodran finally spoke up, and asked, "You won't regret not
making it to that father in time?"

"No, there's nothing I can do about that now," I said, then
leaned across the table to meet his gaze and added, "I meant to
say, I won't regret what happens to you."

"So now you're threatening me?"

"Man, I shouldn't have to threaten you to do the right
thing!"

"But you are," he concluded. "So, what is it then? What are you, O fearsome and mysterious one, going to do to me?"

I leaned back, somehow even more fed up now, and asked, "Does it matter? Really?"

"It might, yeah," he said. "You're important enough to warrant Freyr ordering a hit on you, and you've apparently survived the first two incarnations of the Nuckelavee. Right, and you found my home and just wandered in, that's not supposed to happen. What else? You're friends with the only elf I've ever met who wasn't pledged to Freyr, and your small friend had knowledge of the Anvil of Brokkr that no mortal should have. Good information, too. There's a lot about you that doesn't add up. I've sensed your power, and it's, well, nothing. Maybe not nothing, but close. Next to nothing. I get the feeling that I'm looking at the tip of the iceberg with you, and I can't see beneath the water. There's a lot I don't know about you, but I know that it's dangerous. I don't like either of those facts. So, come on, tell me. What do you have in mind?"

Oh my god. I can't believe it took me this long to see it, but there it is. Kodran is afraid of me! I don't know if it's because I'm actually standing up to him, or if because I'm just that much of an unknown, or maybe both, but he's sweating me right now.

"There's only one way to find out for sure," I said evenly.

Kodran chuckled at that. "You don't actually know, do you?" he asked.

My chest felt heavy with the guilt of knowing that I was about to do something unforgivable, and I replied, "I know exactly what I'm going to do to you, and I really hope you don't make me do it. Because I know I'm going to have to cross a line to get there, and what I'll do to you is something I wouldn't wish on anyone. Please don't make me do this."

He stared at me, unblinking, his fingers drumming on the table unconsciously. "You're serious, aren't you?"

"Here's your cocoa, Kenny," Nancy chirped, seemingly appearing out of nowhere. She turned that smile toward me and asked, "You sure I can't get you a water or anything?"

"I'm sure, Nancy, I should be going soon," I said, flawlessly returning the smile. "But thank you!"

Nancy left, and Kodran was studying me now, unsure if I was just a really scary looking insect or a predator he'd made the mistake of getting too close to. "There's one thing I really need to know," he said cautiously. "Why can't I find you?"

"Did you look under your couch cushions?" I asked with a shrug.

"I mean it, I need to know this," he asked. "I've been scrying for millennia, longer even; I can find just about anyone. I might not be able to pinpoint someone, but, even with the best cloaks, I can still locate a general area; I'll, at the very least, circle on a region. With you and your friends, I get literally nothing. You don't exist. Not here, not in any of the nine realms. I would call you ghosts, but even ghosts are somewhere. Freyja herself couldn't hide someone that well. So how do you do it?"

"Is that actually a question you thought I would answer or ...?" I let the second half of that hang in the air.

"Yeah, you're right," he replied. "You probably don't know anyway; I might have been giving you too much—"

"Dude, save it," I said cutting him off. "Look, just do the right thing. Or don't. You've got over a decade to think about it, so take your time. In the meantime, pretend I wasn't here. You have a real woman with a very real problem coming in here, not a damsel in distress, so maybe keep your head in the game and actually hear what she has to say, and don't spend the whole conversation staring at her breasts. Everyone notices, and everyone is grossed out by it, okay? You're not sneaky, and you're old as balls. Like, the kind of balls that would make archeologists wonder if baseball was invented in ancient Egypt. Right, done with this all now. Bye."

I left him reeling. Kodran obviously had a lot more that he wanted to say, but now was the time to take my leave for a few reasons. First, I had no idea what sort of damage I'd already done to the story by being here, but if I could get out of here before the main stuff was supposed to happen, it might not be that bad. Second, and just as concerning, was the fact that the longer I spoke with Kodran, the more I might let something slip. I started to get pretty heated in there; I'd have to replay the conversation later on in my head. Not that any of it would matter soon, I felt like I was sprinting toward a conclusion with him one way or the other. Either he would call it off, or else...

I didn't want to think about the "or else." I wasn't lying when I threatened him, I had a solution to all of this, but I wasn't sure I'd be able to live with myself after. This would be something I would be forced to do, was something I was going to have to convince myself. Kodran was given an out, I reminded myself. He had the chance to change the story, to fight fate, just as I have. The future is never written in stone; we can make things better. He's going to make things better, or I'm going to make them worse.

When I was on the street, I decided that I didn't want to go home, at least not right away. Maybe it was just curiosity, but I wanted to see how this played out firsthand. See if the story changed, if Kodran stuck around to help like he was supposed to or if he'd go home to focus on the unknown. I'd feel pretty terrible if that happened, I'd hate to be the reason someone was abandoned in their time of need, but to be fair I hadn't expected to actually frighten Kodran, I came to appeal to him. And I guess perhaps stain his shirt.

The air was still stale and cold, and I dug my hands into my pockets as I walked across the road. The door didn't open behind me, which felt like a hopeful indicator that Kodran was going to stick around for a bit. There was an old hotel, kitty corner to the diner, and I sat on the little wall which separated the driveway from the street, just out of his view, but not really, and I waited, watching the customers and staff clean and rearrange the bits of mess until there was no trace of my entrance. I watched a customer leave, I watched another stop in just long enough to chat with Nancy and get a to-go order. I watched Kodran sit patiently.

"Penny for your thoughts?" an elderly man spoke from behind me, startling me for just an instant.

"Okay, putting me on the spot here, but how about these," I began. "Think outside the box, but also get out of that box, it's very cramped and wasn't meant to hold people. The customer is always someone who is trying to exchange money for goods or services. Listen to your heart, and if it begins to speak, call an exorcist. Before starting any medication, ask your doctor about the existence of sentient—"

"Okay, easy," the old man said. "I only have so many pennies."

"Hey man, you asked," I said, looking back at the diner.

He nodded in agreement, and said, "My own fault I suppose. May I sit?"

"Sure," I replied absently.

He sat and asked, "Are you waiting for someone?"

"Nah, I just like staring at diners until a Norman Rockwell moment happens spontaneously."

"You're an odd duck, aren't you?" he asked.

"Lucky duck," I replied without thinking, then added, "I don't know, maybe."

"You know, I know everyone in town," the old man said, and I turned to look at him as he began. He looked older than even his voice would have indicated. He was a Native American with stark white hair that was thinning to the point that it looked like gossamer, and his eyes that resembled the blue of a lake in winter were focused on me. "I've been here since the beginning, never left. I haven't seen you before, and I know that I would remember you. Passing through?"

"Yeah, something like that," I said, turning my attention back, watching with relief as a woman walked into the Cornerstone Cafe and sat opposite Kodran.

"Ah, I see," he said with understanding. "Friend of yours? Lover, perhaps?"

"Ugh." The disgust came out of me before I could stop myself. "No and double no."

The old man put his head back and laughed, a throaty sound with a smile that touched his eyes. "We have something in common! I never did like the man, he's not good for this town," he exclaimed. "Tell me, young woman, who are you?"

"Elana, pleased to meet you," I offered, just about ready to go. "And you are?"

"No one important," he replied. "I just manage the inn."

"Well, both of those statements can't be true," I said, standing up, satisfied there was nothing left for me to see. "You provide hospitality to travelers. Seems pretty important to me."

The old man made a gracious nod with his head, and said, "Thank you. On your way, then?"

"Looks like it, lots to do. Great meeting you," I said, not pressing for his name. He didn't want to give it, and I wasn't sure that I needed it.

"And you as well," he said standing. "I should get back to work; you never know when a stranger will need a place to rest."

He offered me a handshake, and I made a hurried excuse to not take it, something about coming down with something and offered a fist bump instead, which he accepted awkwardly. I began to walk away when he called out to me.

"Oh, Elana, don't forget," he said, and I turned back to see his cupped hand outstretched toward mine. I placed my palm under his, and he dropped a coin into it. "I promised you a penny. Safe travels, now."

I studied the coin for a moment, a worn, copper Indian head penny with the date 1864 on it. I looked up to thank the old man for the gift, but he was gone.

24

The way back wasn't any more arduous than taking a long walk on a hot day in a thick coat, so okay, it wasn't easy. Nothing tried to kill me though, and that was nice. Even the trolls didn't give me any hassle as I passed through their city. A couple of them gave me suspicious looks, either due to recent events, or the fact that I had magic, or maybe both; but most of them didn't do more to acknowledge me than give me a slight nod or gesture me though. I'm just glad none of them were offended that I didn't stop to try the local cuisine.

The doorway back into the shop wasn't touched either, which to be honest, I just guessed that something from The Knowing could enter through it, but either way, nothing had, and that was a relief. The instant I entered the darkened back room, I could hear the sounds of a crowded store, and I was reminded of the days when I'd feel a sense of panic over being late to work. I'd almost forgotten that this was still the week before Christmas, of course there would be a rush. I silently cursed myself for the fact that I'd left Claire to run things herself. Absentmindedly, I removed my book bag and jacket, and felt every drop of sweat that caused my clothes to cling to my skin, the slight breeze from a cracked window giving me a chill. I would have liked to change before walking out, but my clothes were all in my loft space, so there was nothing to do but make an entrance.

There must have been at least ten people in the shop that I could see, but at the sound of the door creaking, Claire spun around from her place at the cash register so fast that I was concerned she might fall over. Her face was a blend of astonishment and relief, but she turned back toward her customer and hurriedly finished the sale before announcing in a loud, declamatory tone that she needed everyone not to try to give her any money for the next five minutes.

"Are you okay? Where have you been?" Claire asked in a hushed, concerned whisper, walking me behind a row of books.

"I'm fine, thank you. Pretty hungry, and I could use a nap, but otherwise all good," I replied as casually as I could muster, trying to reassure her. "I'm sorry that I'm late back, my precision with time isn't always great. What time is it?"

"It's Thursday o'clock," she replied sternly.

"I haven't had a Wednesday in weeks!" I exclaimed in response.

"Not funny," she said in that voice that implied I didn't realize how serious the situation was.

I gave a nod of acknowledgment and replied, "No, you're right, but seriously, I've skipped the past two Wednesdays. That's concerning, right?"

"Yeah, probably, but you have bigger things to worry about, don't you?"

A thought suddenly occurred to me, and I asked, "Real quick! Where were we this weekend?"

Claire glanced over her shoulder and looking back whispered, "We probably shouldn't be talking about this now, but it involved a bridge and about nine hundred dollar's worth of damage to my van."

I felt deflated at that, and all I could manage in response was, "Oh."

Claire's nose turned up in curiosity at my response, and she asked, "Wait. Why would you ask that?"

"I thought I could change things if I just...forget it, I didn't accomplish anything." Disappointment grew in me as I thought about our conversation. I had thought maybe when Kodran didn't leave and spoke with that woman in the diner that maybe I had gotten through to him, that he'd just eventually be a better person, but nope. He still went through with it; he sent the Nuckelavee after me and Bill Greenwood was still dead.

"You went to see him alone?" she asked in astonishment.

"Not that it matters now, but yeah," I answered.

Claire sighed and considered that for a moment. "Okay, the last thing you need from me right now is a lecture, and besides, I'm lost on all this, so I wouldn't be the right person to give it anyway. Just, I don't know, grab a muffin or something and take a nap. You've got a big couple of days ahead of you, and I want you at your best."

I was tempted, but I said, "No to the nap, yes to the muffin. Honestly, I've missed an entire day and, holy crap, look how busy the store is! No, just let me get a quick change of clothes, and we can handle this together. The last thing I need right now is more sleep."

Claire chewed her lip for a moment and finally agreed. I wasn't sure if it was just a matter of not wanting to argue, being tempted for the sweet relief of an extra pair of hands around the shop, or simply respecting my wishes, but I was grateful that I didn't have to do anymore to convince her. There was no time for a shower, and I wasn't about to shower with a store full of customers anyway, but I figured that between the clean clothes and the application of most of my deodorant, I was probably presentable enough for the public.

The foot traffic didn't let up for a minute the entire day which was perfect for both Claire and myself. Claire needed the money, and I needed a distraction. It was good to keep my hands busy, receiving an assortment of wishes for merry or happy days, openly approving or silently judging the purchases of countless customers. Neither of us took a lunch break, and in fact, we stayed open an extra hour just to handle the additional sales. When the last people left the shop with their books in hand, grandparents who bought a stack of Dragonlance books for their grandson, a gift that I had to admit was pretty cool, but also made me wonder how old those books were, exactly; Claire locked the door behind them and looked ready to pass out.

"Come here," Claire said drowsily as she sat in one of the reading chairs. "I want to high five you, but I'd never make it to your side of the shop."

"Yeah, I can do that, but it's a one-way trip." I smiled and received the weakest of all possible high fives as I sat across from her.

Claire sighed heavily and tried to adjust her back against the fluffy seat. "For as glad as I am that you survived your trip, I am equally grateful that you made it back in time to help me out in the shop today. That was insane, right?"

"Dude, seriously," I agreed. "Since when did everyone start buying books?"

"Don't question it, enjoy the literate population while we can."

"I can get behind that," I chuckled.

Claire shut her eyes for a moment, and as I thought she might be ready to take a nap right then and there, she said, "Let's talk about you for a minute."

I shifted in my seat as well, and without seeing a way out, I said, "Okay."

"Don't think for a second that I don't appreciate everything you've been trying to do for here lately," she began. "But are you doing okay? I need to know that you're taking care of yourself."

"You know me, always hurtling toward an endless void filled with danger and kittens," I joked.

"Okay, but you're not though," Claire replied, her voice understanding. "All of the danger stuff is very new, at least from my perspective. You've been a shut in forever, at least that I've seen. You like what you like, and that's cool. I ride a motorcycle, Olivia goes on crazy hikes; even Ann stands in front of a bunch of strangers and makes fun of herself. You read. You watch TV."

"I camped the Hall H line four nights in a row that one time, I practically lived there," I interjected. "I can be rugged."

"Well now, yeah! You fight monsters! I'm still kind of barely accepting that there are actual monsters." Just saying that out loud seemed to make her somehow even more tired. "I watched you fight one. That thing is supposed to be unbeatable, right? You've done it twice, I know you'll find a way to do it again, it's just that I'm worried that this is all going to come too quickly for you, or that it already has. If it's not this, I think something else is going to catch up to you."

My hands pressed hard into my face, and I moved them up my face and to the back of my head, feeling the tension move through my entire body. "You want the truth, Claire?" She nodded in response, and I said, "Everything hurts, and I'm borderline anxious almost every second of the day. I just want to get through this, and I have to believe that one day I'll be free. My head is just, ugh, tight. All the time. And I guess The Knowing has been healing me, but it's not doing anything about the stress. Look at this." I showed Claire the back of my hands, pointing to the raised blood vessels. "This isn't normal! I'm probably going to have a stroke! I'm pretty much only sleeping when I'm too tired to stay awake, and for as much as I'd like to complain about all of this, I can't. Because it's all going to happen one way or the other, and no amount of whining is going to stop it, it's just going to make me insane. I have people relying on me; people can be hurt or worse if I screw up. Lucia might die this weekend, and I think maybe she hates me now? I don't even know. I'm trying to stop Olivia from getting herself killed as well, and I have no idea how that's going to work out. I probably won't even make it to Sunday, which might have been what the Aos Si's entire prophecy might have meant."

"Wait, what?" Claire asked.

Everything is terrible.

"Nothing, it's probably nothing." I tried to recover, but I knew instantly that Claire wouldn't let this go.

"There's a whole lot of what you said that I'm fairly sure you haven't shared with me, and I don't really think there's time to let you decide when I get to know. So out with it."

So I did. No real use hiding it anymore anyway, I suppose. I told her about what the Aos Si had shown me, or let me believe, I didn't know what to think there and wouldn't know for sure without another conversation with him. I let her know all about the baby Gardeners, and my vision of Lucia and what it meant to her when I didn't come for her. None of this was anything that I actually wanted to tell her, but as I did, I couldn't help but feel relieved that I was making a huge mistake. Or at least getting one out of the way.

Claire had a far different reaction than Logan. She just sat there. I sat there with her, afraid to break the silence. She stood up after a minute or so and began to pace.

"Help me understand something," she said finally, but she didn't continue right away. I began to count the seconds after a moment. Eight, nine, ten, eleven… "I don't know Lucia, I never did. But why do you feel responsible for her? Because you knew her when you were young? Because she had a hard life? Because she gave you this power?"

"Maybe all of it," I replied, thinking about the question.

"None of that is on you," Claire said. "You made a friend, but she wasn't the only one. You have other people now who care about you and rely on you. Her parents checking out, her having whatever it is she has in her, that's rough, but you couldn't have affected that in any way at any time. And her sharing that power with you, it sounds like it was well intentioned, but you never asked for it. At best it was a gift; you're not obligated to throw your life away for her now."

"I'm not just going to let her die though," I said. "Whatever else, even if she's not my friend, I'm still hers. I'd do the same for you or any of us."

"I know you would, and that's probably the most admirable thing about you, but I don't get why you're so convinced you have to do this alone."

I sniffed at that. "Do you have a hidden army I could borrow that I don't know about?"

"Okay, so I don't really know anything about your whole world or any of it, but I'm looking at this from just a practical standpoint. Resources, that kind of thing. My working theory is that both the Ashy—"

"Aos Si," I corrected.

"Yeah, that thing," Claire continued. "Both it and the Gardeners are right. And maybe so are the folks who want to abstain. Or none of them are. You have all of these mysterious, mystical forces and they all have different answers. And take the unknown elements out of it, like prophecy or whatever, and what are you left with? A date, a time, where your friend will be. So, think of it in more sciencey terms. Everyone feels they have one shot at this because it's a once in a long-time phenomenon, like a total solar eclipse. You can't see it from everywhere, and your window for it is pretty short. And yeah, maybe something terrible will happen to her, but maybe it won't. It seems to me like you need to just pick a team and hope for the best."

"You're kidding, right? Last I checked there wasn't a team interested in saving her life."

"There doesn't have to be, does there? Lie your ass off! You just have to get close enough, and, well, I don't think you can on your own. Look, when, not if, we take down that monster on Saturday—" as Claire said that, I felt a twinge of guilt for not letting her in on my plan, but that was absolutely off limits—"you simply won't be ready to go fight like, literally, everyone else. Jason very nearly killed us earlier this year. Bres very well could have if he wanted to. You're going to jump into the middle of a battle with potentially all of them? Come on, Elana, what part of that makes sense?"

It was something to consider for sure, and I had to admit that outside of the trolls, I didn't have a lot planned. I was really kind of hoping for a *fog of war* sort of thing, and then just sort of improvising. I know that's something that I probably rely on too much, and my friend's life deserves a better plan, but how do you come up with a strategy for that sort of chaos? I didn't have a lot of time to consider it because, as I was thinking about what to say, I heard a knock at the front door.

"Hold that thought, I need to let Olivia in," Claire said, walking to the front of the store. "She's been texting me all day; I thought we could all grab dinner."

If I had a sixth sense for knowing when I was about to be busted for reasons that were entirely my fault, this was a horrible time to find out about it. As soon as she said that, I had a bad feeling for what was coming next, and it was too late to do anything about it.

The door opened, and I saw Olivia walk inside like she was ready for a fight.

"Hey, Claire," she said briefly before marching over to me. "Yo, Elana, what the hell?"

"Olivia, listen—"

"No, you listen," she interrupted. "Did you think Logan wasn't going to tell me? Seriously?"

"I am trying to—"

"Help, right, I got that." Olivia was nearly shouting now. "By trying to decide what I get to do with my life? By going back to Kodran without telling anyone? God, after all of this, after everything we've all done to be there for you, you're still not learning anything, are you? You don't get to decide—"

"Stop!" I yelled loud enough to make everyone jump. "I am so sick of this! Do you get it? This isn't something you can handle! It's not something I can handle, but I don't have a choice in this! You do!"

I was fuming at this; the stress must have gotten to me because I had taken this conversation to a height I didn't know how to get back down from. "I get that you all want to be involved, and I appreciate it, but do you realize how frustrating it is trying to keep you alive? Whether or not it's true, or a vision of the future, or even an outright lie, I've watched you die! Do you get that too? I have watched you burn until there was nothing left. And honestly? I don't know if it was worth it. You definitely die, so someone else maybe doesn't die. And god, every time I time I think about it, every time I close my eyes..."

I trailed off and sat back down; the room was deathly quiet for a moment. "I don't know what's going to happen; I just know that I have to try. But I don't want anyone else to get hurt. Do you want to be mad at me forever? Fine. It's worth it if you make it out of this alive."

"This is tough for all of us, but good intentions or no, you are not making my decisions for me," Olivia said carefully. "So, I'll make this quick. I'll be there for you on Saturday, and if you tell me otherwise, fine. That one is on you. But I'll be there for both you and Lucia after that, and you don't get a say in that because it's about more than just you. Do whatever you have to do, I'll be back tomorrow. I'm suddenly not that hungry."

Olivia marched right back out without another word, and I didn't feel much like eating either.

25

Chalsarda lead me through the grounds of the estate of the Aos Si, and for once I felt a sense of unease about it. Part of that was due to how unusually quiet Chalsarda was with me. Unless we were training or in immediate danger, she usually had the comfortable presence of an old friend, but it was something else. The atmosphere felt oppressive. Call it anxiety, or a sixth sense, or generic dollar store brand intuition, but I didn't feel safe in what should have likely been the safest place possible for me. I searched Chalsarda's face for any kind of indication, but I wasn't reading anything past her pensive expression.

As we strolled through the grounds, I took a chance and asked, "Hey, so, is everything okay?"

"I think we both know it is impossible for everything to simultaneously be okay." She smiled brightly very suddenly at that and offered a wink, and I knew in a moment that something was off. I recognized what it looked like to see her slip into party mode, she'd been trained in etiquette after all, but her answer was disarming and non-committal, and the smile was not genuine.

"If something was wrong, I want you to know that you could tell me," I offered, hoping to crack the facade.

"I appreciate that. You are my friend, and it brings me joy knowing that I can speak openly with you when appropriate," she replied, emphasizing the last word in that sentence.

We walked a bit more, and didn't enter through the front door this time, but instead walked around to the side of the home. Quieter, I said, "Call me paranoid, but if I wanted to turn around and leave right now, would you allow me to?"

Chalsarda's eye went wide with concern as she stopped suddenly, making eye contact with me and almost imperceptibly shaking her head no. Her voice remained charming and pleasant though as she said, "What a delightfully odd question! I know things are stressful for you at the moment, but after your chat with my master, I am to return home with you to prepare for tomorrow's battle. I don't believe it will take long."

I decided to stop asking questions. Maybe we were being listened to, maybe not, but something was up. I had to wrap my head around the fact that Chalsarda couldn't lie, but she was blatantly letting it be known that I wasn't entirely safe. I knew of only one person who could possibly tell her what to do, specifically detain me or worse if I tried to leave, and he was the one I was on my way to see right now. Still, I had trusted her with my life more than once now, and she hasn't let me down yet, and besides, part of her answer was that she was to take me home after this, and I believed that was her subtle way of letting me know that I'd walk away from this.

"I trust you…are right," I said to her, allowing a brief pause for emphasis, before continuing. "The Aos Si can get kind of busy, right? It's cool that he even sees me at all."

Chalsarda nodded and showed me a smile that was one of understanding and concern. My Spidey-senses were still on high alert, but I was confident that whatever the danger actually was, it wasn't from Chalsarda herself. So, the Aos Si didn't intend to kill me, nor did he plan to keep me captive. I knew both of these things from the fact that I was to return later. So, was he planning to attack me, teach me a lesson somehow? Was it just that I had to see something? Hear something? Know something? I didn't feel like I had enough information to figure this out, but to continue asking questions might put my friend in danger. I'm tied to the Aos Si in my own way, but I recognize that it's far different for Chalsarda. She is bound to him by some sense of duty, and it felt like if he gave her an order, she would have no choice but to obey. I witnessed it the first time with Kodran. Even being asked to go against his orders began to hurt her, and I wasn't sure what he could have done to her to make that happen. The implications of that sort of power made my skin crawl.

I reached out and gave her hand a small squeeze. She was startled for a second, but she returned the reassuring gesture as we continued. No knowledge had passed between us, that wasn't what I was after. I just wanted her to know that everything would be okay.

Around the back of the house, and through a twisty series of turns through a garden that I would have been for sure lost in on my own, we came upon a small greenhouse that looked barely large enough to be an outhouse. "Down at the bottom of these stairs you'll find him," Chalsarda said, opening the door to reveal a winding stairwell. "I'll be waiting here when you return."

That she wasn't coming with me wasn't my favorite news, but it didn't change anything. I offered my thanks as I made my way down, taking each step very carefully. I'd never been back here before; I didn't even know this place existed. Right now, two people in all of existence knew where I was, and one of them was a literal god.

Nothing to worry about, right?

The light became dimmer as I descended, and just as I was beginning to worry about the climb back up and falling down in equal measure, I saw a light coming from a room as I made another turn down the odd staircase. The light was enough to illuminate the way, but not the surrounded areas. It was cold and musky, with dampness in the air that told me there was little in the way of a man-made structure. All of this, with the exception of the stairs, was wet soil.

I could see into the room now, it looked like a cramped study, only the shelves were made of hardened adobe and held containers of liquids, and roots, and god knew what else. The books that were present had not been handled with care, and there were just as many loose papers as there were books. In the center of it all, the Aos Si stood next to a thick iron hoop, maybe eight feet in diameter, and it lit up the room with a pale blue glow.

"Can you feel it, Elana?" the Aos Si asked without looking at me, his eyes shut, his neck craned back. He had the smile and contented voice of a man who needed nothing else. "It's coming back. *They're* coming back! Oh, but can't you just feel it?"

I felt something, but I couldn't tell you for sure what it was, only that it was powerful. It was unlike anything I'd ever felt before, different than Freyja's power, different than what I'd felt in Kodran's world. I tried not to focus on it, completely fine with not drawing its attention, assuming it was something I should worry about. Better to worry about it and not have had to, than to not worry about it and realize that I should.

"Is it weird that whatever I'm feeling is making me nervous?" I asked carefully. My pulse began to quicken just acknowledging the energy in response.

"When you accomplish great things, when you're in uncharted waters, anxiety is a natural response," the Aos Si replied. "It is important not to lose your focus in those final moments. It is important to remember that you feel uncertain because nothing has ever been certain, only probable. And when you challenge the unknown, when you become a pioneer, you no longer have the mistakes of those before you to learn from. There's no roadmap, no handbook; only you. And you will succeed, or you won't, based on your own merits. Do you understand?"

"Are we talking about me right now or are we talking about you?"

The Aos Si opened his eyes and lowered his head. "It is a trait that we currently share, of course," he said thoughtfully. "But my path is not your concern, not yet at least."

"There's something I need to know, right away," I replied, hoping to keep the conversation on the track I needed it to be. "Did you intentionally trick me? Is Olivia actually fated to die?"

"No," the Aos Si said plainly.

"No? No to which one?" I asked.

"Neither," he said. "I mean, no, I am not going to answer questions just because you ask them. I may be your guardian, but that doesn't mean I am your servant. I do not take orders from you, and you should understand that by now."

"What I understand is, that despite not being able to lie, you've found quite a few ways of not being honest with me," I retorted.

The Aos Si stiffened at that, and said, "I have done much for you, more than is required of me. You would do well to consider that when speaking to me."

"I've been thinking about that," I told him, walking around the ring toward him as I did. "Why is that?"

He didn't move as I made my way toward him. "Elana, within you, is the potential to be a great hero, but that path is never easy. Heroes don't just inherit that title; they earn it with tragedy, and courage, and blood. Sometimes their own, sometimes others. But for every hero, there are a hundred would-be heroes who never make it. They fall or back down when their journey becomes too difficult. I have taken it upon myself to see you reach your potential."

"Is that why you haven't helped me against the Nuckelavee?" I asked. "Because I need to face this challenge on my own, on my path to becoming a hero?"

"You can't expect me to fight every battle for you," he replied.

"And see, that's not an answer," I replied. "You've saved me in the past when I've faced an unbeatable challenge, so I know it's not a matter of letting me fail. And you've allowed Chalsarda to fight by my side against the Nuckelavee, so I know it's not that I must face it alone. So it's something else."

"You've defeated it twice now, without my help I might add," he countered. "And I am tasked with protecting you. If I were so inclined, I could keep you here until the Mither O' the Sea returned in the summer to reclaim the Nuckelavee. Do you know why I haven't done that?"

"Enlighten me," I replied.

"Because you can win. Because it is not your time to fall. Because of the lives it would take. Because you'd never forgive me for the damage it caused."

"And that is important to you? That I respect you?"

"Of course," the Aos Si said sincerely. "I value you and wish to see you protected far more than my duty to you requires."

I was upon him now. I stared him down for a few seconds, searching his ethereal eyes.

"But that's not the only reason, is it?" I asked. "Come on, dude; you know where I'm from. Los Angeles isn't a city; it's a bunch of tiny cities all inconveniently spread apart from each other, pretending to be one city. And if there's one thing I've known my entire life, it's when people make excuses for never being able to get to you, making you always come to them. And that's exactly what you've been doing since the day I've met you, isn't it?"

The Aos Si didn't answer, so I answered for him. "You can't visit me. Chalsarda can, presumably other creatures from The Knowing can, but for all your power, you can't travel to my world, can you?"

I refused to let him break eye contact with me, and even as he let the silence become uncomfortable, I could see he was looking for an out.

Finally, he just stated, "I don't have to answer that."

"I think you just did."

"Fine," he snapped. "You're right. I can't leave this place and visit your world. Congratulations, detective."

"Why hide that from me?" I shouted. "Why not just tell me that from day one? I would have understood."

"I don't believe you would," he countered.

I was getting worked up now, and I continued to shout, and demanded, "Stop making excuses!"

"I was protecting you!" he roared in a voice closer to a lion than a human.

"Oh, you are so full of—!" I stopped myself and thought it through for a second. "No, you're telling the truth. That was a definitive statement. You really believe you were protecting me by not telling me. Why can't you travel to my world?"

"You're the reader, you tell me," he said, his voice tired. "Think about my history."

"I still don't know who you are," I replied.

The Aos Si settled his jaw, and definitively said, "No, and you won't know until I decide it is the right time to tell you."

"You could have just asked for my help, unless there's nothing I can do." I was calming down a bit at his revelation. "Could I? Help, that is."

"I have been alive for longer than you can comprehend," the Aos Si began. "I've experienced difficulty you don't even know is possible, at least not yet. And I've gained the wisdom one only gains by working through that sort of trouble. Not asking for your help is a deliberate action on my part."

His answer hurt. He didn't say that I was incapable of helping him, he just didn't want it.

"And everything else? Olivia? Freyja? The Nuckelavee? When are you going to give me answers?"

"I'm asking you to trust me," he asked sadly.

I sighed at that. "You're betting my life tomorrow that I can do what no one else has ever done. You've shown me the death of my best friend and provided me with no context. It's a lot to ask."

"I want you to survive tomorrow. I want what's best for so many," he said. "So I will ask for your trust."

"You can ask, but I'm not ready to give it. Not yet."

His lips pursed at that, and he nodded briefly. "What can I do to earn it?" he asked.

"You can start by answering some questions for me," I said, removing a fist sized hunk of gold from my bag. "Starting with this."

"A Singing Stone," he said fervently, a hunger flashing in his eyes so briefly that I barely noticed. "Well. Someone is trying to impress you with fancy gifts. Freyja, I presume? One of her domains is gold; I hope you're not too impressed. It's an elegant gift, but it's not like she gave you a magic absorbing rod or anything."

I blinked at that. "Are you jealous?"

The Aos Si inhaled sharply through his nostrils, and ignoring my question, put his hands behind his back and said, "I can offer you new information of your Singing Stone, but in return, I would ask—"

"I also brought you this," I interrupted, reaching into my bookbag and producing half a gallon of cream in a tightly sealed mason jar. "And I don't intend to offer you anything else today."

I had gambled that the Aos Si wouldn't let me leave here without every advantage for my confrontation tomorrow, but he'd also ask something in return. The cream was important to him for some reason, and I hoped that it would placate him and get me out of here without owing any more favors.

He eyed the jar for a moment, and continued, "What that is, Elana, is your key to surviving the Nuckelavee. To face it headlong, however, would be suicide."

"That wasn't my plan."

"Coming from you, I find that difficult to believe," the Aos Si said suspiciously. "And just what is your plan?"

"My gut says that if I told you, you might try and stop me," I replied. "Maybe we can focus on the Singing Stone?"

"Very well," he agreed. "May I see her? You have my word, I will return her to you."

I was uncomfortable about handing it over to him, it was by all accounts the sort of things that gods themselves fought over, and for some dumb reason I had it out in my hands all alone with a god, but he'd given his word, and if he just wanted to take it from me he could have. Cautiously I extended it to him, and with cupped hands, he accepted it from me as if he were handling a newborn.

The damp, earthy room began to inexplicably echo with the sound of a gentle song sung by the Aos Si in a language I'd never heard with a voice that could not be human. He slowly began to rock it back and forth as he did, gracefully walking it around in a semi-circle as if he'd engaged in a dance.

"Well, that's fine, because I'm not looking to possess you," he cooed to it, and for a split second, I thought he was speaking to me. "There is someone else who needs your help far more than I."

The Aos Si turned his attention me, and asked in a voice usually reserved for the parents of newborns, "Did you know that she likes to be sung to? You will need to do that more."

I just watched dumbfounded as he went back to his tender coaxing. "Without you, she'll die, you know. And your mother would be quite cross, wouldn't she? Yes, she would. There, there, you wouldn't want to disappoint mother."

This went on for several minutes, until he gently passed it—well, I guess *her*—back to me. I put the Singing Stone away in my bag, and the Aos Si said quietly, "Take her outside every so often, sing to her and encourage her to sing. She will be quite useful to you, though I assume by now you know the dangers of her overuse."

"I only know that I shouldn't rely on it...umm, her...too much," I admitted.

"That is all you need to know for the moment," he conclud-ed. "But you need to have faith in her as well. You've only tapped into her when you've been afraid, and it hurts her feel-ings. Give it a try sometime; you might be surprised at what she can do."

"Why can't I hear her?" I asked.

"Because she doesn't want you to hear her yet," he an-swered simply. He chuckled softly and added, "This conversa-tion didn't go the way I thought it would."

I paused at that, and asked, "What were you expecting?"

"Something else," he answered carefully. "You should go. If you'd like my advice? You'll have many challenges in the near future, and while I believe in you, nothing is promised to you. So tell your loved ones goodbye. Say anything that you feel must be said now. The last thing I want to see for you is the inevitable moment where you fail and lose someone, and you aren't prepared for it. To have that later moment stolen from you...I do not wish that for you."

The Aos Si looked unbelievably sad as he said that, and I turned to leave, feeling less sure about anything than I had in a long time.

I arrived behind the Book's End with Chalsarda, immediately noticing that slight chill in the air that would usually portend rain and a temporary end to the unending warmth of Los Angeles. The sun had gone down long before we returned, and my friend had remained silent the whole time. I didn't care to push her, knowing what I did now. She had been worried about something, and I suspected it had to do with the glowing ring under the garden, a location which had been well hidden by the Aos Si. The concern didn't leave her when we arrived, but the silence ended the second we made it back.

"Elana, please forgive me, I wasn't able to speak earlier!" The words spilled out Chalsarda almost too fast to understand. "Are you alright?"

"I'm fine, are you okay?" I asked just as quickly. "You had me worried back there!"

"I apologize, I didn't know if he was listening, and there are still things that I am not allowed to say besides." She seemed relieved now, like someone who was just out of harm's way from a recent near-accident. "What did you see down there?"

"You've never been down there?" I asked.

Chalsarda shook her head. "I am forbidden, but I have my suspicions."

"There's something down there like a study, or work space, or something, but it's not like, straight down," I said trying to recall the details. "It's barely lit, I don't think I could give you a location relative to the rest of his home."

"And what was in the study?" she asked.

"Can we talk about this inside?" I asked. "I have my coat, but you have to be cold."

"If you don't mind, I'd like to speak in private," Chalsarda replied, looking around nervously. "For their safety. The fewer who know, the better."

"I understand," I agreed. "Though I don't know how dangerous this knowledge is. There were clay shelves, moldy books, and random pages. Bottles and jars filled with reagents or whatever Celtic gods keep in jars. Weird thing though, he had this big metal ring in the center of the room, maybe the size of a kiddie pool. And it glowed blue, lit up the whole room. He seemed so pleased by it, too. Not quite worship, but something close to it."

The worry in Chalsarda's eyes seemed to intensify as she asked, "Did he say what it was?"

"No, but he asked me if I could feel it. He didn't say what he meant by that, but I did feel something, maybe dread," I explained carefully. "He stated that they were coming back."

"Creators, no," Chalsarda trembled. "Try to remember, what were his exact words?"

"Just that," I told her. "They're coming back."

"Elana, I think I know what he's doing," she said hurriedly. "He's going to—"

Chalsarda winced hard as her lips clamped shut involuntarily. I reached out to comfort her, to put a hand on her shoulder, and she gripped my forearm faster than I could see her move with a strength that nearly made me shout with surprise. I recovered from the initial shock long enough to decide to endure the pain quietly, and after a moment I began to stroke her arm and softly whispered, "Hey, it's okay, I don't need to know. Don't tell me."

Her gripped softened, and I began to massage it at once, trying to circulate the blood where she held me.

"Thank you," she said, her eyes shut for a second to adjust. "Elana, you have to listen to me. I do not believe he will allow me to return once he gets what he wants. I can stay here for a while, but once he realizes that I'm not going back, he will employ other methods of retrieving me that will be less than pleasant. So I need to show you something vital, and I need you to pay close attention."

"Of course," I said, watching her produce what looked like a large seafoam green piece of chalk from one of her pouches, and as it moved through the moonlight, it appeared to have swirls dance across it for just a moment.

"I cannot move the way you do," Chalsarda began, holding the chalk-like item up to the light. "Very few can. And while I cannot travel to the many worlds that you do, I can travel anywhere in this world or within The Knowing that I can imagine, which is to say I've likely seen almost none of it."

Chalsarda flashed me a brief smile at that, but her heart clearly wasn't in the right place for jokes. "That's amazing!" I told her sincerely. "So much of The Knowing is uncharted for me. Moving off the path I create, even for a moment, I could—"

"You could do so much more than you realize, and in time, if we all live that long, you will make my trinket obsolete," she finished for me. "This is adamantine, treated with the blood of a Kapre, and tempered with the heat of a dying star. Or so I'm told. What I know is that it is indestructible, and even the knowledge of its existence can put its owner in danger, which is why I would appreciate it greatly if you didn't discuss this with anyone. Very few people know of it, one of them would be the Aos Si who gave it to me."

"He just gave this to you?" I asked.

Chalsarda shook her head. "It is rare that those like him give away anything without a cost attached. There are those who would pay dearly for this, and well, that's exactly what I did. It is a deal I will likely regret the rest of my life. So, any questions?"

"A billion, I think," I replied, trying to keep up all the pieces in my head that were clicking into place. "What's a Kapre? Isn't adamantine just literary shorthand to mean super hard? How did they get it out of a dying star, and oh! Who are 'they'?"

"Wish granting tree elementals, it's a real material, and I'm holding it, and then I don't know about the last two," she replied. "Any relevant questions?"

I wasn't sure what constituted a relevant question, but I asked, "How does it work?"

Chalsarda knelt down, and with one end of the adamantine bar, she tapped it on the pavement, causing a series of cracks about the size of my hand to form on the ground. "Without instruction, it's just a remarkably dense piece of metal. But when you think about where you would like to go or what you would like to see, you then use it to write the first words that you hear in your mind, and a path will open to it."

"Not that this thing isn't awesome," I said, kneeling down to run a finger over the cracks. "But what's the catch? These things always tend to have a drawback."

She considered this for a second, and said, "For one thing, if you travel somewhere, I hope you plan on staying for a while due to how long it takes to recharge."

"So no popping to China for a quick lunch and returning before anyone notices?" I asked.

"I'm afraid not," she replied, handing it to me for examination. "And for another, it loses potency the more it has been seen. So it is important that it's very existence remain a secret."

"The Gardeners know about it." I recalled the text, and somehow Roger had been aware.

"I know every person who has seen it, that is part of its power," Chalsarda replied with another nod. "Roger and some of the others might know that I have a tool, that is all."

"So why would you show me this?" I asked. "If I understand correctly, you've just intentionally weakened your gift, that doesn't make any sense."

Chalsarda shrugged. "You can call it a show of faith and friendship. I would say that this is very important to me, and I would be devastated if I were ever to lose it. I would be deeply indebted to anyone who returned it to me. I'll let you think on that while I go inside to see how the others are feeling."

She abruptly stood up and entered the back door of the shop before I could say a word; I was still holding her prize. I understood at once what she meant. The Aos Si wants to control the situation, going forward, and Chalsarda is making a huge sacrifice to make sure I have a trump card. The fact that she felt this was a necessary step gave me pause. Something bad was on the horizon, and somehow everyone just expected me to survive to see it happen. The Aos Si wants me to believe in him, to trust him, but I'm becoming increasingly worried that I won't be able to.

I sighed and made sure the adamantine was secure in my bag before following Chalsarda inside. I was stunned to see everyone was there, the whole crew, playing some sort of card game in the middle of the store as far as I could tell. Olivia walked right up to me, and before I could say anything, she embraced me in a tight hug.

"What's happening here?" I asked, suddenly anxious. "Is this an intervention? Is this the ending of Big Fish? Are you all Big Fishing me?"

"We're supporting you, idiot," Olivia said, choking back a tear. "I'm not happy with you, but I'm not walking out on you either.

One by one, everyone stood up to walk over and hug me. While incredibly surreal and uncomfortable, it was also heart-warming to see that everyone I cared for cared enough for me to stick around. It was also heartbreaking to realize they couldn't help and that none of them understood that.

"We were wrong to let you face this alone," Teague offered with her hug.

Jason grinned like an idiot, and said, "I just don't want to be left out of the story."

"You're stronger with us than without us," Claire said warmly.

"I'm not a big hugger, but, uh," Ann replied anxiously hugging me. "Okay, yeah, I'm not letting you die alone."

"I don't think you know how to lose." Logan smiled. "I know you can do this, and I will help however I can."

Chalsarda gripped me tightest of all, and given recent events, she might have had more reason than any of us to believe this was the end. As she released me, she said softly, "You once told me that everything was possible, even magic. And yet it is said that the Nuckelavee is an impossible foe. I can't imagine what you'll do to defeat it, but I think one way or the other you will prove history itself to be incorrect. You will see this through."

It was a lovely gesture, but as everyone stood back and watched me, I felt more ready to vomit than explode with love and gratitude. Not that I didn't want to reciprocate, I just really didn't feel comfortable being blindsided like this.

"Okay, so…uh…thank you?" I offered, trying to come up with something worthy of the attention.

"You're welcome!" Jason answered.

My cheeks flushed and were hot all of a sudden. I took off my coat and bag, hoping that might help, but it didn't. "Jesus. Okay, umm, huddle up," I said getting out of the doorway and to a more central part of the room. "I appreciate this, really, but what the hell are you all doing here? And since when am I the huddle up person?"

"You know why we're here," Claire said firmly. "We're here to help."

"Okay, but how?" I asked. "Anyone? You're not all planning to go with me, right? That's crazy. You could literally die, and I don't want that for any of you. For the—it will be Christmas in two days! I don't have family outside of all of you, but I know for a fact most of you have places to be! This thing, this demon or whatever, I don't have a choice. If I don't face it, people die—"

"And if you face it alone, you might die," Logan interjected.

"Maybe, and I really don't want that, but what if it's you?" I asked the group. "How do I explain that to your families? Your other friends?"

"Hopefully not alone," Jason replied.

I took in a breath, trying to get my frustration under control. "This isn't a game! If I die? It sucks, but you know, whatever. But all of you? Every single one of you is going to accomplish big things in your life, you all have every reason in the world to stay out of this."

"Oh, stop it!" Olivia nearly shouted. "Seriously, shut up with this. I'd call you a hypocrite if I thought you actually believed any of the crap you're going on about."

"Of course I believe it!" I fumed. "Chalsarda is the only one of us here who can actually fight, and no offense," I said glancing at her. "But I don't know what a thousand of her could do against what I'm about to face! Given enough time we all might be useful, but—"

"I'm not talking about that, and you know this," Olivia said, cutting me off. "You're telling all of us, right now, with a straight face that it doesn't matter if you die? You're saying that? Elana, I've never met someone in my life who believes more than you how important everyone is. You've personally saved my life, more than once, and you've been willing to break the universe and piss off gods to keep saving people whose names you don't even know. And on top of that, everyone in this room has a history with you! Are you really trying to tell us that your life is somehow worth less than ours?"

"That's not what I'm saying," I tried to reply.

"We know what you're saying," Teague said diplomatically. "We understand that you don't want to see us hurt, but why is that more valid than all of us not wanting to see you hurt? Because someone else wants to hurt you specifically? That's not a good reason; it never will be. Friends are there for each other, that's just what it means to be a friend."

I sighed. "You're not wrong, but it's more than that. This creature, I've seen what it can do, I know what it's capable of. It could wipe out the entire city if it wanted to, and not a thing anyone could do would stop it. And the two I fought were nothing compared to the one coming for me tomorrow. You just don't understand."

"We understand plenty," Jason spoke up. "I mean, you told me vampires exist, and I'm going to be terrified of the dark forever now, and that's just one of the many things I'll never be strong enough to fight. I mean, if a vampire wanted to kill me, that would be it. I would just be dead because, let's be honest, no vampire is turning me, I'd be a worthless vampire. I'm not even a throwaway vampire that gets killed by Blade in a nightclub, those vampires are all leather clad, and understand club music, and how to order drinks, and that is just not me at all, but yes, I'm hearing it now, the point! It doesn't matter if it's this, or a goblin, or a yeti, or some invisible wailing spirit with teeth made out of bones and hate; any of it is more than enough to kill us. But not you, you keep making it through, and we don't want to lose you. So we're going to stand with you."

My friends are the sweetest idiots on the planet.

Okay. All right, they're not going to stop, are they? "Fine. I get it. Let me just see if I understand this, and then I'll shut up about it." I asked, "You're all determined to fight a demon with me, knowing full well that if you get in its way, it will murder you without blinking just to get to me, and it almost certainly will because I have no idea how to stop it. Does that sound right?"

"Afraid so, dude," Ann replied. "You're stuck with us."

I threw my hands up and sat down. "Then I won't argue. You're all free to do what you want. Thank you, sincerely. It means everything to me that you all care about me that much."

Claire moved toward me and began to rub my shoulder. "Anyone of us would do the same for anyone here," she said. "That's just the sort of group you've attracted."

"So what's the plan?" Teague asked. "This is kind of my first monster fight, so what are we doing?"

"For now, we're all getting some sleep," I answered wearily. "In the morning we just start driving north. I doubt we can make Albion again, but there is any number of secluded beaches between here and there, so we just need to keep an eye on the clock. If there's nothing else, you need to get ready for tomorrow, find a chair, or use my bed, or whatever you need to sleep."

Everyone seemed content with the answer and offered me small tokens of reassurance as they settled in. I climbed up to my loft, taking my bookbag with me, and grabbed a couple of key items, shoving them inside. I made myself look busy, absently looking through books or sorting through junk until one by one most of my friends had turned in. When only Claire, Ann, and Chalsarda remained awake, I slipped on my coat, asked for Chalsarda's help with getting something out of my car. Claire and Ann didn't so much as blink at the lie, which made me feel extra awful.

Chalsarda, for her part, saw right through it as we stopped at Big Sister.

"You're leaving, aren't you?" she asked.

"Absolutely," I replied, the word thick in my mouth. "You heard them. They're all willing to die tomorrow, and I can't have that."

"And you're not taking me, are you?"

I looked at her for a moment, not wanting to answer. "I can't," I said finally, knowing it was true, but still feeling it was an excuse. "I only see one way out of this, and if you were there, or even if I just told you, you'd try and stop me. This gets said all too often, but this time it's true. I have to do this alone."

My friend nodded at that. "You will come back. I believe in you. Where are you going?"

"Well, if I tell you that, you won't be able to tell them that I said I was driving to Albion," I replied. "So you can tell them that I told you this: Chalsarda, I am driving to Albion to fight the Nuckelavee."

"I understand," she said knowingly.

"Great. Now if you'll excuse me, I'm off to betray everyone I love."

27

There's no way I could ever tell you I felt good about lying to everyone and walking out on them, but they didn't leave me with a choice. I had expected Claire and Olivia to be there, and I could have maybe reasoned with them, but what I got instead was a mob absolutely bent on sprinting toward oblivion. My phone began to blow up with calls and messages the moment it became apparent that I wasn't coming back, so I turned off the phone. I didn't need distractions for what I was about to do. To start, I needed to find a place to sleep that no one would ever think to look, so I hit the 110 until it ended, and I drove up into its hills until I would be lucky to find my own way back.

San Pedro is a town that can best be described, if I'm being generous, as a dump. It was like an entire city decided to do a low budget cosplay as Robocop's Detroit. I heard a story from a local who came into the shop one day. Once upon a time, back in the thirties or so I believe, San Pedro made a deal with the city of Los Angeles. It was a simple trade, Los Angeles gets the port rights to San Pedro, and in return, the city of Los Angeles will provide police and fire services. If this sounds like an incredibly stupid deal, I would agree with you, but I guess it must have happened. So, to this day, San Pedro gets all of traffic, and pollution, and crime, and filth that comes with being a major port city, but without any of the money. And that's how we have the Port of Los Angeles. A city without a coast somehow has a major port.

And that's where I was going to sleep tonight. Not at the actual port, that would have been dangerous and stupid. No, I drove through the hills of the city until I came across something relatively secluded, a rotting house, likely abandoned, with a distant view of the freeway. The area looked like a place frequently used to dump old furniture and appliances. There were no signs telling me that I couldn't park here, and the presence of two RV's at the bottom of the hill let me know this was probably a safe place to hide for the night, but not indefinitely. With the car parked, I began to munch on a protein bar that I'd stolen from the store on my way out, and went through the motions of charging my bracelet and coat. It was strange doing that in my car out in the open like this, but there weren't exactly rules on when and how I was allowed to do this.

When I was finished and sufficiently tired, I crawled over the back seat and curled up in the trunk space using my bag as a pillow and my coat as a blanket. I placed the Singing Stone next to my face and sang a gentle lullaby to it, trying to feel not completely alone out here. I understood that it could hear me, but I still didn't see any evidence to support that. Still, once I finished I sensed gratitude from it somehow, and that made me smile as I shut my eyes. Now to just not think about what I'd done or what I was about to do.

There was never a fear of not waking up in time, and I wasn't disappointed. There was more than enough time between now and monster time, and I wasn't going far besides. I made a couple of quick stops on the way, a CVS for a travel sized bottle of mouthwash, the gas station, a drive thru for a breakfast sandwich; but then it was back to Palos Verdes. I took a shortcut this time, parking up at Christmas Tree Cove, appreciating the name, despite the fact that it was also called that in July.

I gathered everything I would need before making the climb down to the shore. For as much as this shoreline was rocky, there was a proper sandy beach spot not far off from the cove. There were no homes visible from the beach there, and with the weather as lousy as it was, I didn't expect anyone to be out hiking here on Christmas Eve, which made the spot perfect.

With the beach found, I spent time clearing a spot in the sand as far back from the tide as I could and got to work building a protection circle. This was my second time using this trick, I thought to myself. I'd better be careful about not becoming too predictable. Eventually, I had it just right, and I sat in the center, focusing my energy into it, creating a shimmering purple dome over and around me.

I went into my bag, removing a couple of things. The first was a copy of the most recent book in the Stone Sorcerer series, Enemy of the Lost Ones. I opened the book to the last chapter and began to read. Kodran was spent. He's managed to stop the Lamia infestation, but not without a cost. Several young mages had fallen in the process, and he had to release several prisoners from his cave in order to have a shot at winning. Now he was at the Stone Lagoon, a beautiful and dangerous place filled with shallow caves and tunnels where someone could drown quickly if caught off guard by the rising tide. He was hoping to gain an audience with the Norns and was using the power of that place to call out to them. They wouldn't answer. I found an entrance as close to the end of the book as I could, and when I did, I placed the book in front of me, weighing down the pages with two small rocks.

The second thing I removed was a packet of chocolate covered acai berries. I removed a single berry and placed it in my mouth, savoring it, not in a hurry to finish it anytime soon. Instead, I began to settle my nerves and found clarity.

The taste of the berry in my mouth, the chocolate sweet as it began to melt against my tongue, and the berry tart as it was, alerted my taste buds...the sound of the ocean water, gently washing over stones and sand, crashing, retreating, repeating... the feel of sand sifting through my fingers as I absently scooped up small handfuls and let them fall back to the beach...the smell of the salt as it clung to the air and the rocky cliff walls around me...and the view...the overcast sky was vast and oblique above me, spreading out forever in odd, streaking directions...the calm before a storm...water as far as I could see, the sky infinite before me, ominous even with the violet filter of my bubble.

This was good. I had found my center.

The calm stayed with me, unwavering. The minutes passed like hours, and my mind never ran out of things to consider. As much as I hated my recent decisions, I didn't see many alternatives. Lying to my friends was a move I'd never be proud of, but was unavoidable at a certain point. With the Nuckelavee, I still had time to accept Freyja's help, but I wouldn't do it if it meant becoming an assassin. There's nothing heroic about agreeing to murder to save your own skin, even if the target wasn't the best dude around. No, I had a plan, and I wasn't proud of it either, but it was all that I had left. As far as Lucia, even with a clear mind, I didn't see a clear solution. I wanted to save everyone, but I didn't have a clue how to make that happen. Hopefully, I would make it that far. I'd have to survive what came next before I could really focus on that.

He came at last. His arrival began as a subtle gathering of clouds, but I was watching for them. The clouds gathered and darkened, and they brought booming thunder and streaks of lightning. The ocean began to recede and boil, and my confidence nearly cracked until I took a calming breath and steadied myself. The Nuckelavee walked out of the sea, slowly, and approached until it was no more than ten feet away. It might have been because I was sitting down, but it towered over me, far more imposing than the previous iterations. It wasn't as awkward as the other two; it had better proportions, even if its arms were elongated, but it was still hideous and reeked of death. As it stopped, it looked down at me with both of its heads, and through the humanoid head, it said with a voice like a crackling fire, "You are Elana Black. You are my prey."

"You can speak," I told it.

"I can, and I must thank you for I have not had the chance to talk to my prey in an age. It is indeed a rare thing that I have been freed. Am I to understand that you are surrendering?"

"No, that is not something I can do," I told it more calmly than I could believe. "But I did not expect to be able to communicate with you, nothing I had read about you mentioned speech. May I ask you some questions before we begin?"

"You are the first person who has ever asked," the Nuckelavee replied. "You may, but let it be known that this will end, and I will return to the sea with my prize. You cannot stop this."

"I understand, and I don't expect to defeat you," I told it with a nod of acknowledgment.

"Then ask your questions," it said. "Would you prefer to speak to this head?" it said through the humanoid head. "Or this one?" it said through the horse head.

"Whichever you like," I replied. The humanoid head appeared to smile as the horse head grunted. "Why were you summoned against me?"

"Summoning me always comes at a high price, and with significant risk to the summoner. I am only summoned out of extreme hate or extreme fear. You are someone to be feared it would seem. This very conversation is a testament to that fact."

"And how does that make you feel?" I asked, and before I could finish the question the creature made a sound that may have very well been a guffaw.

"There is nothing I despise more than being used as a tool of revenge by lesser beings, but this is what the universe has asked of me. I have always been what I am, and I always will be."

"So you don't choose to be evil?" I asked, raising an eyebrow. "Your nature isn't your fault?"

"The idea of evil is something you consider because you have a choice," the Nuckelavee growled. "You are so very temporary, yet every day of your life you decide your actions. Even when you feel forced, you are not. Not truly. Why should beings, such as I, be measured by the same stick?"

I considered that for a moment, and when I didn't answer, it asked, "You are angry with me for killing the man that you feel you failed to save, but are you not more upset with the one who sent me?"

"And who are you angrier with," I asked in retort. "Me or the one who summoned you?"

"You are beginning to understand," it said. "And though it is true that I may take the summoner in place of the target, he is not here, and you are."

"Tell me then, are the writings correct?" I asked it. "Can you really find me anywhere, no matter where I go?"

"Child, my lesser selves would have gone to the ends of the earth to find you," it began. "I have no such limitations. There is no realm you hide where I cannot find you. No god can protect you. My hunt is now a matter of fate. I will never stop. I am unable to. Now if we are done, with the questions, shall we begin?"

"Just one more question, just one," I said, lifting the book to the eye level. "Think you can keep up?"

Before the Nuckelavee could respond, I snatched open the book, reading the passage where the way in was marked, and in an instant the sandy beach and ominous sky was replaced with, well, a rocky beach and an ominous sky. The ground I was on was stone, ocean water lapped at my feet, and though the structure I was in has the semblance of being natural, I knew better. The primary difference was that I could no longer see the Nuckelavee, though I knew he'd come. I didn't know how fast he could travel through The Knowing; I just knew that it wasn't as fast as me. The other thing I could feel, overwhelmingly, was the power of the contract being broken between Bres and myself. It was the sickening feeling that I'd done something horribly wrong. It was the moment when you began to run a red light because you thought the yellow would last far longer than it had, or when you knew that your foot should have touched solid ground by now, but it was still descending. And I knew that whatever I had felt, he felt the opposite.

Kodran felt something change as well, I could see him above me, standing on a rock ledge and his face twisted as he began to seethe. "You have got to be kidding me!" he shouted toward the sky as I took cover behind a pillar, removing my rod and shaking out a shield. I just had to not die and buy a little bit of time. "After all the hell I've been through, I ask for the Norns, and I get Elana Black? Yeah, that's right, I know you're here, and I know your secrets, so you can just come out now."

Yeah, screw that.

"You don't want to show yourself? No problem, I'll just come to you." As he shouted this, his hands turned a sickly shade of gray, and I recognized it as the Stoneskin spell he was famous for in his book. "It makes sense that you don't want to show your face anyway, you're a damned thief! Taking everything you can from my world for your own selfish ends! Bleeding us dry!"

"Wait, I'm sorry, but what?" I asked out loud, stepping out from behind the pillar. Kodran leaped down to my level, landing with the weight of a boulder. I knew right away that I had screwed up, but I might as well go with it.

"Freyr told me everything. Just like you were afraid he would," Kodran snarled walking toward me. "Do you know how I found you? Your shield. Once a year, every year I would disenchant my spell on your shield just long enough to take a piece of the magic you left behind, and every time I couldn't trace it to anything. It was like the caster didn't exist."

"Kodran, listen—" I began.

He wasn't stopping as he moved ever closer, ignoring my words. "Then Freyr came for me, as you said, and he told me everything. He showed me the hole in the skin of the world, a Midgard within Midgard, he called it. An entire world that shouldn't have existed, and on it, you. You, with your grand design to steal the very source of life from our world. And now you're here! Why? How did you survive the Nuckelavee? How did you make it past the legion of elves Freyr had guarding the hole? There were thousands of them!"

Oh holy hell. It just occurred to me that even a god was working off of false information.

"I only very recently found out that my world was stealing magic from yours, and I'm sorry that's happening, but I didn't do it and that's not why we're fighting," I said, gripping my rod and pulling in stray bits of magic as he approached. "I never wanted you as my enemy; you're the one who summoned the

Nuckelavee and killed an innocent man. I warned you that this would happen."

"If by this you mean my tearing you apart with my bare hands, yeah, that's exactly what's going to happen," he snarled. "I had to summon the Nuckelavee; you made that clear when you took it down twice. Nothing else I had to throw at you came close. And defeating it doesn't change my orders. I have to kill you, and honestly? I'm not mad about it."

He lunged at me then, swinging wildly, but I was ready. I shut my eyes and channeled a burst of light through the tip of the rod in his direction, sending flashes of red through my eyelids. A shout of surprise escaped his lips, and the sound of a stone smashing against stone reverberated off the walls. I fell back, having been knocked off balance as his body slammed inelegantly against mine. My eyes opened, still blurry from the sudden burst of light, to see Kodran frantically rubbing his eyes with his forearm. The pillar he struck was now weakened with a decidedly Elana's head-sized chunk missing from it. I stiffened at the realization that one punch from Kodran would have caved my head in if it hadn't removed it entirely.

This wasn't going to end well for me if I stayed here, and I think we both knew it. I scrambled to my feet and iced the ground underneath him as I ran past, climbing to the level above as quickly as I could. Kodran must have heard me running past him, but the ice did its job, and he slipped, his vision still apparently not fully returned. There was a ledge up to another level of rocks, and I struggled to get up it momentarily, but the sounds of anger from Kodran spurred my ascent. I didn't have to beat him; I just had to outlast him.

"You tried to scare me, Elana!" Kodran howled. "That's not going to work anymore! You're going to have to do better than fear! You're going to have to step up and face me!"

As if on cue, darkening clouds gathered at an alarming rate, the tide fled from the shore, and the ocean began to bubble in the distance. It was happening.

A single clap of bone rattling thunder erupted, heralding something terrible. Somewhere, I could hear the panicked shouts of Kodran as he pleaded with me, unwilling or unable to accept his situation. "No! Oh gods, what did you do, Elana? What did you do?"

28

ore thunder. More lighting. Bigger clouds.

"You asked what I was doing here," I called down to Kodran, still looking for a place to hide. "And I think you're starting to get it. You made a mistake though; I didn't defeat the Nuckelavee. I don't believe that it can be defeated, but it is a surprisingly decent conversationalist."

"The Nuckelavee talked to you, and you brought it here?" he screamed. "What's the matter with you?"

"I tried to tell you, you killed a man," I said over the roar of the unnatural storm. "You put a lot of people in harm's way, including my friends. And I'm not ready to die for you, but you can still save yourself! You hear that, Kodran? That's a warning call! Call it off! Set it free!"

"You know I can't do that! Freyr wouldn't allow it!"

I spotted a shallow cave, just above me and behind a waterfall. It would be a perfect place to take shelter, but the problem would be in getting there without Kodran spotting me.

"Sounds to me like you have a difficult choice to make. Piss off the god or piss off the cosmic horror." I was stalling, trying to survey the area and come up with a plan.

"Maybe not," he yelled back. "This is one of the most warded areas on the planet, and I just have to finish you off before it gets here. It will be happy to take your corpse back to the sea just as soon as it would take you kicking and screaming!"

Kodran had a point, and though he wasn't certain where I was at the moment, there were only so many places to hide. It was only a matter of time before he caught up with me, not that I needed to let him know I thought that. And the Nuckelavee likely would have preferred to take Kodran instead of me, but the truth was, it would probably take whoever it caught first. Still, the caves and curved stone walls were at least hiding my location for the moment. With everything going on, the brewing storm, the unnatural thunder and lightning, it would be impossible for him to locate me by sound alone, and at least I had that going for me.

There was more than one way up to the top level, but the quickest and easiest way up was a climb that may as well been a staircase with how perfectly separated the jutting ridges were from each other. The issue was that it was about a ten-yard sprint out in the open, and I risked being seen or worse. Still, fortune favors the unnecessary risk-taking idiots, right?

About halfway across the stone walkway I stumbled and barely caught my balance, as the god or goddess of unnecessary risk-taking idiots must have heard my silent prayer and caused an explosion out at sea, something akin to the blast of a torpedo finding its target, a tower of water erupting skyward with the force of an active volcano. I could see Kodran beneath me now; his back turned to me, his attention was on whatever had just happened out at sea.

Okay, I really hope it's this easy.

I wasn't a scientist, but I know certain things don't mix with water. Like electricity or Mogwai, or in this case, stones. And Kodran had two very scary, very heavy stone fists. Maybe just a little push in the ocean would buy me all the time I needed. So I paused and took aim, holding the spell in my mind and gathering just enough power, I imagined the burst of air and allowed it to move out of me, perfectly and whole, striking him square in the back.

Which was just about enough to tousle his hair.

Kodran spun on his heels, eyes hungry as he spotted me. "Did you really just try to use the wind to knock over a stone?" he asked wryly.

"I'm not a scientist!" I shouted, momentarily forgetting the difference between inner and external dialogue.

With a growl, Kodran propelled himself upwards to the next level, gripping the structure with hands made of stone, gripping the ledge with an unnerving crack. That was all the motivation I needed to make a straight dash for my little hidey-hole. I climbed to the last level with relative ease, frantically digging through my book bag as I did. I removed Chalsarda's treasure and hoped that adamantine was as strong as the legends claimed. I placed the tip to the ground, and pressing into the ground with the same force I would use on paper with a pencil, I tentatively began to draw the protection circle.

To both my relief and amazement, the stone began to etch with all the effort of scribbling a note on a pad. Kodran was closer now, but I quickly replaced one treasure with another, removing the Singing Stone gently and holding it up to eye level, I spoke to it.

"Okay, little Singasteinn," I cooed. "I'm still not sure if that's your name or just what you are, but it sounds pretty, doesn't it? I think so. And I think I need your help, but I want you to know that this time it's not because I'm afraid. It is because together I believe we can overcome an enemy of Freyja, and as a bonus, he's just not very nice. But I won't try to make you, okay? If you are ready, give me a little note. If not, I'll tuck you back away where you'll be nice and safe."

It didn't take more than a second for the fist-sized hunk of gold to begin to vibrate gently and for a single, crystal clear note to emanate from it. I smiled at that, nearly laughing with a joy I didn't expect and couldn't explain, and I let my power into the circle in concert with the Singing Stone. The result was wondrous! The dome was thick and flawless, and it was only after seeing the quality of this protection up close that I understood how much my own usual circle could be improved. I was almost embarrassed that anyone had ever seen them in action.

There was a sense as I held the Singing Stone that it was grateful for my appreciation, and I whispered my thanks to it as I placed it back into the pouch inside of my bag. The unholy, localized storm still raged on ever closer as Kodran pulled himself up to the shelf where I'd made my sanctuary. His eyes were mad with frustration now. I could see it as he stared at me through the violet sheen, he wanted to pummel me into a paste. "Come out! Right now!" he raged.

I looked past him, only just now appreciating the view. We were made sixty or seventy feet up, and I had a bird's eye view of the oncoming storm. It was close now, almost on top of us.

"No, I don't think I will," I told him flatly. "Give it up man, look at this thing. You couldn't punch your way through this in a hundred years. Now call off the Nuckelavee before something bad happens to you."

A flash of insight seemed to flash across Kodran's eyes, and he let out a small, knowing laugh.

"Oh wow," he said to himself. Then looking at me, he asked, "Is there anything as satisfying as poking the most glaring hole in the plan of someone who thinks they're just so, so clever?"

I had a bad feeling about that grin, and I held my shield up in front of me in spite of the protection circle, and I asked, "What are you talking about? It's almost here! Think about this!"

"You're right," he replied. "You're right that the Nuckelavee is coming, and you're right that I couldn't possibly punch my way through your very impressive shields. That must have taken a tremendous amount of energy, by the way, good for you. But most important of all, you're right that I just had to think my way through this. So, thank you, and allow me to reintroduce myself! My name is Kodran Osvifsson! But you may know me by another name!"

As he spoke, the ground began to quake and shifted under my feet as his hands shot out to his sides, his fingers curling into fists as he began to gather power from the earth at an alarming rate. "I am the Stone Sorcerer!" he shouted triumphantly. "And just where do you think you're standing, moron?"

I realized in horror, a moment too late, that the carvings I'd made began to groan as the stone they were etched on was pulled apart. My protection circle seemed to fight the stones themselves, struggling to hold together, but it was no use. An imperfection in the circle somewhere must have given way, and the energy of the circle exploded and evaporated into the air around us, falling like sparkling rain.

I stared at a now considerably calmer, more confident Kodran as he looked back into my eyes and, with a smirk, only said, "Fall."

It was a miracle my shield was already up as Kodran threw the punch that sent me onto my back. Purple energy shot out of my coat as I hit the ground with the impact of being struck by a car. My shield nearly burst. I had just a second to recover enough to redouble my energy into it, keeping it and me alive. Kodran fell on top of me and with a long, sustained roar began to hammer away at the shield. My teeth began to grind together so hard that I was afraid they might shatter, but I maintained my focus on the shield, trying to block out the pressure of being beaten into stone, wondering if my jacket might give out, or if just the sheer pressure might kill me anyway. Each shot at the shield strained my ribs; my wrist began to swell, my fingers clenched until I thought the tendons in them would burst. But it wasn't the sound of my body giving way that I heard through the unrelenting pounding. It was the rock I was being hammered into.

It all fell apart at once. Kodran continued to rain blows down into my shield even as the stone shelving collapsed and fell through other, weakened rock shelves, all the way to the shore below. I began to shout in pain and fear the whole way down, creating a horrible concert with the sounds of his rage and the ensuing rock slide. And then all at once, it was done. Kodran was still on top of me, but there was no screaming. No falling rocks. My shield was gone at last. Not even the sound of crackling energy escaping my coat. Just labored breaths. Some were mine. Some were not.

"Kodran?" I asked after a moment.

It seemed that question woke him up, and he bolted upright, face grimaced, stone fist raised high over his head. And behind him, the Nuckelavee.

A skinless, elongated arm whipped toward him, gripping the arm in mid-air. Kodran was barely able to register his shock as he was effortlessly slammed into the shore, the stone walls; anywhere the Nuckelavee's arm took him. It only lasted a few hideous moments, but that was all it took for Kodran to be bloodied and battered.

"You wanted my power. Tell me now," it hissed at Kodran, using its humanoid head. "Are you satisfied with my work?"

It gave him one more slam for good measure, and the Nuckelavee looked down at me.

"It will be sometime before I am whole," the Nuckelavee said to me in that profane voice. "I do not know when I will be summoned again, nor do I know when I will next escape the Mither's grasp. But I do know that you have given a merry chase, and I hope to face you again, Elana Black, if only to determine a victor. I have chosen my prey, be thankful that it was not you."

As the Nuckelavee turned to leave, Kodran's eyes shot open in terror and he screamed, "Do something! He's going to kill me!"

I sat up against the stone wall and told him, "You're immortal. You'll figure it out."

The Nuckelavee slowly made its way back out into the ocean, its grip inescapable on Kodran's wrist.

"I mean it!" Kodran shouted. "Do something!"

"You're the only one left who can do something about this, man," I called out to him.

Kodran struggled futilely to free himself until he was waist deep in the ocean, before finally screaming, "I release you!"

The Nuckelavee stopped, the black clouds evaporated in an instant, the waters calmed.

"I release you from this duty, from your bonds. You are free to return; you do not need a prey! Do you hear me? You're free!"

Kodran watched the Nuckelavee desperately, breaths coming fast and shallow as it regarded him for a moment.

"We hear you," the humanoid head replied.

"We do not care," the horse head said.

Eyes wide with realization, Kodran managed a scream for a moment before the Nuckelavee pulled him under the tide and walked out into the water. And just like that, there was nothing.

Aside from the destruction, there was no sign of either of them and not a sound to indicate that I wasn't alone. I waited, staring out into the ocean, expecting one or both of them to pop up out of the water, or for some signal that this was finished, or just, anything. I waited. I kept waiting. Nothing.

I was at a loss. I knew this was a possibility, but it wasn't what I wanted or even expected. I don't know why I just expected that he would call it off, that this would conclude with Kodran angrily swearing revenge against me or with some kind cataclysm separating the two of us long enough for the both of us to know that we'd be unable to continue or fight, or something equally dramatic, but not this.

This was just empty. Stark.

There was nothing left here for me, and nothing coming. I went home.

I just traded one beach for another. I appeared behind a young couple, a man and a woman in matching USC workout clothes, who had been looking at my book that I'd left in the sand. They almost fell over with shock when I asked for it back, utterly confused about where I came from, but one look at me, and they didn't want to argue with me any further. They handed it back and wandered off, occasionally looking back with uncertain glances.

The hike back to Christmas Tree Cove and the climb back to my car wasn't fun, but it wasn't like I had a choice. I just wanted this day to be over. I made the drive back down to civilization and turned on my phone as soon as I had decent reception. My phone almost seized up with the flood of missed call alerts, texts, and Facebook messages, but the last message was a text from Claire that read:

No one is mad at you. We don't care why you ran off. Just please let us know that you're safe. We love you.

I replied with, "I'm fine. It's done. I'm coming home."

The streets were empty, but the parking lots were full as I made my way home. It didn't feel like Christmas Eve, and the long drive back only forced me to think about what had just happened, and what I'd be walking into. Claire said that no one was upset, but honestly, that was the last thing on my mind right now. I just did everything I never wanted to do, and I didn't know what that would mean for me and everyone else.

Big Sister rattled into the parking lot, unhappy as a car older than myself could be with her workload. The sun was beginning to set, but the shop had likely closed hours ago if Claire even opened up today at all. There were none of the tell-tale signs in the parking lot that she had. I got out of the car, knowing there would be questions, but I just wanted to go to bed. Why didn't anyone ever tell me that the downside of living in a store was that just about anyone could just walk into your home and bother you?

I sighed, seeing that no one had left. No one had even changed their clothes. And again, they were all just waiting for me to walk through the door. "Not in the mood," I announced flatly. "You can all go with me tomorrow. Or not. Whatever. I just need some alone time."

"Jesus, Elana, sit down!" Claire exclaimed, eyes wide. "What happened? Do we need to get you to a doctor?"

Claire gently guided me into a chair, and I wasn't in the mood to fight, so I sat.

"What are you you…yeah, I just want to sleep for a hundred years, is that cool?"

"Hold on, here," Teague offered, pulling a makeup mirror out of her purse and handing it to me.

Ah, yeah, I see the problem. That is a fair amount of blood. And the massive bruise building on the side of my face wasn't putting anyone at ease either. "Blood isn't mine, and that bruise is, okay yeah, I didn't know the bruise was even there, to be honest, but it's cool. I'm fine, really."

"I'll get her some ice," Logan said.

"No need," Chalsarda stopped him, reaching into her bag. "I have a poultice."

She unwrapped two sturdy, ardent leaves and scooped what looked like a bean paste from them with her two first fingers and began to rub them around my cheek and eye. I winced slightly, feeling for the first time how tender my bruise actually was.

"Really?" I asked, trying not to gag on the scent and feeling ridiculous with this paste on my face.

"You're welcome," she said firmly, continuing to generously apply the goop to my cheek.

"We'd like to know what happened," Olivia said. "But maybe we pushed you too hard. You don't have to tell us if you're not ready, we're just happy that you made it back."

Jason handed me a bottle of water, a look of genuine concern in his eyes as he did. It was starting to occur to me that just about everyone here had some variation of the same look. I sighed and gently waved Chalsarda off, trying not to undo her work.

"I want to tell you all that I'm sorry I lied to you," I began slowly. "But I'm not. I hate that I had to lie to you, but I'm not sorry that I did because it meant all of you were staying here where it was safe. You didn't know what I was facing. To be honest, I didn't really know what I was facing, and I'm lucky to be sitting here with all of you right now. And if any one of you had gone with me, you would be dead or I would. Or both. I love you all, but I had to do something terrible, and if I had told you what I was going to do, you might have tried to stop me."

Olivia nodded thoughtfully at that. "You might be right, maybe just walk us through it?"

"Not all of you know this, but the Nuckelavee killed a man last time we faced it. I couldn't get to it in time, and it…the details aren't important. But I went back into The Stone Sorcerer alone, and tried to convince Kodran to do the right thing; I just thought that if I could convince him not to summon it at all, that man wouldn't have had to die. But he did, and he didn't leave me with a choice."

"You killed him," Ann said in a horrified hush.

"No, I didn't, not exactly," I tried to explain. "But tomorrow is our one chance to save Lucia, to keep Olivia alive; just too much is happening tomorrow. And the Nuckelavee can't be defeated by someone like me, and if my guess is right, it can't be defeated by anyone. But it can be called off, and I just thought that if I took it back to Kodran, he'd have no choice, but…"

"But what?" Olivia asked.

"There was only one way to get back fast enough not to get caught, and that meant breaking my deal with Bres. I took the direct route because if it killed me, the deal with Bres would be broken anyway, and I definitely wouldn't be able to keep you all alive then. It was a hard choice, and I think it might have been the wrong one because the Nuckelavee didn't care when Kodran called it off. Kodran tried to kill me, he was going to kill me, but then the—"

I paused, remembering how horrible the sight of it all was. "It dragged him into the ocean. It understood that the contract had been broken, and it said that it didn't care. It was deliberate, and it wanted its prize. Kodran isn't dead, he can't die, but I am genuinely afraid there's something worse than death waiting for him right now."

No one said a word at that. I took a long sip of my water and told them all, "We're all in danger now. More than any of you realize. I traded one monster for another, and our only shot at having a continued existence might depend on my ability to defy fate, and gods, and shadowy organizations, and save everyone tomorrow."

"We need a Christmas miracle!" Ann cried out in realization.

No one humored her. How do you possibly respond to something that stupid and that accurate all at once?

I couldn't help myself. For as terrible as everything was, for as much as the weight of the world was crushing me, I giggled. Then I laughed. Then I began to laugh so hard that it hurt my already bruised ribs and globs of paste fell off my cheek, and I didn't care what anyone thought of what I looked like.

"Oh my god, we literally need a Christmas miracle," I said in disbelief. "I have the stupidest life ever."

29

Imminent disaster or no, it was Christmas Eve, and all of my friends surrounded me, and it wasn't like everyone had nowhere else to go. In fact, it was the opposite, just about everyone here had family or somewhere they could be, so in its own messed up way, this was already kind of a treat. Jason and Logan declared themselves responsible for procuring our Christmas feast, which ended up being a collection of takeout orders from Norm's Diner down on La Cienega. Ann and Teague decided on questing for eggnog, and after three 7-11 visits, they returned with eggnog for all. Ann insisted only the cowardly and weak were lactose intolerant on this day. Claire had a hidden jug of the sort of rum that came in a plastic jug and only pirates with the lowest of standards would be caught drinking. For a brief moment in time, things were fine once again. It had only been weeks, but it felt like years since I'd been allowed to be normal and spend time with my chosen family.

I desperately avoided the voice that told me this might be our last Christmas. The voice that reminded me there was one person who had always been missing from these things and should have been laughing with us the whole time. The insistent, hissing voice deep in my skull that said this was as good as it would ever be for me again, that whatever happened next, things were never going to be okay or normal ever again.

The hilarious sight of Teague nearly doing a spit take with a mouthful of eggnog because Jason said all of the lifts in the Death Star should have been called Ele-Vaders made it that pretty easy to do.

Eventually, we all reached that inevitable point in any gathering where people drifted away to have private conversations, check their phones, or just generally do whatever people do when the group chatting dies down. For myself and Chalsarda, that meant moving upstairs to my loft to prepare for tomorrow. Chalsarda watched with significant interest as I infused my coat and bracelet with their daily charge.

"You're a savant," she remarked. "Had I known that you were putting as much magic into these things, I would have unquestionably tried to stop you months ago. I'm astonished that you haven't destroyed anything yet."

"Hey dude, I don't know what to tell you, I just followed the instructions," I replied, slipping on the bracelet and hanging up my coat. "There are a whole lot of things I struggle with, but this just came pretty easy to me, especially with the rod."

Chalsarda smiled at that. "Finding what you're good at is of vital importance. Just be sure not to get careless with your creations."

"Oh! That reminds me," I said reaching for my bag. "I still have your—"

"Quietly, please," Chalsarda quietly shushed me. "And I think you should hold onto it until tomorrow, at least. Your friends will be expecting you to lead the charge, not me. Besides, I'm becoming increasingly concerned about that."

"What's up?" I asked, letting it slip back into its pouch.

She pursed her lips and took a peek below. "I gave that to you because I expected that I would be fetched by now," she explained. "Forcefully, most likely. It would seem unlikely that he hasn't noticed my absence by now, and even less likely that he would just allow me to join you. For everything I know, I also must admit I don't think anyone ever fully grasps his machinations except himself. So maybe I'm wrong, but in case I'm not and anything were to happen, I feel it's best that you have a path forward independent of me."

"Is he evil?" The question was blunter than I'd anticipated, but it was out there all the same.

"I believe he is well intentioned," Chalsarda answered carefully. "But well-intentioned men do terrible things because they feel they are right. Well-intentioned men, at worst, can cause a war, but well-intentioned gods are capable of much worse."

Chalsarda raised her glass of eggnog with both hands and her brow creased. "I am going to choose my next words very carefully, and for my sake, please do not attempt to follow-up with me about them. Do you follow?"

"Of course."

"Very well," she said, her words coming slowly and deliberate. "One day I hope to tell you a story. It is the story of an elf who was hurt deeply by the good intentions of someone far greater than herself."

I could see as she spoke that she treated each word as a potential landmine, and she might have been fortunate to get just that much out. I kept my voice quiet as I said, "I understand."

This comment brought a small smile out of her, and she walked to the edge of the loft space, leaned on the railing to look down at the rest of the store and said, "I like this tradition. Christmas that is," she mused. "I understand that historically it hasn't always been what it is, but for as long as I've been able to observe it, this has been it. Loved ones coming together, celebrating that they've survived one more year together, always hoping for one more. Hopeful that the next year will be better than the last, while still grateful for the year that was."

I flopped back into my bed, grinning as I thought about what this time has meant for me historically. "Well, it's not always like this," I told her. "Most of the time I spend Christmas alone. No big deal, but everyone usually has somewhere else to be. You know, technically this isn't supposed to be my holiday?"

"Oh?" Chalsarda asked with a hint of curiosity in her voice.

"Yeah, growing up I was always told it should be Chanukah. Elana Ruth Black. First and middle names are Hebrew, last name was also probably Jewish they said. My mom had a decidedly Irish name, but I ended with none of that in my name, so yeah. They always said I should have probably gone the Jewish route if I wanted to respect the family tradition."

"So why didn't you?" Chalsarda asked.

I pulled myself out of bed and joined her at the railing. "Take a look down there," I said softly, barely above a whisper. "There, coming out of the stock room, is Claire Van Amburg. Look carefully; she's doing inventory, but not for the store. She's putting together little survival kits for all of us for tomorrow. I think she sees herself in me, and she's always nurtured me, even when I was a snot who didn't deserve it." I pointed over to the far end of the shop, and continued, "And in the corner, almost hidden from us? Ann Bancroft. She doesn't think we can see her. I can feel her anxiety from here, she's a little excited, but mostly terrified for tomorrow. But if I walked over there right now? She'd never show it. I've known her longer than most here, and no one else has made me feel as good about laughing at my fears and anxieties or encouraged me to try to be different if I needed to be different as she has."

"She has the heart of a hero to be sure," Chalsarda agreed. "Brave enough to stay, smart enough to know that she should run."

"Oh, and those two, sitting in the reading area?" I asked excitedly. "You don't know them as well yet, Teague Chetty and Jason Kelly. They're not from here, Teague came from South Africa, Jason grew up in Ohio, but they both came here for work. Jason has the life I'm going to miss, Teague has the life I'm probably most envious of. Jason has, I am not kidding, more worthless history knowledge than anyone I've ever met. But when you get him going, he's so excited about it that you can't help but feel excited too. And I've always needed that because I do the same thing with my books and shows, and one of the worst feelings I've ever been subjected to on a regular basis is when someone tunes me out and makes me feel like I shouldn't have even opened my mouth. And I know that he's felt that too, but I have never once seen him be anything less than interested when someone is sharing with him."

Chalsarda frowned slightly at that. "Teague though, Teague is great," I offered. "Everything she's done since coming here, her job, who she spends time with, everything has been because she wanted to and no other reason. She is so effortless with people; she makes friends consistently. I'd like to believe that I'm kind and caring, but I know that doesn't always come across well when I'm uncomfortable? Her? Never uncomfortable and she makes everyone feel loved. I admire that."

"All that is left is those two over there?" Chalsarda asked with a nudge, looking down and to my right.

Olivia and Logan were hidden behind our travel section, but I could see them perfectly from up here. "Ah, yeah. Olivia Moore and Logan Kobayashi. Check it out, she's going to take both of his hands, and he's going to kiss her. Wait for it," I said in a hush, focusing on them. Chalsarda leaned in, observing, and after a moment, there it was. Hands were taken. Kiss shared.

"Called it," I said with a hint of satisfaction.

"Well done."

"Thank you," I said with a smile, happy in the moment because they were happy. "Logan is right for her. Olivia dated some of the worst dudes ever in high school, but Logan has been a good fit. He and I would have been friends no matter how we met. He sees the best in everyone, and he'll never lie to you. Not for anything. And Olivia, I mean, damn. Come on; she's my sister. We've fought like sisters, and we've loved like sisters. She hasn't always agreed with everything I've said and done, and sometimes she's tried a little too hard to make me more sociable. But you know what? No one has ever had my back as much as her, shared with me like her. There's nothing I could possibly ask for that she wouldn't give. Do you know how rare that is?"

The question came out of my mouth incredulously. Chalsarda nodded sadly. "I've not had many friends, and I've seen more betrayal than anyone should in their lifetime."

"And I'm sorry for that, but that's over now," I told her backing away from the railing and facing her. "I've said all of their names out loud because they're important. They matter. I never knew my mother and father, and there's a part of me that will always regret not having a childhood the way I was supposed to, or the way that I saw others have theirs. But whoever my parents were, their past doesn't dictate my future. Maybe my dad lit the candles and spun the dreidel, and if he did, I hope it brought him joy. But Christmas for me isn't about the religion, and it's not about traditions started by people I'll never know. It's about the family I've chosen, not the family I've lost. Everyone here means the world to me, and that includes you, Chalsarda. Welcome to my family."

Chalsarda looked stunned, maybe even ready to cry. Maybe I was a bit dramatic, but I meant it, and she needed to hear it. "What do I even say to that?" she asked, her eyes welling up.

I shrugged. "Merry Christmas? Happy Chanukah? Thanks? If there's an Elven equivalent, I guess you could—"

I was nearly tackled off my feet in a hug. "Thank you, my friend," she said into my ear. "No, not that. Merry Christmas, Elana Black."

I returned the hug just as tight. "Merry Christmas, Chalsarda."

She released me, and wiping away a tear she asked me, "And this is why you need to go into battle tomorrow, isn't it?"

I agreed with a nod. "Yeah, there's someone else who deserves to be here. Lucia may very well hate me by now, but that doesn't matter. I've let her down too much; I'm not going to let her down tomorrow."

"Then I'm with you."

Christmas this year was not at all what I had expected it to be. A month ago and I would have told you that my plan involved watching *National Lampoon's Christmas Vacation* and a series of naps. And don't judge me on that, there are a lot of Christmas movies out there, but few that end with a heartwarming kidnapping. Maybe *Die Hard* counted based on that criteria, but—and you can call me crazy if you need to—I just prefer my Christmas movies to keep the gun violence to a minimum. Weird, right? Instead, my Christmas was going to involve, potentially, a whole ton of violence, and magical fights, and I don't even know what?

Mounted Unicorn Lancers? I don't know what these people get up to.

And now I was standing dumbly in front of my friends who were all prepared to run into the unknown like a bunch of dummies. I'm still kind of getting to the point where I need to accept that this is going to happen, but I'm not exactly happy about it either. And the longer I stood here just staring at everyone, the more awkward I felt it was going to get.

"So, uh, are you all expecting a speech or something?" I asked nervously.

"Kind of, yeah," Ann replied. "Feels appropriate."

"Ah, well, I sort of don't want to give one," I answered. "Is that cool?"

"Kind of a letdown, but I guess." Ann sighed.

"So, better plan, I'm going to let Chalsarda explain exactly how off the damn rails crazy this place can be instead," I announced. "Olivia, can I talk to you real quick while that happens?"

Chalsarda began her safety lesson while Olivia and I went somewhere more private to speak. Olivia didn't so much as let me start before saying, "If you're going to try and tell me I can't go, please don't, okay?"

"I'm not, I know that I don't have the right to stop you, but I just," I stopped mid-sentence to collect my thoughts. "I just can't see you get hurt, okay? This isn't the completely unknown, I've watched you die, and I'm telling you now that I won't let that happen. I need you to understand that before you go through with this."

Olivia looked enervated at that and motioned for me to sit. There were no chairs in this aisle, but that didn't stop her. Mildly confused, I joined her on the ground and sat across from her cross-legged. She shut her eyes, and took a deep breath in through her nose and held it momentarily, before allowing it to release slowly. I waited patiently, but uncomfortably for a moment before she said, "You should be doing this too, you probably need it worse than I do."

I decided to oblige her and shut my eyes as well, taking in deep, relaxing breaths to match hers. It felt like a waste of time, we were about to jump into the middle of a battle after all, but if this is what she wanted, I wasn't going to argue. In. And out. Repeat. Try not to think about In-N-Out, now is not the time for that. Just breathe. Let it become a pattern. I could feel the air fill my sinuses, my chest inflate, and after each time, I would come closer to sleep as I felt my shoulders relax while the air left my lungs.

"I know you want to protect me," Olivia said slowly, and the suddenness of it made my eyes dart open. "And I want to protect you, too. I always have, and in some ways, it's been difficult for me to admit that you don't need that as much from me. But it's a good change; we'll always need each other. And, even if you don't need me, I'll still want to be there for you, as you want to be there for me. However, that's tomorrow and going forward. For now, you need to understand that whatever happens once we're in there, you might not be able to protect me. I might not be able to protect you. And that's okay. Before we go, what we both need to understand, more than anything, is that we both have our own reasons for going through with this. And neither of us have the strength to carry both of our reasons. So look out for me if you need to, but appreciate that I am my own person with my own choices, my own consequences, and if something happens to me, that's not your fault. You warned me, you did your best to talk me out of it, and I'm going anyway. And so are you. This isn't just your fight; we will be there together."

I considered that. There was nothing more that I could say to her, which was both terrifying and freeing all at once. I didn't take back what I said, I'd die before I let her get hurt, but she was determined to go. That was that.

"Are you ready?" Olivia asked, standing up. I nodded in silent approval, and as I stood up, she gave me a brief, reassuring hug.

"It's going to be okay," Olivia said. "Let's go."

There wasn't time to learn exactly what Chalsarda had said to everyone while we were away, but every face looked to be in a state of horrified disbelief. "Largely, that's all the worst-case scenario," she continued. "Don't wander off, let the fighters do the fighting, and hopefully you'll all return safe and sound. Elana, shall we?"

I walked through everyone and made my way to the back storeroom, which felt like the safest place to open a portal into a nightmare. "Everyone just stand back," I instructed.

"You remember what to do?" Chalsarda whispered.

"Yeah, I got this," I agreed as I prepared, trying my best to keep the adamantine hidden from the view of everyone else. I did as Chalsarda had instructed. I held the location I'd received from Roger in my mind, along with my memories of the various visions, the pain I'd seen in—

LUCIA.

It rang out in my head as clear as if someone had spoken it directly into my ear. I bent down to write the name, and the adamantine took on a texture like a crayon, the letters spread against the floor like melting wax. The air shimmered above the letters as the way inside began to peel back from nothing. I steadied myself, ready to cross over.

And that's when the hoard of goblins poured into the room.

30

I kicked the very first goblin I saw square in the stomach, much more as a surprised reaction than a deliberate attack. It doubled over in pain all the same, completely unaware of my intentions. It was like stepping on one cockroach only to see its family make their mass exodus from their home in the walls. And the thing with goblins that I don't think most people realize is that they come in many different sizes, colors, and smells. The one that I kicked was maybe three feet tall, a sickly-green, little, twisted thing wearing a rotted tunic and wildly waving a stick over its head wildly with both arms. The next couple of dozen, however, were too numerous to describe. The one that immediately followed it nearly bowled me over and was my height at least; portly and covered in warts.

I heard cries of panic and surprise all around me; it was impossible to tell which noise was coming from whom. There wouldn't be standing room in here soon at this rate, and I had absolutely no idea of what to do.

"Get inside!" Chalsarda screamed over the chaos. "Your opening won't hold for long! I will do what I can here!"

As I watched, it seemed like the majority of them were piling on her. Was she just the perceived threat? Did goblins just really hate elves?

I didn't have time to consider it as I heard Olivia shout at Logan next to me, and she practically dragged him across the threshold and out of view. That made my decision for me; it was now or never. I didn't have another way in, and currently, two of my friends had taken a running leap into the unknown. My present situation was perilous for sure, but Chalsarda said she had it and I had to believe that. I held on tightly to my bag and dashed forward and—

—I was standing alongside Olivia and Logan, facing the Aos Si. In the distance, there was the roar of battle, but it was hard to see anything through the hazy dome surrounding us.

"Aos Si?" I asked, trying to make sense of everything. "What are you doing here? Wait! Did you just stand there while a hoard of goblins ran at me?"

The Aos Si offered a grin that didn't quite touch his eyes. "Hello, Elana. Hello, Olivia," he said. "And you would be Logan, I presume? I admit that I am less familiar with you."

Olivia traded confused looks with Logan as the Aos Si again addressed me. "To answer your question, I didn't allow those goblins in, I ordered them in."

"You what?" I shouted.

He held up a hand. "Everything is fine. No one is to be harmed. They were sent to retrieve my elf," he continued.

"Her name is Chalsarda," I insisted.

"Yes, and I know that you have something of hers, and I know that she disobeyed me on a technicality. You've been keeping secrets from me, but I'm not hurt," the Aos Si said, turning his eyes to all three of us. "There is too much at stake. Allow me to show you."

The Aos Si turned away from us, and with a wave of his hand a patch of haze on the dome cleared up, and we all saw immediately. As if time had slowed to a crawl, the melee and pandemonium of what we'd come to see played out before us. Men and women were fighting, numbering in the hundreds, if not more. There were people that I'd come to expect, those in the various suit colors, but there were others as well. Demons and monsters, the trolls had shown up after all; armored hulking men and women whose proportions were large enough to make me question if they were even human; there were guns, and swords, and spikes of energy everywhere. It was terrifying, and all of it moved slowly enough that I could mistake it for being frozen in place if I didn't look for too long.

But above all, in the middle of it, in a bisected cage that hung high above the streets and illuminated with a pair of spot-lights was Lucia, head slumped forward, her posture loose and resigned. Underneath was a circle painted on the ground, unbe-lievably complex in its mad design, tendrils of a bright blue energy reaching skyward.

"It was no easy task to arrange this, in fact, holding every-thing together right now is taxing even my powers and focus, but we will have time to discuss what's next while we are in here," the Aos Si said, turning back toward us. "No one knows we are in here; no one could penetrate our defenses if they did."

"Lucia!" I cried out suddenly. She was older than I'd re-membered her, and she didn't look well, but it was unquestiona-bly her.

The Aos Si looked uncomfortable at my outburst but con-tinued, "Olivia, you may not know this, but you are the only one who can save everyone and in the process, you can right a great wrong from your past."

"What do you mean?" Olivia asked unsteadily, looking increasingly unsure of herself with everything going on around her.

"I think you know," he continued. "Once in an age, something greater than fate, or the gods, or the universe itself chooses someone in our darkest hour. Someone who can bring about a change, someone capable of driving out the swelling evil infecting everything. Someone who can bring a light where there is none. Lucia Cruz was chosen for that purpose. But now you see before you, the dying of the light. She shared so much of herself, and because of you, she shared too much, and she now no longer can sustain herself. If some of that light is not returned, she will perish, and soon."

Olivia shook her head in disbelief. "That's not...I never meant." Olivia struggled to find her words. "I didn't know!"

"Of course not, I understand what you are going through," the Aos Si reassured her. "I am familiar with exactly how unfair it can be to make a simple mistake in your youth only to have the consequences follow you forever. I empathize with you now more than you could ever know. But that changes nothing. Right now, your friend is dying, and if she dies, there will be a catastrophe. The only way to save her is by returning some of her light to her with love in your heart and of your own free will. And Olivia, you were given so very much. So much in fact, that you seem to have shared some yourself with your paramour."

"You did this?" Logan asked Olivia, his voice confused and hesitant. "The reason I can read those pages, that came from you?"

"I'll do it," I spoke up suddenly. "I've let Lucia down more than anyone, and the Gardeners said as much that it had to be me."

The Aos Si scoffed at that, a bead of sweat forming on his brow. "The Gardeners are fools. You have love in your heart, certainly, but they understand the process is fatal. They merely want you out of the way. No, this is not your fault regardless, Olivia pushed her to this point. However unintentional, if Lucia dies today her blood, and the blood of those who fall next, will be on Olivia's hands. Besides, I have sworn to keep you safe where I can; I can't allow you to do this."

"Elana, it's okay," Olivia said, her voice trembling. "Whether or not I meant to, I pushed her to this point. This is on me."

The Aos Si seemed to be visually strained at this point. "Excellent. Now, when you exit the protection of this circle, you will see a path. Take care to not stray from it or draw attention to yourself, and you will remain obfuscated. It will get you close enough, but not all the way. Pick your spot wisely, because when you are seen, every single thing out there will be focused on you until you are either dead or inside the cage, do you understand?"

"I do," Olivia said walking forward. "Elana, my friend, Logan, my love, I am so sorry. I love you both, but I...I have to do this! I have to go!"

Logan stretched out an arm, tears already streaming down his face. I already hated myself for what I was going to do next.

"Wait!" I shouted. "Olivia, take this, it will help!"

She turned as I removed my bracelet and threw it at her feet. She didn't have time to be confused as I released the magical trigger, coating her body waist down in a quickly hardening sap.

"Get it off of me!" Olivia shouted in surprise.

The Aos Si lost his calm, his eyes darkened, and he began to tremble as he commanded, "Dispel that sap this instant!"

It was a nausea inducing sort of terror hearing a god take that tone with me, but I held firm.

"You do it," I shot back.

"I said now!" he shouted, and I very nearly did as he asked on instinct, but I remembered myself.

"No. And you can't, can you? At least not without letting this all fall apart. Time dilation and keeping us invisible from that many magical eyes? You're at your limit. Thank you for all of your help, I mean that sincerely. But I'm not letting anyone else die today, and you can't stop me."

I turned to Logan and said to him, "You two have a beautiful life together. She's my sister, so you better take care of her or I'll come back and haunt you. If that's an option."

Olivia was screaming at me now as Logan embraced me. "I'll never let anything bad happen to her, I promise. I love you."

"Love you too, dork," I said turning toward Olivia, tears now falling from my eyes as fast as they could be produced. "Thank you for always taking care of me, Olivia. Please don't hate me for this."

I turned and began to run, intent on saving the day, when one word stopped me cold.

"Stop."

As the Aos Si said that, I lost my balance. Pure vertigo overtook me, and I dropped to my knees. I could feel my body wanting to pull in every direction all at once, even the flickering of my eyes felt like something that might cast me into the abyss.

"What did you do?" I cried out.

"I removed your training wheels, I'm allowing you the full extent of your power," the Aos Si grunted. "When we first met, do you remember? You were ready to travel to parts unknown without a thought. I placed an inhibitor on you, allowed you to travel through this place safely, controlled. This is temporary, I promise. Just long enough to prevent you from making the biggest mistake of your life."

"Let me go," I asked weakly.

"I won't, for your own good," he replied. "I see it in your eyes. You're starting to see, aren't you? You came here to save the life of Lucia. You came here to alter the fate of Olivia. And now you understand that you cannot do both. Dispel the sap and save Lucia, or be content in this stalemate and save Olivia."

I stood up, slowly, and began to center myself. I focused on the sound of Olivia's shouts. I felt the pain in my knees from collapsing to the ground. I could smell the ozone and metal musk of the battle even from here. I could taste the salt in the tears that had streamed down my face. I looked to the skyline, eyes opening wide. I focused on the vanishing point where the buildings converged, past and above the distracting mass of the battle.

"I can do this," I told him in defiance, not looking at him.

"You will never make it," he said, his voice filled with concern and certainty. "If you lose focus for even an instant, you will be transported to a place that even I may never find you. You're treading on a billion needles, don't be stupid."

I took a deep breath and began to walk, carefully at first, and said to no one, "It's a really good thing you paved the way for me then, isn't it?"

The ground gave off a luminescent glow narrowly in front of me, but I didn't look down, didn't blink. The skyline, I focused on that and that alone. Everything remained in slow motion around me, and the peace of it all gave me rhythm. The walk became a jog, and the jog became a steady sprint. I kept time with my feet. One, two. One, two. I was doing it! Racing now. Don't stop, control your breathing! One, two! One, two! Lucia was coming into focus now, an oak tree grew out of the concrete in front of me at a forty-five-degree angle, a ramp into the cage.

I'm coming, Lucia.

The glow ended at the base of the tree, and I knew what that meant, but I didn't slow down, I pounded my feet harder than ever, eyes wide enough to strain my sinuses. I held my bag tight, leaping toward the tree with everything I had and—

—I was sitting at a dinner table. I needed a second, what had just happened? The table was, well, extravagant. Golden goblets, nearly every meat and dessert I could imagine, and even more that I couldn't. There were several crystal carafes filled with exotic, swirling liquids. It took me a moment to realize that there was already a plate in front of me, with nothing on it except for a spoonful of pomegranate seeds.

The Aos Si was sitting across from me then. Not that he sat down across from me, he was just there. "I couldn't decide if the seeds were in bad taste or not," he said sheepishly, the first time I had ever seen him like this, in fact. "I had hoped you would appreciate them given the situation."

Lucia!

"I'm going back," I said, standing abruptly.

"Please, sit," he said, and it sounded like a genuine request somehow. "It's already too late."

My legs went weak hearing that. "What do you mean it's too late? What did you do?"

"You are merely fulfilling your end of the bargain. A fair deal made freely. We are sharing a meal," he said with a wave of his hand, indicating the enormous amount of food. "You could break our deal, but you'd never make it back in time, and besides, you don't know the way. You may as well try walking to the moon. The deal will be honored when we have eaten everything or when I decide we have had our fill."

"What do you want?" I asked him.

"To be honest with you, Elana. I want you to understand. I'm not a monster, I was, like you, just someone in an impossible position."

A thought seized me, and my face grew hot as I asked a question before I could stop myself. "If you're going to be honest with me, then answer me this," I said sternly. "The reason for my name, your protection of me, the fact that I can't find any information on my father; is…is that you? Are you my Dad?"

The Aos Si sighed and said, "No, but I certainly wanted to be." He paused at that, clearly embarrassed by his answer. "I'm sorry, I shouldn't have said that. But I knew her quite well... your mother. That necklace you're wearing, I gave it to her as a gift."

I instinctively clutched at the dara knot resting on my chest, stunned by that piece of news. It felt impossible, but it couldn't have been, he was telling the truth. "What? How?" I shouted, realizing my fingers were trembling. "Who are you? I mean, your name. Why are we here?"

"I once told you that I am Aos Si, though right now I am not even that," he began. "And that is still true. Do you know what the Aos Si are?"

"Guardians, we've discussed this," I said, knowing that wasn't the answer he was looking for.

"Of course you don't know." There was mild disgust in his voice as he said that. "No one remembers the Tuatha Dé Danann, and no one knows how to get to Tir Na Nog; you people still think Leprechauns are happy little green men who grant wishes when you capture them! Corner one, steal from one, see how well that goes for you!"

The Aos Si was showing more emotion now than I'd ever seen from him. A range of frustration, anger, sadness; and underneath it was a sense of guilt. "Those do exist now, you know. Thanks to the humans. They're Leprechauns, but they're not Leprechauns. But that's not what you want to know, is it?"

I shook my head, and he said, "No, it's not. People today get everything wrong about us, about their own history. My name is Abarta. Do you know what they called me?"

"I've never heard that name before, so no," I said, realizing how that might have hurt.

Abarta laughed bitterly at that. "You would be right, most of the time they don't call me anything at all," he said. "That

319

anonymity might have been what spared me; I simply wasn't important enough to—" He paused, and continued calmly, "I have been called a trickster god. Let me tell you, what I did was deliberate. I had a plan. I had a plan, and I failed. And when the Milesians drove my people underground, I had already been shunned by my people for the mistakes of my youth. But now, now I have the chance to bring them back. I will once again have my family; the Aos Si will no longer be confined to the mound, all of the heroes of old can return."

"What does this have to do with anything?" I asked. "Why drag me here, why put Olivia in danger?"

"Anyone can keep one promise, Elana," Abarta said sadly. "I pledged to keep too many. I told you that I knew your mother. What do you know of her?"

"Not much," I admitted. "Almost nothing. I never knew her."

He nodded at that. "But Rosheen knew you." Hearing her name gave me goosebumps. It only just now occurred to me that I don't think I've ever heard her name from anyone who knew her. "Your mother had the power to walk between worlds as you do, not with your talent, but she could travel nonetheless. She, however, had a gift you do not, one which is quite rare. She was a Sibyl, one who saw possible futures. She saw the many divergent paths you may take in your life, and mostly she was proud, but she saw how treacherous those paths would become. And more than that, she knew her path was coming to an end. And so, I made her a promise."

"Not a deal?" I asked irritably. "I thought Fae promises always had strings attached."

"No, not with her," Abarta said softly. "I was in love with her, and she…she did not reciprocate. But she knew I would do anything she asked, and her wish was for me to protect you. I told her I would, but—"

"The Aos Si are meant to protect certain things," I interrupted. "That's where they can focus the most energy, yes? A wood, a hill, or even a tree. Oh god, my name might as well be Loophole."

"Your mother was very clever," he said. "And she saw that you could reach heights others would not dream of, if only you wanted to. She loved you before you ever even knew what love was."

"So you couldn't let me sacrifice myself to save Lucia," I said out loud, piecing it together. "But why let me be aware of Lucia at all? Why would you allow my friends to be in harm's way?"

"Many people all throughout history, past, present, and future, owe their ability to travel to Lucia. She changed everything when she did that, or she changed nothing, and she had always done it. Regardless, Lucia was the source. And through your mother, I was able to see the day when I would once again be whole as an Aos Si. They told me, if I could return them, I would be accepted again among them. I was the only one left who could; this was my redemption. So I set my hands to the task of creating something magnificent. When your friend Lucia is restored, there will be a fantastic release of power so primordial that it defies explanation. But she was only loved by two people, yourself and Olivia. Ann as well, but her power is too weak for my purposes. The more power which is returned to her, the stronger she will be. If your friend Ann were here, she would gladly volunteer, and the result would be insufficient. You and Olivia are the only two viable candidates, and I am sorry, but to save my people, your friend must willingly die. This brings me no joy, but I feel it is important for you to watch and say good-bye."

Abarta directed my attention to the other side of the dining room where a mirror began to display the vision of Logan trying to help a struggling Olivia free herself from the trap that I had sprung on her.

"Send me back to her!" I shouted hopefully, exhilarated that she was still alive. "You might be wrong about all of this! If the two of us enter together, maybe we can both live and still return your people and save Lucia! We can all win!"

"I'm afraid not." Abarta sighed. "I am still maintaining the magics, albeit at a distance, and it is taking all of my strength to do so. What you are watching is, how did you put it? Time dilation. Everything is moving differently, our view of this is delayed. By now the spell you cast has undoubtedly weakened, and Olivia is free, it was just a matter of time. Even if I sent you back, this has already happened. Watch."

"Tell her—" a small, uneasy voice began speaking from under the table near Abarta's seat.

"Quiet!" he barked.

I shot to my feet and looked past the table to see Chalsarda at his side, on her knees with her head to the floor, her wrists bound behind her back with metal restraints, her ankles locked together as well.

I stared in disbelief, anger overwhelming me.

"Let her go!" I shouted on impulse.

"I apologize, you were not meant to see that," he said. "The elf is currently being punished for subverting my will. And while you are free to do as you will here, I would suggest you look back if you would like to witness the final moments of your friend."

I was furious, but in a way he was right. I didn't want to see this, but it felt disrespectful not to.

"I don't know how, but I am going to make you hurt for this," I seethed, sitting back down and watching the mirror as a knot grew in my stomach.

"I need you to know that I'm not a monster. I need to know that you'll forgive me," Abarta said, and as he did I couldn't help but believe that he actually expected forgiveness from me.

I watched as Logan stopped trying to help Olivia out of the hardened sap, his arms went limp, and he instead cupped his hands behind her head and spoke with her. She was crying now, so was he. They kissed, and when he pulled away, she was screaming at him. It was then that we all saw the last thing any of us expected.

Logan ran away.

31

We watched as Logan sprinted out of the dome, Abarta feverishly waved his fingers at the mirror to keep the perspective on Logan as he ran. "The fool! What is he doing? He doesn't know Lucia! His power never came from her; he carries only the barest amounts of runoff from Olivia!"

The realization hit me like a cold shower.

"Oh my god. He doesn't need to know her," I said aloud, my mind putting it all together.

"Of course he does!" Abarta snapped. "Without love for Lucia, he'll be utterly obliterated! He doesn't stand a chance!"

"Seriously, you're a trickster god, how are you *this* slow?" I asked. "You're Fae; you understand technicalities in words more than anyone. Logan just has to have love in his heart and sacrifice himself of his own free will. It's not Lucia he's saving, it's Olivia!"

"But he has the least amount of light to give back of anyone! If he succeeds…" Abarta's words trailed off, then his twisted into a portrait of panic and understanding. "No! No no no no!" he shrieked.

In the next instant, we watched as Logan dashed up the length of the hearty tree, the rest of the world around him suddenly moving, and alive, and nightmarish. Bolts of electricity, arrows, spears, flame, and every other conceivable thing someone could throw at him was ready to strike him, but for every measure used against him, someone had a countermeasure prepared. Arrows were deflected, flames extinguished, lightning dispersed across invisible barriers; Lucia raised her head for just the moment long enough for us to register her confusion as Logan hurled himself across the divide and into the open door of the bisected cage.

The house was bathed in blue light as the mirror abruptly went blank. Then just as suddenly, all was still.

Abarta sat forward in his seat, gripping the table with both hands. His eyes opened wider than I would have thought possible, staring in astonishment, mouth half open as he struggled for words.

"My family…" he half muttered.

I didn't dare move as he howled wordlessly, demolishing the table and everything on it, wildly smashing everything in sight.

"Hundreds of years! Hundreds!" he bellowed, his eyes unable to focus. "Everything was planned, guided by fate! This was the worst of all possible outcomes! Had she just died, perhaps another would have been chosen! What he did, he has robbed everyone! He robbed me of—"

He had a look in his eye then, as if he had just suddenly run out of steam. His arms went limp, two wires cut from a marionette.

"None of that matters now," he said flatly, all of the fury now gone from him as he looked me in the eye and said,

"There's just one thing that I need. I need to ask for the impossible. I need to ask you to forgive me."

"Are you out of your damned mind?" I yelled, standing fast enough for my chair to fall over.

"Please, Elana, you don't understand what I've lost today, you are a child," Abarta pleaded. "And I am still sworn to be your guardian. More than that, you are all that I have left of your mother, and you are my friend. Even if it were not my duty, I would do this anyway."

"Holy—! Yeah, you are serious," I said incredulously. "How can you call me your friend when you have one of my real friends held against her will right in front of me?"

"The elf?" Abarta asked, looking down. With a wave of his hands, her bonds vanished, and he said, "You can have her. And the rod, you may keep that too. And I've already restored your focus for travel; you will be okay now."

"Another one of your deals?" I spat.

"No, no deals, no bargains, I give her to you to do as you wish, nothing owed in return."

"Then I accept," I said, and as I did, I felt a charge run through me. Something electric. Chalsarda stood and walked through the mess toward me, but before she was even all the way across I said, "Chalsarda, my friend, you are free. You are your own person, no longer bound to myself or anyone."

There was a burst of something magic in the air momentarily like a balloon popping too close to my head, and Chalsarda gasped for air momentarily, her eyes wide with surprise for half a second.

"Thank you," she breathed. I didn't take my eyes off Abarta.

"Now do you forgive me?" he asked.

"Hell, no," I shot back. "People aren't gifts, you ass."

Abarta sighed. "I didn't suspect it would be that easy. It will take time, I suppose."

"More time than you have after what you did." I glared at him.

"I'm patient." His words lacked conviction.

I dug into my bag and retrieved Chalsarda's adamantine, placing it into her hand. "Thank you for trusting me with this," I said, cupping her fingers around it. "Do you think you can get us back to Olivia?"

Chalsarda shook her head. "It is nowhere near ready to be used again, it will take several hours, at least."

"Damn. Okay, well, is there any other way we could—"

"I could send you back," Abarta interrupted. "With your abilities as they are now, you would discover how challenging it is to find your way out of my home and back to your friend in a timeframe that you would deem acceptable. But maybe Olivia will be just fine in the middle of a battlefield all on her own, and you don't need my help."

Oh damn. I hadn't even considered that.

"Is he right?" I asked Chalsarda. "I know time works differently here, is there any way to get back to her?"

"I'm afraid not," Chalsarda claimed sadly. "I've lived here a long time, and even I get lost in this place. We have no map, and we're in the center of an ever-changing landscape. We would need his help without the assistance of my adamantine."

"To be clear," Abarta spoke up. "I am offering transport to Elana, not you. Elana, I have no intention to harm your friends, the elf included, you have my word on that. But I am not obliged to do them any favors, particularly not this one. She can walk, for all I care."

"How can you—" I nearly shouted, before Chalsarda put a hand on my shoulder.

"I'll be fine; your sister needs you," she comforted me. As I looked into her eyes, I noticed that her face seemed lighter than ever. She didn't have to say it, but I could tell, she wasn't worried about being left behind at all. "I'll meet you soon, just get home safe."

I glared at Abarta, realizing I had no choice, and said, "Fine. Just do it."

He smiled at that, waving a hand to remove the debris between us. "Our meal is complete, and your end of our bargain is fulfilled. Now close your eyes," he spoke softly as he approached, and I did as he asked. "I will see you soon; you may thank me then."

There was nothing, pure silence, and peace for a moment, and then, the soul-shattering noise of Olivia wailing with grief filled me with dread instantly. I opened my eyes to see the aftermath of a battle. Bodies of all types lay around the city, but directly in front of me was one that I wasn't prepared to see. Logan, his head cradled in Olivia's arms, laying perfectly still. And above us, hovering about fifteen feet above the ground, was Lucia, looking at us indifferently as Olivia wept.

"Oh, you're here too," Lucia said to me. It was hard to look directly at her; her body was glowing, radiating a warmth that hurt my eyes.

"Lucia! Help him! Please!" Olivia cried out, her voice straining as she did.

Lucia turned her gaze to the two of them, and regarding them for a moment finally said, "No. You should go."

As soon as the words left her mouth, Lucia vanished from view, taking her bright, oppressive warmth with her. I wasted no time rushing to Olivia's side, but she was inconsolable. Before I could say a word, she screamed at me, "Do something! He's not ...!"

Logan didn't look well, but there was nothing I could do to help him. And the moment I thought that, it occurred to me I might be wrong. I could ask, but it was a long shot.

"Hold on; there may be something. It will be okay, I promise," I assured Olivia. She nodded frantically, continuing to rock back and forth.

I stood up and looking out to the sky I began to address everything. "I don't sense you, but I know you can hear me. Please, I need your help, and I know you want to help me. I'll do whatever you ask, and I'm sorry if I've hurt you, but I really need you right now."

"Hello, Elana," The words came from behind me, and they unmistakably belonged to Logan. I spun around to see him standing near Olivia who was still cradling Logan's dying body in her arms. I tried to speak, but he held a hand up and continued. "No, I am not Logan. I am just the one voice that we chose to talk to you, and I chose this form to do so."

Olivia looked on in bewilderment, and I wasn't sure that I looked any more certain than she did.

"Please! We need your help!" I shouted.

"I know," The Knowing replied to me through this Logan avatar. "But we cannot help you, not in the way that we have in the past. We have healed you, but his wounds are not physical, he lost the light. It was a brave and loving sacrifice, but it was a sacrifice that must stand. To return that to him would be abhorrent. You cannot understand this now, but this is his time. Not by fate, but by choice. So few choose their destiny, you must respect it."

I shook my head at that. "No, you're wrong. And if you won't help, I have no choice."

"What will you do?" it asked me.

With trembling hands, I found the Singing Stone and held it up in front of my face, and said, "I'm going to make a deal."

"You once swore to us three times that you trusted us," it replied evenly. "Did you mean it?"

My battle with Jason. I practically sang the words. I would have been killed, Olivia and Claire would have been killed without their help. I shuddered to think at who else would have suffered in the days to come. "I did, and I do," I said nervously.

"Then trust me now when I tell you this is something you will regret," it said.

"I would regret it a lot more if I didn't try," I told it.

It seemed to consider that for a moment before saying, "Please remember that we tried to warn you. We know you, and we know how treacherous this path is, but we also know that in order to learn you must make your own mistakes."

It looked at me expectantly as if waiting for a response. Instead, I focused on the Singing Stone and shouted, "Freyja! I am ready to make a deal!"

"You needn't shout. I can hear you perfectly well," Freya remarked, strolling through the Logan avatar as it evaporated. "Now, what sort of deal did you have in mind?"

"I need you to save Logan," I said quickly.

"That's more of a request than a deal," Freyja remarked. "What will you do for me?"

I hesitated, knowing the one thing she wanted from me and knowing that it was the one thing I couldn't give her.

"I will help you prevent Ragnarök," I said finally.

"You will kill my brother," she said sternly. "My terms are non-negotiable."

"No, I won't," I replied before I could stop myself. "I know you don't want to kill your brother, and I know you think that's the only way, but you're wrong."

Freyja scowled at that, and asked, "Who are you to tell me that I am wrong? I have considered this plan longer than you've existed! I have searched for every possible alternative! Of my domains, which I have many, I claim war itself, and I have seen every outcome, carefully considered each move. Oh, pray tell then, child, why you would know better than I?"

"Because I know you," I said glumly. "I loved all of the old tales when I was a kid, you were my favorite, but you know, you also had a temper. And I don't know how much of what I read is true, but I know you loved humanity. You saw their beauty and strength. And that's why you're asking a human for help now, I believe. You could ask other gods, make a deal with some demons, threaten a whole ton of monsters or send an army of dwarves, but you didn't. You're entrusting your most important task with me, and I'm telling you what I do. I challenge fate. And that man I'm asking you to save? He wasn't even supposed to be here, and look at what he accomplished. For all of the careful planning and schemes, for all of the prophecies and cryptic signs, not one person accounted for him. He is your proof that there's another way!"

Freyja seemed to stare through me at that, lips pursed. "And what if you're wrong?" she asked. "You don't have a plan, and you haven't thought this through. If you're wrong, everyone dies for the sake of a story! Can you really tell me that it's not worth it to sacrifice just one life to prevent that, even if it is my brother?"

I threw my hands up in frustration at that.

"Look, I don't know, okay? That's a huge question on top of a crap mountain worth of huge things I've had thrown at me lately! But look around you! Olivia and myself were willing to die to save the life of someone who probably hates us, and Logan, that man right there, is about to die because he wasn't willing to see the woman he loved be hurt for any reason." I took a moment to look at the two of them, Logan's breaths coming more shallow than ever now. "They say you should never meet your heroes, and this might be what they were talking about, but I'm really hoping that I'm right about you. I believe that you're desperate. Otherwise, you wouldn't even be considering the path you're currently on, but the Freyja I grew up with would never be able to live with herself if she let anything happen to her little brother."

Freyja took a long look at Olivia as well, her sobs now quiet, though her body heaved at each one. She cast one more suspicious glance at me before walking over to Olivia and kneeling down.

"Shh, calm now my child, it will be all right," Freyja cooed, and miraculously Olivia stopped crying in an instant. "Do you know who I am?"

"Yes," Olivia answered weakly with a sniffle.

"Good. Now, I am going to give you a choice, but you must make it quickly as I can tell there is not much time left. Understand that your decision will come at a high personal cost to Elana, and once the decision is made, it is final. Do you understand?"

Olivia nodded nervously but kept eye contact.

"Your beloved is dying of wounds that I cannot heal, and he did so for you. It is a good death, and if you choose, I can reward him justly. Far from here, I have a meadow, more beautiful than any land you have ever seen. Pain does not touch this place; there is only joy and tranquility there. And at the heart of the meadow, there is a hall, great and fair. And in that hall are those who I have chosen from the battlefield, kind and righteous warriors who lived their life with honor and without hate. If you like,

I will take Logan there, and I will give him a seat in my hall, and he will be at ease forever and ever. Would you like that?"

"Yes, I would, thank you," Olivia managed.

"As would I," Freyja told her. "But it is not without a cost, for you would never see him again. Whatever else happens, however you choose to live your life, your soul will not be mine to claim when the time comes. Before you decide, there is another option. I may give him as a gift to my brother, Freyr. My brother lives among the sun elves who worship him, for he is their god and their king. In extraordinary circumstances, a human may become an elf after death, and your circumstances are nothing if not extraordinary. However, the process would not be easy for him, and he will not be welcomed with open arms. But in time, he will return to you if—"

"Freyr!" Olivia interrupted. "Give him to Freyr. That is my choice, I can't say goodbye forever, not like this!"

"Very well," Freyja said with a smile. "Do not despair, he will not be gone long, so long as you will wait for him."

Freyja stood and walked back to me, and said, "You now know what my end of the bargain will be. Before it is complete, I must know that you understand what you are doing. Elana Black. Are you aware that if you agree to a partnership with me, I will not release you under any circumstances until your task is complete?"

"I do."

"And are you aware that for as long as we have this agreement, my enemies will become your enemies, and your enemies will become my enemies, just as we will share allies?"

"I understand, that's fine."

"Where do you call home?"

"Los Angeles," I said without thinking. "I've bounced around all over it, but it's the only place I've ever called home."

"Then from this day forward, I expect you to defend it in my honor as your home," Freyja said sternly. "Our agreement then is this: I will transport Logan to live in Alfheim in exchange for your assistance in preventing Ragnarök?"

"We have a deal," I agreed.

"Then it is done," she said, pointing toward the building in the distance. "And as such, you have an unwelcome guest in your home, someone who is responsible for much of your pain already. I expect you to deal with him."

I could feel Roger's location in the building somewhere deep in my heart, though I didn't know how. It seemed as if Freyja had pointed to him on a map, and I could never forget where he was. It burned, and though I couldn't explain it, I suddenly felt as if I didn't confront him, stop him from hurting anyone else, that this burning would consume me. All of those wildlings he must have at least known would be killed! Those who were hunted down, or worse, those who had no idea what was happening. How could he not have known? And how much was he directly responsible for? That was nothing to say for what that bastard did to Lucia, what he turned her into, the childhood that he stole from her. I watched as she was taken from that hospital, I'd seen her drugged with my own two eyes! Then there is the world that he's bleeding dry because of her, how could I forget that? She couldn't have known that would be the consequence when she did it, but he was in charge! He should have known!

"Yes, that's good, let me show you the way," Freyja said knowingly. "You have business to attend to; I will see to it that Logan is seen to and Olivia is taken home. Good hunting."

Yeah, let's do this.

"Oh, and Elana?" Freyja said, almost as an afterthought. I turned to face her, and she smiled and said, "Merry Christmas."

I clutched at the handle of my rod removing it from my bag, immediately sensing the enormous amount of stray magic in the air, more than I could ever hold, and I absorbed it until the rod began to glow red and started to burn my hand as my fingers tightened around it. I held Roger's office in my mind, able to see him in there even now, frantic and uncertain, and with a shout, I willed myself there.

I had only done that once before, and I wasn't sure if I could do it again, but in a second I was standing in Roger's office looking at him from across the room, though neither he or Setanta didn't seem surprised by my sudden appearance.

"Now look, before you say anything, I just want you to know that none of us are happy about this. Not you, not me, no one."

"I know," I said gravely, taking a step toward him. "And I'm here to take it out on you."

"Don't be stupid," he shot back. "Setanta nearly killed you last time, and you can bet your ass I'm going to defend myself. Why don't you turn around and just walk out of here while you can?"

"Setanta isn't really Setanta though, is he?" I asked. "I'm sure you even have a full grown Cú Chulainn around here somewhere too, don't you? How does that even work, exactly? Bres isn't Bres, but he is. What's going on with that?"

"Setanta might not be what you think he is, but he's still an indestructible terror who protects me with the strength of a—" Roger began before clutching the bridge of his nose with his thumb and forefinger. "You know what? I'm done taking questions for the day. Setanta, get her out of here."

The besuited child began his steady march toward me, and this time I knew what I was in for, I could feel the power radiating off of him. I had a little power of my own this time, and with a wave of my rod I conjured a gale force wind in the center of his office that didn't last more than a second, but ejected everything between Roger and me out into the streets below, including

Setanta. Every inch of glass in the room was instantly shattered and expelled.

"What in the blue hell has gotten into you?" Roger screamed at me, in awe of the devastation present in his office.

"You did say he was indestructible, didn't you?"

Those words incensed Roger, and any calm or disbelief I'd read on his face had morphed into a rage. "Is this really what you want? You want to feel my full wrath and find out exactly why I'm the leader of this organization? Do you really want a piece of me?"

"Of course I do! Let's settle this!" I challenged him.

"Okay then, Elana," Roger seethed as I braced myself for a fight. "Okay."

32

Roger Nill locked eyes with me as he grit his teeth, straightened his tie, and squared his shoulders. And then he immediately turned and ran out of the room.

"What?" I asked aloud to an empty office. "I'm sorry, but, what?"

I only hesitated for a moment before following him into that long, bright white hall. I was keeping pace with him well enough, but he'd gotten a bit of a head start on me, and between the beatings I'd taken recently, the lack of sound sleep, and as weighted down as I was with the coat and my bag, I wasn't in the shape to catch him. That was increasingly becoming a concern because I had no idea what was behind any of these doors and no idea what he was running for. Some of these doors looked as if they were holding something in, and based on what I remembered from Lucia's memories; they had some nasty things hidden here that I probably wasn't ready to face on my own just yet.

I was about to find out what he had in mind. He reached a door at the end of the hall and threw his shoulder into it, dashing into the room without stopping. Well, I'd come this far, right? Might as well.

I ran into the room as well and stopped in my tracks, unable to immediately accept what I was seeing. What should have been a space the size of a conference room was much closer to a cathedral; the dimensions of the room shouldn't have been possible given what I knew about the architecture of this building from witnessing it from the outside. The floors and walls were pure marble as far as I could tell, and the four corners of the room housed runestones at least as large as I was, the carvings on each glowing with a different color. In the far corners of the chamber, green and blue, and closest to me, red and black. All four sending waves of energy into the center of the room where a white, almost pearlescent maelstrom towered high above me. There was no ceiling in this place, just gaping void and a view of infinity surrounded by hideous tendrils of purple and black reaching out from nothing toward nothing. I'd seen something like this before, and I couldn't immediately place it, but I knew that I would never forget it.

"Hold it right there!" Roger yelled at me from across the room. "Just calm down!"

"What? No! Are we going to fight or what?" I challenged, trying to focus.

"Why would you think that?" he asked.

"What do you mean, why would I think that?" I replied. "Didn't you just threaten me with unleashing your true power or whatever?"

"Yeah, I don't know how to break this to you, but that was a bluff," Roger responded. "I was hoping you'd think twice and just go. No such luck, I suppose. Do you really think I just get to be in charge for being the strongest? That's a pretty simple take, isn't it? I'm more of a diplomacy, finances, deal-making, resource management type of guy. I make sure the trains run on time."

Ugh. "Did you really just make a Mussolini joke?"

"Why not? You already view me as the villain."

"Yeah, because you are," I said carefully. "But we're not going to fight?"

Roger shook his head at that and said, "It wouldn't be much of one considering you came armed for bear."

"That's kind of anticlimactic, isn't it?"

"If you say so, I don't see this as a climax."

I managed to relax a little, given that he didn't seem to be able to defend himself at the moment, and the wonder of the room caught my curiosity.

"What the hell is this place?" I asked in amazement.

"I suppose you wouldn't recognize it," Roger said, circling the turbulent portal, keeping his eyes on me. "I imagine it looks considerably different than what you saw in Lucia's memories. This right here, this is the source of all the magic you seem to love throwing around so much. All the magic on the planet started here. It hasn't been well contained though, that's certainly been an issue."

"This leads into Kodran's world? This portal is what he was talking about; this is how we've been bleeding their world dry of magic."

"Indeed, it is, but it seems a little disingenuous of you to assign an entire universe to him given exactly what you damned him to," Roger said wryly. "Yeah, we know about that. Pretty dark, at least for you. I don't know that he left you much choice, but still. Wow. Maybe you ought to just say the world where Kodran is suffering a fate worse than death?"

I studied Roger for a moment, trying to get a handle on him. "You said it wasn't well contained, what did you mean by that?"

"I mean when opening something this size, it's like, well, you ever been to an old movie theater and seen the film burn at the end of a reel? There's that one initial hole, but there are all those little holes spreading over the rest of it all. That's what we did. One primary source providing magic to travelers all over the world centered right here. Our unintended consequence, however, is countless little holes all over the rest of the universe, because, and this may surprise you, the holes work both ways."

"So, wait a second," I said in horrible realization. "Are you telling me all of the monsters, and mythological creatures, and all of that written and created in that world, can just enter into this world from that one?"

Roger chuckled at that. "No walls safer than the ones we tore down," he mused to himself. "That's exactly what I'm saying, though nothing has tried to cross over through this portal directly. Anything on that side is probably a little concerned by the magnitude of it and doesn't want to risk it. You know, this whole situation is ironic when you consider our mission."

"Why are you telling me all of this?" I asked, trying to process all of this information.

"Because I'm hoping that if you understand what this place is, you won't be so quick to throw around that wild magic you're so fond of!"

"Still not following," I replied.

"Are you serious?" he asked dubiously. "Look around you, kid! Those runestones might as well be porcelain eggs. And I know, I know that in your very limited world view you see us as evil, but—"

"Of course you're evil, how the hell can you possibly deny that?" I nearly screamed.

"Let's settle this once and for all," Roger remarked, his tone becoming more lecturing. "Just what exactly is your problem with us and what we do?"

"How much time do you have?"

"I'm serious, what is your problem?" he asked. "Precisely, please."

"All of this power that you have, all of this responsibility, and think about all of the people you've hurt, you just—" I paused at that, unable to find the right words. "You just could have been heroes."

"Heroes?" Roger scoffed loudly. "Is that what this is all about? You think we should be the goddamn Justice League or something? Foiling bank robberies? Slaying dragons? You simple-minded infant, people don't want heroes!"

"I would disagree with that," I countered.

"Even you don't want heroes. You want avatars; you want someone to cheer, someone to worship. But regular people? Everyone with their boring day-to-day lives? They don't want heroes, they want there to be no need for heroes! Where you have heroes, you have villains or tragedy or worse. You and I used this magic and our talents for the same ends. We try to keep our world safe. The difference between us is that you seem to think this is all some grand adventure and we see it as necessary. You're so bent on doing the right thing you never stop to consider if you might be wrong."

"No man, that's where your argument falls apart," I replied. "You don't get to claim the high ground when the people underneath you have kidnapped and murdered innocent people. And I've seen the people you've chased into hiding, individuals who live their lives in fear of you. And who gave you the right anyway?"

"How are you any different?" Roger asked. "You came here to kill me."

The statement was a sucker punch. "No, I would never, I mean—"

"Well, if you weren't going to kill me, then what?" Roger was agitated at my response. "Were you going to turn me in somewhere? To who? And for what crime? Under whose authority?"

"I hadn't—"

"No, you most certainly hadn't thought this through, had you?" he pressed. "Because that's not how life works. You don't just get to showdown with someone because you don't like them, unless you're willing to follow through or suffer the consequences. Tell me, what does tomorrow look like for you, hmm? Or next week? Where do I factor into all of that? Because if you don't kill me, I have to assume that it's still business as usual for me then, except now I have to deal with you as part of my calendar. You, and that elf, and all your wide-eyed, innocent, little friends. Me and my magic army of highly trained operatives, versus you and what exactly? How are you going to stop me?"

"Well, there's always the dumbest way possible," I replied, feeling my stomach begin to churn at my horrible idea. "These runestones, pretty fragile, right? And they're what is holding up all the magic in this place?"

Roger visibly blanched at the implication of my words and began to plead, "You wouldn't, you don't know what would—"

I pointed my rod in the direction of the runestone to my left, the one glowing red, and cast a cone of ice into it. The runestone shattered upon impact, sending a cloud of red smoke directly into the vortex.

"Oh my god! Oh hell! Oh, my—" Rogers eyes were wide in disbelief at that. "You have no idea what you're doing!"

"Yeah, so, I can't beat you, like you said," I continued, this time pointing the rod at the runestone glowing black, shattering it to a similar effect. Roger howled in fear and frustration as I did. "But I can do the right thing, and please, please trust me when I tell you that this really feels like the right thing; and I get to cripple you all at the same time. This magic doesn't belong to us. You stole it. And it's not the first time either, is it? But if I close this portal, try to stop the bleeding, I allow that world to keep what is rightfully theirs, and your magic army suddenly isn't so magic anymore. It might make my job a bit harder in the future, but no plan is perfect. Seems like a good deal to me."

I started to walk across the length of the room, tilting my head to see the turbulent swirls of red and black now mixing violently with the pearlescent base. It didn't look exactly stable, but it was certainly exciting to watch.

"Wait, wait!" Roger shouted, running behind me. "You don't know what this will do. Hell, I don't know what this will do! No part of this is stable; you might just blow up the whole damn building!"

"Roger, in recent memory I have survived a mythological monster who may or may not have been the literal devil, I've been defenestrated, gotten into fights with not one, but two different gods from different pantheons, I came inches from watching, again, not one, but two of my friends die, I've been punched through rocks, been chased by what I'm pretty sure was every single troll, been forced to lie to my friends; am I missing anything? Probably, but whatever, not the point," I chided him, sending another bolt of ice into another runestone, this time the one glowing green. "I just need you to understand that after the month I've had, deep down, from the bottom of my heart, as sincerely as I can possibly make this for you, I need you to know that I really, really don't care if this whole place goes up."

The vortex was pulsating now, shimmering and creating a painful burst of light, the cracks in the universe above growing now by inches every second.

"I thought you just said that you weren't going to kill me!" Roger shouted cynically.

"Not my fault that you're not running for cover." I shrugged, walking toward the last runestone.

"Hoo boy! Okay, all right, look, it's not too late to fix this," Roger said between deep breaths. "Elana. Elana, just look at me. You've made your point, okay? You hold all the cards here, and that's something we can work with, we both know where we stand. Now, I know we have our differences, and I know deep down, you're a good person. Your intent is noble; you're out there trying to save lives, I get it. I do. But you know, so are we. We have been around a long, long time, and I could show you things you would not believe. Records of not only the worlds we saved, but the worlds we lost. It has been through our failures that we have adapted our strategy over time, and I know how unpleasant it all must sound, but sometimes, hey, listen to this. Sometimes the needs of the many outweigh the needs of the few. You're right, this isn't the first time we've done this, but time works differently and sometimes our twenty or thirty years is a thousand years on their end, and they're never the wiser. And for every time we have to make that sacrifice, countless worlds are saved as a result. I understand that it doesn't seem like it now, but we are right. We were first, and we are right. So all I'm asking you is to stop and consider those oth—"

I fired an ice bolt into the last runestone.

"God, I hate monologues," I muttered as I watched the glowing blue energy add itself to the vortex.

Roger screamed in a panicked disbelief. "Oh, come on, this thing isn't going to explode. You'd have to be an idiot to build something that volatile next to all of the rest of your cool stuff, not to mention where you work."

After a short pause, Roger's face turned pale and he added, "That wasn't a bluff, I really don't know if it will explode or not."

"Oh, dang, really?" I asked, now concerned as well. "Wow, I really read that one wrong. Still, it was the right thing to do, right? Yeah? Yeah, I think it was. Hey! Are you going to miss having magic? I probably will."

The colors danced and swirled, the rumbling grew deeper, and the ground began to shift and shake, and for just a moment I actually started to think that I might have been way, way off. There was nothing to do now though but watching the beautiful lights and contemplate my poor impulse control and hope it didn't kill me. It didn't kill me though. Instead, something miraculous happened. Like that instant where all of the ingredients in your mixing bowl just suddenly work together and looked like it was always meant to, the swirls just hit their stride, and all five colors just worked in harmony. The shaking stopped, and though the void remained constant, the tendrils noticeably stopped growing.

The disbelief on Roger's face morphed from horror to elation as he smiled wide, laughing softly at first, then more raucous as relief seemed to wash over him. "Hot dog! I can't believe it! They were right!" he exclaimed.

"Did you just say 'hot dog'?" I asked.

"Good news, Elana!" Roger said with a little soft shoe for effect. "You didn't blow us up, and you didn't manage to kill magic all around the world! Well, good news for me, that is."

"Okay, well, I didn't stop you from harming an entire universe separate from our own, and the two of us are still standing, and it looks like I'm out of things to break, so…" I let the words hang in the air as I cradled my rod. "What now?"

"If you're open to suggestion," Bres shouted from the far end of the room where I'd entered. "I might have some ideas!"

My blood ran cold as I watched Bres casually stroll the length of the room toward me, blazer opened, held back by the two hands he had shoved into his pockets. I began to take stock of everything around me. Maybe, just maybe, between the rod and the Singing Stone, I might be able to conjure a way out of here. I had no idea if it would be enough, but it would have to be.

"Bres! About damn time, what the hell took you so long?" Roger barked.

"Oh, I've been here the whole time." Bres shrugged. "I just thought it might be a laugh to see how this all played out."

"And what if she actually closed the portal?" Roger asked.

"Then you'd both be helpless. I can't see how that would bother me any, my power isn't tied to their world."

"God damn you, man, I swear one of these days I'll..." Roger tried to compose himself and stopped short of finishing that sentence. "It doesn't matter. Kill her. Now."

"Oh, that is a fine idea indeed, boss man," Bres replied with a grin. "Get me revenge and save your hide all in one go, eh?"

"Yes, now get on with it," Roger ordered.

"Oh, sure," Bres replied slowly and cheerfully. "And how would you like it done, hmm? Quick and easy like with a rake of my scythe? Perhaps I could set her on fire? Or should I just roll my sleeves up and choke the life out of her?"

"I don't care how it's done, you insubordinate clown!" Roger nearly shouted. "I just want her dealt with so we can move on!"

Bres snapped his fingers and looked as if he had an epiphany. "I've got it! Why not something special?" As he asked this, his voice sounded like burning gravel and smoke began to rise from beneath his clothing, his face twisted hideously and changed colors, the mass in his arms and chest seemed to double as his shirt and jacket ripped apart and fell from his body. "Why don't we just make full use of my demon side and rend the meat from her bones? Boil the fat in my blood and let the cries of her agony haunt this place forever as a warning to all who dare oppose you? Is that what you would like, Mr. Nill, sir?"

346

Bres was inches away from me now, and I was too terrified to move or even blink. His hot breaths burned my face like steam, and for a moment no one said anything.

"On second thought," Bres said in his normal voice, resuming his human form, although now sans shirt. "Nah."

Roger blinked in surprise, his face going red. "No? You don't say no to me!" he shouted. "I gave you an order! Kill her!"

"In case you forgot, I'm off the clock until I get a new assignment all official-like," Bres laughed. "And I don't suppose you're in much of a position to be giving out orders. Remember, my orders were to see to the safety of the Cruz girl until she fulfilled the prophecy, and I'm a man of my word. And you there, acting the maggot, demanding I clean up your mess for you, and you couldn't even use the magic word! Oh, the shame of it all! No, fearless leader, I think it's time you led by example and cleaned up your own mess. See you after the holiday break, lad!"

Roger's eyes went wide with fear, knowing suddenly he had no backup. "This is not a negotiation! I am ordering you to—!"

Bres spun on his heels and marched back to a visibly frightened Roger. "In case you forgot, sir," Bres said coldly before backhanding Roger hard enough to send him to the ground in a heap. "I don't like being told what to do."

The two of us watched in stunned silence as Bres strolled back out of the room, whistling a happy tune to himself. Roger looked at me helplessly, the welt on his face getting worse by the second. He scrambled to his feet and put his hands up in defense. "I know you're not going to kill me—!" he began.

"You're right, but shut up and listen," I demanded. "You brought up a good point earlier. I don't have the authority to judge you. But I know who does, and they're waiting for you right on the other of this lovely little door you built. So I'm giving you two choices: Either you walk through on your own and confess, or I kick the hell out of you with every last bit of magic

I have stored in this rod, and then I push you through. What'll it be?"

"You wouldn't—!"

"I absolutely would, but if those prizes don't sound appealing to you, there is a door number three we can look behind."

Roger had the nonplussed look of a man who was starting to realize that his only options were losing or not winning, and one of them would involve cathartic violence.

"Well," he said impatiently. "I'm waiting."

"I made you a promise, back when we first met," I said, extending a hand to him. "I could use your help. Come on. Why don't you give me a hand?"

"The old glad hand, huh?" Roger asked quietly, looking down at my hand with the reverence of a loaded gun, knowing full well what I was ready to take from him. "I'm sorry, but no deal. The things I know, I have to die with."

I shrugged. "Suit yourself, doesn't matter to me."

Roger took a deep breath and tried to gather himself, facing me with a look of defiance. "You do know that I'll be ba—"

I summoned enough wind to take him off his feet and soaring into the vortex. Some people just don't know when to shut up.

33

It took us a little while to find an overlook that didn't already have at least a couple of cars parked for the evening, but that was the beauty of the hills up in that whole Sherman Oaks, Mulholland Drive area. There was no shortage of scenic spots if you were just willing to get a little bit lost. By the time we found one the New Year's fireworks had already began. I couldn't have told you with any certainty where we were, but there were expensive homes and curvy, poorly lit roads. Most important, we had a nice little patch of dirt large enough for Big Sister and then some, and that was all I needed.

I began the ill-advised and utterly dangerous task of backing into our space, Oliva stood outside and made sure that I didn't back my car over a cliff. After a tense minute or so, I was parked and had the trunk open, and I set myself to the task of making a suitable bedding for the two of us. I'd slept in the back of this car recently, and it wasn't a comfortable experience, but I hadn't allowed for any margin of error for this outing. Between the two of us, we'd brought enough pillows and blankets that we would sleep soundly in a quarry. Olivia offered me a small smile while we worked, and whether she was ready to be happy again yet or not, I was glad to see it.

Our task complete, Olivia and I crawled into the mobile pillow fort that we'd built for ourselves, lying on our backs, enjoying the view of the San Fernando Valley illuminated by fireworks exploding. The sounds of a party going on in a house that likely cost more money than I'd ever see in my lifetime was just loud enough to be impossible to ignore, but as usual, I didn't want to be at a celebration, and for once, Olivia agreed with me. This car, hanging out one on one, was where we both needed to be at this moment, though I wasn't sure what needed to be said. If anything even should be said. But I could handle that uncertainty as long as we were together. I was comfortably uncomfortable.

We stayed that way for ten minutes or an hour-and-a-half; I wasn't sure. And even over the distant music and shouting, over the heaven bound pops in the sky, when Olivia broke her silence it startled me.

"I really wanted to be angry with you," she said, almost to herself. "I still want to, kind of."

"Why aren't you?" I asked meekly.

"Because it's not fair to you? Because now is not the time for it?" she mused out loud. "Because we need each other now more than ever, I guess. I've had a few days to think about it, and that whole thing was all just so impossible. If there was a happy ending there, happier than the one we got, I don't see how."

"I'm so sorry about Logan; I didn't mean—"

"Don't," she said quietly, gently, but forcefully somehow. "He's not dead. He's just not here. I'm going to see him again. She said so."

"It still shouldn't have happened; I should have done more."

"What could you have done?" Olivia asked. "I'm not saying this to let you off the hook, we all handled this whole thing poorly, and you might have made the biggest mistakes of any of us, but I mean it. What else could you have done?"

I didn't have an answer for that. I didn't know I just didn't have one now or if I'd think of one five years from now, but either way, the result was the same. I stayed silent.

"You pinned me down and tried to sacrifice yourself for everyone. Literally. For me, especially, in that moment. And you warned me what you were going to do; I just didn't think it would come to that. I'm the one who dragged Logan with me, if anything, I'm to blame. But I'm not. He just did what you and I were both willing to do, just for different reasons."

"He loved you," I agreed.

"Loves me," Olivia corrected. "And I love him. But let's be honest, Logan might have been the only one of us who could have even saved Lucia."

"What do you mean?" I asked. "I'm still her friend, even if she's not mine."

"Come on, Elana, you saw what I saw, you're—" Olivia rolled on her side slightly to look at me. "Okay, that's what I'm talking about. I don't know about you, but there was guilt there. Mostly guilt. The rational part of my brain tells me that we were kids, and not only did I have no way of dealing with all of that correctly back then, I still don't. I could watch every minute of her life through her eyes and still not relate, not entirely. I just know that intentional or not, I played a part in her becoming what she is. You didn't feel any of that?"

"I mean, yeah, of course," I replied. "But that guilt comes from knowing that someone you love is hurting. I don't know how you feel deep down, but I do know that if I hadn't stopped you, you would have gladly died so that she could live. That's not guilt, be real. You buy someone dinner when you feel guilty.

351

You don't kill yourself. And yeah, Logan's motivations were pure, but we don't have to compare the two. We just need to accept that it happened."

Olivia's brow tightened as she turned onto her back. "I still can't believe she just left like that," she said.

"Would that have made a difference?" I asked. "I mean, if you knew that's what she would do, would you have acted any differently?"

"Maybe, yeah!" she almost shouted. "I know that's not the right answer or whatever, but it's my answer. It's an honest answer. We didn't walk into that knowing that Freyja would help. So trading Logan's life or your life or especially my life for someone who doesn't care about us? I'm sorry, but it's not worth it."

I let that answer hang in the air. On principle, I wasn't sure that I agreed with Olivia, but it was hard to argue with her as well. She was probably right, Lucia could very well just hate us all, and that's her choice. Or maybe she'd just been hurt too many times and she doesn't recognize us anymore. Regardless of what Lucia thought of the two of us, she still saw a stranger save her life, and she didn't tell Olivia that she couldn't help him, she didn't so much as show emotion one way or the other. She just said no, and that was it. No. Not with a touch of sympathy, or explanation, just no. I wasn't sure how I was supposed to forgive that, let alone understand it.

"I had to lie to his parents," Olivia said flatly. "I still have his phone; I sent his Dad a text from it saying he was going to work on a movie set in Brazil for three months. Then I took the battery out of it before I could get a response. I hate myself for doing that, but what could I do?"

"I hadn't even thought about that," I told her.

"They probably won't forgive me, when they find out. I can't imagine how they'll take the news. I don't know how I'm processing the news myself. I'd like to talk with Chalsarda at some point if she'd be cool with it. I just—I don't know anyone else who I could remotely think might have answers for me."

"I'm sure she would, but I haven't seen her much since we got back, and even then, it was just for a minute," I said. "I'm glad she got back okay, but she just went through something we can't imagine. I was around her most of the year, and I never suspected, not once. She's had to endure god knows what for who knows how long, and now she's truly free for the first time in a long time. We're just going to have to give her as much time as she needs."

Somewhere at the party, someone shrieked in a celebration of life loud enough to be heard over the music and the rest of the background noise, and that sound was met with applause shouts of agreement. A cloud opened up overhead somewhere and provided a few seconds of rain, just enough to tease us. I pulled at a handful of a blanket and burrowed my way into the blankets just a bit more. A slight chill accompanied the rain, and snuggling in made a good substitute for talking.

"You're going to have to teach us, you know," Olivia remarked after a while. "Something happened after all of that, and I can see the ways into things now. Ann too."

I'd actually known about Ann before Olivia. Ann saw her first opening into a story the day after and had the good sense to shut her comic book the instant she did. Olivia saw the way into the middle of an episode of The Outer Limits that was running as some marathon. She wasn't even trying to watch it at the time, so she wasn't sure what she was looking at until it was almost too late.

"I'm still looking for someone to teach me," I laughed bitterly which drew a side eye from Olivia. "Sorry, yeah, of course, I'll tell you everything I know, but there's still a ton that I have no clue about. Do you want to hear a piece of advice I got once?"

"Sure."

I tried to recall the exact words Abarta spoke to me at that party, and I tried to ignore whatever hidden meaning he might have had behind them, and I repeated them for Olivia. "Be ready and be brave."

Olivia nodded in agreement with that and said, "Don't worry, I don't think I'm ever going to be afraid again."

There was something dour about the way she said it; the words were wrapped in sadness and determination. "Well, teach me how to do that, because I'm pretty much terrified constantly," I admitted.

I looked at her as I said it, and her face went from something hard and unrecognizable to the carefree smile full of joy and mirth that I had missed for so long as she laughed in spite of herself. I joined her, unable to help myself. It's true, laughter is contagious, no matter how temporary it might be.

"Do you want a drink?" she asked, sitting up.

"Yeah, but just the one, remember? I gotta drive us back."

"Good, because I only brought two anyway," Olivia said, finding her backpack under a pillow. "I wasn't exactly ready to party tonight. No offense."

"None taken," I told her as she handed me a bronze colored can. It had the words 'Champagne Velvet Brand Beer, The Beer with the Million Dollar Flavor' written on it. "Champagne beer, huh?"

Olivia sat cross-legged on our pillow pile, and I did the same. "You know it's classy because it has their slogan written right on the can," Olivia remarked as we opened our cans.

"Sure, I've heard dumber things," I agreed with a smile, raising my can. "Sláinte!"

"Ooh! I like that one!" Olivia perked up.

"I know, right? I just learned it."

"Well, cheers," she said, clinking our cans together.

I took a long, deep swig from the can and my body began to convulse in disagreement.

"Oh god, I regret everything about that!" I choked out.

Olivia made a face to show her revulsion and exclaimed, "I think we were supposed to drink them cold!"

"Why would you do that to us?" I asked, examining the back of the can.

"I don't know; it just seemed like a fun idea at the time!"

"I will never get to be a person who didn't drink this!" I complained.

Olivia burped loudly, and added, "It tastes like a pork mimosa. I can taste it in my nose."

"Maybe the million dollars is the prize for actually finishing one of these," I said. "Also, not worth it. Do we have to finish this?"

"I want to say no, but I also think we kind of have to," Olivia replied. "We don't want to end the year as quitters."

"I will keep your secret if you'll keep mine," I offered.

Olivia responded with a second, though smaller, burp before squinting her eyes and nodding her head vigorously. "Yeah, okay, I'm good with that."

"May we never speak of this again," I said as we leaned out the back of the wagon, pouring the foul liquid into the dirt.

Olivia pulled a couple of water bottles out of her backpack and tried to wash the taste out of our mouths, laughing wordlessly for a little while at the experience. For all of the crap we'd been through, and for everything that I knew was to come, this moment felt good, and I couldn't have been happier to see Olivia feeling unburdened.

"So, what about you?" she asked as we sat, sipping our waters.

"What about me? I thought we established my opinion on that devil elixir," I said.

"No, not that, your life," Olivia said. "What's next for you? Do you really work for a Norse goddess now?"

"Yeah, I don't know if that's a partnership or if I'm her employee or what, but wow," I replied. "I genuinely don't know how to deal with her. Got any advice?"

"Let's see," she said thoughtfully. "Fear nothing, be yourself, and of course don't do any of that! Dude! She's a freaking goddess! How do you plan for that? Aren't you supposed to, I don't know, leave fruit at an altar for her or something?"

"How should I know? Maybe she likes milk? No, that's stupid," I said, thinking out loud. "Whatever it is, I'm sure she's going to let me know sooner or later."

"Thank you again," Olivia said. "Whatever it is, you're not going through it alone. I owe you for making this deal, I'm going to get to see Logan again because of you, and I'm not letting you pay for that alone."

Before I could respond, the music shut off at the party nearby, and I went to check my phone. It was 11:58 pm, but I was sure that was about to change any moment. I put my phone down as Olivia moved to edge of the trunk, to watch the fireworks.

59! 58! 57! 56!

I sat next to her, looking out over the San Fernando Valley with my friend, and she put her head on my shoulder. I wrapped a blanket over us with my free hand and placed my arm around her shoulder, giving her a comforting rub.

42! 41! 40! 39!

"I'm going to see him again," Olivia said murmured. I gave her an extra little rub and tried not to think about everything that had happened this past year. I tried my best to pretend that when the clock hit midnight that we'd be given a cosmic do-over, a chance to go back to a time before magic and gods invaded our lives, before the threat of monsters and shadowy organizations.

19! 18! 17! 16!

"I am going to see you again," Olivia said with more conviction in her voice. That one didn't feel like it was for me, and I didn't respond. Thunder rumbled ominously in the distance.

5! 4! 3! 2! 1! Happy New Year!

God damn, I really hope so.

ABOUT THE AUTHOR

Danny Bell is the Amazon #1 Best Selling Author of The Black Pages and he nearly had an out of body experience when he realized that the song Mr. Brightside by The Killers is thirteen years old and that would surely mean that he was also older than thirteen. Older than double in fact! Certainly not triple. He has three cats, Mister, Jameson, and Koala, and they all tolerate each other. He would never compare himself to Robocop, why would he do that? He plans to continue to write books forever with hope that one day there will be a Quantum Leap style thing where Dr. Sam Beckett will help fix his life, or failing that, the time-traveling ghost of Samuel Beckett, the author, will tell him that he has been pronouncing 'Godot' wrong the whole time. He isn't sure why anyone ever wants a bio, but if you're willing to read random things about him that may or may not be true, he's willing to provide you with them.

https://www.facebook.com/ElanaRuthBlack/